I0738059

The Brambles

Leah Erickson

ISBN-13: 978-0-578-42528-3
ISBN-10: 0-578-42528-9

Book design by *Caryatid Design*
Cover design by *Caryatid Design*

For my husband and daughter

ONE

The dead girl haunted the minds of the townspeople like a half-remembered dream, a tune once well known, the words vanished into silence.

Many times they had seen her over the years, riding past on her bicycle or walking on foot, dreamily, down the road's dusty shoulder. Often her skirts were long and dark colored, crinkled cotton or crushed velvet. A colorful yarn Guatemalan bag hung with its long strap crossing her chest. She was like a figure from another time, though it was hard to say *which* time. Dressed like a sixties flower child, but with her long dark hair pinned up primly from her pale neck, she looked more Victorian, like a girl from a cameo. A silhouette of yellowed ivory, distinct in its delicate lines, but at the same time featureless.

One remembered *seeing* her, but the girl was always in the peripheries of inner vision, just at the edge of consciousness.

Summer or winter, there had always seemed to be an air of remote *coolness* about her. As though she hadn't much to do with the roads, the landscape, the town and its people. On her way to the library where she sat alone at a study desk. Or going to the market to pick up some things for *the mother*. (About whom much was whispered. Thought to be a solitary and odd woman who had homeschooled her daughter, though the public schools were excellent …)

The girl's name was Elizabeth, though few had called her by her name. She had lived in the town for years, and though seen by many, she was known by few. Seventeen years old at the time of her death, according to the news reports.

An elderly man, Ernest Stevenson, who suffered dementia and sometimes wandered around, lost, found her hanging by her neck from the limb of a white oak tree, deep in the woods that rimmed the edge of her backyard. At the moment in the early morning when the girl's mother first realized that Elizabeth was not in her bed, Ernie was outside in his striped pajamas and bare feet in the woods, like an apparition in the mist and the ferns; he stood looking at the girl's lifeless form as she swayed from a creaking rope in the soft early light, an expression of stunned wonder on his face.

Once the police came, news traveled fast.

What was there to say? People shook their heads. The girl must have had troubles that no one knew of. She and the mother kept to themselves, living in a house of a modern, Japanese design, with siding made of blackish charred cedar. The windows, irregularly sized and placed, had panes of frosted glass that looked like rice paper, impossible to see through. They obviously had *money*, because the mother had had the chic house custom designed. But no one had ever visited the house. If the girl was suffering, how could it be anyone else's fault?

A polite girl. Her voice was deep and level when she spoke to say please or thank you. Adult in her directness. No trace of an accent, though she had something vaguely foreign about her. Dark hair and eyes, dusky voice.

The more people tried to remember details about Elizabeth, the more elusive she became, as though in the mind's eye her identity was *pixilated*. She had died in the autumn, a time of year when she walked down the road and the sun burned low and golden behind her, turning her into a silhouette. She had lived among them, invisible, for so long, that no one could agree on exactly what she had looked like.

Except for the girl's eyes; penetrating, strange and feral looking. She'd suddenly turn to look back at you as you drove past her and make your heart stop, as if a painting or statue had come to life and now saw *you*. No one could forget those eyes, which still seemed to hover from the shadows, watching them. Once seen, never again unseen.

Two

The Lab Rabbit

William "Mack" Mackenzie gunned the engine of his dented red Dodge pickup and raced down the long stretch of highway that sloped through the countryside; he enjoyed seeing the flare of alarm in the eyes of Kirsten. Beautiful Kirsten with her long blonde hair and perfect pink skin. Her father was a personal injury lawyer with his photo on billboards all over town, looking like a rugged star of an action movie, shirt sleeves rolled up, and arms crossed, above the slogan RELAX, I'VE GOT THIS. Kirsten was one of the most popular girls in school. Her face was usually calm and composed as a china doll's, but now her eyes had grown large, and she said, "Mack, slow down!" as she swatted him on the arm.

They had been in homeroom together all through school. Everyone expected that they would eventually hook up. It was understood. Their first date had an air of inevitability about it, and somehow that gave Mack an impulse to recklessness that evening.

He gave her his best sheepish grin. With his bristly black hair and brown eyes that squinted engagingly when he smiled, even *he* knew he was handsome. He liked to drink and to mess around with the guys from the football team. Everyone liked Mack. He had friends in all social groups. He lolled and clowned in most every page of the yearbook. He could have any girl he wanted.

Though lately, now that it was October of senior year and the end of high school was closer and closer in sight, a question had begun to enter his mind, sometimes in a whisper and sometimes in a shout. Does anyone here really know you?

People *thought* they knew him. But Mack kept his secrets. Like how hard he studied, relentlessly pushing his stubborn brain up against the hard white wall of obstinacy, again and again. Like the neat and immaculate way he kept his room. Dusted, vacuumed, sports trophies gleaming in the dull afternoon sun in a way that sometimes made him feel unaccountably strange when he looked at them in the long stretch of a solitary Sunday afternoon. It felt as though they didn't really belong to him, but someone else.

It made him feel better to rev that engine, to whiz down the open road. He loved nothing more than a good stretch of open road, even though he didn't much care for the countryside. Something about the empty fields, the old barns, even the tang of manure, made him feel, for some reason, lonely. A rooster crow, the sound ghostly, recalled long ago times. He could almost hear the trot of horse hooves, the rumble of wagon wheels.

He liked to drive out here because when he was done, it made him feel happy to go home again.

He turned on the radio and dialed up the thrashing heavy metal rock that he liked to crank up when he drove. He drummed his fingers on Kirsten's knee, hammering out a frantic, staccato rhythm.

"Where are we going, Mack?" Her voice placid, cultured, with just a touch of giddiness. She was going to Yale next year. She had dreams of a career in telecom, life in a big city, exotic travel. But right now, the night wind blowing in the window carried her voice away. She had a beer buzz and a hiccup of laughter when she spoke. This girl was happy, really happy. He clutched at her hand, hoping it would conduct through her straight into *him*, this clear sense of grace and surety in her place in the world.

Because, he had applied to only one college, Brown, where his father had gone, and where he dreamed of Mack going one day. People said he was crazy, that he should have safety schools to fall back on. But in his mind, it was Brown or nothing. And if they said no …. well, best not to think so hard about it.

He suddenly slowed the truck and swerved, pulling over to the side of the road.

"Come on, you have to tell me what we're doing."

"I'll show you." On the grass shoulder, he parked the truck at an angle and turned off the ignition. The headlights he left on, illuminating a cornfield. "It's fun! I used to come up here with some guys when I was a freshman."

"And do what?"

"Get loaded and run through the corn." The air was brisk, the moon low and full as though weighted down with sweetness; he felt glad they had left the party in Mark's basement rec room, Crowded and noisy, humid with beer fumes, a sharp headache throbbed behind his eyes. And an electric, panicky feeling in his very bones. It felt as though he would jump out of his skin and he grabbed Kirsten's hand and led her out to his truck. Half delirious, half desperate.

His subconscious brain had led him here, to the cornfield, because he had truly had no destination in mind. The stalks swayed and whispered against the deep blue sky, and made him feel incredibly happy. It made him remember being a boy, and loving nature. "Come on, Kirsten. Run, and I'll chase you!"

She looked at him for a long beat, brow furrowed, but then shrieked in laughter when he pushed her forward into the corn. "Run! I'm coming for you!"

Run, she did. Mack entered unhurriedly, to give her some distance. He took a moment to enjoy the whispering shelter of the stalks. The eerie way the headlights illuminated the flickering spaces between.

Every so often, from up ahead, he heard her high, breathless laughter, and caught a glimpse of her running through. She was the girl everyone wanted, and tonight she was his. Blonde hair like corn flax. She belonged here, like some benevolent young goddess of the harvest. He walked forward and concentrated on only her. Finding her. Because if he looked upon her beauty long enough, maybe he would start to want her. And he wanted to feel something, anything right now. Even if it was just lust.

He imagined that she would turn to him when he *did* catch her, and remove her clothes. Her soft, pale white body would glow, and beckon to him. Her cornsilk hair would spread around her as she sank to the ground, he on top of her, and their cries would be lifted away into the night ...

"There you are," she said, laughing, breathless, coming up behind him and breaking his reverie. "I caught *you!*" But when she looked up into his face...

"Hey, are you okay?" he asked. Her face, technically smiling, wore more of a pained grimace.

He was shocked when she burst into tears.

"Kirsten?"

"I'm sorry," she snuffled. "I guess I've just been holding it in, and it just came out at a weird random time ..."

"But what is it?" He stroked her back, trying to calm her.

"It's just, all of the news about the dead girl. Elizabeth. Everyone's been talking about it all day. It's just messing with my head I guess ..."

At the mention of the name Elizabeth, the animation fled Mack's face. He felt a leaden feeling in the pit of his stomach.

Kirsten spoke in a rush now. "I mean, I never knew her or anything. But the whole thing is just so sad. I mean, a girl our age hanging herself. And I heard a story about how when that old man found her, her face was so purple it was almost black, and her tongue hanging out ..."

"Shhh. It's okay. Don't cry." But it was difficult to comfort her. Because he had known Elizabeth, what felt like many years ago. His friends didn't know that, and he didn't want to talk about it. He had thought a night of fun, and making love to Kirsten, would stop him remembering.

"This is so embarrassing." She wiped at her nose with the sleeve of her russet sweater. "I sound so dumb. But I've just never known someone my own age, could, you know ... die. I've always felt like I'll never die. Now I kind of know I'm wrong, that I could ... anybody could ..."

"So let's try to forget about it then."

"I don't know, I just feel really strange tonight."

"You want to fool around?" he asked, hands on her waist, gently. "Nobody here. We can do what we want."

He tried to nuzzle her neck. But she edged away from him.

"Sorry." Then, seeing she'd hurt him, she said in a softer voice, "It's getting colder. You didn't even let me grab my jacket when we left the party, you lug!" She laughed, a flat little laugh. And her eyes, though lovely, now had an opacity about them. Something removed and impersonal. Maybe he should have made the drive on his own, after all.

"Come on, Mack. I'm *sorry*. Don't look at me like that. Like I … I just stomped on your fucking heart or something." She looped her arm through his. "If we go back to the party now maybe they won't have even missed us."

Driving back to the party, Mack had one arm cocked out the window, a lazy half-smile on his face. "So anyway, you wouldn't believe what these fuckers did next. Brent picked up one of those large plastic trash cans, like an *industrial* trash can and hurled it straight through the window …"

It felt grounding, *easy*, to slip back into his school persona. Funny, friendly, hard-partying Mack. He felt Kirsten start to like him again. Even *he* started to like himself again. They had the music going, though not so loud this time, and were relaxed, chatty, trading stories and gossip.

"Hey, Mack, I'm hungry. Why don't we go get something to eat first? All they had were, like, *chips* at the party."

"You got it, dude. I could go for a burger or something …" But he really wished they could stay just like this. Driving aimlessly, with no destination. It was the only time he felt truly at ease.

He drove the long way, by the back roads through different neighborhoods. In a lull in conversation, Kirsten squinted forward and said, "What's *that?*"

Cars had lined up on the side of the road, a bucolic, wooded area with each house spaced far apart. A place that Mack knew well; he had lived there when he was young, when his parents were still married, and his big brother still lived with him. Oh, no, he thought with sudden realization.

Deep in those very woods, they saw a corona of light that seemed to come from many flickering candles. Damn, why did I drive this way?

"Oh, shit, I know what that is," Kirsten said, "It's the vigil. For Elizabeth."

Mack's heart sank in his chest. The previous morning he had walked into the living room to find his mother watching the news, frozen, coffee cup forgotten in her hand. There had actually been a tear running down her face. "Jeez, ma, what happened?" he had asked, and then she had really started to cry.

His mother tended to be emotional, he told himself. And he had only known Elizabeth when they were kids. But still, Mack had felt a sad, guilty lurch in his heart every time he thought about what had happened. And also that skin-crawling sense of panic, which is what had sent him out to the cornfield that night. He had tried so hard not to dwell on it. Until now. Damn it.

"You think we should go?" Kirsten asked, serious now. Her eyebrows puckered up at the inner corners, giving her an anxious look. "We kind of have to, right? The girl was our age and everything."

Mack sat with his hands frozen on the wheel for some moments, as though in a trance.

"Mack? Are you listening?"

"Yeah. I mean, naw, I don't want to. It's not my kind of

thing. Let's go back to the party."

"Oh, come on, just for a few minutes? I'll bet there will be kids from school there."

"I dunno …" Looking at the haze of candlelight seemed to play tricks on his mind. It seemed to grow in brightness. Get bigger. Something about it made him feel a vague sense of doom, and he wanted to leave. But what could he say? "Well. Just for a minute, I guess."

He parked the car, and they walked toward the gathering. "What's wrong, Mack? You look funny." Kirsten took him by the hand.

He shrugged. "I feel weird about it, I guess. I sort of knew the girl. Once."

"No way?" She looked wide-eyed for a minute, but then her face collapsed into such an expression of sympathy, *pity*, that he felt embarrassed; exactly what he'd wanted to avoid. "Mack, are you really sad about it?"

"Well, when I say I *knew* her, I mean just barely. A long time ago when we were kids." They had been seven years old. It all felt so hazy and dreamlike now. He pictured her, a little girl with short dark hair. Her intense eyes. She and he rarely spoke aloud to each other, able to play for hours, absorbed in what they were doing, with a kind of silent, shared ecstasy, overturning rocks, looking for bugs to put in a jar. Picking wild blackberries. In these same woods, they'd built shelters from large broken branches then camouflaged them with leaves. Finished, they sat in the cool leafy shelter and said nothing, but felt a great tired satisfaction. How wonderful it was, to communicate without having to speak! How he had loved those quiet leafy shelters.

Elizabeth had not sounded like other kids when she *did* speak. Her words had a strange, skipping cadence. Her voice sounded furry and rarely used.

He remembered her mother, who hovered, watching and listening, from a distance. She had long, curly silver hair and stood on her house's back deck overlooking the woods, leaning on the railing, still as a statue.

They passed this very house, now. Elizabeth's house was so different from the others. Clean and simple in its lines, almost like a modern art museum. Odd-shaped translucent windows on the front. And the vertical wood siding, so dark that the house blended, almost invisible, into the woods behind it.

"Do you think her mother even wants these people here?" he asked. "Aren't we invading her property or something?"

"A lot of the woods back there belong to the town, my dad said. I guess she can't say anything either way. If it's like, public."

For so many people, maybe forty, fifty people gathered in the woods, it was oddly hushed, their footsteps silenced by the fallen pine needles as they threaded their way through the trees. Candle-lit faces of all ages loomed in the darkness. Most looking solemn and speaking in low murmurs. Some old folks, some people his parent's age. Lots of high school kids; who didn't look quite so solemn, but stood in little packs, talking quietly.

"Hey, there's Mack!"

Reflexively, hearing his own name, Mack pumped himself up, a genial smile on his face, half raising a gangly arm, ready to wave to a group of kids from school, ones he didn't know well. But everyone knew *him* because he played on the football team.

"Hey, what's up?" he asked, approaching the two guys and two girls, rubbing his hands together. The night was turning brisk, crackling with autumn. The guy who had spotted him he knew from biology class. One of the girls saw Kirsten and waved, with a shy smile on her face, ducking her head.

"It's some sad shit, isn't it?" asked the guy. Brendon? *Brandon* Mack suddenly remembered. Blond guy with a buzz cut who wrote for the school paper.

"Yeah, sucks, doesn't it?" The candlelight flickered on the undersides of the leaves. The gathering felt all at once very strange, too many people here, in a space where they should not be; Mack experienced an overwhelming feeling of doom. He badly wanted to leave, though he knew he had to *look* cool, at least.

"The girl, Elizabeth, I guess was some kind of shut-in? Her and the mom?" Brandon's eyes always burned with unusual intensity. He had looked, Mack remembered, with the same bright-beamed attention upon the rabbit they had dissected together in class, sprawled on the lab tray, its legs surprisingly long and thin; Mack had felt that there was *tension* in those rabbit limbs, as though it might spring away at any moment. "I used to see her around, though. I always thought they were Amish or something. She had that *look*, you know."

"Yeah. I know what you mean. I guess"

Brandon came closer, edged up to Mack and spoke low. "I have an uncle works for the news station. He told me all the details. The girl's face, well … you wouldn't even recognize it. People don't realize how ugly hanging really is, it's fucked-up." He shook his head. "They're doing an autopsy and everything. I guess that's what they have to do, even though it all seems pretty clear-cut."

"Clear-cut?"

"*Suicide.*"

Brandon whispered the word in a low hiss then peered into Mack's face as though to gauge his reaction. Mack stepped away, rubbing his chin, looking around. He didn't like the annoying way Brandon kept looking at him like that, in that clinical, *fishy* kind of way.

And when Brandon silently mouthed, *"She was a virgin,"* Mack had such an impulse to hit him in the face that he actually made a fist, clenched deep in his pocket.

"And the mother, well, he said the mother had to be sedated. She was out of her mind. They had to give her a knockout shot. I mean, they *had* to, right?"

"Yeah." Where was Kirsten? He couldn't see her anywhere. "By the way, is the mother here?"

"Oh, hell no. She's laid up in the house they said, zonked out. Who can blame her?"

"Well, shit, maybe we all shouldn't be here. What if she doesn't want this?"

"Come on, the town has to mourn. These are good people, coming together. Just showing support." He smiled a tight little smile. "Did you see the tree?"

"No!" Mack was slowly becoming pissed off. Brandon wasn't taking any hints.

"It's over there," he pointed.

It was a large white oak tree, so tall that he could not see the top of it. At the bottom of its large, gnarled trunk was a little shrine comprised of large pillar candles, their flames flickering deep into the melted wax, and a hand-drawn tacked-up sign that said, ANGEL GONE TOO SOON. Heaped at the bottom was a mound of plastic-wrapped florists' bouquets, and, weirdly, stuffed animals. Teddy bears and bunnies and mice. The firelight reflected blankly in their dark plastic eyes.

The sight unnerved Mack. "But…but this isn't her at all!

It's like it's for some other, *imaginary* person!"

"What do you mean, bro?"

"Mack knew her!" Kirsten emerged behind them from the darkness. Mack had wanted to find her. Now he wanted to lose her again.

Concerned faces turned toward him.

Whispers. He knew her. Over there, that tall guy … a friend of the girl's …

Mack shrugged, speechless. He actually felt his ears turn red.

"Hey, Lillian!" someone called, looking around "Where is she? She knew Elizabeth, too. Is she—"

"That's okay," Mack said, "I'm leaving any—"

But they'd located Lillian and brought her to him. "Hi, Mack," she said, looking awkward and giving a little wave.

"Hi," he muttered, his voice hoarse. "How's it goin'?"

Lillian, too, had been one of his childhood playmates in this neighborhood. But Lillian had lived down aways, in the biggest, nicest house in that neighborhood; her parents had let all the kids race their bikes down its long, sloping driveway.

Lillian was so small, he could rest his arm on the top of her head. She looked like the dancer and gymnast she had always been. Small, compact, with dark bobbed hair and large, earnest brown eyes. Tiny as she was, she possessed a frenetic energy that made her seem somehow larger. She was fond of causes and petitions. PETA, Amnesty International. Bake sales for charity. Although friendly acquaintances since the old days, she and Mack now ran in different circles.

"Oh, Mack, it's so awful, isn't it?"

As though on cue people began to back off, to give the two of them some space, although they continued to stare.

Wringing her hands and bouncing on her heels, she looked up at him. "I-I hadn't talked to her in so long ... I just ... I should have gone to say hello.... I could have, I don't know, been a friend to her or something ..."

She talked fast which made him nervous.

"Dude, it's not your fault," he said, cutting her off. "It was hard, you know, for her to keep in touch when she didn't go to school and all. I lost touch, too. It's natural."

"But you don't live in the neighborhood anymore. I do! And now I just, just can't stop thinking about it, and what it must have been like to be *her*, you know?" This had always been the other side to Lillian. Bright and earnest and ebullient most of the time, but she could turn stuttering and anxious when things went wrong. She reminded him of a spooked horse.

"Lil." He hadn't called her that in years. "There's nothing you could have done. Really. It was what it was, right?" He idly gazed out over the illuminated branches, and a memory suddenly surfaced into his consciousness. "Hey, remember the firefield?"

He'd sometimes played with Lillian and Elizabeth, together, in those woods. With no other boys in the neighborhood, at that age, it hadn't bothered him to play with girls. One other girl had played with them, too. Vanessa.

The woods had seemed enormous and magical. One day they'd followed a young doe through the dark green woods and eventually broken through into an unexpected meadow, one they'd never seen before. Mack remembered the light, brighter than nature in the overexposed film of his memory. Bright flowers, goldenrod and Queen Anne's lace, all ablaze in his imagination. The landscape had struck him as inverted: the field brighter than the sky above. Even now, to him, it was something too painfully bright to look at.

He caught Lillian's eye and knew she remembered it, too. The present and the past felt all mixed up; in that moment, they were friends again.

Lillian smiled. "Yeah. That was fun, wasn't it? Everything seems so much larger when you're a kid." She frowned. "I wonder how we thought up that name. Firefield?"

The four children had played there until dusk, games now mysterious and almost tribal. Games of circles and rocks and stones, moon, and sun, strange things. It was funny, though, that at some point during those games Elizabeth disappeared without saying goodbye. Look up, and she had gone.

Lost in his thoughts, it took a moment to realize that Lillian was holding his hand. Tight.

THREE

Vanessa Davis was in love with words. Her parents joked that she loved them more than boys, and they weren't far off from the truth. The shelves of her bedroom were lined with dictionaries, not only in English but Japanese, French, and Greek. Though she went to a rigorous private day school, she also signed up to take college courses in linguistics at the local liberal arts college. Her parents, as always, were uncomplaining about paying the fees. They did worry, though, that sometimes Vanessa was too fevered in her drive to *learn*. She never went to dances or had a steady boyfriend or even a regular group of girlfriends to bring back to the house.

It was true, Vanessa stayed in her room a lot. But what they did not realize was that her inner life was huge, echoing, and enormous. She could stay happily occupied in her own head for hours, and not get bored.

That morning when Vanessa opened her eyes, she lay in bed, still in that twilit state between sleeping and waking. It was a lovely lull of space in which words lit around her like brightly colored butterflies: *Natsukashii.* Scintilla.

Sillage. Offing. Stretched out, prone, it was as though the words fluttered and settled softly over her body like a veil. The music of language stirred pleasurable tingles through her limbs. It *could* be a compulsion, she figured. But such a lovely one. She loved nothing better than to capture a word with her net, pin it down, and trace its heritage.

One word was larger and more gaily colored than any of the others on that particular morning: *Kairos*. The word was one of her favorites. From ancient Greece, it meant supreme moment. Delicate, fleeting rightness of time and place. A doorway of opportunity.

The word eclipsed all others as she stirred beneath her sheets. Though it preoccupied her drowsy morning thoughts, she thought it had actually first popped into her head the night before. Working at the computer in her bedroom, she had intermittently looked out of the window at the vigil for Elizabeth Gray, right down the street. Though her parents had walked down to pay their respects, Vanessa had stayed behind. "General principles," was the reason she tersely gave them. "But Vanessa, you used to *know* her," her mother pleaded. But Vanessa did not feel comfortable joining the throngs of people. To her, there was something about the ceremony that rang hollow. Some working-out of a false emotion.

She felt the same way about the memorial site set up in Elizabeth's name online. It was *creepy*, like a digital graveyard. Instead of a headstone, it featured a picture of Elizabeth as a young girl. Just a snapshot, and not even a very good one. The girl's face was half turned in shadow, one hand at her mouth, her eyes mistrustful and hesitant. It was odd, strangers coming to this site and posting maudlin greeting-card type memes, In deepest sorrow for a flower plucked away, unbloomed! There are no endings, just new beginnings! Vanessa rolled her eyes.

Many people, particularly middle and high school students, found Elizabeth to be a romantic, tragic figure. They not only posted memes but shared song lyrics and movie quotes, as though Elizabeth had been their friend and shared their tastes and private jokes. Vanessa found the whole thing to be distasteful, and frankly, weird.

"They are making this death all about themselves. It's a sociological phenomenon." She tried to explain without hurting her parents' feelings, as they put their jackets on to go to the vigil, without her.

Her mother had sighed. A big, warm woman who always hugged her friends and wore tie-dyed scarves and lots of turquoise jewelry. Sometimes it was hard to believe she and Vanessa they were related at all.

"Honey, sometimes I wish you wouldn't talk about people like they are ... just a walking heap of *concepts*." She stroked the side of her face. "Life is more complicated than that. And I know this must affect you deep down in ways you don't realize yet. That poor girl. And *Annabel*. My God ..." Vanessa's mother was one of the few that had been friendly with Elizabeth's mother, though they only made small talk in passing. "I can only imagine what she's going through. I'm taking her a casserole. And I'll ask if she needs any errands run."

"Well, I have a paper to write for AP English. A big one."

"Then you can stay home and watch your little brother," her father said, patting her on the back. "Make sure he's in bed by nine."

So as Connor played computer games in the den, from which tinny Japanese music emanated, Vanessa sat at the keyboard in her room, composing a paper on *Middlemarch*.

But the provincial life of Middlemarch in her head, and her own thoughts and words on the screen, intermingled with the noise from outside. It sounded almost celebratory, as though people were on their way to a carnival; she paused and looked out of the window. Without streetlights on their road, it was black save for the headlights of cars that washed through again and again. She regarded her own reflection in the window, a seventeen-year-old girl with long, dark blonde hair twisted carelessly into a topknot. Her chunky-rimmed glasses tapered and angled up, hiding the top of her face in a kind of mask. Often she tucked her lips into a small, ironic-looking smile, of which she was rarely aware until people asked "What is so funny, Vanessa? What are you always thinking about?" To which she never had an answer.

She knew the crowd was headed to the woods behind Elizabeth's house. The place where they had played when they were kids. The place where, three days ago, they had found the body.

Concentrating on her work was hard. Her mind kept wandering. She tried hard to remember the last time she had seen Elizabeth. Although they lived a three-minute walk from each other, and she had seen her from afar from time to time, the last time they had spoken together face-to-face was five years before, when they were twelve. That was the time they had stolen ammonium nitrate together.

Vanessa had been restless. It was the end of a long summer. School was not in session for another week. So she had gone out to ride her bike around, aimlessly, in big lazy loops, looking up at the sky, not really thinking anything at all.

She became aware of the quiet hiss of bike wheels behind her; she slowed and looked over her shoulder.

It was Elizabeth. Vanessa had not seen her in ages and was shocked by how different the girl looked. Already she looked like a young teenager, with long muscular legs, dark bangs that swept down low across her forehead, and full, almost insolent looking lips. Not only did her body look like that of an older girl. It showed in her eyes, her face. That was the most striking of all. Her expression was that of an adult's, as though she had seen plenty in her lifetime, though she was only twelve. She reminded Vanessa of a photo she had seen in a magazine of child soldiers in the Middle East.

Her presence was so shocking, dazzling, as to be nearly hallucinatory. Had Vanessa conjured her up out of woozy boredom?

Stopped in front of each other, they regarded each other in silence over their handlebars. And then Elizabeth spoke, in a voice that was low and quite flat. She said, "I know a secret."

"So?" asked Vanessa, crossing her arms over her flat chest. She wanted to hide the fact that the girl made her feel intimidated and shy.

But Elizabeth motioned with her head to follow, and they rode their bikes down a long narrow lane that went off into different neighborhoods, where the houses were more run-down and further apart. They snuck into the barn of a small farm, where Elizabeth showed her various scary implements, things with cogs and blades and sharp edges. And the big bags lined against the wall, one of which was split open. Full of fine white crystals.

"Put your hand in, I dare you," Elizabeth urged her,

and Vanessa did. It was so cool and pure, running through her fingers.

"You can make that into a bomb, you know. Terrorists use it."

She looked up and their eyes locked. Vanessa didn't know whether to believe her or not, but the idea fascinated her: crystalline beauty. Compressed explosion. The girls filled their pockets with the stuff and then ran out, giggling.

It was such an odd memory, and to think it was the last one she had of this girl. Now she was dead.

It stunned the mind. Vanessa had never known anybody dead before.

It made her feel so incredibly odd, lightheaded, sitting there at her desk. And for the first time, sad. But in a way, she could not share with others. They wouldn't understand.

Her parents were subdued when they came back and gave her extra-long hugs. She went to bed and had strange dreams in which some roaring, void-like entity was chasing her through the woods, trying to annihilate her. For hours, she ran and ran, trying to get away.

But she woke in the morning well rested, and she even forgot, at first, that Elizabeth was dead. And that was when the word *kairos* started to nag her head, like a message of great import. Perfect time. Sacred time of action.

She didn't know its significance.

Located on acres of hilly green land, Windsor School occupied a cluster of tasteful Spanish-style stucco buildings with tiled roofs. It had always reminded Vanessa of a high-end retirement community, except teenagers ambled down the long curving walkways.

At lunchtime, she liked to smoke behind a manicured privet hedge with the few other scholarship kids she hung out with. Most other students thought Vanessa was "hard," a "ball buster," a shrew with a mean edge to her. Mostly because she did not laugh at their stupid jokes, and had a way of looking at people levelly, staring, until they looked away first. So she always sat with the smokers, the derelicts of the school. They were watching two girls in tennis whites, whacking a ball back and forth across the tennis court, the sound of it echoing hollowly.

"I want to burn this place down," said one girl.

"Fuckin snobs," said the boy sitting with them. "They don't know they're living in a dream world. We don't even exist on their plane. What do you think, Vanessa? Don't you fuckin hate this place?"

Vanessa shot smoke through her nostrils in a stream. "Doesn't affect me. I'm already gone. Mentally, anyway."

"Nothing bothers you, Vanessa."

"Hopefully I'll be in New York this time next year, and this place will be ancient history." She had applied to NYU and Columbia. She didn't yet know whether she had been accepted. But she liked to think that she could will it to be so.

She smiled to herself, imagining walking down a gritty sidewalk, sun-blocked out by glistening buildings of dizzying height. A veil of pigeons lifting in the air.

"Oooh, boho intellectual girl in da city, look out! Livin' the LIFE!"

Vanessa just smiled her mysterious smile. Her eyes closed; in her imagination, she was transported. "The life of the mind, baby."

The story ran in the local newspaper. Vanessa clipped it

and hid it between the pages of her French dictionary:

WELLSLEY, Ct – State and local authorities are continuing to investigate the death of Elizabeth Gray, 17, who was found hanging from a tree branch in the woods near her Wellesley home. Resident Ernest Stevenson, 84, discovered the body the morning of October 2nd. Coroners estimate that the girl had been dead for several hours.

According to sources, all signs point to suicide. However, there are some questions now that toxicology reports show evidence of Flunitrazepan, aka "roofies" in the girl's system. Officials now are interviewing townspeople for any information they might have about the girl, who reportedly lived a reclusive life with her mother, Annabel Gray, 55.

Adding to the complexity of the case, the Connecticut Department of Health Services says that there is no official record of the girl's birth.

"No social security number, no nothing," says a source close to the case. "Supposedly Elizabeth was homeschooled, but that wasn't possible. She was never registered with the district. It makes you wonder, how could this happen? How can we declare the girl dead if we can not even say she was born?"

Annabel Gray claims that the girl was born at home and that the midwife filed for a birth certificate to the best of her knowledge. Mrs. Gray continues to be questioned. The midwife may be subpoenaed if necessary.

"Suicide investigations must be handled with enormous care," said the source, "especially a case like this one. While no conclusions have been reached in this matter, we must do our due diligence."

Anyone with any information having to do with Elizabeth Gray's life or death is encouraged to call the Wellesley police department.

So it should have been no surprise at all the evening that her father appeared in her doorway, knocking softly on the frame.

"Honey, we got a call from the police station. They want you to come down so they can ask you some questions about Elizabeth." He was blinking, as he did when he was uneasy. "Nothing to be nervous about. It's just because you knew her way back when, and, well … you know, they need to do their duty, and you need to do yours, yadda yadda. I told them you'd come down tomorrow night since you've got class this evening. Is that, I mean, are you—"

"Dad! It's *fine!* I'm not nervous about anything. I just—"

"No need to snap. Just … tomorrow, okay?"

She didn't know what she felt. Just blank, as her father wandered away and she continued to sit at her desk, her calculus book spread open and forgotten before her.

She had been pressing her pencil against the desktop so hard that the lead snapped.

Intro to linguistics class took place in a small room with flickering fluorescent lights, students and instructor sitting around a long conference table. The instructor was an intense young man with dark circles under his eyes, who swiveled his gaze up and down the table as he intoned:

"Consensus is that there are two layers. The surface structure of language, those sounds that we hear with our ears, and the deep structure, which is internal. Deep structure exists in the mind …"

The class comprised mostly adult students, Vanessa, the only high schooler, and Nick, a scruffy boy in his twenties in a denim jacket who worked in a pizza place by day and took classes at night.

Vanessa couldn't keep her eyes of Nick. They had talked a little bit before. Pleasant acquaintances. But something about the newspaper article had made Vanessa feel unmoored. It made everything seem somehow more fragile. Like reality was brittle as a mirror. Anything could shatter in an instant.

She approached Nick as class ended. "How's it going?" she asked.

"It's going. What's up with you?" His body was slight. But she envisioned that he was wiry with taut muscles. She pictured him as a car mechanic. Or with an acoustic guitar in a coffee shop. It was enticing to her that he could be anyone.

She shrugged and smiled the half-smile that people found so mysterious and compelling. "You need a lift home?" Nick usually walked back to his apartment building that was just off campus.

As they drove into the night in her ten-year-old Honda Civic, she switched on the radio, tuned to the campus jazz station. Lonely alto sax and keyboard. It was only minutes before they pulled up in the parking lot.

"You want to come in, or…" The boy, who was at least five years older than her, lowered his eyes. He may have been blushing in the shadows thrown by the utility lights.

Vanessa had always regarded her virginity as a complicated thing. It made her feel in control, Teflon-hard. To lose it made her fear losing perspective, her only strength, as far as she was concerned. Losing it would make her ordinary.

And yet, at the same time, it was a burden she wanted to shake off so that her real life could begin. And she adored the beauty of the young man in her passenger seat. Having him there made her feel alive, and grounded in her body instead of lost in her mind. And she wouldn't have to think about *tomorrow*.

"Yes," she said, eyes unwavering. "I would like to come up."

FOUR

THE PHOTOGRAPH

The room was down a flight of stairs, basement level. Everything in it was a different shade of brown. Brown paneling on the walls, brown imitation wood table. Brown carpet with indentions where furniture had been moved around.

Against this room, Lillian Harris stood out vividly in her red-and-white cheerleader uniform, with sweatpants worn underneath. She sat straight-backed at the table, hands folded in front of her, all quivering lines of tension. Though her brown eyes were large and liquid and down-turned at the corners, her lips were held in an eager smile in anticipation of anyone who might look her way.

"So thank you for coming down …" the man looked at a paper by his hand "… Lillian, I can see you came straight from school."

"Yes," she stuttered a little, her smile fading "I … I'm sorry about the outfit. I don't know if it's appropriate since th-this is such a serious matter."

"Yes, it is a serious matter," the detective said. He was a tall man, muscular, with a wide neck. A shaved head and a gray goatee. "But you are not in any kind of trouble, miss. We are just interviewing all the folks from town who had ever been in contact with Elizabeth."

"Yes. I-I know. And I want to help in any way I can." Her smile was back, bright as ever, but her eyes looked strained; this room, to her, felt tinged with other people's suffering. An energy trapped in its depressing brown stagnancy.

"When did you know Elizabeth?"

"Mostly when we were kids. Although we still are neighbors. Or, were. I would, like, honk the horn at her when I was driving by. She never really smiled. She always just kind of gave a little wave. I never took it personally. Just …"

"Just what?"

"I don't know. She just always acted sort of different. I thought it was because she was adopted."

"She told you she was adopted?"

"Not exactly." She fumbled with the zip of her cheerleading jacket. "It was just known, I guess? That she was adopted from a Russian orphanage? The kind where the babies aren't hugged, and they just lie there in the cots with a bottle propped up?" Her large eyes went glassy and vacant for a moment, as though she saw something troubling. Her voice had faded away into a croak.

The man nodded, no expression on his face. "And when was the last time you saw her?"

"I think um … when I talked to her mother when I went door-to-door last month selling raffle tickets for the Boys and Girls Club. I saw Elizabeth watching from behind, but we didn't talk. Just looked at each other. Waved."

"It sounds as though you are a very active girl."

"I try to be. I'm trying to get into the best school I can.

My grades are okay, I guess. But I'm not exactly setting the world on fire." She rolled her eyes with a little laugh. "So I just try to do a lot. I guess I just really want to make the world a better place? Some people say I take on too much, but it's hard to *stop?* If I get too stressed out, though, I like to ride my horse. I have a Morgan named Midnight. She's boarded. I ride her on weekends, mostly." Lillian's heart swelled and bloomed in her chest just thinking about Midnight. Her happiest times were spent alone on her horse, galloping with the wind in her ears, shutting everything else out. She had none of the racing thoughts that usually tormented her when she rode Midnight. They merged into one, they were so in tune. She loved to brush Midnight until her coat was glossy and bury her face in her side. She was most herself in a barn full of snuffling, gentle horses.

The detective smiled at her, nodding. "So it seems you and Elizabeth kind of took different tracks as you got older."

Lillian looked down guiltily, saying nothing for a moment. "I-I wish I could have reached out to her more. But it's hard when you don't go to school together."

He opened a folder and took out a scanned photograph and pushed it over to her. "So this is you together when you were young?"

She held it up in front of her. It was a photo of Elizabeth's seventh birthday party. The only party she remembered the girl invited her to. The children, four of them, posed, grinning in her backyard, arms around each other. In the background was the picnic table set with a tablecloth and a lavender birthday cake with a unicorn on it.

Stunned, Lillian said, "I've never seen this before!

Where did you get it?"

"Mrs. Gray, Elizabeth's mother, provided it. So that is you?"

"Yes," she whispered. It was her seven-year-old self, skinny and knock-kneed, wearing terry shorts and a shirt with a sequined floral appliqué on it.

"And the others?"

"Oh. Well, that would be Mack right there. The other little girl is Vanessa. Vanessa is still my neighbor, too. She goes to a private school outside of town, she's really smart. Mack and I go to Wellesley High together. He's on the football team. He's a really good guy, the most popular guy in school, practically...."

Her voice trailed off as she gazed at the picture. Mack with his spiky dark hair and missing teeth, like a little Jack O'Lantern. Vanessa, even then, composed and mature beyond her years with that close-lipped smile.

And Elizabeth. In retrospect she seemed tragic and haunted in this photo, even though she was just a little girl in a sprigged sundress, smiling shyly with watchful, deep-set eyes.

"I-is the interview over?" she asked. "I don't know if I'm feeling so well. I think I need some air."

It was a relief to be back in her own bedroom, where every surface was cushioned, draped, full of things that made her happy. On a large board on one wall of padded pink satin, crisscrossed with pink ribbons, she kept all her photographs. Many of the photos were of her and her older sister, Megan, who was a pre-med student at Emory.

Megan had always been a star student, and she would become a doctor like their father, who was an obstetrician at the women and infants' hospital. The two sisters looked somewhat alike, dark hair and brown eyes, but Megan was taller, more graceful. Confident enough that she did not ramble and stutter as Lillian did when she was nervous. She feared she had made a fool of herself at the interview.

Also on her pink board were photos of her riding Midnight on a sun-dazzled spring day the previous year. One captured Lillian with the cheerleading squad, hugging her teammates, grinning as though she would burst with happiness. All of those girls doted on Lillian and called her Bug or Ladybug. Lillian was always good for a sympathetic talk or a hug. She always remembered people's birthdays and brought them a card or a balloon.

Images of Lillian and her boyfriend, Jack, peppered the board. She and Jack had been together for a year and a half. He was away in college but saw her on most weekends. He was kind, with tousled blond hair, and wanted to be a special needs teacher. She didn't know if she loved him. She often felt wound-up and over-talkative in his presence. Though she knew she shouldn't, she most liked spending time with him in bed. Sex still new to her, she wasn't sure if she liked it, or was good at it. But she liked the lull afterward when he lay in her arms, vulnerable and panting and she stroked his head. He reminded her of one of the horses, an elemental creature she could relate to, spirit to spirit. She'd soothe him, and feel so moved that sometimes she'd burst into tears for no reason. She'd have to tell Jack yes, yes she was all right. Nothing was wrong. It was just something she had to do.

Sometimes she felt the same impulse to tears when she was in church with her parents. It was a stately Episcopalian church, and when she heard 'I Want to Walk as a Child of the Light' played on the organ, she couldn't say she felt the presence of *God*, exactly. (She even doubted sometimes that she believed in God.) But her body was like an unsheathed nerve. The faith of other people in the room made her feel lightheaded with emotion, made her want to run out down the red-carpeted aisle, with her eyes closed and her hands over her ears.

But her room was safe, a soft, rosy place where she could talk to friends on the phone, their distant friendly voices lifting her up. Here, she felt anchored. She felt real.

She propped herself up on the white wicker bed frame and dialed Mack's phone number and closed her eyes, listening to the far off, digital tone of the ring.

Two, three times. "Hello?" There was the sound in the background of muffled screaming, explosions, gunfire.

"Hi, Mack. It's Lil." It was funny how her voice could in an instant be bright and sunny and bell-like. "What are you doing?"

"Oh, not much. Just some homework."

"What's all that *noise*, then?"

"I got a movie on while I'm working. But I'm not watching it. Noise makes me concentrate better."

"Okaaaay …"

"Hold on." He turned down the volume. "So what's up?"

"Well," she sighed, "you wouldn't believe where I just got back from."

"Police station?"

She laughed. "How'd you know?"

"Lucky guess. Nah. I was there, too, the other day."

"What happened?"

"They interrogated me. Then they beat me up. Gave me a concussion. Haha, nah, not really."

"Well, what happened, Mack? For real?"

"For real?" He stopped, considering. She knew he had

his eyes rolled up to the ceiling, the way he did when he was thinking. "For real, nothing happened. They asked me some stuff about Elizabeth, and I answered. We were done in about fifteen minutes, boom, I go home."

"Oh." He sounded so casual, so unruffled, she didn't know what to say. "Well that's good, I guess." She scrolled through songs on her iPod, looking for something to soothe her mood and settled on Marianne Faithfull. Lillian had inherited a stack of record albums when her grandmother died of lung cancer and drawn to the covers showing Marianne in her blonde bangs and girlish dresses. But it was her voice that drew her in, especially those early songs where she sounded like an upper-class schoolgirl, but with such wisdom and sadness in her voice. She chose 'As Tears Go By.'

"So how did it go for you, Lil? You okay? You were taking this all pretty hard when I saw you the other night."

"I'm fine."

"Then why do you sound all … I don't know … weird."

She switched the song over partway through, to 'North Country Maid.' It told the story of a country girl who strayed up to London but then wept to go home again. It always made Lil go dreamy and swaying.

"Geez, what are you listening to, funeral music? You're bumming me out."

"It's *folk*. Traditional English ballad! Marianne Faithfull," her eyes ran over the rose pink walls of the room, as Marianne's deep, quivering voice sang in the background of the poor maid's laments. She sighed. "The interview was fine. The interview was *short*, thank God. I'll say that. And it's over now. It's all over."

"Then what's the problem?"

"I don't know. They showed me a picture, and it kind of

freaked me out all over again."

"The one from the party?"

"Yeah."

"That's right," he sighed. "You, me. Elizabeth and Vanessa."

"We were so little! And just the fact that I hadn't seen the photo before is what made it so bizarre. Like stepping into a portal or something. You know?"

Mack didn't answer for a few beats. Then he asked, "You still see Vanessa at all?"

She shook her head, though Mack couldn't see her. "No. We still live in the same neighborhood, but we aren't like, close like we used to be. We run into each other sometimes. We went for a walk once. But I always feel like she thinks I'm an airhead."

"I don't think she thinks that. She just looks at everyone that way. It's just the way her face looks. I think she's cool, just not big on social niceties. No time for bullshit, you know?"

Lil heard the sound of him drumming his desktop with pencils.

"Can you guess the drum solo I'm playing?"

"Mack, come on."

"Here's a clue, Zeppelin. Aw, come on, Lil, lighten *up*." He stopped the drumming and turned serious. "So why'd you call? It's kind of out of the blue. I didn't know you had my number."

"I got it from Jen. I-I didn't know who else to talk to about it. Everyone is getting so sentimental and stuff about Elizabeth, but we were actually her friends. Maybe her only friends. And it's bothering me. A lot"

"That was years ago, Lil. And that was a messed-up situation in that house, sounds like."

"What do you mean?"

"Well, with all that stuff that's come out, you know?" Lillian flushed.

"What? Lil, haven't you been following the news?"

"Well,…"She felt flustered and defensive. "I don't really *read* the news, okay? It's not that I don't care, it's just … me."

"Okay, cool. No judgment," he said mildly. "So you don't know about the roofies?"

"What?!"

"Yeah. Roofies in her blood. Me? I bet there was a guy involved."

"Huh? You think some *guy* had something to do with this?"

"No. I mean, I think she killed herself. It's obvious. But I bet it was over some guy messing with her head. A man, maybe. Some perv."

Lillian stared into space, assimilating this information.

"So I guess you don't know about the other weirdness? No birth certificate? Missing midwife? She wasn't adopted, you know."

"But she was! She had that sort of accent. She was adopted from Russia …" but her voice was trailing off uncertainly.

"Nah, man. I don't think she was, you know, murdered or anything. But I do think things were just more fucked-up than we realized. Her mother must be kind of a nut. She's a real granola hippie, that's for sure. And rich. Too much money can make people strange."

Lillian pictured Mrs. Gray, with her full head of long, springy white curls, the cargo pants and hiking boots she usually wore. "Her mom was always nice! To me, at least." But she had always found Mrs. Gray's eyes to be over-alert, and shrewd, and they looked at Lillian too closely. It made her feel self-conscious, as though she should check her hair or for stains on her clothes. "And she must be smart. Didn't she work in nature conservation or something? Like a Ph.D.?"

"Yeah. Something. There was some business thing with her husband, they split, and she cashed out. I never really knew her to mingle or anything. She always kept her eye on the kid. Smothered her. Sad stuff."

She felt slightly sick, thinking about it all. "I think I'd rather remember Elizabeth as a kid. Things are different when you're a kid, you know? We were more open-minded. Stuff was magical. There was almost a kind of heaven in it. I think about the firefield, and it was like … this plain of existence. We couldn't go back to it anymore because we don't believe. But I'd believe again if I could …"

Mack was drumming on the desktop again, thinking. "Well, forget that, there's no going back. Can't feel bad about what *is*, right? It's all over. Elizabeth was cremated, she's probably in some urn now. I mean, it's over. Done. No funeral but it's done." He cleared his throat. "So. Anyway. You got all your school applications in?"

"Yeah," she said.

He heard dejection in her voice. "Where you wanna go?"

"Don't know. Probably a state school if I'm lucky. I only have a 2.8…"

"Know your major?"

"I have no idea."

"Gonna keep your man? What's his name, Jack?"

"Don't know."

"Dump him."

"Why?"

"He's a smiley-faced cheese eater, that's why."

Lillian laughed in spite of herself. "Go to hell, Mack!"

She was still smiling after they had said their goodbyes and hung up; she closed her eyes and lay back on her bed.

Though she knew that all around her were her pillows, her pictures, and all of her favorite things that made her feel safe, she imagined that she felt the chill of autumn air underneath it all. She swore she could smell the damp scent of rotting leaves. As the warmth of the phone call faded away like a cloud over the sun, any sense of safety and familiarity gradually eroded, surmounted by the feeling that she was not home at all, that there was a forest growing in her bedroom, wind blowing through the tops of the trees, the ground cold and hard beneath her.

FIVE

I Like Your Nightgown

The first killing frosts of November were on their way. Though the sky was blue and the sun still dazzling bright in the sky, Vanessa felt a change in the air.

Helping her father winterize the yard, Vanessa did the raking. He had cut back the hostas and trimmed down the rose bushes. Afterward, they would shred the leaves for the compost pile, the same routine since she was a little girl.

Her father was the one who had taken most to gardening, her mother happy to leave him to it. His career as dean of his school's engineering department and the infighting and politicking that went along with it drove him to get his hands into the dirt whenever he could. Vigorous yard work seemed to energize him. She glanced over at him, a shambling academic with shaggy hair and a mustache, dressed in baggy corduroys and green plastic garden clogs. Would this be the last time they did this together? Already she felt a twinge of nostalgia for lost times; she would be in the city this time next year. She had gotten an acceptance letter from Columbia. And the scholarship money they offered was enough. Close enough, anyway. She could get a work-study job in the library. She smiled, imagining the prolific library stacks. The brilliant people she would meet. All the things she would learn.

Vanessa struggled hard for her to live in the moment, to be where she really was. She made an effort to pull herself back into the now. *Natsukashii.* The small things that bring sudden, joyous memories of the past. Maybe the crunch of dry brown leaves would always be her natsukashii and make her think of gardening with her father.

Her good fortune and happy anticipation of New York made her feel magnanimous; everything felt lovely and dear to her. She smiled to herself absently as she pulled the rake across the dead flowerbeds along the west side of the house. Leaves, sticks. An occasional bit of trash that had blown in. But something else drew her eye, something sticking up from the dirt. An edge of cellophane, with perforated edges. *Film?*

She reached down to grip an edge and pull it out. Not photo negatives. It was *movie* film, the kind that would run through an old 8mm projector. She wiped it off and held it up to the sun.

There were eight frames. She squinted to try to make out what they captured. The film was black and white, and quite degraded and scratched. She figured it must have been buried in the dirt for quite a while.

The film showed a young woman, standing in front of Vanessa's own house. But it must have been many years ago because she was standing next to their mulberry tree, which was enormous now and shaded the whole front yard. In the film, the tree was a sapling with wired braces around it to hold it up.

The fifties, Vanessa guessed. The house was built in the

fifties. It must have been when the tree was planted.

The girl in the photo wore a full-skirted dress with a smocked bodice. Her dark hair was pinned up on the sides and curled in the back, just hitting her shoulders. The frames appeared to show the mid-arc of a gesture: her face raised forward and a hand held out, as though testing for rain. Wind blew her skirt back and tousled her hair.

Vanessa was about to call out to her father, "Dad, come here, I found something neat buried in the dirt!" But then she stopped dead.

Because she knew the girl. The eyes were unmistakable. Sharp and piercing. There had always been something wild, *other* about her. And that presence burned forth, even through the degraded scrap of old film.

It was Elizabeth.

Vanessa felt that her throat had tightened up, as though someone had put their hands around it and squeezed. She couldn't utter a sound. The yard was still sun-dazzled, but through some kind of temporal reversal, like a photo negative, what was bright now dark. What was known and dear a few moments ago now frightening and unknowable.

She held it up again after taking a deep breath and shaking her head. A mistake? A trick of the subconscious, maybe? It had been a month since she had gone to the police station. A month since Elizabeth's cremation, and the news stories had ceased for the time being. She hadn't even been thinking of it, there had been too many other things happening. Why now?

But it *was* her. Vanessa felt a surge of irrational anger, humiliation. Someone must be playing a trick on her. But who would want to mess with her mind this way?

Her eyes darted around the yard. Still a beautiful autumn day. Crab apples still rotted on the ground, a drone of bees as they hovered around the vinegar smelling pulp, her father in the distance, pushing the wheelbarrow into the garage, oblivious in his garden togs.

She said nothing and slipped the scrap of film into her pocket.

Vanessa did not mention anything to her parents, and ate dinner in silence, listening to her excited little brother talk about an upcoming trip to Lazergate. The television broadcast the local news from the other room: early morning showers. Bank robbery thwarted downtown. Harvest Festival days. Vince, the golden retriever, slumbered near her feet, thumping his tail, lost in his dog dreams.

"What's up, Vanessa?" asked her mother, "You're a little quiet."

"Oh, just tired from yard work, I guess."

As soon as she could, she escaped to her bedroom. She lay on her sloppily made bed, among the several splayed-open textbooks and notebooks that she pushed aside. She didn't want to think anymore, so she put in her earbuds to listen to music. She chose Kraftwerk, 'Trans Europe Express.' Something about the song hypnotized and calmed her. The mechanical minimalism of it. The feel of trains bulleting forward, and the trailing Doppler effect. The emotionless, robotic chanting of the title, *Trans ... Europe ... Express* over and over until the words lost any meaning.

And for a time, she did feel lost in that feeling of momentum, the thrill of anonymity and new directions. But then her mind pulled her back to places where she didn't want to go. She looked again at the ruined segment of film.

Elizabeth, in frame-by-frame motion, wasn't holding

her hand up to the rain but holding her hand *out* to Vanessa. An entreaty. Looking right into her eyes. But *why?*

She had gone to the police station, hadn't she? She had done her part. When they showed her the picture of her and Elizabeth and Mack and Lillian, she'd nodded, all business. "Yes, I remember. Yes, that is me."

"What can you tell us of your impression of Elizabeth?" the man had asked.

"Nice girl. Quiet. I always thought she might have had neurological issues, though."

"Oh?" The detective asked, a sharp flash of interest in his eyes. "Why?"

"Just a sense. She talked a little funny. Like, weird starts and pauses. I thought she might have had some brain damage. Fetal alcohol syndrome or something."

Had that been a cruel thing to say? Was it even true? Vanessa couldn't say anymore. She didn't want to be involved. Had not *asked* to be involved. She just wanted to do her schoolwork. Go to college. Become a famous American linguist with her photo on book jackets. She would travel the world. Live in hotel rooms. The future was something she was hungry to consume. No longer would she have to even remember being the gawky, strange girl with the dictionary collection that nobody liked. She would be free.

And yet, this dead girl, trapped in this eternal gesture! Trapped in celluloid, with the little sapling tree that would stay in its braces forever. The image burned into Vanessa's mind; she saw it even when her eyes were closed. It made her feel frantic with claustrophobia. As though trapped *herself.*

What do you want from me?

Later that night, when everyone else was asleep, she

crept outside to where the trash waited at the curbside in the moonlight for the truck to come. She opened a trash bag and slipped the film into it, along with the news clippings she had saved for reasons unknown to herself. With the sense of relief, of a ritualistic cleansing, she retied the bag, looked up at the moon, and went back to her bed.

Mack slammed shut the tailgate of his truck and leaned against it with a ragged sigh, looking up at the night sky. His muscles ached, and the sweat on his body chilled in the November night air.

He was helping his father and older brother move to a new house. "Out in the country! Away from people. So Busby can roam all he wants without a leash." His father had told him this, but Mack had the feeling it was also because his brother Ricky liked to play loud music and shoot his gun at targets in the backyard. Not to mention the screaming arguments he sometimes got into with their dad. This tended to cause friction in their old neighborhood.

Ricky was twenty-four. He had graduated with honors from the military academy and had even served some time as a lieutenant. But he had had some trouble a year into being deployed in the Middle East. Things that had happened there had left him changed. Formerly garrulous and easygoing, he became withdrawn. The smell of burning drove him into contortions of anxiety. He'd speak to Mack sometimes in a low, spooky, monotonous voice, stories about interrogations and "men being put in boxes."

It was thought that he had started experimenting with drugs because of PTSD, and no one knew exactly when he'd escalated to snorting heroin. But he had gone from looking flat-lined to becoming erratic and excitable. Their father, a psychologist, did not want to send him to rehab.

He thought Ricky would do better in a home setting. "He needs love and patience, not an institution!" his father would yell at his mother, though she cried and begged to send the boy away for his own good. She couldn't handle it anymore. So his parents ended up separating, Ricky and his dad in one household, Mack and his mom in another.

Their new place was a rickety farmhouse with a falling-down old barn in back. Even though nothing had been unpacked yet, Ricky went out and climbed up into the hayloft where he made himself at home, lighting up a cigarette.

"Isn't that dangerous? Fire hazard and all?" Mack had asked his father as they watched from the window.

His father had only shrugged, resigned, and shook his head, his eyes dark-ringed and tired. "Whatever keeps him feeling safe. Contained. He probably feels comfortable there. It's like a barracks. He'll be fine."

He'll be fine, his father's mantra. Mack sometimes doubted that his brother was fine. His eyes, large, naked and hungry, trembled back and forth in their sockets as they scanned places, things. People's faces. Ricky wrote Mack actual letters in envelopes because he had paranoid ideas about the Internet and would not use email. The letters, long and rambling, spoke of "extinction events," "civil defense exercises," and questions like, "Do soldiers have free will? Sometimes I think not."

In one letter he described an incident from when he was deployed, seeing a jinn when he was scanning perimeters one night. A jinn was a desert spirit of Islamic mythology. This one was a tall, spindly, long-legged creature that looked like it was made of smoke, and strode straight toward him over the desert sand and then suddenly disappeared. The thing emitted no body heat on the reconnaissance equipment, convincing Ricky that making eye contact with it had made him lose his soul to the jinn for eternity.

Mack and his dad had taken a break and ordered pizza and eaten it with Ricky on the floor surrounded by moving boxes; the house looked badly in need of updates. The worn hardwood floor sagged toward the center of the room. The kitchen linoleum, shades of seventies goldenrod and avocado, had lifted in places. The previous owner's things could still be found here and there. Cooking utensils. Air fresheners. In one closet, a pair of madras plaid sneakers.

"It's okay, Ricky and I are going to fix this place up nice," his father said. Though their previous house had been equally shabby and in ill-repair.

Ricky and his dad drank beers, while Mack drank soda. Mack asked his dad how things at the office were going, and he in kind, asked Mack about college plans.

"No acceptances in the mail yet," Mack said, vaguely. He would not mention Brown.

"Well, I'm sure it will be real soon now, son."

As the other two talked, Ricky was eerily silent. At one point their father asked, "What's up, Ricky? Talk to your little bro, he came here just to see you."

Ricky wheeled around, looking at Mack in a belligerent way. "What the fuck do you want to talk about? Football? Cheerleaders? Keggers?"

"Hey now, Rick. That's not appropriate. Your brother cares about you and wants to—"

"The hell he cares. The hell he understands real life. Stupid kid."

"Ricky," cautious but firm this time, "how about some respect for Mack. Not everyone has to live your life and experiences to be validated, now do they? Respect and boundaries, right, bud?"

"I'm not one of your patients, Dad. Don't be fucking condescending."

As usual, when the two of them argued in this way, Mack willed himself to disappear.

It ended, as it usually did, when Ricky yelled, "Fuck everybody!" and left. He slammed the door on his way back to the hayloft, leaving an uneasy silence.

His father sighed. "Please, don't judge your brother. He doesn't do well with adjustments. He just needs to settle. He's been doing so well recently, you wouldn't believe it."

"Dad? He doesn't seem to be doing well at all."

"What do you mean?" His father tended to slip into this faux easygoing, neutral tone that infuriated Mack.

"Well, come on, really. He doesn't do well with *adjustments?* He's an adult! Twenty-four-years old and he behaves like a spoiled brat half the time—"

"Stop right there. Your brother has not had the typical life experiences of a kid his age. He's seen a lot. He's a sensitive soul, you know that. There is a lot for him to process right now."

"But I think he's still using drugs."

"He's *not.*" His father's mouth set in a straight, grim line. "I'd know. I live with him. And I'm his caretaker. He's not using."

"Dad, I'm not criticizing, I'm just telling the truth."

"But you *are* criticizing!" he said, his voice abruptly loud, arms flying out. "Can't you see that? And it isn't helpful! Don't you see that I expect more from you? You're the mature one! You're the one with a more stable temperament. You must see that you are lucky and you should not be judging those weaker than you when they can't help it—"

Mack had his hands up in front of him, as though to shield himself and kept his eyes down. "Okay, okay, okay …"

"Well, son, you don't live here, and I don't think you understand—"

"Okay, okay, fine, sorry …"

"—what it is exactly that we're going through here." He sighed heavily. "Sorry. Stress."

"Got it. No sweat."

His father sat staring into space for a few beats, then came back into his pleasant, smooth, reasonable voice. "How's your mother?"

"Okay, I guess." He thought she had been watching too much television lately. And the other night she had fallen asleep in the living room, an empty wine bottle on the coffee table that had been full that afternoon. "I think work is getting to her. A lot of parents giving her shit." She taught seventh-grade social studies.

"I thought she was moving to a new school soon."

"Thinking about it."

His father nodded. "You're a good son. I always thought that you and your mom had a tight bond. It's good, it's *good* I mean!" he said defensively, eyebrows up.

"Yeah, but I worry about how she's going to do when I move away." In fact, it made him feel queasy with guilt even to think of it. "She doesn't like to be alone."

"Well, you shouldn't feel responsible."

"Yeah, but shouldn't someone?"

"That someone isn't *you*. You aren't her spouse, you know."

Mack stood up, smeared his hands over his eyes. "No, I'm not her spouse. You were. You're supposed to be her spouse. And you're the one who walked out!"

"Son, Melissa doesn't want me there. She let me know in no uncertain terms. And I'm respecting that."

"You could check in every now and then."

"Your mother needs to respect our boundaries, Mack."

"Don't talk to me in that *voice!*" he yelled, walking out of the room. "Listen, I'm outta here, I have a biology test in the morning, and I don't have time for this."

"Well, Mack, we'd like to see you up here again. Sooner than later. Ricky and I are your family, too…"

But his voice had already faded away as Mack stormed out, slamming his fist into the wall of the mudroom as he went out the door into the night.

From the barn, darkly cavernous in the moonlight, he saw the red glowing tip of a cigarette.

"I heard you talking about me," Ricky, said in a cool, indifferent voice. "I'm tired of your shit, brother."

"Well, I'm tired of yours."

"Go back to Mommy, you little pussy."

Mack swore under his breath as he jammed the key into the ignition and pulled off, turning around in the grass, not caring if he left tire tracks.

Fuck them both, he thought. Let them rot out here in their falling-down house.

Instead of heading home, he drove in the opposite direction. It was a Sunday night, no other cars on the road. Perfect time to clear his head.

He liked having nothing to focus on but the beam of headlights, the hum of the engine. He didn't even turn on any music.

How could his dad be so irresponsible ... why was it so wrong for him to worry about his mother? There was no one else to do it. Though she was only fifty, she'd aged fast since Ricky's discharge from the service. She had shrunk. Her face pallid, her eyes always red-rimmed now.

Mack vowed, once again, that he'd succeed in life, no matter what. He'd walk the straight path. He would be the one to make up for the nightmare of the past two years.

He shifted into gear and flew off down a long stretch of straight country road. What in daytime was dazzling green farmland was unseen in the dark. The moon, bright and full, gave the impression of being stationary and following him as he surged forward, window open, black wind in his face.

But what if he *didn't* succeed? What if he just did not have the willpower? He imagined himself succumbing to weakness, a broken person like his brother. It would not happen. It *could* not happen. He would not allow it. For his mother's sake, he couldn't.

Up ahead, he had to slow down at a flashing railroad crossing. "Shit," he muttered under his breath, hitting the brake hard enough to squeal; a long car chugged by, endless, its whistle a baleful wailing that got to him. He actually wanted to cry. It was like hearing a sappy song or something. He put his head down on the steering wheel. He had felt so free a minute ago, and now the spell was broken.

The train passed, and the striped arm of the crossing had gone back up, and he drove off, slower now. The spirit of anger had left him, and he just felt numb.

Way, far up the road, he saw a figure walking on the shoulder. Which seemed odd; there was nothing around here but some run-down mechanics' shops, closed at this hour, and a rusty old water tower. He craned forward and peered, eyes narrowed, surprised to see that it was a woman. Or a girl, at any rate.

It didn't seem right. Had she been beaten, thrown out of someone's car? He slowed down before approaching her, unsure of what to do. He didn't want to scare her.

He'd only noticed her because of her pale hands and the nape of her neck, which glowed like phosphorescence. Her hair was piled up on her head in a fat, coiled plait, her skirt long and dark, and she wore a long dark overcoat. A dangerous way to be dressed for being out there.

She looks like Elizabeth. The thought, creeping into his mind, sent a current of electricity coursing through his system.

As he got closer, he took a wide berth, driving into the opposite lane. She glanced backward briefly so he could get a glimpse of her face.

Elizabeth. It *was* Elizabeth! His mind went blank with confusion and panic.

What happened in the next five seconds he could not explain to himself, no matter how many times it replayed in his mind afterward. The figure of the young woman *slid* into his path, as though she were an image from a film projector that had swiveled to the left; her feet continued their motion of walking *forward*, but the image slipped into the truck's path in one swift, smooth, sliding motion that made his stomach turn.

Mack screamed and slammed the brakes as he came upon her. The girl turned and looked over her shoulder again. There was *no face*, just a shadowy blank. The apparition flared up for a split second, to the size of a billboard. Mack heard a roaring in his ears, and felt his body pulled inside out as he drove *into* the image; his truck passed right through it as though it were made of air.

Blinded by fear, Mack felt the truck fishtail and leave the road, then roll down a low grassy embankment. His whole body shaking uncontrollably, he came to a stop, All he could do was gasp for breath.

Elizabeth! He must find Elizabeth (or the thing that looked like her.) He jumped out from the truck and hurried up the hill, his breath rasping through his mouth.

"Hey!" he called out, looking to the right, looking to the left. Nothing. But there had to be … something. His mind reeled, scrambling to make some kind of sense of what had just happened.

He ran across the road and into the scrub of woods on the other side. Hushed and dark, a small creek burbled through. He cried out again, startled by the thrashing of an animal running through the brush, inches away from him. He recovered himself and stumbled on. He found a shoe, but it was a woman's pink canvas sneaker, crushed flat. Empty beer cans, a cracked cell phone, dead. But nothing else.

Mack dashed back across the road, back to his truck, askew, down the embankment. Surely, if he had struck a person, there would at least be a dent? But there wasn't. He got in, put his face in his hands, breathed, breathed, breathed. Then put the keys in the ignition with shaking hands and eased back up onto the road's shoulder.

Lillian had been feeling off all day. She was edgy and irritable. Jack called her from school to plan what they would do over Thanksgiving break, and she started a fight with him for no good reason. Then she felt guilty for it afterward.

She didn't want to hang with her friends, either. The girls from cheerleading had invited her out for a late dinner, but she turned them down, saying she had too much homework. But it wasn't true. She simply wasn't in the mood for company.

She ate little that night, and after watching a movie with her parents (some confusing detective drama, people muttering in English accents) she excused herself and went to her room, changing into her long flannel nightgown with the sprigged flowers, the one that she wore when she wanted to feel like a little girl again.

Unable to sleep, she tossed and turned for hours.

The moonlight drained her bedroom of its soft pastels, its familiar amalgam of rose pink and cushions and white wicker. Everything looked silvery and very flat, lacking dimension. What had always been her safe place, all her life, looked alien to her sleep-deprived eyes. She had not had a full night's sleep all week. Maybe, she thought, that's why she had been so out of sorts.

But sleep did not come easily. It was a long time before her eyelids finally fell shut for good, and her thoughts drifted and skidded into strange waking dreams. Images from the rain misted streets of the detective movie, (an unseen narrator saying, "All was not what it seemed.") Flashes of random occurrences at school. Disembodied voices calling out to her. "Ladybug! Ladybug!" She imagined she was on a stage, about to give a presentation, but she had no notes and no idea what to say. The room was an amphitheater, but it was also a gray seascape, with crashing waves that receded into a wall of mist.

She started out of her reverie, frustrated to be awake again.

To distract and quiet her mind, she started to say the Lord's Prayer. "And now I lay me down to sleep …"

She said the prayer over and over, until her mind spun and unwound itself into unconsciousness. And for a while, there was nothing but oblivion.

But then, a small flicker centered in her brain, like a lone flame, red and orange, violet at the base.

That flame grew larger and lighter. She couldn't say that she was exactly *awake*. But it was a different kind of sleep. No words, just a serene and pervading clarity.

Lillian was aware of the heaviness of her limbs under the rose-print cover. Though she was a small person, her sleeping body had a great density. She stirred her fingers and toes. It felt so freeing to move while asleep. Compelled to sit up, she swung her legs over the side of her bed.

She needed to be somewhere. A great urgency moved her forward, but she could not make out what the destination was. Only that she needed to keep moving.

Out the bedroom door, down the hallway, past her parents' door, past the door of her sister's old bedroom. Down the staircase, past the framed family photos placed at even intervals on the wall, all the way down. Her parents on their wedding day. Baby portraits of herself and her sister. A family vacation in Nova Scotia. Lillian's eyes flicked over them, without really seeing them. She only saw the things in her mind, not the things in front of her.

Out of the front door. It felt natural to be outside in the night. It was her friend. She was supposed to be there. She didn't even feel the cold, though it was November, and she wasn't wearing shoes.

Floodlights lit the way down the walk and down the driveway that curved on a slope down to the street. Lillian moved serenely. This neighborhood had always been quiet and peaceful. But at this late night hour, it was silent, one could hear the smallest noises. The slight buzz from a utility pole. The whisper of night wind softly rustling the leaves of the trees. The barking of a faraway dog. Pitch blackness, but she could still see in the dark, like a cat.

She was Lillian, and yet she wasn't. She felt nameless, label-less. Neither boy nor girl. As she glided down the middle of the street, she felt that there were no limits to her. She and the night were one. An owl, hooting somewhere in the darkness, felt as close as the pulse in her wrist. She *was* the sky and the bright moon. She was the vastness of the stars.

These were not words spoken in her mind, but feelings. All of the houses were dark, the neighbors deep asleep. No one would witness the girl in the ankle length nightgown walking in darkness with an expression of peaceful, but absorbed attunement.

She had a destination, not in her mind, but in her gut. Her solar plexus. Her very center felt gripped by spectral fingers; she was pulled forward as though by a magnet. But the feeling was peaceful and loving, not scary. It was okay to let herself be guided.

The force was guiding her to Elizabeth's house, that large rectangle of blackened wood, streamlined and elegant looking. Unique from any other house. The opalescent windows that you couldn't see into, but at this late hour, light glowed through. The only house with lights on. She made out the footprints that had trampled the grass, back when people had gathered for the vigil. But that had been six weeks ago, in another world.

Everything was so very still. It could have been any time in Lillian's life. Past. Future. Serene and frozen in place.

She followed the footprints, down, down into the woods, to *the* tree, which still had a few candles around it, and stuffed animals, swollen by moisture from the autumn rains, like little drowned things. She looked but didn't go near it.

Farther, down a little path that wasn't really a path, but she remembered it by heart. The ground felt soft and spongy with pine needles, and she dug her toes in with pleasure. The trees enclosed her overhead like a canopy, a canopy that gently whispered and swayed.

To get to where she was going, she had to walk through an area of brambles, which cut her feet and made her bleed, but it didn't hurt. She was too happy just to break through. In a happy burst of wonder, she was back at *the firefield*.

Lillian stopped, and stood still for a long time, relishing the feeling of homecoming. Despite the dark, she felt the power of this place surrounding her. Why had she not been here in years? It had been so close all along. The firefield was a place that gave her a feeling of limitlessness. So secret, and yet so large, it made her want to gallop like her horse, Midnight. It made her want to gulp greedy lungsful of air. It was a place where you could be anything. It was a place where you could play and play. She had just somehow forgotten what this feeling was.

Standing in that state of strange flaring joy, she grew aware that she wasn't alone. And this knowledge did not alarm her. She was in the presence of an aligned spirit, a friend, who felt as she did. And there was an awareness in each of the other. A silent acknowledgment.

I like your nightgown. These words weren't exactly spoken to Lillian. They just seemed to leap into her mind, an intrusive thought, coming from without.

Thanks, Lillian thought, in reply, to whoever it was.

As soon as she made her telepathic reply to this voice, something changed and subtly shifted. As though speaking, a contact had been made. An energy transferred. Lillian felt small ripples of unease, which amplified into waves of fear. Lillian's breathing labored and her heart rate accelerated. Tingling sensations spread to her hands and feet. She felt an urgent need, all at once, to move. To *run*. But she could not move; she was cemented into place, her bare toes digging into the cold dirt and dead, dry grass poking into her feet like spikes.

The presence that she had felt to be inside her soul earlier was no longer a part of her, the *other* now was standing very close in front of her, and it was this *other's* fear that enveloped her. She could not see her, but she knew she was there, inches away from her face. It wasn't a bad energy, but it appealed to her in some way, a way that felt desperate.

Time stood still. Paralyzed by this creature's fear, the pain it transmitted unbearable, Lillian experienced a rawness that was terrible. And moment by moment, a shadowy figure began to form, arranging itself into the wispy outline of a girl with long hair, but before the features were filled in, before Lil could see her face, the image flickered away like a bad radio transmission.

Sky of distant stars, the hum of cicadas. Dampness of dewy ground wetting the edges of her nightgown. Maybe it had been an hour. Maybe two or even three, before Lillian's sluggish and dazed brain formed the words she needed to ask it. What do you want?

And the answer was, I want you to help me. Help me get out of here.

Then, in one searing burst of terror, Lillian felt a man's hands roughly on her shoulders and the sharp constriction of her throat. The surge of adrenalin shattered her trance, brutally transporting her to a wakeful state. Lillian clutched at her neck, willing the airways open, and screamed, a stifled, strangled scream, the sound a rabbit makes when grabbed up by a predator.

Lillian's eyes, awake and aware, rolled around her in terror. A wind crashed through the branches, making the trees come violently alive, thrashing all around her. It took her long terrified moments to figure out where she was. She had no idea how she had gotten there. But she knew she had to *run*.

Six

A Robin In The Window

Into the trash went the pumpkin with a squishy *thud*, along with the pots of purple and yellow mums, which were dead and drying out. Vanessa paused and wiped her hands on the back of her jeans; it was sunny outside, but purple rainclouds swelled in the distance. That pumpkin had sat for at least a month on the front porch, sinking in on itself like a deflated basketball. She often cleaned up her mother's holiday decorations, which she always put up zealously, then was lax about taking down.

On her way back into the house, she stopped. It took her a moment to recognize Lillian, who watched her quietly from the street, just standing there. Vanessa raised a hand in vague greeting. Lillian came forward.

The two girls had been neighbors for many years but rarely saw each other except in passing. Vanessa already felt defensively tongue-tied; Lillian had always been the type of girl who made her feel leaden and awkward, at a loss for what to say. Those who were so effortlessly cheery and outgoing threw her into confusion. Sometimes Vanessa acted haughty, even rude, to cover up her discomfiture.

Pale, with dark circles under her eyes, Lillian did not look her usual self. Whereas usually she was naturally effervescent, Lillian now looked … withdrawn. She had her arms wrapped around her chest as though chilled in her oversized gray sweater. Her rolled-hem jeans and boat shoes with no socks suggested she had wandered out in a hurry. Thin red scratches covered the tops of her feet. Fresh.

Vanessa's gaze moved from the feet, up her body, settling on her face, a small delicate face that in this autumn light looked like a small smudged fingerprint.

"How are you," Vanessa ventured, no question mark on the end.

Lillian shrugged. "Good. How about you?"

"Good. Just cleaning this Halloween stuff up, finally."

"Oh." Lillian shifted back and forth, right arm clutching her left anxiously. "Know where you're going to school yet?" The question was jaunty and did not match the watchful expression on her face.

"Yep. I'm going to Columbia. Hopefully, I'll be there early. Summer program. I can't *wait* to blow this joint."

"That's great."

"What about you?"

"Haven't heard back from my schools yet." Lillian glanced up at the approaching storm, avoiding Vanessa's eye.

The clouds blew closer, and a sudden gust stirred up the orange and yellow leaves on the ground. From above, the honking from a formation of geese flying through the sky; the sound amplified in a strange way, coming from all directions at once.

"I wonder how they know where they're going?" Lillian said this softly, to herself, a rhetorical question.

She was slightly startled when Vanessa answered, abruptly, "Pineal gland."

"*Pineal gland?*"

"Tells them where to go. It's at the center of the brain. Comes from Latin. *Pinea.* Like, pine cone. Pine nut."

Vanessa smiled at Lillian, a smile of innocent self-pride that lit up her face and made her look like the young girl she once was; but Lillian looked back at her with her in a searching way, her expression wide open, vulnerable. Lost.

Vanessa, brow furrowed, peered at her more closely. "Lil, would you like to come in?"

The girls sat together at the kitchen table. Vanessa had poured tea into steaming mugs.

"My parents and brother are out at the fall festival, so it's just us."

"Oh, yeah. I went there yesterday with the girls from my cheer squad. It was fun." Lillian held the mug in both hands, up to her face, as if she wished she could burrow into it.

Vanessa, always clumsy in situations that required delicacy, racked her brain for what to say. The girl was obviously distressed. But they weren't friends, exactly. Though they once had been, years and years ago.

So they sat in silence for some moments until Lillian put down her mug with a resolute clunk, sighed, and asked, "Do you remember the firefield?"

Vanessa blinked, puzzled "Sure. That clearing in the woods where we used to play all the time." She stared into space for a moment, recalling the games they had played together there. The games where they turned into statues. Or played "murderer." There had been one sing-songy ritual that, in retrospect, was astrological. They had chanted, "Tail of the dipper, tail of the bear ..."

"I wonder where we came up with all that stuff," Vanessa mused. "It was so weird, some of it. Psychosexual? Did it have something to do with the latency period?" She was taking a class in psychology at the college.

Lillian interrupted this train of thought by blurting out, "I was down there."

Vanessa frowned. "Where?"

"The firefield."

"Why?"

"Because I ... I don't know. I was there in the middle of the night, barefoot in my nightgown. I don't know how I got there."

"Sleepwalking."

"But I was, you know, lucid. It wasn't like that."

"Sleep paralysis?" She looked to the side, tapping the table with her fingers, pensive. "Fugue state!"

"Vanessa, it was something more than that. I think it was something, like, I don't know. Spiritual, in nature."

At the word spiritual, Vanessa stiffened. It was a word her mother and her New Age friends used a lot. It was one that often put Vanessa in a bad temper. A word empty of any real meaning that was used too much. She sighed. "Is that what you came here to tell me about?"

Lillian swallowed. She wasn't sure exactly what compelled her to watch Vanessa's house from afar that afternoon, waiting for the right sign to come over. The right time to act as though the visit was casual and off-the-cuff. "Vanessa, have you gotten any ... messages from Elizabeth?"

"Messages?"

"I don't know. Dreams. Visions. And please don't look at me like that."

"Like what?"

"Like I'm stupid. Sometimes I think everyone thinks I'm stupid."

"I don't think you're stupid. Just maybe susceptible? Making a narrative out of random events? People tend to do that, you know."

She spoke pedantically, but Vanessa's heart thumped loudly in her chest. Adrenalin whooshed through her veins. Somehow, since finding the scrap of film the day before, she had managed not to think of it at all. Even while throwing things into the very same trash can, she had not considered that the film scrap was still *in there*. The memory had somehow been erased from her mind. But now it returned, sending a rush of confusion and panic to flood her system. And she did not like it.

"Think about it," Vanessa carried on, to cover up her own dismay, "it was, what, six weeks ago? The whole town, all the schools, everyone was hysterical over Elizabeth. The vigil, the website, everyone was on overdrive. And now? They've dropped it. Forgotten about it, like it never happened. It was a sort of mass hysteria. People making up stories. Feeling they knew her when they didn't—"

"But we *did* know her."

Vanessa sat, mouth agape. For a panicked moment, she thought of telling Lillian about the scrap of movie film. Maybe she would feel better? Maybe speaking of it would release the strange power the incident had over her mind? The dead girl, lifting up her hand to the viewer from a black-and-white day of the past. The dead girl in front of Vanessa's own house. It made her feel scared and violated. And she never entertained the idea of fear. She always thought of herself as fearless.

She decided she would say nothing about the incident. For now.

"We knew her," Lillian went on, "so I feel like the responsibility is ours, you know?"

"What responsibility?"

"To know more about her. To figure out what happened."

"That's the police department's job."

"Well, they aren't doing it. They gave up. No leads. No ideas."

"I think the writing's on the wall," Vanessa said, evenly. "Sometimes, you look at a picture of something, and the answers are all there. Cut and dried. It was a suicide. A tragedy, but it's an old story. And it's done."

"But it's not done. This is a girl's life. It isn't done yet." Lillian looked at Vanessa wildly, trying to appeal to this girl who was so centered, and so calm. There was so much alert intelligence in Vanessa's pale eyes. But Lillian wanted her to *react*, to put her focus to good use.

She grabbed her wrist, and Vanessa flinched.

"Please, Vanessa. Will you at least do something with me?"

"Do what?"

"Will you go with me to visit Elizabeth's mother?"

"*Why?*"

"To talk to her. To tell her we're sorry about what happened. And I want to see if we can find anything out."

"That makes no sense. Find *what* out?"

"I don't know, okay?" Lillian fiercely wiped at the tears that had sprung to her eyes. "I don't know. Except that I feel like something has contacted me. This spirit. And I don't know what she wants."

"I don't think it is your responsibility to solve anything.

There is no evidence of a crime—"

"But you didn't feel her pain! That's the thing. There was all this fear and pain, enough to tear right through me. I can't sleep again until I do something, and this is all I know to do right now …"

Lillian was so overwrought, she looked almost frenzied. Always the sunny one, always the girl with the smile. Vanessa didn't know what to think of her transformation. She sat very still, and watched her, considering.

"Why don't you ask Mack to go with you? He was part of our little club. You still in touch?"

"Yes, we're still in touch…" Lillian wiped her nose on her sweater sleeve. "But … I just … I wanted to ask you to go with me."

"Why?"

"Because you're smarter than anyone. And you're always so calm. And you always know what to do. And I don't know if Mack would get it. Maybe it's a guy thing, I don't know …"

"So you asked me because I'm a girl?" Vanessa rolled her eyes.

"Sort of," Lillian whispered.

"Have you gotten any sleep at all?"

"Not really."

"You don't look right."

"I know."

Vanessa tapped her fingers on the table again, looking off to the side, through the window beyond them. "If I go with you, will you feel better?"

"*Yes.* Yes, I know so. Thank you, Vanessa."

"Shhh. Chill out. I don't know that the timing is good. Thanksgiving …"

"The day after then? Or two days? My sister is home,

we might be doing stuff."

"Okay, okay, fine. After Thanksgiving, then."

"I'll call you. And Vanessa?"

"What."

"Thank you. For having an open mind."

Lillian stood up, gave Vanessa a one-armed hug, and turned to leave.

Vanessa walked her to the front door. "Well. See ya," she muttered.

She closed the door after Lillian, and watched through the fan-shaped window at the top of the door. Lillian, hunched over in her big sweater, arms held close, looked like a tiny old woman, or an urchin.

Vanessa sighed, closed her eyes, rested her forehead against the door. Why, why, why did she have to come here? The girl on the scrap of film had been submerged deep in her brain, where she had not had to think about her anymore. Now it was as though she had come to terrible life, become animated, flickering and stirring in Vanessa's head. The girl, and the accompanying feelings of dread, guilt, and aversion.

"God damn it," she hissed. She hated it when her thoughts spun and churned this way in her head.

Without thinking of what she did, she turned the deadbolt lock closed with a heavy click.

Annabel Gray's heart raced as it always did when the doorbell rang. But when she opened the door, there were no policemen. No detectives with their pouchy eyes and badges and large black shoes. This time, it was two teenage girls.

One, the taller of the two, with glasses, looked at Annabel steadily with gray eyes that did not seem to blink.

Something about her face was regal, patrician-looking, with a strong nose and high cheekbones. Her dark blonde hair held back in a low ponytail, she had the look of a youth from a medieval painting, a young page or a courtesan.

The smaller one was the complete opposite. Dark-haired and delicate, with large, emotion-filled eyes, fawn-like. Annabel had dreamed recently that she had been chasing a young fawn, through the woods where Elizabeth's body had been found. The fawn had been fragile, and she knew from the way it moved that it was injured. But she could not catch up with it.

She blinked and put her hand lightly over her heart, staring at the fawn-girl. Through the last terrible weeks since Elizabeth's death, she had been unable to sleep, panic cascaded through her synapses like a shower of sparks. By the time the sun rose, the tide of her mind would let out again, leaving her exhausted, beached on jagged rocks.

The only comfort she could find any more were in tail ends of little synchronicities. To open a book, and point with eyes closed, and have the word be *grace*. Turn on the radio, and it would be playing 'Tie a Yellow Ribbon,' a song she had been thinking of moments before. Everything was interconnected, everything lately laden with meaning. Wheels of karma, wheels within wheels within wheels.

"Mrs. Gray?" the smaller girl said. "Are you alright?"

Annabel roused herself at last from her trance "Yes. Yes. I was just … can I help you, girls?"

The taller one spoke. "I don't know if you remember us, ma'am. We are Vanessa and Lillian. We were playmates with Elizabeth when we were children."

The woman stood still and looked very closely from one girl to the other. Yes. Slowly did the features of their childhood faces reveal themselves.

"Oh, my. Oh, *my*." She put one hand forward, fingers splayed, as though to touch and trace the features of each one of them. Like a blind woman. "Of course I know you girls. Elizabeth's little friends. Little angels, you were. Have I … surely I've seen you since then?"

"We're all neighbors," said Lillian with a bit of her old brightness. "We've been neighbors all this time."

"Yes. I— Won't you please come in?"

The girls followed her into the living room. Though the house looked smaller from the outside, it felt incredibly spacious within.

"I had forgotten how nice your house is, Mrs. Gray." Vanessa gazed around her at the clean lines of the place. The bamboo floors, the open design living room all flooded by natural light from the floor-to-ceiling glass that made up the whole back wall. From the wide-planked deck in the back, one could look down and out into the backyard, where solar panels were set into small canopies over her garden. Farther out, and away, stretched the woods. "You have incredible taste." Her eyes were drawn to a plank table set with an arrangement of purple orchids in glossy black pots.

But the room was also very stale and contained pockets of mess. Dirty plates and several cups with dregs of dried-up tea at the bottom littered the tables. A rumpled blanket lay on one long white couch like an abandoned cocoon.

"Thank you, dear. I helped design it, you know. I own three acres of those woods in back. You see, I had once done a site assessment here for a client and the deal fell through, so I snapped it up, back when I was flush with cash. Part of the deal when I got divorced was we would sell our firm. I had a lot of money for a while. And I was *so* passionate back then about creating a perfect home …” She trailed off with a weak laugh.

“Well, it’s gorgeous,” said Vanessa, thinking, I will design a place like this for myself one day.

“Yeah, well.” Mrs. Gray shook out a long cigarette from a pack on the dining table. “I thought one day I’d make my wooded area into a wildlife refuge. But I just … didn’t. Waylaid by life.”

“So … that was Elizabeth’s father you were talking about? The divorce?” Lillian asked softly.

The woman paused, blowing out a long plume of smoke toward the ceiling. “Yeah. We had an environmental consulting firm we started just out of grad school. When I was young, not too much older than you girls.” She spoke calmly, but there was a noticeable palsy in her hands. And she resolutely did not look at them.

“We just came to say that we’re really sorry about what happened. We should have come sooner.” Lillian took a seat closer to her, put a hand on her arm soothingly.

At this touch, Mrs. Gray burst into tears, leaving the two girls looking at each other with alarm.

“I’m sorry,” she gasped, “I should get myself together, I was trying to stay calm, it’s just … having you girls near me. Your energy, that energy of a young girl. It-it makes me feel closer to *her*, it’s like she’s here. A signature, or something, a resonance, and it’s making things unblocked, like a river, a river undammed and I just get so out of control sometimes and I can’t make it stop, and all I want is to make it stop …”

“Shhh, shhh, it’s okay Mrs. Gray,” Lillian stroked her arm, while Vanessa, from the loveseat, looked on aghast.

“Oh, honey, I’m just so out of my mind. Elizabeth was my life, we had no secrets. We weren’t like other mother and daughter. And I just can't accept what has happened. I refuse. And I guess that might make me an insane person. I know I sound like one."

"Of course not."

Mrs. Gray raked her hands through her wild gray curls. "Fuck," she whispered, "I'm so sorry. You're the first real company I've had in a while, and I'm not handling it well, am I?"

"We wanted to visit earlier, but thought it was just too crazy at the time, you know," said Vanessa.

"Yes. It was crazy. And ever since, people seem to stay away from me. They just don't know what to say, I guess. It's just as well. I don't want to talk to anyone. I can't get my head in order. But I'm glad to see you two. Because of course, you knew my girl. You were her friends ..."

Vanessa looked away guiltily.

"... so I feel differently about you two. And though I don't look it, I'm happy that you are here. Truly. "

Indeed, Mrs. Gray sat up, and looked at them avidly, her eyes large and quivering. She looked like a drowning woman, struggling to stay on the surface.

Neither girl knew what to say next. Lillian smiled sadly. "I always enjoyed coming over here to play. I never knew you built this house yourself. So, Elizabeth had lived here always?"

"No, not always," she took another drag, inhaling and glancing to the side. "It was a little complicated in the beginning. I was divorced when I was pregnant, you see. She was back and forth between us when she was small."

"So, she was born here, right?" asked Vanessa casually.

"It *was* a home birth. But not in this house." She stubbed out the cigarette on a dirty plate. "She was born in a little bungalow I rented while this place was about to be built.

Over in Westchester. Sweet little place. Just me, a midwife, and my doula. It was the happiest day of my life." She looked over at them and smiled a trembling smile, for just a flash, and then it was gone.

"It must be so hard for you. Grieving, and dealing with all the … stuff."

"Lillian, you don't even know. It kills me that my child was in such pain, and I have to trust her, that it was bad enough that she had to … do what she did. As bad as that sounds. The whole investigation has been such a violation. I can't take it anymore. When they call, I don't answer. They have to come find me here. In fact, I thought you were *they*. And just the thought of another interview ..."

"Yeah, all the stuff in the papers. I don't even read it." Which was a lie. Lillian had started to read all about it, ever since the night in the woods. It was hard to think of anything else, now. It had become an obsession.

"Well, I'm glad you don't, hon. It's bullshit. Those people are vultures. They call me uncooperative. I call them *heartless*." She lit another cigarette, though she had stubbed the last one out halfway through. "I never wanted to answer the door again, since the morning they came here to say that they had found her ..."

"Who called the police?" asked Vanessa, trying not to stare at the way the woman moved her hands, like two fretful spiders.

"It was the neighbors. Dave, and his wife, down in 117. They border the same woods. That old man with Alzheimer's knocked on their door. *He* was the one who found her." Her voice was stiff and distant again, her eyes out of focus. Just as suddenly, she snapped back into alertness and wheeled to look each girl in the eye. "I have something to show you," she said, getting up from the couch.

The girls exchanged a troubled glance and followed her to the huge, gridded glass window.

"Look," she said to them, pointing at the glass.

First, they strained their eyes outside, toward the woods. But it was not what she had been pointing at.

"It was a robin. I heard the thump this morning when I was just sitting here. It struck the window then fell to the ground, dead." They looked at the glass carefully, and indeed saw the bird's imprint. The dying afternoon sun shone through the window, illuminating what looked like a winged ghost, revealing each individual fiber of the wings and tail feathers.

"Do you think it is … significant?" Mrs. Gray asked, turning to look at them. She seemed to expect an answer.

"How do you mean?" asked Vanessa, evenly. Lillian had gone pale and quiet.

"Well, do you think it is some kind of clue? A synchronicity? That this should happen, and then you girls come to the door on the same day?"

Vanessa breathed in, exhaled. "I think, Mrs. Gray, that it is only coincidence. That's all."

They stood for some moments, looking, not saying anything. Then Lillian put a hand on Mrs. Gray's shoulder and said, "I think we should probably get going. You're tired."

Again, that vulnerable, wild look in Mrs. Gray's eyes. "But you girls will come back, right? I mean, this is good for me. You make me feel closer to her."

Lillian, with a stricken look on her face, kept one hand on the woman but said nothing.

"Of course we will," Vanessa said, knowing it would be unlikely.

Mrs. Gray led them back out the door, realizing too late that she had not offered the girls anything to eat or drink. But she was so absentminded these days., social niceties all but forgotten.

After they'd gone, she walked back and looked again at the ghost bird, and touched it lightly. A funny thing, these patterns. Once you notice them, they exist everywhere, with no linear path forward or backward. You just had to appreciate the beauty for its own sake.

The two girls walked down the street, not saying anything. Lillian finally broke the silence.

"I'm sorry I came up with the whole idea. We shouldn't have done it."

"Why do you say that?"

"I don't know. It's all too heavy. We can't help her. Maybe we might make her worse?"

"I don't think there's any chance of that." Vanessa looked preoccupied. Her words sounded absent as her brain clicked away at … something.

Lillian wanted to go home. She had a craving to be with her own mother. Lillian never felt too old to lay her head on her mother's shoulder and tell her problems. Though she doubted she would speak of this, it would still be nice for her mother to stroke her hair. Make her a snack.

Because something about Mrs. Gray had shaken her badly. And she could not say exactly what it was. The cocoon-like blanket, the drifts of cigarette smoke. The trembling orchids. The delicate anatomy of the bird, with the sun illuminating it from behind …

Vanessa turned to her, interrupting her reverie, and said, "I think she was lying."

Shocked, Lillian gaped at her. "About *what?*"

"The home birth. The father. She acted funny, telling that part."

"Funny how? She's bereaved! How is she *supposed* to act?"

"I was watching her micro-expressions."

"Her *what?*" Lil looked at her skeptically.

"Micro-expressions. She looked to the right and tensed up. Her vocal cords tightened up. But only when she spoke of certain things. I bet those just happen to be the things the cops think she's not honest about, too."

"That's not fair, Vanessa."

"It is fair. I'm not saying she's a bad person. I just think something is going on here. And I happen to know she's had that house longer than she said she did."

They stopped in the middle of the street, looking at each other. Lillian looked annoyed. But Vanessa smiled in an inscrutable way.

"Well, what do we do, then?" asked Lillian, throwing her hands in the air.

"We'll talk to more people," said Vanessa airily. "I want to talk to the folks who called the police."

Annabel Gray retreated back under the blanket on the couch and stayed there as angles of light and shadow crept along the walls until the sun finally set and the room was dark, and the girls' visit retreated into the haziness of a dream.

Her doctor had offered her a sedative, but she had refused. She wanted to feel everything she was supposed to feel, as penance. Her grief was like childbirth. In the end, she hoped to birth a new person, a new Annabel. She would bear witness to her pain, would respect it enough to let it be.

Though she had never given *actual birth*. In her real life.

She remembered the day she had first held her daughter, Elizabeth.

That had been a strange time in her life. The divorce had been finalized, and for three months she had been living in this house, her beautiful new house that she had just built.

She had come here to be free, but sometimes her new freedom was just too much. Sometimes she regretted selling the firm. After all the years of meeting with clients, reviewing data, writing reports, giving speeches, everything was so still. Sometimes it made her panic: I should do something. Set up a fund. A small foundation. Find a project, test the waters.

Instead, she played CDs of monastic chants. She started a compost heap. She watched sunsets that made her think of a great throbbing neon heart dissolving in the sky. At night, alone in bed all those first nights, she listened to the strange, wild howling from the night creatures in her woods. The sound of it gave her goosebumps, so keening and emotive, echoing in a refracted way. She thought of ghost stories of long-dead Indian tribes, their ceremonies, and rituals still echoing out into eternity.

In the day, she spent a lot of time roaming her new woods. Her land abutted areas owned by the town. She constantly argued with Wildlife Services over their predator control program. It had made her furious when she found animal traps on her property. Annabel had already become known in the town hall offices for being *difficult* and *eccentric*, eager to cause trouble.

One day she set out to walk, bringing her cable cutters to disable any snares she might find. Yes, I'm a crazy pain-in-the-ass rich woman, but I own this land. Deal with me. It was so satisfying to cut through the noose-shaped wires, straining her wrists till she felt the powerful *snap*. So far that afternoon, she had found three.

As she walked at a slow pace, clutching the cutter in one sweaty palm, thoughts of her ex-husband fluttered through her head. She and Eric hadn't spoken in months. As she had suspected, he *had* started seeing someone new. A twenty-five-year-old painter with dark bangs and large eyes who wore her long braids in loops. She looked like a Viennese choirgirl. He was dating a *child*. She could not say why this bothered her so much. But it did.

She stopped by the edge of the creek. Annabel liked to go there whenever she was feeling overwhelmed by her thoughts. And that day, she just could not stop thinking. Of Eric out in the Mojave Desert. Testing rockets at a spaceport. No longer a businessman, he'd grown out his hair and beard, looked like his younger self again. Keeping company with young people, too, evidently. How can he slip back into that identity so easily, while I'm marooned alone in middle age?

But, when she felt overwhelmed and despondent, it was infinitely comforting to for her to be out here, to smell the green smells, to hear the twigs snap and the water ripple, and her mind slowly cleared. It felt as though she were laying her head on some great mothering bosom, listening to the shift and ebb and flow of life itself. She let her body relax, and her eyes lazily explored the creek banks embedded with tree roots and jagged mossy stone. As her gaze drifted over the soft dry dirt near her own feet, she was abruptly shocked out of her meditative state by a cry; a wailing, high and piercing and close by, in a secluded spot where she thought she was alone. And it wasn't animal. It was a human cry. A *baby*.

She stood still and listened. Could it be a sound from far away, all just a trick of acoustics? Nearby was the edge of the large property owned by Mitch Cooper, a frail old man who had once been a well-known movie director. Though she was far off from where his mansion stood, sometimes noise carried from his house. Annabel had learned that what she thought were animal noises at night was actually noise from the parties coming from the mansion. Though the place was enormous and formerly grand, it was in poor repair and falling apart. Mitch was rarely seen and said to be in poor health, but he had many people living in his house at any given time. An ever-shifting group of hangers-on and derelicts. There had been many discussions and complaints about the property at the town council meetings, but it seemed there was little anyone could do.

Annabel didn't mind the occasional noise, and thought, *live and let live.* (Though she was irritated by the occasional beer can that rolled into her woods in that first stormy summer.) She didn't care who Mitch Cooper was – quite a few celebrities more impressive than he was had mansions in the town. (The tax rates were reasonable, the commute to New York not terribly far.) She mostly ignored the gossip and whispers, as it did not interest her. It had nothing to do with her life

She strained her ears; it was definitely the crying of a child she had heard. She waited quietly, to hear if anyone was called to it, or tried to calm and shush it. But no one did.

She stood up and moved toward the sound. The cries were now deep, lusty, and hungry sounding. Cries from deep in the diaphragm. How could she not, at least, try to help?

It came from the other side of the creek, the boundary of

Mitch's property line. She untied her hiking boots and took them off so that she could wade through the shallowest part. The water was cool and bracing. She felt stones dig into her soles, and slimy dead leaves, and the sandy bottom underneath.

At the other side, she walked up the bank, wary, and approached the brush. She pushed it aside and made her way, closer, toward the sound, which was louder, and wilder than it seemed it had been just a minute before.

It *was* a child, maybe three years old, though Annabel had little experience with children. She could not tell if it was a boy or a girl, but it had jaggedly cut brown hair. The child wore nothing but a diaper, though surely it was old enough to be toilet trained, and was filthy and covered with scratches. The toddler's skin had a bluish cast, as though it were cold, and slight hollow dents under its eyes.

My God, she thought, outraged, just who are these people?

Without even stopping to reflect on her actions, she gathered up the child in her arms. It looked into her face, its eyes huge, its mouth wide open in a grimace of despair.

Thief. Thief. I am a thief. These words reverberated in her head, giving her a pang of guilt, but also a small thrill of pleasure. Bathing the child in her own bathtub, she poured the water over her head, (for it *was* a girl she could see now) and worked the suds into her scalp. The little skull, so round and perfect. The small smooth shoulders, the delicate shoulder blades, moved her to a fierce protectiveness so strong that it seared like burning. Maybe, just maybe, her love was so strong and instantaneous, that it made everything that came after okay.

And yet, it was undeniable, even that first day. It was

technically kidnapping. It was a crime.

I will be punished. For being a thief. I used to be a good person, I swear! Annabel had never stolen a thing in her life. Never done anything remotely immoral. Well, she and Eric had for a time been part of that "radical" environmental group when they were in grad school. Chained themselves to trees, broke in and set free those laboratory rabbits ... but she was *proud* of those things! Because they were the *right* things to do.

But that moment, sitting in the bathroom, she no longer knew what certainty was. Because now, like it or not, she was a mother. And a thief. And desperate. Like a wild creature, she felt as though she was the one who would be hunted and cornered by the world.

"Excuse me, Annabel, what are you saying? You found what?"

"A child. A baby. Or, a-a little girl."

She sighed, trying to think how to explain. She lay on a lawn chair, looking up at the stars. The girl napped on her bed, wearing a nightgown and a fresh diaper, from a box Annabel had bought at the all-night superstore.

Though she and her ex-husband had not spoken in a while, she still thought of him first as she scrambled to figure out what to *do*. Tensions had eased when the divorce went through, and it was so much easier to talk. She found herself *liking* him again. Until he hurt her so terribly with the new girlfriend.

But when she was most confused, or afraid, it was still Eric she wanted to call for advice.

"And you say you don't know whose she *is*?"

"No! And the thing is, she doesn't talk. She's wild, different., like a feral creature. A forest nymph." She gestured vaguely with her hands.

After a long pause, Eric said, "Hmm. Well, you were always an expert with the field guides. Sounds intriguing. Like those myths you like to read. The pagan gods and whatnot." He chuckled softly.

"Well, I wish you wouldn't joke. This is serious." Her voice had gone tight and strained.

His sigh rustled like the night wind. She heard the distance in all the miles between them. "What do you want me to say? I'm joking because, frankly, I'm floored. I'm too shocked to do anything else. You know the right thing to do. So why are you even asking me?"

"Yeah? What's the right thing to do?"

"Call the *police*, Annabel! What other option are you seriously considering?"

She was quiet for some moments, not knowing how to answer. There was an option she was considering, had been considering since she brought the girl into her home. Given her a bath and rocked her to sleep, singing in a low, flat monotone that seemed to sooth the child, and herself. It felt, for the first time in a long time, that she intrinsically *knew* what to do. She just could not yet name it, even to herself.

"You aren't thinking of just keeping her, are you? Because that's insane. Alert the authorities—"

"And what? She'll become a ward of the system?"

"They'll find her parents."

"She shouldn't go back to parents like that. It's abuse, it's neglect."

"Annabel. Get real. You're scaring me."

"Well, God forbid, Eric! I thought you were an open-minded guy! Living in the Mojave Desert with that little girl, growing a hippie beard and shooting rockets ..."

"Hey. I'm sorry. I'm sorry." Sorry for what, he did not say. "Listen. I'm going to stay out of it. You'll figure out the way. I have faith in you, Annabel."

"You're just saying that 'cause you think I'm nuts," she said, with a rueful laugh.

"Of course not. I believe in you."

This made her smile, the kind of smile that easily leads to tears. She remembered a long-ago night. She and Eric, young graduate students, had just let loose a stolen batch of lab rabbits into moonlit woods behind the college dorm. Eric, so young and beautiful. Oh, his *eyes*, as they had stopped and looked at each other, in love and wonder, as the little creatures scampered away silently to freedom.

"Thank you," she whispered, and not waiting for another word, hung up the phone.

Mack sprawled, knees bent and spread wide apart, with his feet close together, on the worn plaid sofa, watching the raindrops as they trickled and spread down the windowpane. Folk music played low, there was the clink of a cash register, the occasional shout of an order; this coffee shop was the favorite hangout place for the hip local youth. But Mack didn't order anything. He was only there to wait for Lil and Vanessa.

His eyes slid over the passers-by as they hurried, heads ducked, to get out of the chill autumn rain. Why were the girls late? It was already ten-thirty. He didn't want to be there, anyway. He wasn't in a good mood.

He'd been spending too much time with his mother. He loved her, no mistake. And after the strange night out at his dad's, he had vowed to be as good to her as he could. And it wasn't as though he *minded* doing things for her, taking out the trash, driving her home from the eye doctor. Going to a movie together. But something about his mother's love for him made him feel claustrophobic and hopeless. And he hated feeling this way.

He felt a bit claustrophobic *now*, honestly, contemplating this meeting with the girls. He couldn't take any more drama. Lillian had been so strange and cryptic, saying that they needed to talk to him, not a text or call, but a face-to-face meeting. He hadn't even asked what it was about. He had only asked when and where. Too overwhelmed recently, he just quietly assented, no questions asked; he would go there, get it over with, and get out.

At last, he saw them approach the window, huddled under the same rainbow-striped umbrella. How had those two gotten so close again, he took pause to wonder? As they came through the door, Lillian laughed when she saw him staring at them, Vanessa smiled sheepishly, their faces flushed with the raw wet air emanating from them when they joined him on the sofa.

"Hi, Mack, thanks a lot for taking my crazy call. I mean, it's *not* all crazy, the thing it's about, but I know it must seem weird and all—"

Vanessa merely raised a hand in greeting, nodded.

"*Hey*, Vanessa," Mack said.

"Hey, yourself."

Lillian, in the middle, looked back and forth between the two of them. "When's the last time you two even saw each other?"

"Fifth grade, maybe? Dunno." Mack's head felt clogged and fuzzy.

"Sixth," said Vanessa, standing up. "Seventh is when I transferred to private school. That place is hell. *Lord of the Flies* kind of shit, but whatever. I'm ordering. You guys want anything?"

"Nothing," said Mack.

"Vanilla latte?" peeped Lillian, eyebrows up.

They looked after Vanessa silently for a few moments, at her ponytail swinging across the back of her green army jacket.

"You're looking good, Lil!"

"Good? I looked like a drowned rat."

"No, I mean you look, you know. Better. Less stressed out."

"Yeah. I'm feeling better." The visit the week before with Elizabeth's mother had rattled her badly. But once she and Vanessa had started making plans, and shaping a purpose, she had settled down. She was at least sleeping through the night.

Vanessa returned, the girls settled into the couch and looked at Mack.

"What?" he asked, looking from one face to the other.

Lillian smiled wryly. "Have you had any ... strange experiences?"

"What do you mean?" he croaked, blank-faced.

"So. I had this dream. But it wasn't a dream." Lil went on to describe the sleepwalking and finding herself barefoot at four a.m. in the firefield.

Mack didn't know what to say. He shrugged. "Maybe it was just a dream." He jiggled his foot spastically, and would not look at her.

"It wasn't. I can't explain, except to say it wasn't. It felt like ... like a transmission. I felt *her*. I felt her fear. And it's an indescribable feeling. And I know that something bad happened to her. Elizabeth."

Mack stared into space, the close air of the cozy coffee shop suddenly making him feel he couldn't breathe. There was that feeling again, a tingling in his hands. He couldn't just make an excuse and leave, say nothing. There was nothing to do but to speak of *it*. "I guess I had a freaky experience. It kind of fucked me up, to be honest. I didn't tell anyone about it."

"What happened?" Vanessa asked levelly when after several moments he still did not proceed.

He shrugged, with an uneasy laugh. "I. Um. Was driving my truck at night. Out in the country. All the way out past the railroad tracks. There was no reason for anyone to be out walking out there because there *is* nothing there. But I saw her. Elizabeth. Walking down the side of the road—"

"You're sure it was her?"

Vanessa's penetrating and laser-sharp gaze made him lose his train of thought for a moment. "It was definitely her. But it's hard to explain. It was like a movie projection, like an image."

"Aren't we all images?"

"Not like this. The image moved around, it swerved, like a film projector swinging around. In one smooth motion. And it grew big. Gigantic. As big as a building. And I drove right through it. It was crazy. I almost crashed."

"My God," Lillian whispered.

"Yeah. I thought I would puke. I thought I had run over someone. I couldn't process it. I thought I was going crazy. I didn't want to tell anyone."

"So what did you do?" asked Vanessa, looking at him, holding her coffee in one hand but not drinking it.

"Like I said. Nothing! I put it out of my mind, and told myself it never happened."

They were silent for several moments, Mack looking

down at the floor, scowling, Lillian staring ahead in stunned wonder, lips parted. Vanessa sat very still and expressionless. Until she said, without turning to look at them, "I saw her, too."

The other two whipped their heads toward her.

"Except, I saw her in a scrap of old black-and-white movie film that I dug up out of the dirt."

Vanessa told them the story, her voice calm and very even, but the unreality of the event washed over her again. That bright, surreal autumn day, the way the air felt as she was raking and weeding with her father. The sick shock when she held the film to the light. The way Elizabeth held her hand out to her from her ruined black-and-white universe, her face alive and beseeching, communicating straight through the age and scratches and chemical stains of the film.

Mack merely nodded stoically when she was finished, but Lillian openly gaped at her, as though she had just been slapped.

"Vanessa. Why did you not *say* anything? When you knew what happened to me, and I thought *I* was going crazy? I thought you trusted me, and you kept that a secret?"

"Not so much a secret. I just … withheld it."

"Meaning?"

Vanessa wheeled toward her, a strained and hectic look on her face. "I chose to keep it to myself until I was ready, okay? I didn't like it. I didn't understand it. I didn't really believe it."

"Did you believe *me*? About my story?"

"Yes! I just—"

"Come on, lay off," Mack said quietly to Lillian. "It's just a little freaky for all of us. Everyone has their own way of dealing."

"Okay, fine." Lillian sighed and looked at the ceiling. "So this is real, then. We have established that this is a thing, or am I mistaken?"

"A *thing?* Yes. We've had a series of ... shared experiences. Or ones that are, at least, *congruent.* That *has* been established."

Vanessa kept her eyes closed, her hand moving in a stiff chopping movement to emphasize her words. "Yes, yes, *yes,* to *that.*"

"So what now?" asked Mack. "What does it mean?"

Vanessa kept up the chopping movement with her hand; Mack gripped her hand and stilled it.

"It means, pretty obviously I think, that her soul is not at rest." Lillian still looked put out. She scraped her thumbnail against her foam cup. "And we have been trying to figure just what it is she's trying to tell us. That's why we visited her mom."

"Really?" Mack's brow furrowed. He remembered all the rumors he'd heard about the mom. How she was out of her mind. "You sure that was a good idea?"

"I think so," said Vanessa crisply. "The visit was very ... odd. But insightful."

"How so?"

The girls exchanged a glance. Lillian turned to him and said, "Vanessa thinks she's hiding something."

"Well, I'm not the only one. Obviously, the police think she's hiding something, too. You've seen the news. It's all shady, the homeschooling. No record of her birth. They've questioned her. Still are. There are just no criminal charges they can make yet."

"Come on, Vanessa. I don't think she did anything wrong. The poor woman. You saw her. She lost her daughter. That will mess you up."

"I'm not saying she did anything wrong. I'm just saying I feel she's hiding something."

"So where is this all going," said Mack, whirling his fingers in a manner that said, "speed it up."

"Well, we decided we're going to ask around ourselves. You know. Neighbors. People who knew them. People who might know things."

"The police already did that."

"But this is different," Vanessa had a faint smile on her face, her eyes alight. "They have to go through certain procedures that they are bound to. We're more free. People won't be afraid to talk to us. We're kids."

"And we're Elizabeth's friends," said Lillian. "That means something. We aren't official. We're doing this, you know, out of love. I think there is something Elizabeth wants us to know."

"So what, someone killed her?" Mack asked quietly. "'Cause that's a pretty huge assumption to make. What if it's not true? I don't know that it's stuff to play around with. We might stir up something we don't want."

"We're just going to ask our own questions," said Vanessa. She took a long sip of coffee and wiped her mouth on her sleeve. "If you want in, you're welcome to join us. If not …"

He laughed. "So, what? Like, we're teen detectives, or what? Sounds like a cheesy television show."

Vanessa gazed at him coolly. "Don't be dismissive. If you're not taking us seriously, you don't have to go along."

"I'm not putting you down. I just want to know if there is an actual plan."

"The first thing we're going to do is talk to the people who found her."

"So, you're going to interview *Ernie Stevenson?* Good luck. He's tripping on Alzheimer's."

"No," said Lillian, "We're starting with the Manets. Down at 117. Ernie went to their house. They are the ones who called."

Mack sighed heavily. He felt he couldn't think straight these days. Seventeen, and he was completely worn out from his life. The girls both looked at him, gamely. He didn't know what to say. It was all wrong. It was silly. It was juvenile. But at least, he would have something to keep his mind occupied from his troubles

"Okay," he said at last and shook his head as they high-fived each other. "Because I just don't want you getting into trouble alone."

SEVEN

"Sorry, I know I'm not dressed for company now." A genial man in his late fifties, Dave Manet was large and red-faced with grayish sandy hair and a mustache. He smelled of sawdust and wore a t-shirt with faded writing on it, baggy jeans streaked with mud and tar, and a large leather work belt. They told him they had been friends of his neighbor Elizabeth, and unfeigned sadness washed over his features. He removed one work glove and offered his hand to each of the three teens to shake, a large, red calloused paw, missing the top section of his pinky finger.

"Drink? Beer?" He called back as they followed him into the interior of his house. His tool belt jingled, and he listed from side to side, boots clomping. "Haha, just kidding. Coke?"

"No, thank you, sir." Mack felt compelled to be the speaker, though he did not have much of a good idea what to say. "You've been doing some work, I see?"

"Yeah, yeah. Sorry about the mess. Maybe I should set you all in the kitchen?" The house sprawled, almost Habitrail-like with extensions and add-ons to the original saltbox-style house. In the back was the kitchen, full of elaborate cabinets and cantilevered countertops. "I did this kitchen, too. Like to show it off when I can."

"Nice," said Mack. "So you build?"

"Yeah. Got my own business. Not so busy in the wintertime. I work on my own place as a hobby. I'm always adding a room, building a deck. I made my wife her own custom closet. I just get bored, is all. Always a fidgety kid. Can't keep my hands still." He stroked a cabinet as he spoke, gently, almost as though it were too hot to touch.

"We just wanted to ask you some questions, sir," said Vanessa.

"Dave," the man said, snapping to, with a serious look on his face. "Call me Dave."

"Not to be nosy, or gossip or anything," said Lil. "It's just that we knew her, years ago, and we want to make sense of what happened, just because … well. Closure and all …"

"Sure, sure."

"… and we know you called the police. Well, that's what the papers say."

"Yep, yep." Dave rubbed his big hands together and stared into space thoughtfully. How much should he tell these kids? He still saw flashes of the dead girl when he least expected to, whether putting up drywall or falling asleep in bed. It was something he would never unsee. The way she rocked almost serenely side to side, rope creaking like someone riding a tire swing. It took him some moments to even understand what he was seeing. She looked almost peaceful until he saw the front of her.

"Well, I don't know quite what to tell you." He looked at the three kids sitting at his table. Couldn't be more than sixteen, seventeen. The idea of death seemed anathema to their earnestness and potential. It was goodness that brought them, wasn't it? Caring about the girl. He would choose his words carefully.

"Yeah, it was old Ernie from up the road that found her. You know, during one of his wanderings. We've known him for years and known his situation. Usually, we just bring him home when he's lost, if I happen to see him from the window. But that day he came to us. Knocked on our door." He paused, rubbed his hands together again, considering how to go on.

Privately, in his head, he recalled the events of that morning.

The knock, well no, the *banging* on his front door had the sound of flailing in it, almost like an animal scratching and throwing itself against the door. Dave startled at this early hour, opened the door, hair askew and coffee cup in hand. Who would be at the door at *dawn?* Had to be an emergency.

Dave sighed with relief when he saw who it was and said, "Ernest, what can I do for you? What are you doing out this early in the wet and the mud?" He felt kind, magnanimous. After all, Ernest was alone in the world, but for the sons who took turns looking after him. His wife was dead. No sanctuary of marriage. David put a hand on his fragile shoulder. "Won't you come in? Betsy can get you something hot to drink."

But the old man was agitated, wringing his gnarled hands, rolling his large eyes back and forth. "I ... came to get you. You've got to follow me, come outside ..."

"Why? What's going on?"

Ernest grasped for words for a moment, a haze over his eyes. Then he snapped back to alertness and said, "There's a body in the woods. You have to come and identify it."

"What do you mean?" David smiled to himself. He would drive the confused old man home and help him to bed, maybe call one of the sons whose numbers he had stored on his cell phone for times like these.

"It's in *your* woods, down by the creek. A body in your woods! It is *imperative* that you make an identification *immediately*."

Ernest refused to take no for an answer, so David told him, "Hold on, then, I'll be right out."

He walked upstairs to the bedroom to put on his work boots. Then he called out, "Hon?"

No answer; he went downstairs, through the kitchen, through the side walkway that connected the original house to one of the several add-on structures.

Entering the silent billiards room. *Hon?* Up the stairs to the in-law apartment that had no in-laws. Not there. Only one last place. The solarium.

There she was, in her private jungle. Her bountiful ecosystem. Standing at the glass wall, looking out. She had been watching the whole time.

"Hon, Ernest's at the door, he's all hepped up about something. Wants me to see something outside. He thinks it's a dead body. Probably a log or something. I thought I'd humor him, settle him down, and then drive him home."

Betsy looked at him, brow furrowed in confusion.

"I shouldn't be but a few minutes, but don't hold breakfast."

"No," she said quietly. "I'll come with you." She smiled. "Maybe I can calm him down. Poor Ernie."

"Poor Ernie." He put an arm around her, and they stood for a moment before they joined the old man pacing on the front porch; he was startled for a moment when David put a hand on his arm and said, "Okay, we're ready."

It was a cool morning, cleansed by a wild summer storm the night before. The moon was still visible, a faint silver disk in the clear morning sky. It was a milk-glass sky, reflected in the large sheets of water on the ground as the three walked on. "Some hell of a rainstorm we had last night," said David. "I have one big branch down in the back I need to buzz saw, and I think I got a leak somewhere in my roof because there's this—"

The old man looked at him incredulously, as though he were insane or an idiot. He shook his head.

"It cannot be helped," Ernest muttered under his breath. "Such a great tragedy, and it couldn't be helped." In this light, he looked unlike his usual self. He looked shadowy and noble, like a ruined aristocrat, a Russian duke. And he spoke with such somber finality that David had no response. Obligingly, he followed.

They walked down the driveway to the back to the sound of their feet on gravel, and then as they entered the woods, the heavy dripping from the dark branches that still sounded like rain showers.

Ernest led the way, deeper to where it was dark, the ground padded with pine needles. They walked for some time. Betsy whispered, "Do you think we should turn him back now?"

The old man startled the when he lifted his finger and said, "It is *there.*"

David still had a friendly, indulgent smile on his lips when he spotted the girl.

In that stretched out moment of time that seemed to go on forever, in the woods, where things grew wild and disordered, pale sprouts emerged from the rot of tree stumps, life and death mixed together and, for just a moment, he was free from any emotion. Before him was a scene of serenity. The girl from the neighborhood he saw every day. The girl, in dark clothes, head bowed prayerfully, was she floating? Was she levitating? She looked so at one with the scene, the ferns and the mist and the dripping of the dark branches.

It wasn't until his wife screamed that the scene rushed to terrible life. The scream, faint and strangled at first, spiraled in volume, like an approaching siren, until it filled his head, filled the whole world. A deep, ragged scream that reverberated through that tranquil nature scene, echoing against the wall of damp green. Unthinking, he clutched at his own face, digging fingers into his skin. His eyes torn open by the awful sight of the girl swinging around to face them. The swollen tongue. Her blue skin. The terrible contortions …

That scream echoed through his head all the time, still. As it echoed through his marriage. Somehow he and Betsy had been pulled inside out by that terrible moment and never recovered.

But for the moment, he was back in his own kitchen, with these three sets of eyes watching him. These three teenagers. Asking him questions about that morning that he could never, *ever*, answer.

"Yeah. It was Ernie who found her and took us to her. To where she was. I cut her down with my handsaw, which I shouldn't have done. I panicked, I guess." He had tried to save her; there was a dim recollection of her dead weight dropping to the ground, him searching for a pulse. "But then? We called the police, naturally. They were the ones who told her mother. I stayed behind and tended my wife. She was very shaken up."

"Did you know Elizabeth?" asked Vanessa.

"Mostly just by sight. She and her mother seemed like nice enough people. Built that house, what, seventeen, eighteen years ago? Then she had the girl, thought she'd adopted her from overseas. I wasn't too clear."

"What happened then? Did you go to the police station?" Lillian stammered, trying to get the hang of asking tough questions.

"Well, they were very civil. We answered a lot of questions, Betsy and I. Ernest, they let off the hook. He was pretty upset, you know? Not easy to get much coherence out of the man, anyway, unfortunately."

"Do you think he had anything to do with it?" asked Vanessa mildly.

David let out a whoop. "Ernie? No way. He hardly knows his name, most days. Can hardly dress himself. He needs to be in a home. One son is in the process of arranging it, I know."

"But are there any rumors or anything?" asked Mack. "I mean, off the record. About the whole situation."

David sighed and rolled his eyes up. "Weeeell. I don't know. I personally just think it was a suicide. But that's not to say someone wasn't messing with the girl. Maybe someone bullied her. A solitary girl like that. She seemed vulnerable. Maybe a boyfriend? And the drugs. Those came from *somewhere*. It's all kind of odd. But they're not turning up any answers. So ..." he shrugged. "But then you guys might have connected the dots. Since you were her friends."

Lillian looked down and clasped her hands. "We were friends when we were kids. We all kind of lost touch in middle school."

David nodded. "Yeah. She didn't go to school, so I guess that made it tough to keep friends." Poor kid, he thought. The mother held on too tight. Whenever he saw her now, pulling into her driveway, wild gray curls blowing in the wind like antic thoughts bristling around her head, he wondered what it had been like. He couldn't bring himself to do more than wave. He was a coward, he knew. "I'm just sorry you guys had to experience that. Losing a friend. When I was a kid, I remember a couple of older boys dying in Vietnam. That's different, of course, but it's rough, experiencing the death of a young person. Real rough."

"You said you think she may have had a boyfriend?" asked Vanessa, eyeing him.

"It's possible, I guess. Some kids meet people online, but the word is she wasn't allowed on the Internet. I've always had a weird feeling about the Mitch Cooper place. The house isn't close technically, but you can cut through the woods very easily back there." He made a snaking motion with one hand. "It's closer than it looks."

"What would that have to do with anything, do you think?" Vanessa darted a look at Lillian.

"I don't know. Could be nothing. But after what happened, the thought of that place gives me the creeps. Mitch is quiet enough. You never see him. It's the people he's had living there. Bunch of freaks. He hasn't been in the film business in decades, not been in anything I can recall. But he's old. Still has money. A lot of weirdos moving in and out over there. Drifters. Never bothered me, personally. But it's bothered others plenty."

"Have the cops checked it out?" Mack tried to remember anything he had heard about that place. Kids at school said there'd been orgies and satanic rituals. But he'd never taken the stories seriously.

"Yeah, they have. But nothing seems to have come of it.

Like I said, they can't keep track of everyone who's come and gone from that place. The mansion is so big, the property so spread out, it's mostly self-contained, I guess. So who knows what goes on? But the man is free to have guests in his home if he wants to, you know?" David leaned back in his chair for the fridge, pulled out a can of Coors Light, and drank a thirsty gulp. "I keep my mind on my own matters, though. Work on my house. Hammer and nail till I'm deaf."

It was true, he had been working nonstop, and he showed them his latest project, an anteroom, with a skylight. It was empty, with building material and power cords strewn around.

"I'm getting a good deal on a telescope. A high-powered one. I'm going to take up astronomy when I get the time."

He needed new hobbies. Because Betsy, since the girl's death, rarely left the solarium. It had always been her favorite room in the house. All glass, with curved eaves and a figure of eight walkway. She crammed it with tropical flowers, herbs, and orchids. Lilies and citrus trees. The place buzzed and vibrated with vibrant plant life. The room was moistly humidified, and filled with distilled, bright white light. Dave couldn't stay for long in the room. It gave him headaches and dazzled his eyes, like staring into a flashing, glinting prism.

"It's your natural habitat," he'd joke from the doorway and scuff his boot shyly against the tile floor. She would give a weak smile, her fingers in the soil.

But ever since they had found that dead girl in the woods, Betsy spent *all* her time there. The experience had been so rough on her, she'd even gone to the doctor. But he had given her pills that made her feel too empty-headed and forgetful. So she had gone off the pills. So David mostly built things now, to occupy his mind. He actually found the teenagers' company a welcome relief. He had nothing more to tell them, but he didn't want them to leave.

"Sorry if I'm running on. You sure I can't get you anything? You can hang out while I'm working. Listen to some music or whatever."

"That's okay, Mr. Manet." Mack stood up and swung his arms back and forth, looking at the two others expectantly. They took his cue and got up, too, and each shook Dave's hand.

"Shall we say hello to Mrs. Manet on the way out?" asked Lillian.

"Well, I don't know. She's probably messing around potting stuff in her little greenhouse. Best leave her to it." Being in the solarium was like being at the center of a blazing diamond. Too hot. Dave avoided it. "Tell you what, though, I'll tell Betsy you stopped by and sent your regards. She sure takes an interest in the neighborhood kids." That wasn't true. She didn't take an interest in much of anything these days. "You are all getting so grown up now I wouldn't know you to look at you!"

He waved to them from the doorway as they headed out into the cold, clear afternoon. "Come back anytime. And remember, call me Dave!"

Mitch Cooper asked his caregiver to help him to the wicker settee on his back patio. He felt the approaching cold weather deep in his old man's bones. He wanted to enjoy the sun on his face while he could. He closed his eyes and savored the feel of it, though he had had to wrap in a heavy wool shawl.

Mitch had fled the warmth of the West Coast, years ago. As he said in his final interview, given decades before, the excesses of the past made him too queasy to even think of them, and he preferred the quiet charm of his new Connecticut home. But still, a certain jangling guitar tune, a certain slant of golden light, took him right back to that time and place. That house in Laurel Canyon, with its bright Spanish tile, its high-beamed ceilings. The all-weather cabanas where their guests lounged by the pool, drinking, laughing, their soft laughter carried away in the early evening breeze.

Jack Nicholson. Peter Fonda. Carol King and Harry Nilsson. Something had pulled them all into the orbit of the Canyon. Some hot, wavering energy that made them feel reckless and immortal. They were all there, unreal looking, in the old photographs he kept in boxes and sometimes looked at. Friends, friends of friends. His own face among them, Mitch Cooper the magnanimous host, benevolently stoned, he hardly recognized himself. He looked so self-assured, so placid, as though looking into his own future as something warm and kind and welcoming.

> Mitch Cooper was one of his era's most influential actor/directors, pioneering the cinema of the anti-war, counter-culture movement. Cooper was a master of portraying a generation's loss of innocence and ennui of disillusionment. Made on a low budget, influenced by European art house movies, his hard-edged portrayal of outlaws and anti-heroes brought in millions at the box office and changed the Hollywood system for good.

These scraps of his own biography, gleaned online, he found immensely difficult to read. He just didn't believe in them, any of them. Though he still couldn't resist skimming them sometimes, when one of the kids in his house set him up on a computer.

After Cooper fled the spotlight and moved to Wellesley, Connecticut, he became a rather mysterious figure. Now into his eighties, he refuses all interviews and lives a reclusive life on his bucolic estate, a far cry from when he was a fixture of the heady LA party scene of the sixties and early seventies. He has shunned the spotlight since the death of his first wife, Patty Hunter, of a heroin overdose at one of Cooper's infamous weekend-long parties ...

Young people sometimes hunted him down when he first moved to Connecticut, coming boldly right up onto his property. Knocking at his front door in the middle of the night. Or surprising him in his garden, a frail man who dressed his thin frame in seersucker suits, on his hands and knees pulling the weeds out. "Excuse us, Mr. Cooper?" He would look up, dazed, the hairy roots of wild morning glory dangling from his hand, still throbbing with life. "We just wanted you to know we're big fans. It's like, you understand what it's like to be alienated."

He'd close his eyes and turn away. Their youth was unbearably raw and earnest and too painful to contemplate. "Fuck off," he always muttered.

But they kept coming, year after year. And eventually, there came the point where he felt so eviscerated with loneliness that he wordlessly let them in.

It had been forty years since he had moved to Wellesley. His formerly grand house fell into decrepitude. The sprawling Greek revival mansion was in need of extensive renovations that he could no longer afford. There was a worrisome sagging of the grand balconies atop tall octagonal columns. One of the sidelights of the large double doors had been cracked and repaired with duct tape. This view was hidden from the townspeople by the overgrown brush that surrounded it. The dead fountain in the front was full of dead leaves and debris.

Hardly anyone had ventured down the crumbled brick carriage path in ages, except the people who lived there. So many people, he had lost track of who came and went. But it was rare indeed for anyone in the town to ever catch a glimpse of Mitch Cooper anymore. His poor health had made him a recluse.

Now he swam in his elegant suits and had grown as shabby as the house. He wore silk ascots around his neck to hide its stalk-like fragility. He was more and more like a boy wearing a theatre costume, with a young boy's trusting gratitude when a John, his trusted caregiver, lifted him in his strong arms to walk him from his favorite wicker settee, back into his wheelchair.

Mack enjoyed his new job. He worked in construction after school with the road crew, on days that he didn't have football. He got to wear a hard hat and orange safety vest. His crew currently tunneled under Elm Street, submerging a four-foot pipe with hydraulic jacks to run a water line, rushing to get it done before the bad winter weather descended.

The cold didn't bother Mack but invigorated him. After the clamor and noise and stuffiness of school, it was a relief to climb down into the trench and dig the heavy black soil, He could imagine doing this forever; he loved the feel of the spade in his hand. Skipping college. Working road crew jobs here and there until he had money to just travel for a while. He could go to Alaska. Work on a fishing boat …

And he enjoyed *being* with the road crew. No one asked him questions about his future. They all simply had a job to do, and while they worked, they spoke in easy gestures and grunts. (Antonio didn't even speak English at all. He was Mexican, with dreamy, heavy-lidded eyes. He drank cans of coconut milk and sang to himself as he dug.)

They'd break together for coffee at the donut place attached to the gas station and talk about sports and tell jokes – well, they actually didn't talk to Mack that much, but he didn't mind. He was the only teenager. These men were older. Forties, fifties, sixties. And they had known each other for years. He liked Pete, who was his grandfather's age and had a full white beard. His eyes were saggy and pouchy, his face red and roughened. But he took an interest in Mack, asked him about his football games. Told him stories of what a hell raiser he had been in high school. He had lived in Wellesley all his life, and knew everything about the place.

On one of their breaks, Mack asked him what he knew about the Mitch Cooper place.

Pete let out a hoot. "Hoo boy! That is one fucked-up situation over there, no doubt. A damn shame, too. His place is called The Brambles. That house used to be *beautiful*. I mean, that's why people like that buy places out here. Buy a big old house, enjoy the quiet and peace. Get into New York City in half hour, forty-five minutes. Hell. We've had all kinds of famous people living out here. And they have a nice little life, and no one bothers them—"

"But what about this guy? What's his deal?"

"His deal?" Pete ran a napkin to wipe donut glaze off his lips. "His deal is that he hasn't worked in years, and he's holed up in that place shooting dope with a bunch of derelict squatters is what his deal is."

"How do you know this?"

"*Everyone* knows it. He was once a pretty big name, way before your time, I know. He was famous when I was a boy. Respected. Actor, director, whatnot. Won some awards. Dude would have had it made if he'd just laid low, got a grip on his life. Have a good accountant, you know what I mean? He ain't got nobody."

"But how do you know all this?"

"Well. There's a guy I know. Name of Martin. Martin's around … forty? Forty-two? Looks about sixty. He's burned out for sure. *Way* burned out. He drives for UPS, or FedEx or one of those outfits. Lives in a place out past the railroad tracks. He lived out at Mitch's house for a couple years."

"Really? How did that happen?"

"Oh, I guess he was one of those nutty young people obsessed with Mitch. One of the so-called cult following. Showed up at his doorstep, impressionable young boy. And what do you know, he was taken in."

"When was that?"

"Nearabout about twenty years ago. He was just a boy. And I hate to tell you, but the young can be *stupid*."

Mack felt his excitement deflate. Twenty years ago? May as well be a lifetime ago. He needed to know who was there *now*.

"But, I'll tell ya, Mack. There's young and stupid, and then there's just plain evil. Martin could tell you some stories, man."

Mack grew alert again. "How? What kind of evil?"

"You know, debauchery and whatnot. These are people who don't know the value of life. All they do is get high and *rut*, from what I understand. The place is filthy. And there's this one no-good dude who runs the show there. Took advantage of Mitch, sort of like a manservant, but now feeds the old man his drugs. Freaky guy, still there to this day. It was smart that Martin got out of there. Not that his life's improved that hell of a lot since, but. You know."

"So it was that messed-up, huh?"

"So he says, yeah. The thing he didn't like was kids being involved."

"Kids?"

Pete looked both ways and then got close enough so that Mack could smell is cigarette-scorched breath. "He says he thinks they killed a kid." He drew back to look at Mack's face. The waitress, wearing a pink uniform, refilled their coffee and Pete waited for her to walk away before he asked, "Believe it?"

"What? A *child?*"

"Not so much murder. He thinks it may have been neglect. Little kid running around. No one taking care of it. Then it just disappeared, and no one would admit what happened. He thinks it came to a bad end, and they put it in the ground someplace." He smiled wryly, eyebrows raised, checking to see Mack's reaction.

He had none. He had gone still as a statue.

He recovered himself and remembered to act bored, nonchalant as he asked, "So … you still know this guy Martin?"

EIGHT

"There. A beautiful crane. See him flying? Look at his wings! Now, it is *your* turn."

Small pink fingers lifted up a sheet of paper, a special paper colored black on one side and white on the other; Annabel watched, willing her little girl to get it right. This was the best preschool in town, with a limited number of kids, and they had made the waiting list.

"Origami, as they say, is the science of the practical," murmured the woman interviewer who sat with Annabel and Elizabeth at the child-sized table. "And then, there is the Eastern symbolism. Crane, cat, fish, dragonfly ... so much is integrated. That is why we teach it in our school."

Annabel half-listened, watching her little girl she'd named Elizabeth after her favorite grandmother. Though she did her best to listen to the interviewer, she felt Elizabeth's increasing consternation at this task. She sensed her stillness, the hairs bristling on the back of her neck. The feral alertness of a cornered creature that is about to run. Or bite.

She had cared for the child for the past year. A year! No

one had come looking for her. Annabel had now lost the option of calling the police. *I'm a thief! Punishment will be mine. When I least expect it …*

"So you say Elizabeth has not attended a school previously?"

Annabel shook her head. "No. I have kept her at home."

The interviewer scribbled down something in her notebook. "I notice her posture … well … Elizabeth seems to thrust her head *forward* a bit. A kind of *lunge*. Has her pediatrician—"

"*Yes.* Yes. She's fine." She willed those small fingers to fold on the proper lines. *Come on.* The instructor helped her, showed her where to make the crease. She was too close to Elizabeth, and the little girl didn't like it. Annabel almost felt the tremor of a growl deep in the little girl's chest.

"And … has she been screened for learning disabilities? She doesn't say very much. At what age did she begin talking?"

"There is nothing *wrong* with her!"

The interviewer drew back a bit, surprised by Annabel's sudden rancor. "Well, I didn't mean to suggest otherwise." She again wrote something in the notebook. "We are a very selective school, and we screen accordingly." She stopped and looked up at Annabel, removing her reading glasses. "What lead you and Elizabeth to apply to our program?" Her eyes were intelligent and piercing. "What brought you here?"

Annabel stopped and looked around the room. The school was built to resemble an ultra-modern barn on the outside, of stone and unfinished shingles. Inside, the room was spare and elegant. Skylights bathed everything in a dappled golden light. The space was free-flowing, the lines beautiful. Tables of hand-painted wooden blocks. Looms of vegetable-dyed woolen yarn. Handmade cornhusk dolls. Down the center ran a trough fountain of water and glistening stones, its murmuring ripples so peaceful. And all of these rough-hewn little wooden chairs, empty, waiting.

Annabel let out a harsh little laugh, put her hand over her eyes, and shook her head. Would this, any of this, be possible for her girl?

"Well, I, that is, Elizabeth ..."

What could she say? That this place was a kind of heaven to which many aspire, but few could enter? That what was real and pure and true was so elusive, but here, a child could hold it in their hand? That she could pay cash on the spot, fund a new playground, build a greenhouse, if they would just let Elizabeth in? That when you are the mother of a foundling, the world is working against you, and time is always running out?

But as she tried to remain calm and confident, pulling all the right words from her head, the sudden crash of a chair kicked over, the whisper of scattered papers sliding across the floor, accompanied a long, lusty howl.

"Martin. The guy's name is Martin."

"And who told you this again?"

Both girls sat in the cab of Mack's pickup as he bumped over the railroad tracks and turned right, headed out on the country road. The season's first snow dusted the landscape, the light a stark, blue, winter kind of light, the kind that shows every twig, every blade of dead grass in sharp relief. Mack felt in ill humor. This was near the spot where he had seen Elizabeth walking by the side of the road. The memory still made him feel vulnerably unmoored.

"I already explained."

"You were actually incredibly *vague*," said Vanessa, looking out the window, looking worried. "Where on earth does this guy live? There are hardly any houses out this way!"

"He gave me directions. Yes, he lives out here. A guy I work with gave me his number. Martin said we could come out today. He knows stuff about Mitch Cooper."

"And ... because ... *why?*" asked Lillian as she arched her eyebrows ironically.

Mack swatted at her. "Stop trying to make me feel stupid. It's because he used to *live* in Mitch Cooper's house. Look. There it is, that's his building."

Solitary, in a weedy lot, stood an old building of whitewashed brick. Written in ghostly, faded paint on the side was BILLIARDS, though it had been a long time since anyone had played billiards there, surely. The plate glass windows in front were boarded up.

"You have to be kidding me," sighed Vanessa. "He's squatting in an abandoned building?"

"He lives in the back," Mack said defensively. And sure enough, there was an old black Camry parked behind the building. A rickety metal fire escape led up to a back entrance.

Mack led the way up the metal stairs, rusted through in places. The guardrail threatened to snap off in their hands. He knocked on the door of splintered wood once painted red but aged into a blood-like maroon.

There was no answer. The girls looked at him doubtfully, and he shrugged. "Relax, okay. The car's here. He's *here*."

He rapped again, louder. There came a stirring from inside. Then a moment later, the door opened.

He was a smallish man, though barrel-chested. Around forty, but with shadowed eyes and roughened red spots on his cheeks. His hair, still black and thick, fell in shaggy bangs on his forehead. Waffled creases on one side of his face, as though it had been pressed against a couch cushion, intimated he had just woken up.

"Martin?"

The man did not answer, but tilted his chin down and peered up at him, an almost reproachful look on his face.

"I'm Mack. We talked on the phone? You said I could come by?"

"You didn't say anything about bringing friends," he croaked.

"Sorry, man. Is it okay if we come in for a bit? Cold out here." He rubbed his hands together and gave what he hoped was an ingratiating smile.

The man regarded him solemnly. Then rather formally held out his hand for a handshake. He shook each of their hands, then, unsmiling, led them into his living room.

Living *space* was more like it … bedroom, living room, dining room, and kitchen seemed to be one. "Hold up one sec," Martin said, as he moved some blankets and heaved the bed back into a fold-out couch, then patted it down, motioning for them to sit.

The teenagers looked around at the bleak surroundings in silence.

"Doesn't the noise from the train bother you?" asked Lillian.

"Not hardly."

From one corner, rustling and soft mewing, and a gray cat emerged from a pile of clothes lying in one corner. It padded over, regarding them all shyly with large yellow eyes.

It rubbed against Vanessa's leg. "Who is this?" she asked, stroking its muzzle and making it purr.

"That's Bukowski," said Martin, eyes softening, drumming his fingers on the ragged armchair where he sat so that the cat came bounding up. "He's a stray. We've hooked up together, been buddies a long time."

"You've lived here a while?" Lillian asked. The place was depressing. But the man had a certain gentleness about him. She felt bad for the tired slouch in his shoulders.

"Mmmm, two, three years I guess? It suits me. No one bothers me out here. Rent is cheap. What can I say?" All of a sudden, he was all business. "So what is it you kids want?"

"We wanted to ask about Mitch Cooper. That's why Pete gave me your number. Remember? I'm Mack that he works with?"

"And this is what, a school report?" asked Martin with a bemused look.

"Something like that."

"Well, I'll tell you whatever you want to know. It was in my past, though. My drinking days. I'm in recovery now. Which is one reason why it's good for me to be living way out in the sticks. Less temptation. I go to my meetings mostly. And work. Delivering packages. Those Mitch Cooper days all feel like a dream to me."

"Well, how did you end up there? Living in The Brambles?" Vanessa's eyes scanned his face, trying to see into the workings of his mind. But he was a man of few clues.

"I was a stupid kid, that's why. Twenty years old. I'd just gotten out of a stint in prison. Just for some petty little stuff, selling speed to high school kids. I was in for two years. That period did my brain in, though. Too much time thinking about stuff. I watched Mitch Cooper movies as a teen, I identified with that lonely rebel shit. It kind of expanded in my mind when I was penned up. I read his biography in there. I was impressionable, I guess you would say. Smoke?"

"No thanks," said Mack lamely. "I play football."

"I'll take one," said Vanessa. The others looked at her strangely. "I sometimes smoke, not a lot. It calms me down."

Martin lit her cigarette with a silver lighter, then his own. He settled deeply into his chair.

"Anyway. There came the day when they let me out of jail. 'Cause of overcrowding. I had nowhere to go. My family would have nothing to do with me. I had no job. No car. It was early morning when I was released, still kinda dark outside. They gave me the clothes I was wearing when I went in there, which was my old Sunday school suit I'd worn to surrender myself. I had lost weight, and the suit was big on me. The pants sagged down my ass. They gave me a bag with my stuff in it, my keys, my wallet, and a folding knife. All I could do was walk. I started walking in the direction of Wellesley. I planned to show up at Mitch Cooper's mansion and throw myself at his mercy. Why? I guess the same reason I wore that stupid suit to turn myself into jail. Some obscure point to prove. Some glory in my own destruction. I was, in other words, just a dumb fucking kid.

"I thought I would be walking alone the whole way, but that wasn't the case. Not far out, this other guy joined me. He was a prisoner, too. Let out 'bout the same time as me."

As he told the story, Martin re-experienced that moment in time; he had just made it far enough that the metal gates of the prison yard were no longer in sight. The long stretch of highway before him was almost vertiginous to see, after living in a small space for so very long. It had been early morning, scarce traffic. Everything had looked amped up and over bright. The sunrise had throbbed, electric, *unreal*.

It was a while before he became aware that he was not alone. At the footsteps behind, Martin glanced in back of him to see a figure, blurred by the morning mist. He touched the folding knife that lay deep in his pocket. As the person caught up and pulled even with him, Martin turned his head to the right. Martin recognized the man from inside, tall, with thick white hair and pink skin full of broken veins, though he had never spoken to him. He wore a large, jangling backpack, as a camper would carry in the woods. He didn't turn to look at Martin, but kept his eyes on the horizon and nodded a greeting. He kept up a good speed, but in the silence of that hazy summer morning, Martin heard the man's labored breathing.

Martin kept his fingers on the knife. But in time, they came to tolerate each other's presence.

They walked this way for a while, side by side, never speaking. City became country. Hunger became ravenous. At midday, Martin left the highway to inspect a house that looked empty. The "FOR SALE" sign in the front looked aged, and the yard was overgrown. The white-haired man followed him.

The house was a ranch with a carport, standing next to a cornfield and a tin-roofed chicken house. The house's satellite dish lay tilted on its side on the ground. The chickens ran free, and one had made a nest in the satellite dish. Martin and the white-haired man gathered the fresh eggs. Chickens watched them from where they perched in the trees.

A funny thing happened then. Martin had paused for a moment, thinking no particular thought, when one of the hens swooped down and landed on his shoulder. It perched for a few moments before taking off again.

The white-haired man laughed. "You put me in mind of St. Francis and his nightingale!" he said. "St Francis, who wandered the streets of Assisi with a bolt of cloth under his arm. He wanted to be a knight, you know."

He looked Martin in the eye, nodded curtly but with a smile twitching his mouth. This man was much younger than Martin had at first thought. Early to mid-forties, but roughed-up like an ex-boxer, with prematurely white hair; Martin thought again of his knife. It had been his great-grandfather's knife. The handle was mother-of-pearl.

"Then again, the birds flew away from him whenever he started to preach. I won't make that mistake. Better to build nests for the doves. Or chickens, as it were! Yes. True joy is in keeping patience." He smiled a dazzling smile.

As they cooked the eggs over a fire in small skillet produced from the backpack, the man told him that he was a defrocked priest. "I used to be respected, a man of *dignity* and *grace*. Haha! The man with the answers. Then I made a few mistakes. Hurt a man in a fight, but didn't kill him. Did my time for it, though." He showed Martin a bad prison tattoo, a crudely drawn predator-like bird on his arm, wings arched out like an emblem from a heavy metal album. "Now, I'm homeless. My faith has been tested, surely!" he said this theatrically, as though from a pulpit. But then he dropped the persona, and held Martin's eye with a look of queer intensity. "But you think I'm gonna live in some fucking halfway house, with the television goin' all the time and meth heads eating canned clams with their fingers in the hallway? Fuck *that*. I'm finding something better."

Martin told him he was also a newly released prisoner. The priest (Martin now thought of him as the priest) nodded. "So it is, brother. So it is. I recognized you and thought you might appreciate the company."

They camped that evening in the chicken house, on the floor scattered with grain and dung. The priest fell asleep right away, snoring obliviously. Martin lay awake.

The last week Martin had been in prison had been spent in solitary confinement for getting in a fight with another inmate. He knew the experience had done something to his mind. Language was painful, gestures were empty and meaningless. The priest's words, St. Francis, chickens, a bolt of cloth, rattled at the bottom of his consciousness like jagged rocks. They *hurt*.

He wondered if he would ever be able to live among humans again. All he wanted was to walk east. Find The Brambles. Then he would figure it out from there.

He finally did fall asleep, but it was only to dream of a metal door. With faraway voices shouting words through it that he couldn't understand.

Martin looked up and paused for a moment in telling his tale, and noticed that the three kids were looking at him, completely absorbed; it had been so long since he had told this story to anyone. It surprised him that they seemed to show such an interest.

"I don't know how you seem so normal now." The dark-haired girl looked almost as if she was about to cry. "But I guess I've never met anyone who's been in prison."

Martin laughed, one harsh syllable. But then he smiled. "Oh, honey, I'm not normal. But I *am* a good guy. I am good now, but it took a lot to get here from *there*." He'd finished his cigarette but had been sucking hard at the butt without noticing. He dropped it into the ashtray before starting another. The girl with the long hair and the penetrating eyes held out her hand for another cigarette.

He settled back into the story. "Anyway. I kept moving on the road with this priest. Ex-priest. His name was John Leary. I told him where I was headed. He didn't say anything about it for a long time. Just let me talk. Like I say, I was young, and stupid, and got excited about stupid things. Sometimes you gotta beware of someone who will let you say too much, without putting their cards on the table. Anyway, the wheels were turning, and the next day, he asked if he could come with me, he wanted to meet Mitch Cooper himself. Said he'd been a fan, too, and had seen all his movies. He never mentioned a one, though.

"We were able to catch some rides, and made it into Wellesley in less time than I thought we would. I didn't have much trouble finding the house. I asked at the Esso station where it was, and they told me whereabouts, that it was far back from the road but that there was a stone monument at the roadside with the name on the plaque."

"The Brambles," said Mack, dreamily. He had his chin on his hand and stared into space.

"Yes, sir," said Martin, shaking his head. "I guess they told me where it was because I looked young and harmless. Everyone said I had a baby face back then. Anyway, we found the house, and I just …" he shook his head at the memory. "…I just can't tell you how strange it was. Strange that it was just so easy to get inside. A young hippie guy answered the door, hardly asked us any questions, just figured we were okay and let us in. This was twenty years ago, but the place was already a mess. A big scorched place above the fireplace from when someone didn't open the flue. Just dirty all over. There were already plants growing through cracks in the house. Actual *plants* creeping up the walls that eased right in. I'd never seen anything like it.

"So we were allowed to stay, no questions. There were a few others there, and it wasn't such a bad scene in the beginning. Just chaotic. Mitch Cooper was the big star, but I never would have recognized him. He was smaller than he'd looked on the screen. Childlike. And a personality like a child's. He wore a fancy smoking jacket much of the time and seemed kind of out of it. And I can't say just what that made me feel. I thought he would have been different. Bigger, somehow. It was a disappointment. Made me almost kind of disgusted. But not disgusted enough to leave. No way."

"So how long did you stay?" asked Vanessa. She looked most comfortable out of all of them, feet on the battered coffee table, smoke blowing in a stream from her nostrils.

"Two fucking years, believe it or not. At first, it was all right. But more and more drifters came in and out. After a while, it no longer felt like kids at a slumber party. I guess you could say the main trouble was coming to be John, and I became real sorry that I had brought him."

"What was the trouble?" asked Lil gently.

To which, unexpectedly, Martin grew flushed with anger; his eyes flashed like gas flames. "Well, I suppose the main *trouble* is that the man is a con artist. And evil. And a piece of shit." He stabbed out his cigarette, moved his hands through his hair restlessly. "He tricked me, first. When I met him on the road, I was lonely. And he has this really eloquent way of speaking, I guess from when he was a Catholic priest. He sounds so worldly and intelligent. And he can flatter you, that's the hell of it. He made me feel like there was no one else in the world. I mean, yeah, I saw his seedy side, too. But I thought it made him more real.

More honest. I trusted him.

"But then, things changed when we'd been living at the mansion for a while. He spent a lot of time with Mitch. Just the two of them. I mean, it was a crazy time. I was drunk and high a lot, just like everyone else, so some of it is hazy. But John had Mitch's ear, and I didn't like it. He counseled him, gave him advice and shit. I don't know what all.

"He had an agenda. He was going back to his old role, but this time it wasn't Catholicism. He was starting his own church. It was called the Ministry of Presence. Some half-baked New Age shit. But he said he'd got the calling when he was in prison. He convinced Mitch that *he* had transcended common humanity, too, because he had been a celebrity, a false idol, and had fallen from grace, but he could be redeemed. So, yeah. Mitch was John's first disciple." Martin relit his cigarette. His eyes jumped around the room spastically.

"Jesus, it sounds like Scientology or something," mused Vanessa.

"Don't ask me what all it's about, I couldn't tell you. But I wouldn't have any part of it. They found plenty of others, though. They were called the collective." Martin snorted. "Their worldview was all based on these mantras. Mitch supported everyone financially, but John was in control. It was just foul. Dirty. Druggy. John didn't get *quite* as drugged-out as most. But he certainly had a lot of sex. The women in the group were like a harem."

"So why did you stay if it was that messed-up?"

"Well, I was messed-up myself. I got myself a little job in a store stockroom and started staying away more and more. Then eventually I took off for good when the thing with the kid happened."

The three teens were all leaning forward now,

transfixed. But no one said a word. The sound of a train clattered in the distance. Bukowski roused herself and stalked away with a pattering of feet.

"One of the girls had had a baby, supposedly John's. I don't even know its name. But I mean, for an innocent kid to live in that kind of squalor. Just … disgusting. No one cleaned the baby or spent any time with it. She started to walk and just wandered around that place, completely neglected. Yeah, I was no angel back then. But that broke through to me. What happened was, one day the baby disappeared." His face flinched, and he looked away.

"Are you trying to say that …" Lillian's voice was a whisper.

"Do you kids understand that this is no *joke?*" Martin's voice had gone harsh, and he looked each in the eye, one by one. "You think it's easy for me to talk about this shit? It's not. What if they killed it? What if John's spaced-out acolytes killed that child and threw it in a ditch somewhere? I don't even know what I was privy to. I could have spoken up. I could have done something to stop it. And I have to live with that for life. It scared me enough to go sober. I been in AA for fifteen, sixteen years." He motioned to a pile of AA chips on the top of a broken old dresser. "But it's not enough. It's not enough to change the thing that happened, and my gut says it was something bad. I think you kids should go now," he said suddenly, standing up, hands defiantly on his hips, but his eyes swimming with tears. "And you," he said, swiveling toward Vanessa. "I know that's a voice recorder you been fiddling with in your pocket. I'm not stupid." He ran a hand through his hair as the three kids quickly filed out. "At least not *that* stupid."

The very first memories Elizabeth ever had were from when she was three. Less coherent memories than *impressions*. Impressions of sun filtering and flickering through green leaves. The wind rustled the branches of the trees, and it made her laugh. The woods were her first friends. The trees and the creek and the hum and throb of hidden insects.

Also, she remembered her mother. Her mother's presence was like the warmth of the sun. It emanated from one place. But it was also everywhere at once. The two of them were never separated. To be separated from her mother felt like death. It would send her into a blind rage of terror, kicking and screaming. So, it was decided there was no need for separation.

Her mother's hair was white then, too. But her face was less tense and lined. And she laughed more. She was never a loud woman, but she was quietly intense in her joy. The joy of being with her young daughter, outdoors. Time didn't seem to exist back then. One afternoon seemed to go on and on, never-ending. One season to another.

A rock. A veined leaf. A cloud. Everything was there to be investigated, looked at and exclaimed over. Elizabeth would always remember the wonder of lifting a chunk of sun-dazzled quartz to find a string of ants emerging from an anthill. They were so tiny, and so distinct, tiny beads of scurrying insect-panic.

She didn't learn to talk until she was four. But her mother didn't worry and didn't pressure her. In this honey-sweet time of her life, she didn't need words. She communicated with her mother with touch, with facial expression. It was her mother who provided the words, until she could, too.

Rock. Leaf. Cloud. Each word as distinct and wondrous

as each of the ants, spilling forth to protect their queen.

Days that went on forever, yet seemed to skid by so quickly, like a cloud racing across the sky on a breezy day.

And yet there was more underneath. Just outside the peripheries of sentience. There was an unknowable time that existed before Mother. This was a time and place that was dark, rather than light. And disordered. It was a general feeling of being cold and hungry. There were no faces, just legs of grownups, legs of furniture, television always on in the background, and a sweet sickly scent of rot. To (not quite) recall it filled her with a sense of dread and emptiness. So she did not think of it. Though it was always there, underneath.

Now, in death, Elizabeth could be all places at once, past and present. Just like she could be all things at once. But mostly, she was the woods. She dwelled in the damp forest floor, the twisting of roots stretching for nourishment. She was the rock, she was the leaf, and she was the cloud. Mostly she was just *being*, silent and peaceful. Sometimes she was a presence that watched. Sometimes she was a presence that felt wild currents of emotion, like lightning. But that, too, in its own way felt peaceful.

She was in the trees, whose branches she once laughed and smiled at as a three-year-old. She once was a girl, now she was a tree. Strong and silent and arching out into the limitless sky. She saw the ones she loved best and felt her love, still, in a way that echoed endlessly like waves on the shore.

NINE

MINISTRY OF PRESENCE

"Jesus, Lil, what difference does it make?!"

Mack and Lillian had started arguing halfway through the walk; they were taking the back way through the woods to get to The Brambles, and it was a longer hike than they thought it would be. It was cold, and the woods had a grayish, barren look to them.

"I'm not saying we should have gone in disguise. I'm just saying you could have worn a baseball cap or something, pulled down low—"

"I don't wear baseball caps. I would look like a douche."

"—and I just think it is not a good idea for us to be recognized. That's why we aren't driving, right? If we don't want them to see any of our cars, then why would we want them to recognize us from the neighborhood."

"Well, that's the goofiest thing I ever heard. If I wear a hat, I look like a different person who they couldn't recognize? Please."

"Would you two just shut up?" Vanessa had slept badly and was in ill humor. As a matter of fact, they all seemed to be in bad moods and fighting a lot ever since talking to Martin. No one had said a word on the way home from *that* little jaunt. They had communicated mainly through texts since then. No one seemed happy about this trip to The Brambles. But it was almost as though they couldn't stop the momentum of what they were doing. It didn't feel like a choice anymore. And it made them all irritable. "All we're doing is just going there to do a little … reconnaissance. There are three of us, we're all grownups here. No one's going to murder or molest us, it's going to be fine."

"Yeah, but we haven't even discussed our plan," said Lillian, in an anguished voice. "We don't even really *have* a plan."

"We're going to knock on the door and say we want to meet Mitch Cooper. We're starstruck teenagers. We don't need a plan."

They had, the night before, watched a barrage of clips of Mitch Cooper movies online, from the sixties and early seventies. There had been one movie about teenage hooligans in reform school. One about motorcycle gangs in the Arizona desert. One from the seventies about a hitman in hiding in the city. Cooper had always starred as the main character. Back then, at least, he was a small man, but wiry and tightly wound, with a hard glint in his eye; it was easy to see the man's power of immeasurable presence.

That was why it was hard to reconcile that image to what they had heard of the old man now living in The Brambles. As they broke through the woods out onto the edge of his estate, the back of the house itself appeared ahead. Imposing from far away, the nearer they were, the more evident the ruin. Hedges overgrown. The house itself looked sagging and dirty, with vines growing up the sides.

They circled around to the front of the place, and it didn't look much better. They passed an empty, weed-choked fishpond with an old, rusted wheelchair lying in it, on its side. For some reason the sight of it made Lillian's throat go tight with dread.

Large double doors of splintered wood. One of the broken door surrounds was patched up with a large piece of cardboard printed with the words FROZEN CHICKEN CUTLETS. Nylon folding lawn chairs were on the balcony overhead and a case of beer.

The knocker was shaped like a large golden ring, and Mack rapped it three times. Shortly, the door creaked open, and there stood a young man in sweatpants and a striped, woven Baja shirt. He didn't look quite at them, but past them, and said, "Are you delivering the food?"

"Nah, dude," said a bemused Mack.

"Then what is it?"

"We want to see Mitch," said Vanessa, deadpan.

"Mitch don't want to see you."

"How do you know?"

"'Cause I don't know who the hell you are. Peace." He started to close the door, but Mack held it open.

"Come on, man. We came a long way. On foot. Can we at least just come in for a little bit?"

The young man looked again right past them. Then he winced slightly, and walked inside, without saying anything at all. The three of them exchanged glances and followed him inside.

In the large center hall, an elaborate crystal chandelier hung from a perilously sagging rotted ceiling; no one wanted to walk beneath it. An elaborate double staircase swept up grandly, but it was covered with debris. A clothesline hung down from one, with grayed, ragged looking garments pinned to it.

Their host had disappeared into one of the side rooms.

They looked at each other, and then slowly walked forward. To the left, they found a library, with built-in shelves all the way to the ceiling, full of leather-bound books. Also a grouping of burgundy leather couches, with brass studs, beautiful but for the cracks and cat scratches. Someone, a young woman, was asleep on one of them, wrapped in a ratty bathrobe.

The three sat together on another sofa across from her.

"It smells here," said Lillian at last. "It smells like cat piss."

"Shhhh," said Mack, motioning to the sleeping form.

By and by, another person entered the library, an older looking man with overgrown hair of grayish-blonde, transparent at the crown. He wore a Pink Floyd t-shirt stretched over a thermal shirt and dirty sweatpants. He walked past them without comment and went to a bookshelf. He walked, running his eyes along it as though searching for a book. But he found what he was looking for, a baggie of weed and wrapping papers, and took it down, sitting in an adjoining armchair to roll a joint.

"Cold?" he at last asked, without looking at them.

"We're good," said Vanessa.

"There's some blankets around here somewhere. Place is always freezing. The windows are fancy, but they're for shit. The old man don't heat the place well. He's cheap."

"You know him?" asked Lillian.

"Yeah. Sure. Everybody knows him that stays here. You guys staying here?"

"No," said Mack. "We live in town. We just came to hang out. We want to meet Mitch. Is he home?"

The man snorted. "Home? He's always *home*. Whether

he's available is another question. He might be napping. He might be getting his meds. His IV drip is by the bed, so he stays there a lot."

"How can we see him, then?"

"John's the one to ask. But he's up there, too. And I don't know if he's in one of his moods or not. Sometimes you gotta feel him out."

Vanessa sighed. "What exactly do people do around here?"

The man shrugged. "Hang. Get high. We have our meetings once a week, but that's the only structured thing."

"Meeting?"

"Ministry of Presence. Usually on Sundays but it changes." He licked the edge of the rolling paper, looking up at them at the same time. "You guys can come if you want. Meet John and everything. He could answer your questions."

"Here?" Mack motioned around the room.

"Nah. In the ballroom. Across the way. Just come and you'll find the group if you listen."

"So you are a member of this ..." Vanessa gestured vaguely.

"Church?" the man fired away a hit, held it, and streamed it out contentedly. He did not offer it around. "It's not quite what I would call a church. More a philosophy. A state of being. Y'know."

"And you're into it?"

"It's awesome. John is a really different kind of guy. A prophet, if you ask me. For real, though. There's no Ministry without John. And I know he'd love to meet you kids. For real."

"And Mitch is at the meetings?"

"Mitch is always there, for sure!" He laughed, then

began to cough and choke. "Mitch ain't no prophet though. Mitch is the vessel. But that's just as important, if you ask me." He took one more hit. The smoke surrounded his face like a veil, a corona, from which he shared a benign smile.

Mitch sat dozing in his wheelchair, which John had positioned so that he could look out of the windows overlooking the back balcony. His IV stand stood to the right of him and poured medication into his fragile veins, through which a sensation of merciful coolness blossomed and spread through his aching body.

The medicine made him pleasantly drowsy, and apt to fall into twilit, waking daydreams. He sometimes felt a transcendent ecstasy at its peak, and that's what he lived for.

He felt a similar ecstasy, years ago, while watching his children being born, and he could still remember it now; the babies had had such bluish skin, glistening wet, such slow, uncoiling movements as they became acclimated to life. His three children, now adults, born to his other wives. The ones who came after *her*, his first. But he had never loved another woman the same way he had loved Patty.

Love, my love.

His eyes fluttered behind his closed lids He took one deep, shuddering breath, and almost glowed with incandescence as the drugs reached a climax. She had been like sunlight. Her beauty had always stunned him, he had forgotten how much. Her *face*. It opened up worlds to him. In the background of the everyday noise and bustle of The Brambles, he thought he could hear the soft roar of waves, the cries of gulls. In his mind, he suddenly saw an image of her in a bright floral bikini, stepping into the surf with her hair blowing back on a late summer day in 1973.

"Patty, oh Patty," he said, but it came out as a croak. An

old man's feeble plea.

And then his eyes opened to reality, to see that he was in his very own master bedroom, in a wheelchair, looking out the glass doors at the winter woods in back of his house. Frost covered the glass. He was crying, just a little bit, but John was sitting nearby in a tufted chair, reading a book.

John always noticed what was going on; his bright eyes always alert. He came over and said, "It's okay, Mitch. I'm right here." His hair was snowy white but still thick and bristly, his eyebrows still dark. "You need anything, my friend?"

Mitch shook his head in a jerking, palsied manner, and closed his eyes again.

He saw something new outside the glass doors when he opened them again. Down below, coming out of the woods, were three young people. Two girls and a boy. His heart fluttered at once. His children? He was the father of two girls and one boy. Was that them, coming inside after a tramp in the woods?

Then he remembered his kids were not young anymore. They were middle-aged themselves and living back on the West Coast. He hadn't even seen them in years. Not since John had come to live with him.

He raised his finger and pointed, turning to look over at John, trying to form the question on his lips. But it only came out as a pleading, questioning sound.

"What's that, Mitch? What's the matter?" He came and stood next to the wheelchair, bending down to his level, his eyes narrowing, scanning the horizon. But the three young people were no longer there.

"It's nothing. The meds might be giving you floaters or something. Nothing out there at all. Go back to your nap, okay?"

Elizabeth was five when she noticed the little boy for the first time. She watched him shyly, secretly, from the safety of her front yard, not used to being around other children, since it was always just Mother and her. Other children always interested her, though, when she saw them at the store or on the playground. Looking into their eyes was different from looking into the eyes of an adult. There was an openness, a vulnerability there that matched her own. Were they the same creature that she was? Did they think and feel the way she did? With grownups, there was an opacity, a wall of separateness. She wanted to be near another child, badly. Just to see what it was like.

And this boy was out on their street every day, in the afternoons of those first warm spring days. He had a bright blue bicycle, a two-wheeler, which he rode in looping circles, wobbling back and forth, standing up as he pedaled. She liked him because he had spiky black hair and large eyes. She watched him, every day, willing him to stay upright and not fall. What was he thinking, as he rode back and forth up their street? Sometimes he sang bits of songs or talked to himself a little. Elizabeth talked to herself all the time. Mostly told herself stories. But she wanted to know what *he* was saying.

She wished she could be his friend; somehow he didn't seem real enough for her to approach. Some people were real and some weren't. Mother was real. The trees and the creek behind her house were real. They were like friends to her.

One time she saw a man in the woods. He had white hair and a pink face. Though he said nothing to her, just looked at her from the other side of the creek bank, she wasn't sure if he was a grownup or a kid. His eyes did not seem like a grownup's. They had looked straight into hers with the candor of another child. They had looked into each other's eyes a good long while before her mother called to her.

She turned to her mother's voice, to answer. But when she looked back the man was gone. Though she did not see him again after that, she thought he was real. And he was her friend.

But she wanted to know the little boy. There came a day when he was riding back and forth as usual, wheels humming on the pavement, when he hit the curb with his front tire, and the bike spilled to the ground. He let forth a thin wail of shock and hurt. Elizabeth went forward and approached him; he looked up at her in surprise.

"Does it hurt?" she asked.

He looked at her dazedly for a moment, his pain forgotten. "Are you a boy or a girl?" he asked. Elizabeth, when she was young, had short hair and wore jeans and overalls, the gender-neutral clothes that her mother preferred she wear.

"I am a girl," she said, aggrieved. "You are a boy. And you are bleeding."

"Where?"

"Right there." She pointed to a rip in the knee of his pants, at the raw-looking scrape showing through from underneath. Her throat constricted. She felt the angry pain of that wound.

"Mother will fix it," she said, pulling him up by the arm. "Come with me. You need a Band-Aid."

Annabel was surprised when Elizabeth called her to the front yard. She knew a little boy lived up the street but did not know the family.

"The boy hurt himself, Mother. He needs help."

Annabel brought out the antiseptic, and applied a Band-Aid to the boy's skinned knee, and noticed the way her little daughter hovered nearby, unable to take her eyes off of him.

His tears stopped. The boy turned to Elizabeth and said, "Do you want to play?"

Annabel watched them. A friend. Elizabeth should have a friend, she knew. The child needed some normality in her life. I do not want my daughter to grow up freakish, just because her mother was weak, and a thief, a fugitive from the law.

The two children were so beautiful together, bent over a caterpillar they had found in the grass; she *wanted* her daughter to be happy. But what she didn't want was intrusion. Questions. Scrutiny. All the complications that outside contact could bring into their life.

"You guys can play together," said Annabel, "but I want you to play here, okay?"

And so it was that Elizabeth made her first friend. Mack came over most afternoons, and they played outside, whole blissful, silent hours where they played in the dirt and under the branches of trees.

There were more friends to come. Mack knew other children who lived nearby, two little girls named Lillian and Vanessa. Elizabeth, though she did not talk or show as much exuberance as the others, experienced the most radiant joy when she was with those three. They liked to pretend, just like she did. Sometimes they came up with the ideas for games. Sometimes she did. But every day she laughed, she ran herself ragged with joy and slept soundly at night. The woods, which had once been magical only for her, became a kingdom of four.

Her mother watched and listened from the house, but otherwise did not intrude.

It would always, in memory, seem to Elizabeth to be the happiest time of her life. She completely forgot about the child-man with the white hair. She had real friends now.

The ballroom looked as though it had been very grand at one time. The wainscoting had beautifully carved neo-classical ornamentation, but pieces had broken off. The grand marble mantelpiece had been made into a sort of altar, covered with candles, crystals, mirrors, and a gold statue of Ganesh.

Other than that, there was nothing in the large room, no furnishings whatsoever except for a scattering of faded oriental rugs, and near the fireplace, what looked like an office chair on wheels, covered with a piece of gold lamé fabric.

All of the people sat on the floor, so Mack, Lillian, and Vanessa did the same; although the youngest people in the room, many there appeared not to be much older than thirty. Young men and women dressed in hippie-ish garb, flowing fabrics and scarves. A few older folk who looked sadder and seedier, like the man they had met in the library earlier, who was still wearing the same Pink Floyd shirt he had on the other day.

No one showed any surprise that they were there. A few murmured "welcome" or "praise be," but other than that did not say much else.

They sat there for what felt like ten minutes before the room grew quiet, an expectant tension in the air. Through the door entered two men. The eminent one had thick white hair and dark eyebrows. He was thick chested, broad of shoulder, and muscular. He looked like he could be a bouncer. He had a large stomach, but it did not make him look weak, but even more solid and formidable. He wore narrowly cut black jeans and pointed black leather boots.

He pushed the other man in a wheelchair. This man was very old and frail and dressed in a seersucker suit, expensive looking, but too large for his thin frame. He wore a colorful pashmina shawl around his shoulders, a style usually worn by women. It was carefully wrapped and arranged, but it still did not hide the IV stent still in the top of his gnarled hand; the man smiled in a soft, unfocused way at the room at large, like a baby.

The wheelchair was placed next to the mantelpiece, facing the crowd. Then the white-haired man himself stood before the group, smiled beatifically, and made a little bow with his hands clasped together in front of his heart.

The people watching repeated the gesture back.

The man cleared his throat. He scanned the room, and his eyes alighted on the three new people, who sat toward the back of the group and to the right.

"I see some new friends have come to join us," he said in a low, sonorous voice. "Let me welcome you. I am John. We are very glad you are here." Several faces turned toward them and smiled. The three smiled and nodded back.

"I think you will find this to be a welcoming congregation, if you would like to call it that. But we aren't that formal here. Some might call me the leader, but all I do is speak through the collective." He closed his eyes and smiled warmly to himself, touching his hands together by the fingertips, as though he were considering something deeply. "I am a vessel. As well as Mitch here."

He turned and smiled at Mitch, who moved his jaw back and forth but didn't look up. "It is Mitch who draws a lot of folks here, initially. Through the power of his celebrity. But that's not a bad thing," he shook his head back and forth, eyebrows quirked up. "Not a bad thing at all. He was a manufactured deity," he patted Mitch's shoulder, and now Mitch feebly looked around, and up at John, and smiled shakily. "You know, it was meant to happen. *Every moment means something.*"

With that, the three teenagers were utterly startled when John walked to them, and instead of shaking their hands, knelt and enclosed each in a tight, crushing bear hug, almost lifting them off the ground. The man was even more enormous close up. And strong.

After the hugging, he looked each in the eye with a searching gaze; tears welled in his eyes, and his face glowed a hectic pink.

"Excuse me," he said in a choked voice as he made his way back to the front of the room. "I get emotional when I meet new people. Because … because I know what's coming, and it's beautiful, man. Doors will open for you," he flicked his hands open like a set of chapel doors, "ones that you didn't even know existed. And it makes me so happy."

He wiped at his eyes and then brusquely shook his head as though to clear it. Then he smiled ruefully. "Don't mind me. Everyone here knows how I am." There were appreciative chuckles all around. "But seriously, though…

"It wasn't always like this. I was lost, too. For a very long time. I took a lot of drugs, drank a lot in school. Then I turned back to the Catholic religion of my childhood. I went to seminary. I became a *priest*." He made scare quotes in the air with his fingers, and there was gentle laughter all around.

"Believe it? Well, it's the truth. I was a priest. And I

thought I was living the right life. But something just … swallowed me up whole. My soul, that is. There was something dark lurking there that I did not, could not confront. I did good in the daytime, a servant to the people, I thought. But I started slipping into bad habits. Hiding booze in the church office. Going out at night to where people didn't know me. Getting into trouble. This whole *double life*. And there came a breaking point. One night, I got into a fight with someone. Some dispute over money. Anyway. I beat the guy senseless. He ended up in the hospital with some brain damage. And the long and short of it was, I went to prison. A priest, behind bars. Believe it?"

This time, no one said a word or made a sound. John made a solemn face and nodded, eyes closed. "Of course, that was as it should have been. It was what I deserved. I lost everything. I was, as the parlance goes, *defrocked*. I no longer had an identity. I was in prison for nine months. My darkest moment. But also, my awakening.

"You see, I had time on my hands. I did a lot of reading in that place, trying to find some answers as to how to move forward. A lot of self-help books. *Tibetan Book of the Dead*. The *I Ching*. Numerology. Astrology. Everything I could get my hands on. And things slowly changed for me. The doors opened to corridors that were brand new to me. You know what blew off the top of my head, really? The Hindu belief that all is one and one is all. I mean, when you really understand that?" With his fingers, he mimed an explosion bursting forth from his forehead.

"Yeah. It's just that simple and just that complex. I saw, from my previous work, that people had a need for community and religion and coming together … but … but … it can be so alienating to some of us, man! I mean, am I right? I saw that there was a void out there. There is a need for a religion that is all-inclusive and accessible, but not like a traditional church. And I had *so many insights* to share about my rebirth! I could see it all in my mind! And I knew what I would call it. One day they had put me into solitary again, for my misdeeds, of course, and I was frustrated. I was banging my head against the padded wall in real, human, painful, *frustration* … and it came to me, just at that moment when I stared down into the dark, empty void of myself, that I should start my own movement, and that I would call this movement … Ministry of Presence."

At that point, there were joyful murmurs. One voice shouted out, "And so it was, Brother John!"

John scanned the room with an electric, beaming smile. Vanessa leaned forward, lips parted in amazement. This guy is on fire. He reminded her of those powerful politicians who can move a crowd through sheer supersonic charisma; all the people in the room were in thrall. That is power, she thought. Simultaneously, one of her pet words, like a quick little bird, alighted in her mind: brontide, the low rumble of distant thunder. Just as quickly, the thought was gone.

But the noises at that moment in the room were emotional and joyous. At one point John had all the people in the room join hands in an enormous circle ("The anchor of all of our meetings") and the voices gathered together to say, "Om."

The *om* went on and on, seeming to echo and ripple, but also to rise and gain in power. It was as though the room opened in the center into a large vortex of human energy. It was hard to know where one person ended and another began. Vanessa had to concede that it was awesome, in a literal sense. John had harnessed something. But to what end, she did not know.

Om. Chanted again and again, like a groundswell. The man in the Pink Floyd shirt had one of her hands in his large, cool, dry one, and he was crying.

But then there was another sound underneath that great human breath; it was a rattling noise. It came from Mitch, who seemed overcome, gargling and choking. John, who held his hand, calmly broke apart from the circle to attend to him, tilted his head up, and massaged his trachea. And so then came the end of the circle, and the meeting, when John raised up the other free hand and said, "Go now and love each other."

Some people slowly drifted into other rooms. Some lay on the floor where they had been, and the house quickly settled back into torpor.

"Dudes, I don't like this," Mack was the first to whisper as they stood in a cluster and prepared to leave. "That guy is a freak."

"Sssshhh," said Lil, flicking her eyes to indicate the man and woman intertwined nearby under a dirty blanket.

"But I'm telling you, man, I have a bad feeling."

"He's electric," murmured Vanessa.

"So what, you're falling for this hoodoo? You're whacked."

"No, Mack, I am not saying that. I'm observing, neutrally," she whispered so quietly they could barely hear her. "And I want to know more. Just because I'm fascinated by him—"

The three of them jumped when John appeared behind them, his face transcended and rapturous with a thin coat of sweat.

"Sorry if I get a little excitable," he said, "my work brings it out in me." He grinned at Mack. "I'm just so pumped, to share new things with the young people. If you'll stay. If you give me a chance, it … it …" He rolled his eyes up, at a loss for words. "If you only knew how it could be. To live in love, all the time. Sleep, breathe, and eat love." He motioned around to the inert forms that still dotted the room. "Everyone here, was just like you, at first. And they became reborn into love. Everything your parents probably taught you? Were *lies*."

The three looked at him, dumbfounded.

He looked at Lillian, imploringly. "Oh, did I misspeak? I didn't mean to, I—" He turned quickly to include Vanessa, who looked back, frowning. "I don't mean to insult your parents. If they simply don't know any better. But if you kids only knew …" he slowed down to catch his breath. "We live in this house independently. It's a kind of paradise. You don't need credit cards. You don't need a college degree—"

Mack snorted at that.

"Everything society says you need, you don't. We live in love and faith, and the universe provides. I have so much to share with you. If you would like to come back." His eyes kept being drawn back to Lillian's. He smiled and touched her forehead, making her flinch in surprise. "I see so much potential in you. That's your third eye, right there. You're sensitive, like I am. I can always tell."

Lillian's eyes puckered up again, as if she might cry. His touch lingered there, like a burn.

He put an arm around each girl but spoke to Mack. "Will you all come back? Give me a chance?"

Mack, without realizing it, was nodding his head.

"A party? Tomorrow night? Celebration is a big part of religion, always, and so it is with ours. It brings us all together. What do you say?"

Mack was speechless. But Vanessa said, "We'll be there." Lillian looked at her, aghast.

John shut his eyes, smiling. He backed away from them, and made a small bow, as he had at the beginning of the meeting.

"I know you won't regret it. Thank you. Thank you. You have made me so happy."

As though by magic, he disappeared again. He hadn't even asked their names.

TEN

A Broken Mirror

"The Battle of Towton was fought in March of 1461. The Lancaster faction was led by Queen Margaret of Anjou, who was a brilliant and relentless strategist, feared by her enemies near and far ..."

Annabel had started Elizabeth on eleventh-grade history, even though she was only fourteen, and the girl's favorite part of the homeschooling regime was by far was the history chapters being read aloud. She had her eyes shut, the better to take in her mother's voice reading the story of the Wars of the Roses.

"Begun with arrows, the battle soon evolved into hand-to-hand combat. More than ten hours long, the battle was waged in a whiteout snowstorm. 40,000 men were killed, and the river of the beck was said to be flowing red with blood ..."

But as she read that day, Annabel's mind kept wandering from the lesson at hand. She was not a big history buff herself, always preferring the empirical sciences. History did not seem real to her, the way that her love of the natural world did. And today's lesson, with its bloody snowstorm and beheadings, the young princes in the tower … well, it seemed she was reading aloud from a particularly gruesome novel. Should it disturb her that her little girl seemed so riveted, as though she could not get enough?

As much as Elizabeth felt a part of her, she knew there was something inside of the girl she would never truly know. Something locked away. She tried not to let it frustrate her. At least not too much. But it felt unfair to her. She was a loving mother. And sometimes she wished she had the key to the locked room of her daughter's mind.

She tried to get the girl out of town, as much as she could. They would spend three-day weekends in the city. One thing Annabel was thankful for was her money. There was money for a lovely suite at the St Regis. They would take a cab to the Guggenheim. Elizabeth loved the skylighted atrium, and the cylindrical ramp spiraling up and up like some beautiful postmodern cathedral.

This was the only religion, besides the wonder of nature, that she could teach the girl. The holiness, the beauty of the students lost in their sketch boards in the serene slant of city light. The grandness of the city itself, which was their own rich secret. The magic of yellow taxicabs and corner bodegas. The bustling sidewalks with hidden little leafy parks, if you knew where to look for them. And at the end of their day, the clean, pristine and impersonal luxury of their hotel room.

She wanted her daughter to know there was more to life than Wellesley. And more than just the two of them, alone.

But it *was*, most often, the two of them alone. And Annabel didn't know quite how to make it otherwise. Elizabeth had had friends, for a while when she was a little girl. But they had not been around in years. Annabel saw them, or thought she sometimes did, around the neighborhood. The same, but changed. Like polite young adults, who smiled and waved when they saw her, but that was about it.

She admitted it was a relief, really. Because the older the kids were, the more they would see, the more questions they would ask. But all the same, it worried her that homeschooling the child was isolating her.

If she could, she would take the child away from Wellesley entirely. Then they could live a whole new life.

Crazy thoughts and schemes ran through Annabel's head as she fell asleep at night. Could she draw up a fake birth certificate? A phony social security number? How would she even do such a thing? What type of shady underground people would she have to associate with? She had always been (most of the time), an upstanding person. Done well in school. She'd been a successful businesswoman. She liked to think she had done her fair share to protect the environment and make the world a better place. She might do more good things, still.

But right now she was preoccupied, day and night, with her own fears. Thief, thief, I am a thief. My number will be up, sometime, somewhere. My luck will run out.

Would they put her in prison, if she were caught? She went to the library and scoured the Internet for information. It appeared she could be in a lot more trouble for constructing a false identity, rather than providing none at all.

I have painted us into a corner. Just me, and the girl. Not fair to her.

She would ideally like to get Elizabeth a passport and leave the country. She fantasized about fleeing to England. The French countryside. The spent volcanoes and black beaches of Iceland. There were so many places they could go, and she had the money. They could have a great life, somewhere, where no one knew them, and they could start over again.

But for now, she was too afraid to do anything at all. She was immobilized.

Elizabeth seemed happy enough. She was a quiet, reserved young girl, and did not show her feelings a lot. But they got along well, didn't they? Enjoyed the comfort of each other's company? Enjoyed those excursions to the city, their homeschool sessions. Cooking healthy meals together. Exploring their woods with their battered little field guide that Annabel had had since college.

Her ex-husband was the only one who knew of her predicament. And Eric would keep her secret. He would never tell anyone, and he said that they should never speak of it again. But still, she was tempted at times to call him and ask him what she should do. Because she had to do *something*.

In the park years ago, when the other young mothers she saw asked her questions, she implied that Elizabeth had been adopted. She knew that that was what people still thought. And it was an accepted fact. And that was a good thing.

All was well enough, for the moment. But she knew she had to let the girl go a little bit. She needed her independence.

Annabel got Elizabeth a bicycle for her fourteenth birthday and told her she could ride where she wished. As long as she took her phone. As long as she took care.

As long as she doesn't get too close to others.

All were silent in Vanessa's car as they drove down the long private road to The Brambles. As they approached the house itself, up the brick carriage path, they could feel the vibration of the music. Speed metal.

"Those guys are into Motorhead?" said Mack, bemused. "I thought it'd be more like the Grateful Dead or something."

They parked behind a small line of cars and got out, the night black and icy cold. A line of motorcycles was parked on the dead grass of the lawn. As they got out of the car, someone threw open the door to the front balcony overhead, and the volume of the music intensified. Two people seemed to be chasing each other, cackling. Then something large flew over the balcony and landed on the brick path below. A large gilt-framed mirror crashed and splintered into bright dagger-like shards.

"The *fuck?*" shouted Mack up at the two people, who froze, silent for a moment, two shadowy figures silhouetted against the light coming from the door behind them. It was hard to know if they were male or female; they laughed, and they ran away.

"Soooo," said Lillian in the stunned aftermath, looking down at the mess. "What exactly is the plan here tonight?"

"We're going to party, and we're going to enjoy it," said Vanessa with an ironic twist to her lips.

"Yeah but, I don't know. This place makes me queasy. Seriously. The energy is just … bad."

"Wooo, the energy!" said Mack impishly, waggling his fingers. "Ooooh!" Smiling. *He* hadn't been to a party in ages. He hadn't realized how uptight he had been feeling the past month; not himself at all since this whole business had started. For a long while he had been anxious, and quiet, and depressed; freaks or no, he was in the mood to pound a few beers with someone, anyone. Parties energized him. Annoyed as he was by almost being hit by a mirror, his spirits lifted as they got closer to the throbbing music and the sound of excited shouting voices.

"Don't make fun of me. I don't really want to be alone at this thing. No one had better leave me."

"I won't leave you, Lil," Vanessa said. "But you'll have to try to just go with things. Blend in. That's the whole idea. This is how we are going to find out what's what."

"You girls can stick together," Mack said, walking ahead of them. "I'm doing my own thing."

The double doors were already partially open. Again, the large center hall with the swooping staircase. They had only been there in the daytime before, and the place had a whole different feel at night. It looked a bit less shabby in the low light; a lot of the wall sconces were burned out. But the music was loud, and the place smelled of vomit. And there were more people than they had seen before, not only regulars but different people who seemed to have come just for the party.

People moved every which way, in and out of the various rooms. They passed by the library, where a crowd had gathered around a woman dancing provocatively on a coffee table. Most people seemed concentrated, though, in the ballroom where the Ministry of Presence meetings were held.

This was where the makeshift bar was. A man wearing a motorcycle jacket and a bandana around his head was opening a new case of beer. He didn't blink an eye when Mack dug into a sweaty cooler for a bottle of lager. Lillian got herself a light beer, knowing that getting buzzed would make this place easier to tolerate. Vanessa poured herself a plastic cup of red wine from an open bottle on the table.

Bobbing his head to the music, Mack surveyed the room as he wielded the bottle opener. Not all hippies as he had expected. Some of these looked like a motorcycle gang or something. He ambled into over to where a group played quarters on a table dragged into in one corner; before long he was feeling amiably tipsy and cheering them along.

"Lemme play," he said, "I'm always good at quarters."

As he bounced the coin into the shot glass, again and again, he felt himself go into a zone of mild elation. He *was* good at quarters. Just as he was good at all sports. It gave him such a rush to aim for his target and make it, again and again. Not through effort. But a perfect zone of slightly unfocused intent. Like magic.

After chugging a second beer very fast, he tried to explain this concept to a girl who had taken to staying near him. Woman, really, not girl. He recognized her from the service. She lived there. Cute enough, in a slightly messy way. Very thin, though. Her dark, curly hair was dirty, and her blemished skin unnaturally pale, her mouth painted red, like a wound. But it worked with her look. Dirty, ragged jeans, lots of chain necklaces with little silver emblems. Henna tattoo on her hand. Mack could dig it. He didn't have a precise type in women. He was open.

And she seemed to like talking to him. It was free and easy, just talking about nothing, laughing about nothing. So different from being cooped up with Lil and Vanessa all the time. Things had been so serious with them lately. He wanted to have a night *not* to be serious.

The girl's name was Sapphire. She shouted the name into his ear, the room so loud it was hard to hear anything. "Your name is … what?" he asked, puzzled, and she only laughed, a full-throated laugh showing the fillings in her back teeth.

Lillian and Vanessa stood together, huddled, as they

watched Mack exit the room with the girl.

"God, he's annoying me so much right now," Lillian murmured. "We're here for a purpose. All he's doing is getting shitfaced."

"Well, I don't care," said Vanessa, after a long sip of the acid-tasting cheap wine. "You and I are the ones on top of things. If he wants to act like a dude, bro, and get wasted … just whatever."

They looked around, uncomfortable, not knowing how to proceed. Lillian had been to plenty of drinking parties, but this one was different. She was used to high school kids. This was a rougher crowd, *adult*, and she found it hard to relax.

"Come on. Let's walk around." Vanessa set her jaw, her tone grim. "We won't get anywhere if we don't mingle. Have another beer if you want. I'm driving."

From the top of the staircase, John stood leaning with his hands on the curved rail. He had just put Mitch to bed, after helping him to the shower; someone was needed to make sure he didn't slip on his way in and out of the invalid's shower seat he had to use. He was so thin, his bones protruded delicately up and down his spine like a perfect string of pearls. He was a little *too* thin. John would need to remember to give him an extra can of Ensure tomorrow.

John's pants were still dappled with water, and he was a bit tired, but he was pleased to hear the bustle and noise of a party going on. It made him feel good to know that he was the center of things. It was his party. He was feeling magnanimous and good-natured as he made his way down the stairs to see how things were kicking.

Crossing the front hall into the library, he saw the two girls. The young ones. High school, he guessed. They had that look about them. There was still that curiously bedazzled aura of childhood that lingered around them, like a fresh mist. He enjoyed most working with people in their mid to late teens. They were still so open to wonder, to possibilities.

The taller of the two girls, the one with the long darkish blonde hair and glasses, he couldn't read too well. He had seen her giving him these *looks* that were indecipherable. A thinker, that one. He would appeal to her intellect. She could be won over.

But it was the smaller one he felt especially drawn to. With her dark swinging hair and dark liquid eyes, a brittleness to her when she smiled, as though she were easily broken. He imagined her heart in her chest, beating as quick and shallow as a small hummingbird. He imagined her wrist in his hand, the way her pulse would flutter.

He followed them as they entered the library, talking softly. He thought he heard the brainy blonde mumble, "God, this is like something out of ancient Rome. Caligula. You know. *Primitive* …" He made the girls shriek aloud in fright when he came up and threw one arm around each of their shoulders and hugged them to him.

"Haha, scared you, didn't I? Am I really that scary, though? Oh no matter, no matter, it's not your fault you spilled beer on me, ha! Besides, I was wet anyway. I've been helping Mitch with his shower. He has to be helped so he won't fall." He smiled at them, one then the other. "You girls making out okay?"

"We're good. It's just a little … new to us, I guess," said Lillian as she gazed nervously at a pack of boisterous men in motorcycle leathers headbutting each other for sport.

Again, John grinned, abashed, waving a hand. "Oh, *those* guys, you mean. They're harmless, good guys. They're a club, you know. Called The Lone Horsemen. Whatta you think of *that* name, huh? But they're good, it's all good. I've known their founder from a while back. Real, real loyal guys, you know?" He looked each girl in the eye, in a serious way now, biting his lip as though holding something back. "You know I don't judge. Anyone, or any lifestyle. If someone is a friend, they are a friend. Forever."

He gazed at those men now, with a fond smile, then turned back to the girls. "So, you have everything you need? Another drink? Anything I can get you?"

"We're fine," Vanessa said, looking at John, again completely absorbed by him. She caught herself; people often told her that it made them nervous when she stared at them. Sometimes she couldn't help it, though. "Good turnout you have. You throw a lot of parties?"

John laughed at the stiffness of her question, then slapped her on the back, as though she had told a joke. "Yes. Oh, yes. I have a lot of practice at it. I love to bring people together. New friends, and old. It's part of what the Ministry stands for. Celebration, that is. And as you can tell," he winked, "I don't check ID here. You wanna know why?"

"Why?" Lillian asked softly, dazed as a sleepwalker.

"Because I *trust* you guys. Just because you are young, doesn't mean you can't make your own decisions. I believe all human beings have their own agency. I know that you will drink responsibly."

"How do you know that?" asked Vanessa with a crooked little smile.

John returned the same smile to her, a mischievous smirk, looking into her eyes a beat or two before answering, "Because I know that you are honorable and responsible. If I respect you, you will respect me. That's how it works."

"Simple as that?"

"Simple as that."

They were silent for a few moments, standing and surveying the room together, until John turned to them and said, "Want me to introduce you to some folks?"

He led them over to a group sitting on the floor in one corner, passing around a glass pipe, shaped like a crocus bulb covered with red studs.

"Hey, guys, how's it going?" asked John, sounding both perverse and paternal at the same time.

The faces all turned up to him, eager as blooms opening in the warmth of the sun. These were young people, two girls and two guys. Lillian and Vanessa right away recognized them from the meeting of the Ministry.

"Hey, gimme a hit!" John took the glass pipe, lit it with a silver lighter from his pocket, and inhaled deeply. He handed it to Vanessa, holding the smoke in his lungs but quirking up his eyebrows at her.

Vanessa had never smoked weed before, only cigarettes. But she put the pipe to her lips and inhaled the sweet but acrid smoke. She shut her eyes, to concentrate on what she was feeling, and handed it to Lil.

"No thanks, I'll stick with this," she said and held up her beer. "When I smoke that stuff I get all sweaty and paranoid."

No one seemed to mind. John made introductions all around, though the girls did not remember all the names. Then just as suddenly as he had appeared, he was gone.

"We saw you at the meeting," one of the boys said in the lull of John's absence. He had pale blonde hair, and was somewhat angelic looking, despite his dusty-looking all-black clothes, and ragged, black painted fingernails. "Didja like it?"

"Yeah," said Vanessa, feeling oddly removed from the

moment. "It was really, um, different. So you guys are all members?"

"Uh huh," said a girl, with a broad, pleasant, makeup-free face and a simple plait in her brown hair. "We all live here. We're part of the co-op."

"So, what about …" Lil motioned vaguely toward the noise and commotion around them.

"Oh, I don't know," the girl laughed. "This is just one of John's affairs. A lot of these people are just old friends of his. He likes to entertain."

"How long have you guys lived here?"

"Oh," the boy rolled his eyes back, thinking. "I guess in our group, we've all been here about a year or so, right? But others have been here longer."

"And it works out okay? All these people together?" Lillian feared getting a contact high, the smoke was so strong, so she breathed shallowly.

"Oh, yeah," said the boy. "It really is like a family here. You get that feeling of unconditional acceptance. Which is a whole lot better than I experienced at home. It's very open and accepting here. And John absolutely knocks me out. I go talk to him alone a lot. He can just riff on all kinds of things. Theology. Mysticism. He always has a take on things that will blow you away."

"He seems pretty cool …"

"More than cool," the boy said with a sudden ardency. "He went through a lot in his life. The priesthood, and then going to prison? Imagine that. I think he's pretty enlightened. Actually, I consider him a real father figure. No shit." He smiled. "No matter how many of us are here, he always finds the time to nurture us individually."

"So,…" Vanessa asked lightly, "Can you become a member without, like, living here? That's kind of a commitment, right?"

There was an odd beat of silence. The group looked at her as though composing what to say to the newcomers.

"Well," said one of the girls, guarded, "I think John prefers that we live within the community. But it's not like there are any hard rules here. But it's kind of … understood?"

"Besides, man," the angel-like boy said, with radiant serenity in his stoned eyes. "How could anyone not want to live in a place like this?"

The bed had no sheets, just a bare mattress, and the white canopy above was in tatters. But it was vast and high, a king-sized bed, and Mack was rolling around on it with Sapphire. It felt joyous, it felt like play. They were two children tussling on a large white raft in the mystery of a dark ocean.

It had been a while since he had slept with a girl. And she was so generous, so willing. And it felt so good to be holding another body against his own. It felt like a medicine he had sorely needed in the last couple of grim months. Everything was here, in this girl's simple body that was offered to him. The sanctuary of all that dark, wild, curly hair that fell over his face and shoulders, something soft that he could hide himself in.

Afterward, with this strange new girl in his arms, he felt more relaxed than he had in a long time. Her body was slight and delicate, very pale, and made him feel protective. Sapphire had looked sad to him, her eyes slightly swollen. But he was wrong. She was bright and funny and cheerful and seemed to really like him. They talked and laughed together, and it felt so simple. His mind for once untroubled by either thoughts of his family or his future. A gentle haze had, at least temporarily, settled over his life, making everything more tolerable. He didn't worry about his mother's neediness or his brother's mental illness. His father being an asshole. He could barely even remember the grim task that had brought them to this house in the first place. He hadn't wanted to come here, had dreaded it. But it had ended up being just what he needed.

And so he drifted off to sleep, the deepest sleep it seemed he had had since childhood.

"Where is he? I could kill him." Lillian scanned the room for Mack. He'd simply disappeared, and he wasn't answering his phone. It was one in the morning. She didn't want her parents asking too many questions. They had to get back.

"He could have left, for all we know," said Vanessa. They were walking from room to room together, craning their necks, searching for and not finding his spiky dark head.

They passed again through the front entranceway. John sat alone on the bottom of the stairs, legs spread out, lost in dreamy thought.

His gaze alighted on the two girls. "You aren't leaving so soon, are you?"

"We're looking for our friend." Vanessa was at once drawn to and repulsed by his contented, kingly manner. He always looked like the most centered person in the room.

"You mean the guy you came here with?"

"Yes. His name is Mack. Have you seen him?"

"Oh, yeah. A while back. He's spending time with Sapphire. I don't know where they got off to. But I'm sure it's fine. She's a good girl. A very fine sensibility to her. I'm sure they're somewhere ... talking." He fixed his eyes on Vanessa, and smiled, and said, *"Nescis quid serus vesper vehat.*"

Vanessa blinked. *You know not what nightfall may bring.* "You speak Latin?"

John laughed. "I was a priest, remember?" He winked. "I could just *tell* you were a Latin scholar."

"I've taken it since middle school," she said, feeling a bit faint. "We have to go now …"

"Do what you need to do, and it's perfectly okay if Mack wants to stay over. Sleep anything off that he needs to, you know?"

"That's fine," said Vanessa evenly. "You can tell him we left."

After the girls recovered their coats and went out the door, John remained sitting on the steps, feeling pleasantly sleepy.

His mind slipped into a sort of waking dream, a memory of when he was still in the priesthood. There even seemed to be the scent of frankincense in his nose, a sort of olfactory hallucination. Not unpleasant. A woody, earthy smell. It had always made him feel transported when he walked the aisle at mass, swinging the thurible back and forth with its glowing beads of incense. Oh, what it had been like, to feel that he was blessing the church, its altar and its people merely with *smoke*. It had been a power so rich it almost made him delirious. For some reason, being near the dark-haired girl Lillian had drawn forth this remembered feeling in his spirit. Those holy wisps of smoke dissipating in the high eaves.

"So what'd you think?" asked Vanessa, fishing out her car keys as they walked. The night was frigid, with bright cold stars in the black sky.

"I think I feel sick," Lil said.

Vanessa looked at her and saw how unsteady she was on her feet. "God, how much did you drink?"

"Enough," she said glumly. She had been nervously downing cup after cup without realizing it. She hoped she wouldn't puke in the car.

They looked down at a crunch beneath Lil's foot. The crushed mirror shards. Their arrival felt so long ago that they had forgotten about the smashed mirror. The jagged chunks of silver reflected the moon's quiet presence above.

The place where Elizabeth lives now feels like the place she has always been. But more and more, recently, she is preoccupied with that other, living dimension. The one that she used to occupy, back when she was a living girl. Because even though she is at peace as she is now (not exactly happy, but a blissfully neutral state, experiencing herself as one with the woods and the leaves and dirt, a blissful serenity of death's indifference), she is pierced by her intimations of those still alive in her former life.

She can feel her mother's pain and confusion. Sometimes she tries to will herself back into form, to give her mother comfort. She can feel her mother's mind, a machine that never stops ticking along, racing, ruminating and obsessing until it exhausts itself into an uneasy sleep. She feels that if she cannot still her mother's mind, she can never rest into forgetfulness herself.

She still feels, too, the last tremors of terror before her own earthly demise. The terrible flame-like eyes and the booming voice of the man who killed her. The last thing she can remember of that *life before* is the ferocity of his intent, a rage so strong it was the whole of the universe crushing down onto her, compressing her like dark coal into a diamond. Her girl's life crushed out into one brilliant crystalline spark.

She knows the man still lives and walks himself, and that his appetites are unabated. She can feel the bloodlust rising up in him again. The need to own utterly, to control the life and destiny of another. His soul is like that of a pale, albino-ugly lizard. Slave to its instincts and appetites. Nothing will stand in its way until it achieves satisfaction.

Elizabeth's sense-memories are lately more and more vividly alive, and won't let her rest. In some way, she has to act. She knew she had to harness the power of her pure essence and form to have some kind of effect on what was happening in the present. Or else it would be like a never-ending cycle of pain. The terror would ripple out and never end. She feels herself burning ever more brightly, every day. She is growing larger and stronger every day, like a soft, heavy cloud full of lightning. A glittering electrical field that is invisible, yet undeniable in its powerful presence. In a way, she feels more real than when she was alive.

"What the hell?" asked Lillian when she saw Mack in the school cafeteria. He had been absent for several days and had not responded to phone calls. Now he was sitting alone at one of the tables, hunched over, drinking chocolate milk and eating distractedly from a foam tray of tater tots.

He didn't turn around, just raised up a hand in greeting.

Lil sat down beside him. "You just disappeared in that house and didn't say anything to us? We were actually pretty worried about you!"

He still said nothing, just shrugged.

"Well, what's been going on, Mack?"

He finally turned to her, and she was shocked to see that he had a black eye.

"What the—"

He grinned, sheepishly, and shrugged. "Accident. No big deal."

Then nothing.

"Why have you been out of school?"

"Just been busy. Some family issues. And I wasn't feeling too hot. So." He stretched his legs out and leaned back, and yawned massively.

Lillian slammed her hands on the table. "Mack, why are you flaking out on us now? It isn't fair that—"

"Now you listen to me!" Mack hissed, wheeling around on her. "I don't owe you anything, and I don't have to *tell* you anything. I am my own person, I do what I want, and you can't just—"

"But it's different with us! You know that."

"Why? Because a girl died, I'm bound to you forever?"

"She wasn't just a girl. You're awfully cold-hearted, you know. Drinking and sexing, like we were there just to party, when we were there for a different reason."

"I'm seventeen years old for Christ's sake! It's what I'm supposed to be doing!"

"I thought you were different."

"Well, sorry to disappoint you for not being as morally superior as you are. You think you're better than other people. You know what? You're not."

Now Lil's face flushed red, her mouth drawn tight. All around them echoed happy voices and laughter, sneakers squeaking on the linoleum, but it all seemed far away.

Mack felt a wash of shame seeing her face look that way; he had really hurt her. But then the shame gave way to righteous anger. "You are not my mother! You are not my sister. Neither is Vanessa. I'm sick of all of this, and I don't want to talk to you right now."

He pushed his lunch away from him and unwound his

long legs from the benched table and stalked away, muttering, "Fuck fuck FUCK!"

Lillian stared after him, immobile and speechless.

"It was awful. It was bizarre."

"And you said he had a—"

"It was *huge*. Purple and yellow. The whole eye socket. Like someone really socked him."

Vanessa stared thoughtfully into space, trying to assimilate the information, her phone gripped in slippery gloved fingers. She had taken her little brother sledding. There had been a half-foot snowfall the night before. He stood at the top of the sledding hill with a clump of chattering mothers wearing parkas and yoga pants, their hands clasped around cups of take-out coffee. They looked over at Vanessa curiously; she glared back at them and turned away.

"And he just wasn't even acting like himself, was the weird thing. I don't get it. What do you think is going on?" Lillian said. There was a long silence. "Vanessa? *Vanessa?*"

"I'm here. I'm just thinking." She watched her brother slide down the hill, belly down, on his sled. But she only noticed it dimly. Her mind was on other matters.

"Well," Vanessa said at last, "I think for right now, leave Mack be. If he wants space, we'll give him space."

"But he seems to be in some kind of trouble."

"Don't worry, we'll find out what's going on. In time. But for right now, I want to go back to The Brambles."

"I hate that place. I feel like that's where all the trouble started. It's bad luck," Lillian said.

"Nonsense. There's no such thing as bad luck. And I have plans. We have to go back."

"I don't even know, I mean, are you going to sleep over

at my house this time, or what?" The night they had stayed late at the mansion, Lillian had slept over at Vanessa's because Vanessa had no curfew. Lillian would have a harder time providing excuses to her own parents about being late, who were stricter.

"Don't worry, Lil. You can stay at my place as much as you want. They don't mind."

Lillian grew embarrassed all over again, wondering if Vanessa's parents had heard her vomiting in the guest bathroom; she would watch how much she drank next time.

"Well," she said, "My parents might start asking why I stay there so much. And they'd love to have you over. They think you're a great influence. Scholarship girl."

"Well, let them think it. It's good that they like me. I like them, too." She paused, then added, "You must miss your sister," Vanessa herself didn't know where this came from.

Lillian sighed. "Yeah. I do. Medical school takes up a lot of her time, so we don't talk as much. I really miss her." She scanned her bedroom looking at photos of herself and her sister, beaming and hugging, and the images seemed like wonderful long-lost dreams; even when she was around now, she was more grown up. More tired. Not the same. "Anyway. I'll let you go now."

"You alright?"

"Yeah. Mack just said that stuff that kind of messed with my head. I thought he was my friend."

"Disregard Mack for the time being. He's being an idiot. I want to go to the next Ministry of Presence. I'll text you. Okay?"

"Okay."

"Don't worry about anything. Okay, Lil?"

"Sure." But when she put her phone in its charger, she felt an old, heavy sensation of despair that sometimes fell over her like a suffocating blanket. It was a feeling that she did not ever tell others about. She feared that it would frighten or disappoint people. After all, she was Ladybug. The one with all the energy and enthusiasm. The one who always lifted other people up, not down.

Sometimes she felt like a ridiculous juggling clown. No one knew how low her moods could go. How shocked would everyone be to know that she sometimes carved into her own thigh with a sewing needle? Little etchings in bright blood. It was a pain that anchored her back into her body when she felt scarily disconnected. But she would be so ashamed if anyone knew. Her friends. Her family. Especially her sister.

Sorry for not being as morally superior as you are. Maybe Mack was right? Everyone must think that about her. She wanted to talk to someone but didn't know who to share her shameful feelings with. She liked Vanessa and saw her more than anyone else recently. But it was hard to ever know what Vanessa was thinking. Her face was so inscrutable. Sometimes she looked at Lil like an entomologist studying a pinned-down bug. Ladybug. Darling of the cheerleaders. Sometimes when the squad tossed her in the air during their formations, she felt suspended there, defying gravity, part of neither sky or earth.

Tears streaked down her face. She held the sewing needle in her hand, bright and sharp. She jabbed it into the pad of her fingertip, drawing a bead of blood, which she sucked on.

The large mirror on her bureau replicated an image of a girl, lying in a bed of pink roses. Cabbage roses, large, almost like faces, all around her. It reminded her a little of certain Victorian photographs of the dead.

She looked at herself, her eyes bleary and unfocused so that her mirror image almost looked like a stranger. The girl there became a sort of mute company. Maybe that was all she needed, a witness.

Slowly, a kind of serenity came over her by degrees, little by little. The darkness and anxiety seemed to simply *drain* out of her, with no effort on her part. Hypnotized by this mirror image, she could not look away from it. It seemed like a trick of the mind, but the image seemed to be a presence.

Elizabeth? Lillian crawled to the end of her bed, stood up, and came closer until she was inches away from the mirror; it was no longer Lillian in the mirror. Elizabeth gazed straight back into her eyes.

She was the exactly as Lil had remembered her. (She had wondered if she could even remember what Elizabeth had looked like anymore.) At that moment, Elizabeth was really *there*, she was solid and real. But death seemed to have changed her, but in a way, Lil could not put her finger on. There were many dimensions, it seemed, layered one atop the other. Looking into this teenaged girl's face, she saw all her other selves, all the Elizabeths all at once, baby through the elderly woman that she never got to be.

She put her nose inches from the silvery surface, trying to make it all out. Elizabeth's face was narrow, a bit hollow-cheeked. And her eyes, which were always the most striking thing about her, did not have the hard, challenging expression they had had in life. She looked into Lillian's eyes with a deep, abiding empathy. No one had looked at Lillian that way, not in a long time. She could not move from where she stood.

Time seemed to have stopped. She remembered the dream from months ago when she had sleepwalked into the woods. She had felt Elizabeth's pain and fear, and it terrified her still to remember it. (And often willed herself to forget it.)

But this experience was utterly different. The dead girl's mirror-gaze kept her locked in, and she did not want to break away. Even though not a word was spoken, what was happening felt like a great comfort. What a feeling it was to be known! Because it seemed that Elizabeth knew the turmoil in her heart, and her confusion, and all the dark, difficult things that she couldn't communicate to anyone else. Lillian felt like a newborn baby, gazing into its mother's eyes, and finding an ineffable connection. How wonderful it was, to really be seen!

But, at some point, Elizabeth slowly faded away, and Lillian looked at her very own self again, though it took her some time to realize it. It was not a shock, and not a sorrow to find herself alone again. As Lillian crawled under her covers, she felt a kind of holy peace had come over her.

She turned out the light on her nightstand. It was the quietest her mind had been in a very long time. Even though it was still a dark winter afternoon, she felt sleep come about her, enveloping her in a warm embrace.

And before she fell into a dream, she knew what they were doing was right, that it had a purpose. That even though it felt scary and wrong, that she and Mack and Vanessa would go back again to The Brambles. That they had to do whatever it took to discover what had happened to Elizabeth.

With a renewed sense of spirit and purpose, she shut her eyes peacefully.

Mack sped up the winding road that led to The Brambles, his truck's suspension taking a pounding from all the ruts and potholes. But he hardly noticed the jolting. He glared out of the windshield, his hands white-knuckled on the wheel, Primus blaring from the speakers. He braked abruptly in the carriage path, parked sloppily at an angle; he did not care.

Now that was staying here, he did not have to knock. He pushed one of the battered double doors open and went in, hurrying two steps at a time up the grand staircase, and up to the bedroom that Sapphire and he now shared. Not many people at The Brambles had their own bedroom, so he guessed Sapphire must have been there longest. She was in the four-poster bed, still with its bare mattress of stained ticking. Asleep, dark curls spread up and out over the bed like a girl floating under water.

Mack stopped for a minute. He wanted her awake. She was the only one he wanted to talk to anymore. She was older than he had at first guessed, twenty-one-years-old, and though she hadn't told him much about her own life, it seemed like she knew a lot. He wanted her to hold him and talk to him until he felt better. But he didn't want to be the one to wake her up.

Slowly, carefully, he slid into the bed beside her, claiming part of the rough blue blanket wrapped around her. It was okay. Just having her close was enough for now.

His eye socket still throbbed from when his brother had punched him. It had happened only a few days before, but the bruise was uglier than ever, a supernova of purple and yellow and orange. He prodded it with his finger and it felt tender and inflamed.

What a night *that* had been. He still didn't like to think about it. The night of the "intervention." His mother, without telling him, had invited his father and brother to their little house. "I was just trying to help!" she had cried, later, after everything had gone so wrong.

She had called his father and brother over to talk to Mack about his "downward trajectory." That was what his father called it. His "self-destructive life choices." Mack told him he didn't want to hear shrink talk from his own father, that he wasn't one of his patients.

Mack started to lose his head when his father said, "I'm here to validate your anger, son. It is natural,"

His mother had called his father to tell him that Mack had been rejected by Brown, had not applied to any other colleges, and had no fallback plan. That he had been gone all night the evening before, coming back hungover and incommunicative in the morning. She didn't know what the matter with him was. He'd been losing weight and acting not himself, ever since that poor young girl died.

"I'm sorry, Mack," his mother called helplessly as the two men circled his father's SUV, in which Mack's brother sat, smoking and glowering. "I'm in over my head with you."

"So what is this? Some kind of intervention, like on television?" Mack yelled at his father.

"What? Can't I visit my son when he's in trouble?"

"You never come here! I'm always the one who visits you! Why change things now?"

"That's just because Ricky likes stability. Going between the two households throws him off balance. But in this case, I thought that—"

"There is no case. Mom shouldn't have called you. There is *no problem.*"

"Hey! Don't you beat on my car with your goddamn fist! Control yourself, son."

Ricky, agitated by the fighting, got out of the passenger seat and flicked his cigarette aside. "What the fuck is your problem, Mack?" His eyes blazed, his movements more jerky and spasmodic than usual; he looked worse than the time Mack had seen him last.

Momentarily struck dumb, looking at Ricky, he said, "Chill, man, chill."

Their father took Mack by the arm and pulled him away. Under his breath, he said, "I expect more from you. I'm very disappointed."

"*What* do you expect from me?"

"That you will not upset your mother, for one. You're all she has. Her main focus now. She's terrified that you'll turn out like …" he flicked his eyes in the direction of Ricky, who was pacing agitated, and muttering, "Fuck, fuck, fuck."

"And besides which, I will point out, now you've upset him, too."

"You can't keep him coddled and locked away, Dad, or he won't be able to handle *anything*."

"That is none of your concern. Your concern should be your mother. She depends on you and loves you very much, or she wouldn't have called me."

"Why do I have to be the one in charge of other people's feelings all the time!" Mack was yelling again. He knew he should cool it, but he just couldn't take it anymore. "Why don't you both get out of here—"

"We're here for you—"

"If you want to help me, then go away and mind your own business!" He pushed off his father's hands when he tried to rest them on Mack's shoulders. It was hard enough that his father stumbled back a bit.

At that instant, Ricky stopped pacing and lunged toward Mack, as quick as a cobra strike, all the energy and madness in his lithe body whiplashing him forward.

Mack saw sparks as his brother's fist collided with his

eye. And then everything went red, and he heard Ricky shouting at him, "Who are you? You are not my brother. Tell me who you really are, motherfucker!"

Of course, he had to get out, he told himself in this blessedly quiet room, with this lovely girl asleep beside him. He'd had no choice but to pack a bag and his laptop and the few odds and ends he thought to grab because it was so hard to concentrate, to think, when his mother chased after him begging him to forgive her, begging him not to leave.

"But where are you going?" she asked in a heartbroken wail. "You can't leave me! I love you, son. You're my whole life—"

"Just let me go! I can't *be* your whole life. Find a life of your own."

He blanched now at the cruelty of those words. Best not to dwell on it, because it made him feel like a monster. He couldn't think about his mother or any of his family, or it felt like his head would explode.

"I just need some time to think." He actually murmured this aloud to himself as he burrowed his face into Sapphire's hair, that soft darkness that smelled like smoke, and herbs. A dirty but comforting scent. He wanted to just obliviate himself in it for the moment. And so he did. All he needed to hear was the steady, even sound of her breathing. Perhaps it was best she was asleep. He didn't want to talk anyway. At least not now.

A brisk, cold Saturday morning. The sharp winter sun shone straight through the window, into his eyes. After a while, he turned over on his other side.

His eyes drifted vaguely over the dark wooden nightstand beside him. Tissues, old coffee mugs, and an overflowing ashtray covered the top of it. And there was something else about this nightstand, something he hadn't noticed before.

The wood was full of dings and scratches, but the harsh sunlight revealed something previously unseeable. Words scratched into the side of the thing. Something that a person could only see from where Mack lay. Right at eye level, he saw that someone must have used the blade of a knife to scratch out, lightly: Elizabeth was here

The last summer of Elizabeth's life still glimmers in her memory with a vibrant intensity. It is clear, crystalline, like a snow globe, something with a smooth heft to cup in the hand. The life inside it miniature, but extremely precise in its detail.

It was the summer she kept the ammonium nitrate in her closet, her secret. She stole it scoop by scoop from the neighbor's garage and hoarded it in a plastic bag. She loved to run her fingers through the cool white crystals. That potential for spark and explosion entered through her fingertips with a thrill.

She stole other things, too, the summer she turned seventeen. Lipstick from the drugstore. Fashion magazines. All the things her mother did not want her to have because she wanted to keep Elizabeth pure. But I'm only pure like ammonium nitrate, she would think with her hand wrist deep in the bag.

She loved her mother but wanted, needed, to have secrets of her own. So her secret was the internal world she created for herself that was small and perfect as a dollhouse, but enormous at the same time. Like an expanding universe.

Her world was populated by romance and stories and drama; she spent much time at a large corner table in the library reading books like *Tropic of Cancer* and *Lady Chatterley's Lover*. She loved the tension and drama and forbiddenness of the words. They spun and reverberated through her head as afterward she rolled around lazily on her bike, down back roads of wooded lots and newly built homes in culs-de-sac. The summer started off mildly, with that smell of sawdust and the new, tender weeds poking up toward the blue sky.

I could be anyone, she thought, breathing the fresh, fragrant air as she coasted, spokes chattering like a roulette wheel. Anything in the world might happen to her, in the vivid world she created just for herself. She was not merely a strange girl in a small town. (Though she knew that people here thought she was odd, even pathetic, she clammed up tight as a clenched fist when the librarians tried to make conversation with her.)

All I need is to get out of here, she thought, and never look back.

Maybe it was because she kept the same schedule most days that the man with the white hair took notice of her. She saw him in the library when he started sitting at the end of her long table. In that hushed atmosphere, his silent presence reverberated like a struck bell. That hair. The dark eyebrows. The neck so thick, it strained his collar. There was something different about him. Something barely contained and not of this town. He wore rumpled button-down shirts and when he rolled up the sleeves, she saw, on one arm, the bottom of a tattoo that looked like bird talons. On the other arm was a symbol that looked like a snake eating its own tail. She looked away, then back again, intrigued. It was the third day he had been in the reading room. She wondered who he was. And why there was something so *familiar* about him. She had the eerie feeling that she remembered him from a dream.

He was reading a small paperback book whose title, *The*

Soft Machine, was printed across the front in bright, jangly letters.

He saw her looking at the book, a smile flashed across his face, and he held her eye. "You read Burroughs before?" he asked in a friendly voice.

"No. But I've heard of him." She knew vaguely that he was an old man who wore a fedora, but nothing more. She looked back down into her own book, *Zen and The Art of Motorcycle Maintenance*. But she could no longer concentrate on the words. She was only looking at the page, the letters like lines of swarming ants.

"Well, you should. Read him, I mean. He had a technique to writing, a cut-up technique. Really neat. My favorite quote by him is 'Be just. And if you can't be just, be arbitrary.'"

At this, the man smiled at her, conspiratorially, as though they shared an inside joke. Elizabeth found herself smiling back, she couldn't help it. She liked the quote.

The librarian, walking from the stacks, glared at them as she walked by, a finger to her lips.

After she had gone, the man shocked her by whispering, "Bitch should mind her own business. You ever get close to her? She smells like Bengay and wet wipes."

Laughter snorted through Elizabeth's nose before she could contain it. The librarian turned around to give them another warning glance. Elizabeth and the man exchanged mischievous glances. But then at a signal, a re-lowering of a curtain between them, and the man went back to his book as though they had never spoken.

He was there the next day, too. They nodded in greeting, then read in companionable silence. She found she enjoyed the company, even though they weren't exactly *together*. It made her feel okay in her otherness. This man was *other*, too.

And he seemed educated, urbane, probably from New York. Their shared presence was like a warm circle of light.

One day he slid a book across the table to her, a paperback with a man on the cover, holding a typewriter over his face, and the title, *Naked Lunch*.

"I think you'd like this one. It's a good one to start with if you're just now reading Burroughs. He said that 'naked lunch is the frozen moment when everyone sees what is on the end of every fork.'" He looked at her in a moment of wonder and excitement; he was very boyish, in spite of his white hair. "And the thing of it is? You don't have to read it in order. Just start anywhere. Move around. Backward and forward. Doesn't matter."

She tried it, opened it somewhere in the center. The book was confusing, like someone describing an endless dream, of orgies and dildos and "canceled eyes." It made her a bit lightheaded.

She looked up at the man, and he smiled. "See what I mean? Wild stuff. Man was a visionary."

Elizabeth willed herself not to blush but felt heat go to her cheeks anyway. Partly embarrassment. Partly a rush of pleasure that someone who was so smart and sophisticated regarded her as an equal. She wanted this new friend to see that she was unique, not like other girls her age (not that she currently knew any) so she met his gaze and did not look away.

Was this what it was like to have a father? Elizabeth had never known hers; her mother had broken up with him when she was pregnant. Her mother was very close-mouthed on the subject, though her eyes always grew pained and tremulous when Elizabeth asked about him. There were some photos in an album, and her mother did not know that she knew where it was. Sometimes she snuck it into her bedroom at night and looked at the photos with a flashlight. There, in the quivering beam of light, was her young mother when her hair was reddish brown. There were photos of her with a lanky young man in steel-rimmed glasses. A lot of times they were out in the woods, in khakis and hiking boots. Sometimes with metal sticks and clipboards. Some showed them at a large conference table talking to people in suits. In one they were laughing in front of a lighted Christmas tree, her mother unwrapping a gift and howling with laughter, though you could not see what the gift was. The young man looked on, adoringly.

She could not make much sense or narrative out of these few images. She knew they were environmentalists together. Scientists. But her mother would give her no details about the marriage or why it had broken down. They looked so happy in the photos. What could have happened? It sometimes made Elizabeth very angry to have no answers. To be shut out of her mother's life in this way.

It was that anger that made her feel driven to do whatever she could to maintain this new friendship. You won't tell me who my father was? Then I will create my own.

The man's name was John. He was a father himself, he said, but did not see his daughters. He missed them. They were near Elizabeth's age, and she reminded him of them.

"What are they like?" she asked the first time they hung out outside the library, on a bench outside, under a shady oak tree. John needed to go outside for a smoke.

"Well," he said, lighting up and exhaling a silvery plume. "They have beautiful dark eyes, just like you. And they are smart, just like you. And have beautiful souls, just like you ..."

She smoked her first cigarette, ever. It made her cough at

first, but with practice, she got used to it.

After leaving the library, thoughts of the girl who was his daughter permeated John's mind. He could be in the middle of anything, re-strapping Mitch's catheter to his leg when he was helping him dress, giving a sermon in the ballroom, or even just sitting in a chair daydreaming. The thought of the girl transported him. She was his in a way that no other human being had truly been *his*. Not even Sapphire.

Of course, he had known about her for a long time. She had lived at The Brambles when she was a baby. But John had been out of his mind, literally, at that time. Things had been out of control. He'd had nothing really to do with the baby, and merely tolerated the baby's presence, when he was even aware of it.

He had told Natasha that she could have the baby. She seemed to have wanted it. At least she was not averse to being pregnant, and never mentioned getting an abortion. She was a winter-pale girl from Ukraine. A good girl. She'd come to the US hoping to be a model or an actress but started dancing in clubs and never quite stopped, at least until she came to live at The Brambles. She had a smack habit, but didn't a lot of them? (John did not. John was tangled up with meth in those days, but he never ever shot up. A filthy habit, he thought, for filthy people.)

Natasha was one of many of his girls, but she was his favorite at the time. And she seemed to have taken to the baby, who was born in one of the black-rimmed bathtubs on an arid frozen day in February. He could still remember Natasha's shrieks! It had fascinated him, to stand in the bathroom doorway, watching, as her face contorted into something not quite human, her lithe young body grotesquely distorted beyond recognition. Honeybear had assisted with the delivery and signed the birth certificate as attending physician. And so it was.

A mistake? Maybe. Natasha knew John liked the baby kept away from him most of the time, though he did occasionally hold her when she was newborn. It tripped him out looking into those grave, blue-black eyes. She had looked like a wise little crone there to impart some knowledge to him. What, he did not know. He recalled that the baby's name was Darja, some type of family name, Natasha had said.

Beyond those few moments that he held her, he didn't remember much about the girl at all in those days. He vaguely remembered her learning to walk, because she got around a lot more into places she shouldn't. Harder to contain. It annoyed him, but when he spoke to Natasha about it, she hardly responded, she was so limply passive.

Plus, the baby smelled a lot of the time. He told Natasha she should bathe the child, and at least put clothes on her instead of leaving her half-naked.

He knew, now, that he was the one who should have taken responsibility for the child. But his mind was destroyed in those days, he was tripping balls. It had to do with just getting out of prison. Maybe the freedom was too much to handle.

The drugs weren't his only problem, but they were his main one. So he stopped. Got his head together. And that was when the Ministry really took off.

It wasn't exactly true that he conceived of the church, the Ministry of Presence, while in prison. Rather, he would invent all kinds of things in solitary. Experiences. A whole life. He imagined birth. He imagined a childhood, a happy one. He invented every detail of his house, his school, his friends. He imagined that he had grown up to be a carpenter. He would be a simple man, a good man. He built a house from scratch. He poured the foundation, nailed every board. Every shingle. He lived in that house. He had a wife. He had children. He imagined that he would like to look out of the window in the evening and see the woods on a mountain ridge above in the distance. It was his phantom life that could have been.

The life, he realized in his saner moments, of a *chump*. He needed more. He deserved more than everyone else. It was his destiny to be great. He just didn't know how.

John didn't believe in the arbitrary, in chance. The thought of the randomness of chance made him queasy. He believed in signs and symbols. Significance.

It was no matter of chance that that bum kid walking on the road had led him to The Brambles, and its owner, Mitch Cooper. He had been planning to mug the guy simply because seeing his spindly weakness pissed him off, but a voice in his head told him, *no*. And he had listened. It had been meant to be. The Ministry, his new role in life, had come together for him in an instant when he shook the old man's hand for the first time.

The same sense of the profoundly holy drove him to reconnect with his daughter. True, back in the day, he had hardly realized his daughter had gone missing. It took him a while to get himself cleaned up and on the right path again. He had gotten lost. But that was okay.

Natasha herself had gone away, too, not long after the child had disappeared. It was through the grapevine (one of the crackheads in his Ministry meetings) that he had heard that his daughter hadn't gone far away at all. That she was being raised by a woman whose woods abutted those of The Brambles.

Yes, he knew who she was, he had peeked at her in the

woods when she was a little girl, out of curiosity. Then when she was older, he had seen her on her bicycle, dark skirt hiked up, rolling past with a bright yarn-woven bag across her chest, as though she was delivering mail or newspapers.

He had seen her, walking by the side of the road like an apparition. Sometimes she would turn to look at his car as it passed by. He had thought the expression on her face was a haughty one. Prim. Almost queenly. She was singular, that one. Those strong dark brows, the defiance in her eyes, came from *him*. This was a daughter who could be his equal. She was pure. Special. Not a common slut like Sapphire.

Now, more and more, whenever he saw her, his feelings were more intense. He was getting older, and he sometimes wondered if anyone in his life really loved him. This girl, his queenly daughter, would love him if she knew him. More and more, he felt an urge that he guessed must be paternal. There was a desire to know, to possess utterly what was *his*, that rendered an ache in his chest that he guessed must be love.

ELEVEN

THE SILK SKIRT

Vanessa heard the adults in the living room, the same small group she had known since she was a child. A mix of her mother's friends from the library and people from her dad's department at the university, gathered in the living room, drinking wine and listening to Neil Young. It was a group she had always felt comfortable joining. They were all fond of her and spoke to her as an equal. Her nickname among them was Rat Girl, because when she was small, she liked to cuddle a large stuffed rat that was her favorite toy.

"Hey! There's Rat Girl! Where you been? You been making yourself scarce lately."

She froze. She had been trying to slip into the kitchen to find a snack, and sneak back to her room.

She stood in the doorway. A group of friendly wine-flushed faces, lit by the glow of the roaring fire, tilted up to her.

"Oh, Tess. Is everyone going to call me Rat Girl for the rest of my life?" But Vanessa smiled and went around, accepting hugs and pecks on the cheek. Her mother scooted over on her place on the couch, making space for her, knocking over a glass in the process ("Damn it! Nick could you be a doll ...") then put her arm around her daughter and gave her a hug.

"Vanessa has just been busy with school and things." She patted her with a hand bearing many chunky silver and turquoise rings. There were turquoise necklaces, too, across her cushiony bosom. In certain lights, with her long plaited graying hair and intelligent pale eyes always squinted in laughter, she resembled an Indian tribal elder. A mother goddess, a friendly shaman. "She's starting college in the summer. Then we won't have her anymore."

There were admiring murmurs – Columbia! Wow! – and little spatters of applause. Vanessa looked down. She felt embarrassed, always, by others' praise.

"And you're still sure about linguistics?" This was Artie, her dad's best friend.

"Absolutely." She had always wanted to be a linguist. It was the one true certainty in her life.

"Good girl. Another academic in the family."

"I guess so."

Something in her tone made her mother turn and look at her keenly. Though her mother was gregarious, sloppy and fun loving, she was shrewd enough to pick up when anything was wrong. Vanessa could not meet her eye.

She sat immersed in the warmth of congenial conversation as her little brother dozed on the carpet by her feet. Her father even let her drink a small glass of wine. These are good people, she thought, looking around her. Why don't I appreciate them more?

She went up to bed after everyone went home. She listened to the homey sounds of her parents cleaning up, the clink of bottles in the recycling bin, the stacking of plates and the hum of the dishwasher, the two of them talking quietly.

I know I'm lucky, she thought. It made her feel bad that she lived so furtively. There were so many parts of herself that she could not share with her family. She just wasn't the same type of person that they were. There must be something fundamentally cold about her, she thought.

The love and concern in her mother's eyes felt like a reproach now. Because what could she tell her? Her parents knew she had been out late recently, but as long as her grades were stable, it was not an issue. But they must suspect something was up. And she couldn't tell them a thing about it. She did not know how.

Lillian would belong more in this family than she did. Her mother was very fond of Lil, and always gave her long hugs and asked about her life. And Lil was grateful and bubbly, and eager to share in a way that Vanessa could not.

Maybe, deep down, I just don't care about people.

Sometimes this felt like a strength. For example, she was not afraid of The Brambles. She was not afraid of John. She just wanted to figure him out, like a game or a puzzle. And she intended to. The whole place, The Brambles, was like an enormous web, John the spider at the center, aware of every ripple and twinge. A creepy guy, sure. But an equation that could be solved, if she knew the variables.

She just had to keep Lillian calm and centered. Being so sensitive that everything hurt so much must be painful.

As for Mack, she would figure out on her own what was up with him. What a disappointment he was turning out to be. Falling apart in this way, hungover with a black eye. Snapping at people. Vanessa would die before falling apart like that. It was her will that held her insides together. If one stitch came undone, she feared she would never put herself back together. So she had to be strong. Even if most people thought her cold.

She drifted off to sleep, these thoughts tumbling through her head.

She woke up to a bright cold Saturday when everyone else was still asleep. Sunlight poured through the window by her bed. Idly, her glance fell over the window. With the sun at this angle, she could see a pattern of frost on the pane. She gazed at it sleepily for some time before her eye discerned something.

It was not a random bit of frost. It was the imprint of a bird that had flown into the window. So delicate. Every feather visible, like a small feathery ghost. Her brain was slow, still waking up … recalling what in her mind? A sense memory formed deep below her consciousness.

The day in Annabel's house, when she and Lil had gone to ask questions. The woman's pain and helpless agony. (It was overwhelming for Vanessa to remember this, the raw emotion was too confusing, Annabel was like a woman on fire, oh please stop stop stop …) Yes, she had taken her to her window and showed them the same bird ghost and asked the stunned girls to tell her what they thought it. A sign, a symbol?

Vanessa's heart raced when she saw something else. A word spelled on her window, underneath the splayed angel.

Mitch had been dreaming of the first time he saw the woman who would become his wife. 1969. A silent screen test. She had been luminous, even in black and white. Minidress with full poet sleeves. Hair piled high on her head with tendrils falling down. Double false eyelashes made her already large eyes consume her small face. She held up her own clapperboard: Screen Test 3/69. Director: Mitch Cooper. She could always, she told him later, find the key light by its heat. She smiled at the camera, bravely, but with a little tremble about the lips. Vulnerability in those dark, kohled eyes. Lips silvery pale and waxen. Just a girl, really, with a girl's clear-eyed curiosity. He knew right away that he not only wanted the girl for this part, but that he would marry her. That she could save him from his darkness. In the shadows of the screening room, he watched those silent lips moving, and she spoke to him, to his soul alone.

In real life, of course, the screen test was silent save for the flicker of the projector. But in this dream, she actually spoke to him. She said, "Mitch, I'm afraid! Come and get me! Where are you?"

But before he could do anything, the camera veered into a close-up of her face, so close that he couldn't recognize her anymore. Closer. She was a being of shadow and light. His dream-self lunged at the screen as though he could break through it. Get to the real Patty. That was when he woke up, alone, an old man in bed with a catheter tube.

The dreams he had been having! Sometimes even when he was awake! What was it that John had said about the dreams? Never mind the dreams. Just random neurons firing. Just a bunch of nonsense.

But they seemed more real to him these days than his waking life.

His waking life was sometimes unbearable. There were times when he felt he might jump out of his skin with anxiety. Surely this decrepit, heavy body pulling him down was not his? He was Mitch Cooper. Movie star and director. Someone other than this.

He had been a strong man, able to stride across a soundstage on long, muscular legs. His mind had been quick and sharp. Driven. He worked all the time. That was how he had made his way from boyhood poverty to Hollywood and beyond. Relentless, punishing, occasionally rewarding, *work*.

People had thought way back then that it had been *he* who saved *her*. From bland obscurity. From the endless ocean of girls desperate to be starlets.

It was different from that. It was Patty who discerned *him*. Saved him from his circumscribed life. He had always been living in the shadows and didn't even know it. In spite of his success, he had been the dark-eyed boy who lived alone with his mother in the old walk-up tenement in Brooklyn. Patty saved him from that crampedness, that shame of fatherlessness, of poverty, of beans in the pot and sad yellowed sheets flapping on the line.

Mitch was able to escape this inner prison once and for all. With her, he no longer felt the heedless drive of ambition at all times. She was such an elemental being, as though she were made of sunlight or flame. She taught him to live.

He had never been a true celebrity, with his picture in the magazines, until *her*. Never truly had friends. But then, the beautiful people flocked to them. Deep inside, he knew it wasn't about him. It was because they saw something in Patty. Her brilliance and beatitude. It rubbed off on him. And then? Theirs was the exalted life. And why *shouldn't*

he feel this ecstasy all the time, he thought? He deserved it!
Had been starved of it all along.

A new kind of life, never lived before, was what they
thought they would have. They wanted to go always
further. There was a kind of beautiful momentum. They
wanted more. More beauty. More love. More of everything.

Was it she or he who started shooting smack first? He
truly didn't know anymore. At the time it felt like a
spiritual ascension. A cosmic *yes*. Together they
experienced love in its most brilliant, crystalline form as it
filled their veins with light. Together they embarked on an
ocean of bliss, and their hearts, minds, and bloodstreams
felt as one.

After a time, other people, their friends, tried to
intervene. Told them it wasn't good to be locked up
together in the bedroom for weeks at a time, wasted out of
their minds. That it was *going too far*.

But going too far was the whole point! The life they had
together was a beautiful garden they never wanted to
leave. And other people, especially friends with their
righteous "good intentions," were increasingly unwelcome.

He could not even now, a ruined man who used a
wheelchair, bring himself to think of Patty's death in 1973.
Sometimes involuntarily, in his mind's eye, he saw a flash
of his dead young wife. The blue skin and the unseeing
eyes, the needle still hanging from her arm. The party in
the next room, strident glam rock on the stereo, insistent
and throbbing. Screams and panic as the girl was pulled
out of the bathroom and laid on the living room floor.

This was the point when his mind short-circuited, and
brought him back to the present, with no feeling anymore,
just a dull numbness (though how his hands shook!).

It wasn't your fault, Mitch. She did it to herself. You

aren't responsible for her bad luck. We each have our own fate, man.

It never made sense to him that it had to be her, and not him that died.

He had cleaned himself up after that, sweating it out on methadone. His life had gone on. He had remarried a couple of times, had kids. Made more movies. But it was never the same again. He knew he should have been a dead man. He didn't deserve to be happy.

That was why he eventually fled to the East Coast. Connecticut and The Brambles. He could still do production work in the city. But he had to stay away from LA and its bad memories. Laurel Canyon, 1973, all of it.

He told fans to fuck off when they sniffed him out and made their way to his front door. At first. But one thing led to another. He was lonely and bored. At least those screwed-up kids were company. Little by little he slipped into old, bad habits. Drink and drugs.

And then, one day he met John. Not a kid, but a grown man with white hair and rough pink skin. Not the usual type to show up at his door.

John did not say much or reveal much of himself at first. He kept in the background and observed, his arms folded high over his chest. Muscled arms and chest. He looked like an Irish ex-cop to Mitch. He made him nervous.

But he wasn't an ex-cop. He was an ex-priest.

Mitch did not know this until several days after John began living in the house. Mitch had been feeling low, sitting on a kitchen chair, a bottle of gin on the table before him. Not thinking anything cogent, just feeling tired and empty. John came in, sat at the table and watched him for some moments. Unexpectedly, John rose from his chair, fell upon his knees, looked Mitch in the eye, and chanted/sang, something in Latin:

Agnus Dei, qui tollis peccata mundi,

Miserere nobis …

Mitch was not a religious man. Born Jewish (his last name was really Cohen) but did not practice. He did not know what John was singing. But the fall and rise of his voice was soothing and hypnotic. Something ancient and healing about it.

John kept looking into his eyes when he was done, and Mitch had the overwhelming feeling that he had been forgiven his sins. That this man understood him, and forgave him, and had the power to heal him.

John surprised Mitch again by bowing his head and crying.

That was nearly twenty years ago. An enormity of time that had gone by in a flash. And yet Mitch felt frozen in place. John had become the person he trusted most. His best friend. His brother, really. (John even called him that, *brother*, even when they were still new to each other.)

John was the one to help him as he grew older and weaker. Who was he to complain? He was thankful. It was hard to get about without the wheelchair. (Though he could, if he tried, get around with a walker.) John had always understood, and not judged, the fact that Mitch needed to medicate himself. It is not a weakness, John said confidingly. You are just more sensitive than most. He said this most kindly as he tied his arm off and inserted the needle in the vein, delivering sweet oblivion when he most needed it.

In fact, he had grown to love John. So why did he sometimes fear him? There were sudden, nightmarish instances where John morphed into a monster. Crude; calloused. He would shove Mitch roughly when helping him to the toilet. Or leave him locked in the bedroom for an entire day without food or drink. Mitch always felt lightheaded with relief and gratitude when John let him out. He needed John to help him shuffle down the stairs, or more often, John would pick him up fireman-style and carry his light, twig-like body down the stairs, muttering and swearing the whole time.

Sometimes John said cruel things, too. Called him a shriveled old geezer or that he smelled like piss and denture cream. Then the next instant, so kind and warm that Mitch doubted that it had ever happened.

Mitch had not seen his children in years. John thought it better if he did not contact them. "I'll take care of it," he always said. "Don't worry about things. Past is past. It is time for you to move on to a higher plane in life. Sometimes that means leaving others behind."

But it made him so sorrowful, sometimes, that he could barely remember what his children looked like. Two girls and a boy. Carrie, Angela, and Patrick. Grown up now, adults, but when he thought of them, he remembered only three innocent children. Was it right for him to leave them behind? Such questions filled him with regret and pain, and he needed his drugs. John, or Honeybear, was always happy to oblige.

He remembered blearily that one time he thought he saw his children, all teenagers, crossing the back lawn to his house. He still sometimes felt a barely submerged hope that they were coming to take him away from The Brambles.

In fact, the boy teenager, he had noticed hanging around the house. He tried to catch his eye at John's parties or church meetings, but could not. He had a feeling the boy was staying in the bedroom on the floor below his, but he

wasn't sure. Always there were muffled voices from below
the floor, behind the walls. Who it was, was confusing to
his addled mind. But he dreamed and hoped of a strong
young son and imminent rescue.

"No, silly. Not like that. Like this."

Sapphire pulled her hair back with one hand and
leaned over the nightstand, snorted up the line of white
powder and then dabbed at her pink-tinged nostrils,
delicately, with a henna-painted hand.

It was interesting, to Mack, that her henna tattoos were
so lovely. The rest of her was never that well maintained.
Her dark curly hair, his favorite part of her, was snarled
and sometimes even matted. It was true, also, that she did
not bathe very much, and tended to wear the same long
embroidered blouse and patched jeans for days at a time.

It was probably because she had been neglected as a
kid, Mack guessed as he took his turn at the nightstand. He
wasn't used to cocaine. He'd done it once before at her
urging, but it hadn't made him feel anything but like an
over-revved engine. Heart racing. Unpleasant.

Why did she like it so much? He wondered what went
on in her mind. Sometimes she liked to look deep into the
mirror for long periods of time, as though she were all by
herself. It was as though she was looking for something, an
answer to a question, in the mirror.

"What did you want to be when you grew up, when
you were a kid?" he asked her once in the beginning.

"I wanted to grow to be a junkie since I was fourteen,"
she said and laughed. But there was something earnest in
her face. Plaintive. He saw that look more and more, as he
got to know her.

Eventually he learned more. She told him one night that

she had been homeless for a short time. Followed an old boyfriend's band across the country. Hitchhiked. Worked as a bartender.

"What did your parents think of all that stuff?" he asked, holding her in bed.

"My mom doesn't know what I do. She's upset that I ran away to find my father."

"Who is your father?"

"John."

She said this in a small voice, pained as a purple bruise. Mack was so surprised that he did not say anything. John was her *father?* He'd never seen anything resembling a father-daughter relationship between the two. And what kind of father would let his daughter live in a place like The Brambles?

Ever since she had told him, he had seen Sapphire differently. Even when she was happy, telling stories in a breathless rush, eyes snapping and sparkling, he was careful to be extra kind and gentle with her. Even though she was so much older than him, he knew he was the one who needed to care for her. In fact, he was coming to believe that he truly loved her.

As they lay on the bed, high on cocaine, he felt anxious and churned up with adrenalin. Sapphire was speedy and antic, eyes too bright. Electricity even seemed to snap straight through the ends of her hair. He was afraid if he touched her, he would get a shock.

But he also felt a swoon through his soul. I will protect this girl because no one else has.

He thought he would become a new, carefree person when he first moved into the house. But he felt himself slipping into his old self. In the clear light of day, he was annoyed by the shabbiness of the mansion. Mack found himself driving his truck out to Home Depot to pick up caulking and spackle so he could perform little jobs around the place. Patching up holes. Putting weather stripping under the doors. The house was an absolute wreck, and everyone who lived there seemed indifferent to the fact.

And as for the people he lived with … not everyone was as young or together as he'd thought in the beginning. Some were old and burned out and depressed him somewhat. But, he would not consider leaving. He had not spoken to his mom, his dad, or his brother since he left, and did not want to now. It was all part of getting his head together. How could he know who he was if he was contaminated by family drama? The only way he would even have a chance in life was to be away from them.

He had to admit, for all the faults of the people at The Brambles, at least they supported each other. Well, they were generally on the same page, at least. The same loyalties. It was live and let live. No one hassled or judged you. And John was the benevolent patriarch. He really cared about everyone. No one spoke ill of him, at all. In fact, there was a general reverence where John was concerned. Whenever his name was spoken, it was always in a hushed tone, eyes cast down.

It was kind of weird, but he got it. John was an extremely smart guy, who had been through a lot of things, and gained a lot of wisdom. Mack respected someone who had really lived life, the good and bad. He loved talking to him about how he got his prison tattoo, or what it was like in the seminary as a young man. Who else had lived so much or learned so much, as John?

But why wasn't he taking better care of Sapphire?

Mack tried to reason that John was a good person. He took *total* care of Mitch. He'd never seen anyone that devoted. He'd asked John once if it was hard to commit that much time to someone else's care, and John looked at him, incredulous. Then he pursed his lips into a trembling line, almost as though he might cry. Then he said quietly, "I love him."

And Mack knew not to ask any more questions after that.

It was hard to believe Mitch was only eighty. He looked, to Mack's eyes, to be about a hundred. It tripped him out, a little, whenever he made eye contact with the old man, who was supposedly once such a powerful, famous person. (John had shown him a scrapbook of old photos of Mitch's life. Many of him hanging out poolside at parties with tiki torches, or drinking cocktails and grinning in groups of people with tans and blinding white teeth. John had pointed out various famous folks, but the only one Mack recognized was Jack Nicholson.)

Hard to believe the man in the photos was Mitch. Grinning, ruddy-faced and magnanimous looking – and such a beautiful woman at his side, dark-haired with large beaming eyes, leaning into his side and looking so in love.

I wish that could be me one day.

But look what had come of it all. Mitch seemed happy enough, he guessed, but he was so old and so weak and sometimes, he frankly looked sick. Though John took good care of him and said that he was fine.

It was true. Mack didn't know exactly what he was doing at the moment. As long as he stayed in school, he told himself, he was at least holding things together.

He had been pretty mean to Lillian, true. But he just didn't want to be sucked back in right now. Sometimes the only way to keep his distance was to be a jerk.

And yet the words he had seen scratched into the

nightstand haunted him, Elizabeth was here. He *knew* he had seen them. They had been scraped in lightly, but deep enough that he felt it with his fingers. And he had run his fingers over those words in wonder. And terror. But the next day, when he had planned to show them to Sapphire, they had been gone.

It had been *real*, though. This experience had been as real as the girl that had walked by the side of the road had been real. He had driven right through her, but she had been *real*. Thinking about it all made his thoughts race. And when his thoughts raced, there was no way to keep up with them. It was like a current, a riptide that could pull him under.

That was when he would stop thinking about Elizabeth. It was just too much. He would find solace in bed with Sapphire. Or drinking beer with the burnouts in the library. He would get a job. Soon. There were no roadworks jobs in the dead of winter, but he would be able to find one somewhere. Working for a contractor, putting up drywall? He needed money for gas and take-out and to go in with people for weed, and all the things that made his life at The Brambles possible.

The next day, he lay on a couch in the front room, thinking too much about everything and feeling bummed out, when John walked into the room.

"You look kind of down, Mack. Something on your mind?"

Mack laughed weakly. "I just don't know what I'm doing with my life is all." He felt a bit nervous around John now; shouldn't he be concerned that Mack was sharing a room with his daughter? Shouldn't it make him angry?

But John clamped a hand on his shoulder, and looked deeply into his eyes, and said, "You put me in mind of St

John of the Cross, 'If a man wishes to be sure of the road he treads on, he must close his eyes and walk in the dark.'"

As a joke, Mack closed his eyes and flailed his hands forward like a blind man. John laughed.

"That's advice from a verified saint. Old Saint John. Not this John. I ain't no saint!" He walked from the room, his steps echoing. "But don't we all try!"

"Wait. These things here are the foot pegs. Keep your feet on them even when we're stopped."

The man with the reddish beard raised the kickstand, straightened the motorcycle up, and motioned with his head for Vanessa to get on behind him.

Forced to put her arms around his large muscled torso, she felt awkward; she had only really met Bobo for the first time that evening. It helped, though, that she was halfway drunk. The only way she could fit in and feel even remotely comfortable with the motorcycle guys was if she kept drinking with them.

Bobo was the one out of all of them who was the kindest. He was, at least, friendly to her. Others in the group were indifferent, or openly hostile, or else so drunk that their hyena-like laughter frightened her. Bobo looked to be somewhere around her parents' age. His long, auburn hair streaked in places with gray.

And off they went, for a quick trip up the country back roads. It was in the forties that night, not bad for February. But still, the openness and the wind on her face shocked her. She had never ridden on a motorcycle before. It was a feeling she had never experienced – the lack of a seatbelt to hold her fast, the wind blowing her hair crazily. The powerful vibration of the engine was like a rocket-propelled horse. She tried to explain this to Bobo, but it came out garbled and incomprehensible, the engine noise and the wind so loud he couldn't hear her, anyway.

"Lean with me." This was all the instruction he had given her, and as they sped up on the open road, she tried to do what he did. Lean forward. As though she were one with the bike, and lean into momentum itself.

Never, in her life. Such freedom and velocity! She knew she should be frightened. But she wasn't. Bobo smiled at her through the little rearview mirror, his pale eyes twinkling. She smiled back.

She had agreed to go for a ride because she had wanted the guys to trust her. Vanessa had come on her own to The Brambles because she knew it was a party night. And she planned to make inroads with this group called The Lone Horsemen. Ever since she had seen them that first night, she knew she could get the *real* information from only them. The people who went to the Ministry of Presence meetings were fanatical and slightly secretive. She wanted to know how The Lone Horsemen connected to John because they seemed to have some kind of a long-running bond between them. Especially between John and the leader.

But first, she had to get into their circle. The only way she knew to do it was to play it all as being patently absurd and improbable. She obviously didn't fit in, so she acted the straight-laced scholarly girl out to expand her horizons.

It worked. The gang was so bemused by her, they tolerated her presence for the evening. And Bobo jokingly offered her first motorcycle ride.

What she hadn't expected was that she'd *like* it as much as she did; when they arrived back at The Brambles her face stinging from the cold, her hands numb despite her leather gloves, she felt exalted. Transported.

Bobo laughed to see her expression in the moonlight. "So you liked that, huh?"

She could only nod dazedly, as though she had been conked upside the head. She found her voice and said, raggedly, "When can we do that again?"

Bobo stopped for a moment and turned to look at her straight on, his face serious. "Again? Does that mean you're planning to keep hanging around this place?"

"Maybe. So what?"

He shook his head. "Watch yourself, is all I'm saying. You're jailbait to these guys. I don't think you get it."

"I can look out for myself."

"That's all fine and good and everything, but what are you doing here? Kid like you. Doesn't make a whole lot of sense."

"Yeah, well what are you doing here? And how do all you guys know John?"

Bobo laughed. For a moment he said nothing, and they heard only the thrash of loud music coming from the house. "Well now. That's a long story. Flash is the one who knew John way back when."

Vanessa knew who Flash was. Older guy, small, with a handlebar mustache. His eyes disturbed her. They were too large and startled and scanned the room too much. The guy looked like a tough customer. She instinctively avoided him and didn't like when he even looked at her.

"Flash knew John from prison."

Vanessa took this in. "Okaaaay. So they were locked up together?"

"Nah. This was back when John was a prison *chaplain*. He'd been bored with cooling his heels in church. He asked to be sent to the prison. And he was. He counseled Flash. They got to know each other pretty well. Got close, you know? Holy Spirit. Trinity and all that shit."

Vanessa looked at him with her brow furrowed. "He was working at a prison? I thought he was *in* prison. It's in his sermons. It's where he had a spiritual transformation."

Bobo guffawed. Vanessa looked at him, perplexed.

"Good lord, those fuckin' sermons." He shook his head. "Yeah, he worked as the prison chaplain. It was *later* that he did something where he got put in and actually did time in the same place he used to work. Ironic, innit?"

"He said he went to jail for assault."

"Did he tell you why?"

"No. He was kind of vague about it. Just said he had a falling from grace."

Bobo nodded. "Well, when John was prison chaplain it kind of brought him into this other gig. He started running a Catholic halfway house. Men lived there who had just gotten out of the joint, or had drug or alcohol problems. He did that for several years as I recall. He'd bought this big, run-down house in a crummy part of town where no one cared what went on. He lived in one of the bedrooms, the other went to these other men, druggies or ex-cons. They were mostly men he was sort of buddies with. I don't know what John was supposed to be doing, keeping an eye on them, I guess? But it was a huge party house." He cut his eyes at The Brambles. "Kinda like this place. Except this is helluva nicer. Johnny's moved up in the world, I'd say."

Vanessa gazed at him, impassively. Trying to understand what she was being told. "So?"

"Yeah. Anyway. From what I hear he got into some kind of misunderstanding with one of his tenants. Guy called Shorty. Shorty owed John money and had trouble paying up. I don't know exactly what happened. I think Rooster was living there at the time, or else he was just hanging out. Honeybear was around then, too."

"Which one of you is Honeybear?"

"He's not one of The Horsemen. He's a doctor."

"A *what?*"

Bobo laughed at her confusion. "Friend of John's. Medical doctor. Saw some of the hard cases in the halfway house and gave them methadone and stuff. And now he doctors Mitch. You've probably seen him, he's…unmistakable. *Anyway.* But where was I … Shorty. There was alcohol involved that night, there was a huge fight, and John hurt the guy pretty bad. He just flew into a rage when Shorty said something to him he didn't like and just beat the shit out of him. Rooster did say that John's face was completely …" Here, Bobo made his eyes go dead, and passed a palm over unseeing eyes, "… just not there, like a robot. He'd already hit Shorty in the head with the base of a table lamp, knocked him out and just kept beating and kicking. Blood sprayed across the bridge of John's nose, and he didn't even look fazed. Just kind of laughing, panting, as he just went *off* on this guy …"

"Jesus!" Vanessa had, without thinking, put her hand over her mouth. "I can't imagine him act anything like that!"

"Well, didn't he say he had some *transformation?*" Bobo wriggled his fingers. "Life changing shit? I don't know how he's spinning it to those burned out freaks that follow his every word." He shrugged. "I don't judge, either way. I'm cool with the man. He likes to party. He likes his women. He's generous, likes to share …"

"Yeah, but—"

"Yeah, but I wouldn't cross him." They slowly meandered back to the house, from which metal music emanated, guitars howling elliptically.

"But, Bobo, what exactly is the deal? Between you guys. Why do The Lone Horsemen stay so tight with John?"

"That's all down to him and Flash. Blood brothers. Do anything for each other."

"What? So it's some kind of business deal or something?"

Bobo turned to look at her, with a surprised look on his face. Maybe she had gone too far.

"I don't know what goes down between them. And I don't care. I don't judge, and I got no problems. John is gold as far as I'm concerned. Guy has earned his way. But." He cuffed her on the cheek with his large paw, heavy silver rings on each finger. "You need to get wise, little girl. Get away from this place. You're gonna get raped or drugged or worse if you don't stay clear." He pointed a finger in her face. "Consider that a friendly warning, 'cause Bobo's a good guy. I got nieces. One's around your age. And I would never let them *near* any of these guys." He walked ahead of her, not looking back. "You're not like the others," he said in a singsong voice. "You better stay away from John. And stay away from The Horsemen, for real."

She stood just inside the foyer for a moment, trying to shake her head clear. Bobo had already disappeared back into the party.

Vanessa didn't look for him again. She wanted to find one of the bathrooms and then go home. She felt sobered up now and overwhelmed and overstimulated.

Someone was throwing up in the downstairs guest bathroom. She started up the small back stairwell because she didn't want to talk to anyone else, just get her bearings and leave.

There were some people on the second floor, but it was much quieter. In her state of abstraction, she hardly noticed that the guy she nearly ran into on the landing was Mack.

They stared into each other's eyes for a startled beat of silence. She saw the black eye that Lil had described; fading but still there. He also looked like he had lost five pounds since she had seen him last.

"Mack," she said with hoarse astonishment, "you look like shit."

"Thanks," he muttered, looking down and away from her. "What are you doing here?"

"I came to the party. You know me."

"Lillian too?"

Vanessa paused. "Nooo. I thought I would leave her out of this one. Sometimes I work better on my own." She looked him up and down. He wore no shoes and was carrying a stack of dirty plates. "Well, you look ...at home."

He said nothing, just shrugged.

Vanessa looked at him, incredulous. "Is this where you have been the whole time? Are you *living* here?"

He shrugged. "What's it to you?"

Vanessa burst into laughter, and he glowered at her.

"I just can't believe it! Or maybe I can. Nothing surprises me anymore, honestly." The motorcycle ride had loosened up something in her. She felt reckless and slightly madcap. More laughter tumbled out of her.

"Vanessa. Are you, like, okay? You don't seem yourself. Are you high?"

This made her laugh anew. "High on life, I suppose." Her face abruptly changed into a more serious expression. "Do you know that John is evidently a complete psychopathic maniac?"

"How you figure that? He's just eccentric. I thought you would be the last person to care."

She raised an eyebrow. "Well. I'm learning more about him. And my eyes are opened now. Which is more than I can say about you. You're the one who looks doped up."

"It's none of your business what I do. Or anyone's." He sounded righteously defensive. But there was hurt in his eyes.

"I don't care what you do. I suppose you're shacked up with *Sapphire*."

"Why do you have to say it like *that?* It's her name. I'm seeing her, yes. And it's only temporary, but I *am* staying here. John's an all right guy. He's been great. Supportive."

"Yeah, well, something sure is off about him. He's crazy violent apparently." She lowered her voice. "And I think he's running drugs with The Lone Horsemen."

"That's stupid."

"Is it?" She took a step closer to him, and whispered, "And I think there is a real connection."

"With?"

"You know what I mean. Or who, rather," she whispered, "Eliz—"

"DON'T SAY HER NAME!" He threw down the stack of dishes and they crashed, splintering on the stair steps.

Vanessa instinctively moved away from him, watching him warily like he was a crazed animal.

"Sorry." He held his head between his two palms, as though afraid it would split apart. "What I mean is … what I was trying to say, is that makes no sense. Just because he's different …"

"This guy is beyond different."

He threw up his hands suddenly, backed away from her. "No, no, no. I don't want to talk about this stuff anymore. Don't tell me. I'm through playing detective."

"Why? 'Cause you're living in never-never land? You

look like terrible, Mack. I don't know what's going on here, but it's not good for you. I think you should just go home." And suddenly, she felt the truth of this. Mack looked weak to her. In need of defending. A scared boy. "Come on. You can leave tonight. You don't owe anyone anything. We don't need you. Please."

They looked into each other's eyes, for a long, silent moment that seemed to go on and on. It was almost like when they were children, and so attuned and in harmony with each other that no words needed to be said. It had always been that way, between Mack, Vanessa, and Lil. And Elizabeth.

It was Mack who looked away first, muttering, *"Fuck."* He stalked up the stairs, and she heard the slam of a door.

Vanessa was left stunned and alone, looking at the broken dishes on the landing, shards radiating like an explosion.

"But, hon, do you want me to go with you?"

Elizabeth's mother usually walked with her through the woods. She looked up at Elizabeth now, from the living room floor, her body bent into a complicated yoga position, the camel pose, spine bent back, knees tucked under her, her muscles shaking with the strain.

"That's okay, Mom, I thought I'd just go by myself. To clear my head. I'm seventeen now, I can take care of myself. Besides, you're busy. Keep doing your thing."

She just wanted to get out, *out*. She was wearing the nicest things she could find, a sleeveless t-shirt and a new skirt, a long wrap skirt made of raw silk in an India print, blues, and pinks.

Annabel looked at her daughter. The skirt. Annabel had bought the skirt for her at the summer arts festival downtown, where they had recently gone together. It had been a gorgeous day, with a soft golden light in the air. The streets of the downtown were shut down so that pedestrians could fill the streets lined with stalls. People sold paintings of the local coastline. Hammered silver jewelry. Hand-poured candles and jars of dark, golden honey. The smell of fried dough and cotton candy wafted through the air and shuddering bouncy inflatable houses filled with the delighted screams of children.

Elizabeth had paused here and there to look at a tin garden sculpture, a tray of glistening glass rings. Then she was drawn into a tent where a woman was selling homemade clothes; everything was so bright and lovely. A gaggle of girls Elizabeth's age tried on velvet patchwork hats. They chatted happily, pulling faces in front of a large full-length mirror on a stand.

Elizabeth found the skirt and held it up to her body to see what it would look like.

Annabel said to her, gently, "Hon, why don't you go use the mirror so you can see better? I'm sure those girls will make room for you. They look nice." Annabel so wanted Elizabeth to make friends of her own. Though it scared her to imagine the implications. Teenagers would ask too many questions. So where were you born? So why don't you go to school?

But still, she wished the girl had companionship. Her heart beat in anxiety, watching Elizabeth approach the teenage girls. Please, let her in.

But as Elizabeth's wan reflection appeared behind their own in the mirror, a ripple of unease passed through the group. Elizabeth held the skirt to her body and stroked it, lifting the fabric between her fingers and smiling with pleasure at the soft touch of it. She said nothing but smiled at the girls in such an appealing, dreamy way.

But it was as though Elizabeth carried a chill around her that cast a pall over the group like a cloud passing over the sun. The energy changed. It was as though those girls sensed death in their midst, and things grew quiet and strange. They put back the hats and moved on.

It all happened in just a small moment, a fraction of time. As Elizabeth looked longingly after them, Annabel quickly strode over, paid the exorbitant price of the skirt, put it in her arms, and said, "Here, here, darling. Never mind. I love you."

But Annabel's jaw clenched, her face flushed red with anger at the unfairness of it all. It upset her still.

"Well, have a good time, hon. Don't stay out too long."

Elizabeth hurried. The skirt was very beautiful and brighter than anything else she had ever worn. The fabric swung around her legs like a soft, gauzy curtain as she walked, shimmering iridescent in the sunlight. She knew she was doing the right thing, the only thing. It was the first time she had agreed to meet him outside the library, and she was terribly excited.

He had explained to her, where it was that he lived. They realized together that their backyards practically touched. The grounds of his house could be reached through the woods in back of her house. It seemed natural that they could meet there, it was easiest. He promised to show her the grounds of The Brambles. It's amazing, he had said. A lot of history to it. She would have to see it.

She had arranged to meet him at the creek.

Elizabeth smiled to herself. She liked having secrets that her mother couldn't guess at. It made her feel rich.

She walked barefoot, sandals in her hand; the delicate

straps had slowed her down, and she wanted to move fast. The grass beneath her feet was springy and damp from an early morning rain shower. But now the sun was out, warm on her face. Only a few fleecy clouds raced through the sky. It was one of those moments where Elizabeth felt truly, and simply, *happy*. She felt her own youth coursing through her veins, pumping through her heart. She made a couple of tiny leaps, like a frolicking deer.

She crossed from her sunny lawn into the shadow of the woods where it was hushed and quiet; pine needles cushioned her footsteps, muffling them. It was cooler and wonderfully sweet and damp. She heard the rustling of small animals in the brush, the high whine of insects. Noises dear to her, because they were so small and delicate.

At last, she approached the creek, with its small rivulets chucking over the rocks. Here she stood still. It was one o'clock, wasn't it? This was the time they had agreed on? Because John wasn't there.

It's okay, she told herself. He might be a little late. She dipped her foot into the water, shockingly cold for late July. Dug her toes into the gravely, sandy bottom. Tried not to feel worried. Maybe she had been tricked? Maybe he had simply lost interest in her. It could be that he had even forgotten about her altogether. As these thoughts spiraled, she chastised herself for being a fool. What had she been thinking, that an older, educated man would want anything to do with someone as silly as her?

Her feelings rushed and swirled like the water over the rocks. Just when she was about to sink into despair, she heard someone clear his throat.

John. He stood on the other side of the creek, his brightness emphasized by the darkness of the surrounding woods. With his white hair and ruddy skin, he practically glowed like a paper lantern. She wondered for a moment if she was hallucinating, until he said, "Hey, lovely!"

In spite of herself, a huge grin stretched across her face. So she turned it down and away from him.

"I'm glad you're here," he called, with a courtly flourish. "I wasn't sure you'd remember."

"I thought the same thing," she said, blushing.

Then he surprised her by suddenly, like a clown, walking forward into the creek. He always wore the same short, sleek black boots with pointy toes. Now, these boots were submerged, the water up to his ankles. He looked at her and smiled, impishly. She laughed like a child and held a hand to her mouth to stifle it.

"You know what?" he said, splashing. "I've had these boots for years. Made by Crockett and Jones. English. Handmade. Calf leather and single leather soles. Once you've worn handmade shoes, you can't go back." He looked at her and shrugged. "But you know what? I don't give a shit if I've ruined them. They are only things. I can't let my ego attachment rule my life."

He stood beside her now, beaming, his black jeans soaked from the knees down. But the boots looked fine.

He took Elizabeth by the arm and asked, "May I escort you, madam, through the creek?"

She giggled as she took his arm. His large feet made great plunking, splashing sounds as they crashed through the water. Handmade English boots! And he was willing to ruin them for *her*.

Her own bare feet sank into the sandy muck. Every so often, there was a sharp stone that dug into her foot painfully. But she said nothing. Her own sandals she had forgotten about and had dropped them on the other side.

"Yep, the ego," John said as they scrambled from creek

bank to sloping grass. "A thing best eliminated. I lost mine some time ago, during a real low point in my life, that maybe I can tell you about later. But one thing I can tell you *now* is that low point became my salvation. To walk without ego is to walk free. I've never felt as alive as I do now, *ever*. Free to just be. In the moment."

Elizabeth tried to think of something clever to say but came up with nothing. She didn't know if she had an ego or not. But she desperately, now, wished to shed it if it would make her as wise as John. "So, your house is up this way?" she at last asked, blushing at her own dullness.

"Yep. Just a little walk up the trail. I do love this trail. Just to walk, and clear my head. You see, I live with friends. And I love them all. But I don't always get a lot of opportunity for quiet. The woods are good for that."

"I know. I come here a lot, too."

"Oh yeah? Do you come alone?"

"Usually I walk with my mom. As a kid, I used to play here with friends. If I'm really bored, I'll come out with my guidebook and identify trees."

"No *way?*" He turned to smile at her, brimming with sudden wild enthusiasm. It threw her off for just a second, made her forget what she was saying.

Then she recovered herself and said, "This one up ahead right here is one of my favorite trees. A white oak."

They both stopped and looked up into it. The tree was enormous; the wide trunk had many growths and bumps and gnarls in it.

"Just look at that trunk, Elizabeth! Think how old this thing must be. Lotta rings in there, I bet."

Elizabeth was happy to talk about something, at last, that *she* was knowledgeable about. "I like the shapes of the leaves. Almost like little fingers." The branches were incredibly long, some drooped all the way to the ground. She picked a leaf and held it up to John. "And in the spring, the leaves grow pink. Just for a couple of weeks."

John stood next to the girl and together they looked at the leaf, *through* the leaf. They could see its tender veins even though the light was low here. Elizabeth was so earnest, it made her seem even younger than she was.

For a moment, looking at the leaf, John remembered his solitary confinement, where he did a *lot* of thinking. The padded room was a sort of cocoon, or a womb, in which his next life was gestating. He'd reflected on his life choices at the time, and knew he had gotten out of control. He wondered if it would be possible to curb his appetites and become what others would think was a *better man.*

But the problem was, then and now, he wanted things too badly. He wanted this girl, his daughter; he wanted to possess her completely. His desire was like the sound of steam in his head, getting louder and blocking out all these thoughts of being a good man. And he was staring into that void-like tunnel of his needs all over again.

Rage overtook him when he couldn't have what he wanted, almost like a blackout. The smallest slight or insult and blackness spread through his brain and nerves like a drop of dark ink in water. All rational thought obscured. Just like that time that Shorty had held out rent money on him. And in the heat of their argument, called John a freak and a perv. John's brain blanked out and he jumped Shorty, pounded the fucker's head till blood ran from his ears.

John found it most prudent to get what he wanted when he wanted it. No use even thinking about it. Or someone would get hurt. Like that hooker who insulted his manhood as a young man before seminary. He got inflamed even now, and remembered what it had been like to throttle her until her eyes rolled back …

He still needed what he needed. He would just be more careful from now on. That way, everyone came ahead. No one would get hurt.

"Well, it certainly is a beautiful tree, Elizabeth. Almost something stately, Biblical about it, I would say." He looked up at the topmost branches as they swayed, very slightly, even though there was no wind to speak of. He took the leaf from Elizabeth's fingers, and looked at the delicate thing, for a moment with real wonder in his eyes.

"Whatta you say we move on, kiddo. I have so many things to show you. And the afternoon is getting by."

Through the woods they walked until suddenly, they were out. The woods ended, and they were on the sunny edge of a great sloping lawn.

"Grass is a little shaggy," John said. "We have a service come and do the mowing. But I don't think they were here this week. At least I haven't seen them."

But Elizabeth wasn't quite listening; she was too transfixed by the house. Surely, this wasn't the one where he lived? It was like something from a movie set. Even though they approached it from behind, it was still dazzling. A large, sprawling house, a mansion really, on an endless lawn. A tiled swimming pool. True, there were quite a few properties like this in town. But they were hidden from view behind woods or gates. And she had never known anyone who actually lived in one.

"So this is really *yours*?"

"Yep. Yep, yep. My very own abode. It's called The Brambles. But I call that pretentious shit. Imagine, a house having a *name!*"

"It's beautiful." She admired the great stone terrace,

with what looked like a grape arbor arched above it. Great iron lawn chairs were pulled together in random, messy clumps, as though there had just been a fun party the night before. "How long have you lived here?"

"Dunno. Lost track. A long time. Twenty years, last count."

"Did your daughters grow up here?" She tried to imagine, living on an estate like this. It would make her feel like royalty to live here.

John looked at her strangely for a minute. Then snapped to attention and said, "No. No. My daughters, unfortunately, are a closed chapter in my book. Not that I don't love them, and dream of them every night. Beautiful, beautiful girls. With dark hair and dark eyes." But it was Elizabeth he caressed with his gaze as he said this.

As they drew closer, Elizabeth wondered if anyone was watching them approach from the rows of windows. So many of them. She thought maybe she saw a face, in a second story window. A woman with long curly hair … but then she was gone.

The house was three stories high in some places! Multiple chimneys, a beautiful, slated roof. Was there staff there? Surely there was a staff. What would they think, to look out and see their master crossing the grounds with this young woman? Because that is what she felt like at that moment. An adult. A mysterious, interesting adult, whom John thought worthy enough to befriend as an equal.

Would they think she was his girlfriend? She felt a fluttery embarrassment. Don't be silly, no one is watching you. But just the same, she turned away from the house, and looked up at John, arranging her face in a rapt smile. "Who is here now?"

"Who is here *now?*" he returned her smile, but it was

droll and lopsided. "There is no telling who is here at any given moment. People come and go."

"Yes, but who *lives* here?" They were approaching the back terrace. The house didn't seem quite as grand as it did from far away. The house was badly in need of a new coat of paint. The pool, though it had pretty, Moroccan-style designs along its side, needed cleaning. Several plastic cups and a single red flip-flop floated in it.

"Oh, a jolly old bunch. You'll like them. They make my life so much richer. I would hate to live in this space all alone. I believe in the sanctity of friendship." He looked at her with a solemn expression as he led her across the terrace; he opened a French door and motioned her inside.

The large, sunny room should have been airy, but it was not. The air she breathed seemed queerly stale. Somewhere around them, a fly buzzed, trapped and beating itself against the windows.

It was some type of game room. A large pool table dominated the center. Ping-pong table. There was also a table for card games. In one corner was a bar. Bottles still littered it, and sticky plastic cups.

"Did you have a party here?" she asked. Funny. Her voice did not seem to echo at all in this large room, absorbed instead by the stale stillness. Everything felt muffled. For a moment she felt a flutter of panic, as though she could not catch her breath. As though a jar had been lowered over her.

"Oh, yeah. Just had a few friends over. Some of them stayed late. Haven't gotten around to cleaning up yet. Forgive me." He made a funny little bow, and she smiled again. He was such a funny man. He didn't take anything seriously. So different from her mother, to whom everything seemed serious.

"Oh, it's fine. It must be fun. Having guests over. I mean, this place is so amazing, I never—"

"You ever played pool?" He practically leaped over to the pool table. His hands moved around busily, gathering up the bright colored balls from the pockets, arranging them in the triangle.

"No, I never have ..."

"You'll love it. It really passes the time. Here." he hurried over to a rack, and chose a cue stick, looked at it carefully and then looked at Elizabeth.

"Here. This seems about right for you. Not too long. About a medium tip." He handed it to her then chose another for himself. "It's real easy to learn how to play. I'll show you a few things first. This is the cue ball. The other important one is the eight ball, in the center there. Now, the first move is called the break ..."

The time that followed seemed to Elizabeth to both stand still and fly by. The July sun filled the room so that it glowed with a radiant white light. The sound of the clacking of balls on the pool table accompanied John as he showed her how to play the game, in what order, and the different ways to hit the ball with the cue stick to make it go where she wanted.

Relaxed and chatty as he did this, he smiled, made little jokes, but when he stopped to look at her when he made a point, the intensity of his expression made her feel disoriented. Sometimes he gave her a fleeting glance where he almost looked worried or a little scared, but she might have imagined it, it was as quick as an indrawn breath.

At last, he gathered up the balls again, sliding the triangle formation to the center of the table. "Okay, kiddo, I'm going to let you make the first break. You ready?"

Doing what he had shown her, she made a loop with

her thumb and pointer finger, and leaned forward, angling the stick through it.

"Good, good, but let me show you something." He came behind her and put his arms around her, gently repositioning her hands. "Just a little more this way, see? Feel the difference? Line it right up."

But his voice was a little tight, a little strained. And then his strong arms were wrapped around her. It was something she had imagined happening to her someday. And she was ashamed by her childish fear now that it was happening for real.

And suddenly he gave her a big smacking kiss on the side of her head, but she didn't know what the kiss meant. Did he see her as a little girl or a woman? What was happening?

She felt his weight collapse on her. She was holding him up! And could it be, he was crying? Very softly, he whispered, "You are a good girl. A very good girl. Different from all the rest of them …"

Elizabeth froze and went somewhere else in her mind, where she didn't have to feel his middle-aged weight anymore, or the soaking of his tears into her shoulder, which she found repulsive. She went hard and cold all over like an ice maiden made in a fairy tale.

TWELVE

The Blue Wheelbarrow

Lillian walked the halls of her high school as the bell rang to let out the second period. A faint smile on her face, there were small, sharp creases centered between her eyebrows, etched in, new to her.

I know I should appreciate this time of my life. It is almost over and done.

People were still always happy to see her, eager to pat her on the back or muss her hair and say, "Lil!" or more often, "Ladybug!" And she would beam her warmest smile at them, but then the smile would falter as they passed by, and it was almost a relief to slip back into herself again. Though what she thought of as "herself" felt vast and more mysterious every day.

Just the other day, her ex-boyfriend, Jack, had sent her an email. *What's up? I miss you. You were like a ray of sunshine in my life and I want you to know that. If you want to give things another try, I'm there. Your mother told my mother that you're pretty stressed with school and everything right now, but if you want to talk about anything ...*

But she didn't want to talk to Jack. Not that she didn't like him. Or miss him. She missed having a solid human being in her life who would hold her tight. Hold her in her skin and keep her grounded.

But that wasn't enough to go back with him. She feared he had the wrong impression of her. She was no ray of sunshine. If he knew all the things that went on her mind, or the way it raced and raced just beneath the surface of her cheerful demeanor, she feared she would repel and frighten him.

The only person who looked the way that she felt these days was Mack, with the dark circles under his eyes and his clothes that were too large for his frame. It wasn't that they weren't friends anymore, exactly. But things were a bit strained and awkward.

Vanessa had told her that Mack was living at The Brambles, with that girl, Sapphire. Sapphire made Lil nervous. While most people (thought) they adored Lil right away, Sapphire always had a closed-off look to her face when Lil said anything to her, and it made her feel at a loss for words. Sapphire reminded her of one of those girls who smoked behind the dumpsters. Girls who had that hard and uncared-for look. The look of being a *not-daughter*. Lil thought she must look ridiculous to them. If Lil was anything, she was absolutely a daughter. Darling Daughter, her father used to call her…

The only other person who Lillian felt truly connected to was Elizabeth., It had made her feel at peace, as she never had before in her life, when Elizabeth had visited her through the mirror; she had felt enveloped by a golden light that stayed with her for days afterward. But little by little, that goldenness had dissipated, leaving her feeling naked and vulnerable to the world again. And this time, it felt worse than before.

She stood in front of that same mirror when she got home from school, trying to conjure up the benign, loving companionship of a dead girl who knew her better than anyone else. But all Lil was able to see was herself, no matter how long and hard she stared, and wished, and prayed. It was only Lillian, in her small girlish body, with her wan face and large anxious eyes, her bedroom reflected behind her with its cheery photo collages and large, dusty pink roses. This place that had been her habitat for so long. It used to feel homey and safe here. Now it looked like a room that belonged to someone else.

Giving up, she burrowed under her blanket. (Which was messy, tangled with the sheets; she had not made the bed that morning, had stopped making the bed at all; so much energy in such a meaningless gesture.) The good thing was, she had gone from having insomnia to being able to sleep anytime she wanted, long deep naps that took her away from life for an hour, two hours at a time.

She slid slowly down the tunnel of unconsciousness, her thoughts skidding and spinning again into strange places. She was back in kindergarten, wearing a smock and pounding a mound of white clay. She was swimming in a lake of sun flecks and minnows with her sister at their summer place, in the mountains of upstate New York. She was riding Midnight, her beautiful horse that she had neglected so much recently; they were clearing a jump, then speeding up, faster and faster, her eyes were closed but she felt Midnight's beautiful, fluid energy flowing through her.

Then she was somewhere else. Someplace she didn't know. A house, but it seemed to consist of nothing but hallways, lined with locked doors. One leading to another, like a labyrinth. And someone was following her. Panic closed her throat tight, as she hurried faster, considered opening one of the shut doors, to hide. But somehow, she knew what lay behind the doors was worse.

A voice, from within and without, said in a husky girl's voice, "Use the key. You've had it all along. You just forgot."

"What key?" Lil asked. "What key? And what door?"

Adrenalin pumping through her limbs must have been enough to wake her, because she was back in her bed again, gasping for breath, heart pounding.

In her sweaty, clenched right hand nestled something small and sharp. In disbelief, Lillian opened her hand. In it was a bright silver key on a chain.

The next morning, full of new energy as she got ready for school, she dressed in her favorite oversized blue fuzzy sweater and the flared skirt that made her look like an ice skater.

"You're looking … happy this morning," her mother said, eyeing her over the rim of her coffee cup.

"I am. I feel good this morning," Lillian said brightly. Her mother squeezed her shoulder as she walked to the kitchen sink.

As she pulled into the school parking lot, where the snow piles had yet to melt though it was April, she felt a great serenity, clear and sure. She was sure this serenity emanated from the little silver key, now around her neck, under the striped shirt. It had been cold at first, but now it gained heat from her body. She liked the weight of it there, swinging back and forth when she moved, like a secret pendulum.

Without hesitation, she strode toward Mack when she saw him shoving his things into his locker with an absent look on his face; recently, she had given him a wide berth, so he looked puzzled when she stood right in front of him, with a smile on her face, looking into his eyes.

"What?" he asked after a long, confused pause.

"I think I have it now," Lil said, quietly.

"What?"

"The key."

"Key to what?" He was a bit worried by her demeanor. Was she going off the rails? Her mood swings made him feel concerned. She was a girl who felt too much, always reverberating like a struck cymbal.

She pulled the key on its long dangling chain over her head and swung it in front of him, without a word.

"Lil?"

She was subdued, but there was something quietly rapturous in her smile. "Elizabeth gave this to me."

"How?"

"In a dream."

Mack said nothing, and looked into her eyes for several long moments; Lil caught herself losing her nerve as she remembered waking up in her bed, key in hand. She had been alone, mind thrumming, looking up at the ceiling of her bedroom, wondering, can this be real? She was feeling the same way now, but instead of a white ceiling, she was looking into the face of Mack, one of her oldest friends. And she couldn't read his expression at all. If he believed her. If he thought she was crazy. Her lips twitched and faltered as she waited for his reaction.

Incredibly, he smiled at her; she smiled back.

"I don't know what it means. I don't pretend to know anything anymore. But it's great, Lil."

He patted her on the back, and she beamed. It was as though he was proud of her. Though she hadn't done anything, not really. But she basked in his smile. It had been so long since she had seen it.

He took the key from her, looked wonderingly at it, and then placed it back around her neck, as though putting a gold medal on an athlete. "I've gotta go. We'll talk later. Promise."

With that, he swung around and walked down the hall as the bell rang, and the last straggling students ran to their classrooms, leaving Lillian alone. But not feeling that way.

Mack was a bit spaced-out the rest of the day. The teacher asked him a question in French class, and he was so baffled that he didn't respond at all, setting the other kids to titter nervously. Someone greeted him and he just waved in an abstracted way, no mood to talk. He couldn't wait until the final bell, to get into his truck and drive away.

He drove out into the country, aimlessly onto the back roads, just as he always had, to gather his thoughts. He felt mentally exhausted. But oddly calm and centered since talking to Lil. It was good to return to what was familiar.

Things had not been great at The Brambles, and he wanted to move out. Especially, things had been getting complicated between him and Sapphire, ever since the day he had seen the marks on both her wrists. Bruises that made it look as though she'd been bound.

"What the hell is this?" he asked, astonished and angry. They had been fooling around in bed one Sunday afternoon when he had seen them in the slant of light from the window. So ugly, so glaring. Unmistakable. "Who did this to you?"

Sapphire pulled her wrists away and looked at him with distaste.

"Well? Who?"

She looked away and shrugged, and in a very nonchalant manner said, "It's nothing. It's all just fun and games."

"That's a pretty fucked-up looking game. Was it one of The Lone Horsemen?"

She laughed, a sudden, harsh bark. "Why do you care so much?"

"Because I love you!" he cried out, surprising even himself; in response, her expression was one of dismay; her eyes widened and her lower lip trembled.

"What? That doesn't make you happy? Don't you love me, too?"

Sapphire looked at him, her face even paler. Lips painted so red, so raw.

"Mack, I don't think it's a good idea for you to l-l-love me."

"Why?"

"Because you don't know what I am."

"You are Sapphire, and I love you."

She threw her arms up with a bitter laugh. "Well, I love you, too!"

"So what is the problem here?"

"You can't love me. I'm nothing. I sleep with other men."

He paled, but he said nothing.

"Not because I want to," she said hastily. "Because I have to."

"Says who?"

"Says my father. He would kick my ass out if I didn't."

"Your own father pimps you out? That son-of-a-bitch. You should leave!"

"I can't leave. I just … can't." She sniffed, covered her face. "And don't say bad things about him …"

"Why? I could kill him!"

"Don't. It's me. It's all my fault. I know how pathetic I

am. I'll do anything for my father to love me. Even be a whore. And when I was a kid I wanted to grow up to be a junkie just so my father would try to r-r-rescue me …"

"Ha. He doesn't care about *you*."

Sapphire slumped as though she had been shot. Mack went closer to her, he wanted to embrace her. But he was scared to touch her. So he let her cry.

"I … guess I know that. He had another daughter. He loved her way more than me. She's dead now, but it still doesn't make me feel any better."

"How did she die?"

"Killed herself. They found her hanging from a tree."

Mack felt electricity shoot through him, rendering him speechless.

"He even *brought* her here, last summer. I watched them from my window as they walked from the woods to the house. They looked so happy together, and it just hurt me so *bad*. The way he looked at her … he never looked at me that way."

Mack was incredulous. "She was … your sister?"

"Half-sister. Different mother. She didn't even know John was her dad. But he knew. He loved her and he stalked her. He was obsessed," This came out as a wail of torment. "God, he never even paid the least attention to *me*, no matter what I did for him."

Mack put his hands forward to touch her. But he couldn't. She wasn't looking at him anyway. He started to pace. He wanted to punch a wall.

"I gotta …" he panted, "I gotta … go get some air." He kissed her on the forehead and hesitated, watching her crumpled in torment, then feeling helpless to do anything, he went out the door.

Mack went down to the kitchen. He wanted a drink,

and he wanted one *immediately*. There was always beer in the fridge.

The kitchen was enormous, with racks of pans and pots and utensils that no one in the house used, so they hung there dusty. He couldn't think straight. He could barely see or hear anything. There was something so evil about this place, and the darkness was infecting him, seeping into his bones.

Have to get out!

He grabbed a cold bottle and searched for an opener; looking around, he was startled to see Mitch's wheelchair pushed up to the butcher-block kitchen counter. He'd been there the whole time. A glass of water and a plate of cold toast sat in front of him, neither of which looked touched. Mitch was so still and silent, staring straight ahead, that Mack feared he was dead.

But he wasn't. Just waxy-pale, his fragile neck swimming in the shirt collar under his seersucker suit. He looked as though he would be at home tucked into a coffin, a clutch of white lilies in his hands.

But his large eyes moved in their sockets, rolling up to settle on Mack's face, and life sprang to his expression, lighting it up.

"Y-y-you came back," he said, his voice furry and faint. Almost like a yell echoing from far, far away. Then his lips kept moving, not shaping any words.

Mack felt bad for his struggle, and covered it up by grinning good-naturedly; funny how that instinct came back to him so quickly, no matter the circumstances.

"How you doin', Mitch, my man? You're looking good this morning. I always love your suits. I want to wear a suit someday like that. When a man wears a suit, it's like the world pays attention." His words were friendly, but his voice strained. He slammed the beer down his throat as quickly as he could.

Mitch continued to goggle at him, still stuttering and gasping for what he wanted to say. "M-m-my s-s-s-son. My b-b-b-boy. I've been w-w-w-waiting for you to visit for so long—"

"Oh, I've just been busy with school and everything. You know."

He took another draw while looking at the old man; he could tell Mitch used to be someone. There was still a nobility in his bearing. He must have been a *handsome* man when he was healthy. Mark did not know just what Mitch's affliction was that made him so weak. But he vowed that it would never happen to him if he could help it.

I will never allow life to beat the shit out of me.

He was alarmed to see that tears were streaming down Mitch's weathered cheeks. Those eyes, so rheumy and pleading. God, he couldn't take this place anymore. He would move out tomorrow, maybe …

"I-I lu-lo-o-o-ve you, my son. Please, take me home?"

Mack glanced desperately around the kitchen. Should he just pretend not to hear?

"Little … blue … wheelbarrow. Remember?" Mitch smiled wistfully, nodding.

"Right." Mack stood up, put the empty bottle in the sink, and grabbed another to take with him. "I've gotta get going." He patted the old man on the shoulder, which felt like nothing but a coat hanger under his suit.

Now that he was *away*, behind the wheel of his truck, eyes on the yellow line of the road but not really seeing it, he felt a little better about life in general. Seeing Lillian at school, her shining expression and the silver key in her hand, showed the rest of his life to him in sharp relief.

Maybe he could feel hopeful again. He could get away from the sickness in The Brambles, before it made him sick, too.

He did a U-turn and made his way back to town, to the old neighborhood of his childhood. The house on the corner with the cedar shingles, owned by somebody else now. But that was okay, it didn't make him sad anymore. The sight of the house made him smile, at the memory of innocence and secret childhood games and rituals. Long afternoons in the dirt and grass. Secret codes. Magic.

He pulled into the driveway to Lillian's house, her car parked out front.

He raised his hand to ring the doorbell but the door opened.

"How did you know I was coming here?"

"I just knew."

Behind Lil's shoulder was Vanessa, smiling that inscrutable half-smile; he never knew what Vanessa was thinking. It used to make him nervous. But now it didn't; it made him feel safe. He looked her in the eye and smiled back. "Long time no see," he said warmly.

"Get in here," said Lil, pulling him by the arm. "We've been waiting for you."

Lil's mother called out to him as they went up the stairs. "Mack! I haven't seen you in the longest time."

"Hello, ma'am." He grinned goofily. He had always thought that Lillian's mother was as beautiful as a model. She still was.

"You doing well?"

"Yep! Can't complain." He leaned over the railing to see her; she was sitting in the living area, all done out in white carpet and white couches. Her hair was pulled back in a twist, and she wore an exotic looking caftan.

"And your mother?"

"Doing well, as always." He had actually not spoken with her in quite a while. A small fluster of shame overtook him, and he looked away. He would see her soon.

"Good! Vanessa is staying for dinner. You too?"

He lit up. "That would be great. Thank you, ma'am."

"I'll call for take-out." She made a little sweeping motion with her fingers. "Well, scamper off! You three were always thick as thieves. Go catch up."

Lil rolled her eyes good-naturedly as they closed the door of her room. "God, she always loved you. Thinks you're a little angel."

"Who can blame her?"

"You've been a bad boy lately, Mack." Vanessa wagged her finger. "But you *can* redeem yourself."

"Oh, yeah?"

Lillian pulled something from her purse. A little paper bag with the name of the local hardware store on it.

"Here. I had two copies made."

She dropped a key into his outstretched palm; he held it tight, like a good luck charm.

"So what's the plan, girls?"

"The plan is that we're going to find out what the key opens. Even if we have to try every door, every file cabinet, and every chest of drawers in the whole place." Vanessa had taken off her glasses and hung them from her front pocket. Without lenses, her eyes pierced him like laser beams.

"The Brambles? Do you guys know how big that place is?"

"We are aware of that."

"So how are we going to work this out without calling attention to ourselves?"

"Very slowly and carefully." Lillian was sitting on her bed with her knees tucked up under her chin. Her body was so small, it was easy for her to tuck up in on herself. Maybe that was why they called her Ladybug, he thought idly. "We're relying on you to cover the most territory since you actually live there."

"Yeah, well … I don't know for how much longer. Besides, I don't have business being in most of those rooms."

"Well, everyone there is stoned most of the time, so I don't think it will be much of a problem. As long as *you* stay sober."

"I *am* sober, Vanessa. I just went through a phase."

"Some phase. You still look ill. And it's a good thing Lil's mom didn't see your black eye. It's almost gone, though." Something in Mack's face made her stop and peer at him more closely. "How exactly *are* things at The Brambles? Are you still seeing that girl?"

"I don't want to talk about it. Yet. But let's just say I hate John."

Lil and Vanessa exchanged a quick glance.

He told them everything. That John was Sapphire's father. That she was Elizabeth's half-sister. That John had stalked Elizabeth. He felt darkness creeping in just *talking* about it all. But at least he was the one with valuable information; he wanted Lil and Vanessa to like him again.

After a long silence when no one said a word as it all sank in, Vanessa clapped her hands together, breaking the spell, "Okay, then. We've been on the right track all along, and now it's full steam ahead. Mack, you are going to lay the groundwork. You know when people come and go. Go through every room you can. See what you can find."

"That's fine, but the place is *huge*. As you know. And

some places are impossible to get to."

"Such as?"

"Well. John doesn't like anyone in his bedroom. If his hippie minions wander in, he gets pissed as hell. He says it's sacred. It's the place where he prays and meditates."

Vanessa let out a loud snicker, but Lil looked serious and determined. "Well. That's probably exactly where we want to go, then."

"Well, the only people who go in there are the girls he sleeps with. I glanced in there once. It was kind of weird."

"How?" they both asked at once.

"It was really *really* neat. The bed made up like in a hotel room. Just so. It wasn't like the rest of the house. The only other thing I remember is an electric guitar in one corner. On a stand. Old Stratocaster. I'd kind of like to see it."

"Lil, you can probably get in there. John likes *you*."

"Vanessa! Don't be gross!"

"It's true. He watches you."

"Well, he makes me sick. Why don't *you* try to seduce him?"

"'Cause Vanessa prefers men in motorcycle gangs," Mack sang out; Vanessa glared at him.

Lil frowned. "Huh?"

Mack sighed. "I was joking. Joking. Let's just focus on one thing at a time. I'll go back there tonight. I'll see how far I can get. But I hope you guys realize that this might take a while."

"I don't care," Lillian said calmly, "I know we're doing the right thing. If it takes years, I don't care. If someone in that house killed Elizabeth, we *will* find out. We're so close right now. I just know it. She knows it, too. That's why she's guiding us."

"Also, I'm guessing you guys didn't see the morning paper?" asked Vanessa.

"No, we don't get newspapers at The Brambles. Why?"

"The cops are still going after Elizabeth's mother. Taking her in for further questioning. Evidently they became aware of some phony documents she had drawn up? A birth certificate, social security number … I don't know, it didn't give a lot of details."

"Yeah, they're barking up the wrong tree," muttered Mack. "And she's in a bad enough state as she is. Bastards. They need to leave her alone."

"I had no idea," Lillian said, astounded. "I wonder what it means? I don't think my parents tell me this stuff anymore. They don't want to upset me. Mrs. Gray might lose it under the pressure. She might make herself look more suspicious, and she's not the guilty one!"

"Which is why we need to get on this, *now*," said Vanessa, decidedly.

"Kids!" A voice called up the stairs. "Come down and eat. I got Thai, I hope that's okay with everyone."

"Coming, Mom." She eyed the two others, biting her lip. "We can't argue anymore or get mad at each other again. From now on, we're like family. We stick together no matter what."

The blue wheelbarrow.

Mitch could see it right now in his mind's eye, standing there beaded with morning dew. A rich, bright, primary blue, straight from a child's paint box.

It wasn't *his* wheelbarrow, really. It was the gardener's and usually kept in the shed at the edge of the large Malibu property. Oh, the place in Malibu! Where he lived those years with his second wife. The place where his three kids had been born. The place where he thought he would start all over again. He had sweated it out at the methadone clinic and vowed he would never get lost again. He'd worked out and ate healthy food. He worked hard, making a film a year in those days. And he was a *family man*.

His wife was beautiful. His children were beautiful. His garden property in Malibu was like a rich pastoral landscape that belonged in a frame. Jasmine. Lavender. Blazing rose bushes. Paths through the olive groves. And a view down the meadow to the infinite sea, glaring misty and gray in the distance.

But sometimes, a sense of unreality still pervaded it all. That *this* was only a dream. And *reality* was the past, the darkly blurred days and nights back in Laurel Canyon. His first wife (the one he would always love the most) was eternally blue-skinned, eyes rolled back, a needle in her arm. Though people told him differently, he knew it was all his fault. That he was the one who deserved to die.

And yet there he was with his (other) wife. That house, that garden house. His children. Those miraculous children, who loved him, their father. Father! It never failed to stun him that he was the father of three children.

And he'd loved them, too. As much as he could back then. The truth was, he didn't feel much of anything in those Malibu days. In a way, he felt like maybe he *had* died, back in 1973. And now he was a ghost haunting this home and family.

He liked to push his children around in the blue wheelbarrow. The gardener, an older Latino man named Luis, would shake his head and laugh, "Ay, Mr. Cooper, don't hurt yourself, heh?"

Two girls and a boy. They had had them so close together. They must have been three, four, and five when he used to push them around, speeding along that huge green lawn that Luis kept so immaculate, all of it *his*, speeding blurring green, the heady smell of lavender, three squealing children, two dark-haired and one tow-headed. An incredible bounty that no man deserved. Running as fast as he could …

"Daddy, *whee*! Faster Daddy!"

Even as he laughed with joy, he had been afraid his heart would explode.

Certainly his body was frail and damaged from those years back. Lost years. He imagined keeling over from a heart attack on his beautiful lawn, with three terrified children gathered around him, eyes huge…

But that didn't happen. He'd race the kids in the wheelbarrow, then catch his breath and have a smoke, leaning against a tree. And though the kids begged, "Again, Again!" he shooed them off. The ride was his gift to them. That crazy blurring speed was all he could give. He didn't know how to talk to them. He felt so hollowed out and empty in those days. And not just because he was working so hard.

He had not seen those kids in nearly twenty years. They used to love him unconditionally when they were small, just little things with large round heads and stocky little bodies. But when they grew up and became thinking, rational young adults, they saw the deadness in their father's eyes. They saw him for what he really was.

And then the divorce, the mother turning the kids against him. He didn't try to fight. He let them all go. Maybe he had let go too easily?

Of late, though, he had been dreaming more and more of that blue wheelbarrow. Freshly painted, glazed with dew, just waiting for him on that green meadow. Waiting for him to fill it with his children. His greatest good fortune – that he didn't deserve. Was it too late? Could he ever go back?

He hadn't expected an answer to that question. Until that day when, looking out the bedroom window from his wheelchair, drip in his hand, he saw the three young people crossing the lawn to his house. Two girls and a boy. Coming to his house. Looking for *him*, their father? Even though he had abandoned them! John said it was healthier just not to think about it at all anymore, but he couldn't help it. He wanted to see his children.

And they were somewhere in The Brambles, looking for him. He had known it. And waited.

Until finally the boy found him, sat with him at the kitchen table. He couldn't believe his eyes. Forgiveness? He tried to talk to the boy, a fine boy, with dark hair and dark eyes like he once had. Couldn't believe his eyes! Tried to make his mouth work, but the words weren't right. Perhaps the boy didn't recognize him?

But it was okay. It would be okay. Mitch would be patient. His children had come back for him.

THIRTEEN

CRAYONS AND PUPPETS

Annabel kept the documents hidden away, in an envelope tucked into a coffee table book of Kandinski paintings, at the bottom of her bookshelf. She did not take them out often but was always aware that they were there, and her eyes often traveled up, glancing to the book's spine. *Kadinski in Theory*, in orange letters on black.

Sometimes, when Elizabeth was out at the library, she would succumb and take the book out and look at them. The birth certificate and the social security card. Both with her daughter's name on them. That is, the name of Elizabeth Rigby, her ex-husband's last name.

Now I've really done it. I'm a criminal.

But I just own them. I don't have to use them. Yet.

It was her ex-husband she had at last called for help. She hadn't spoken to Eric in years. But she could still trust him. He understood her conundrum. He did not want to know details or to get involved. But she knew he still had the contacts she needed.

It was Stan she wanted to get in touch with. Stan, now a college professor of environmental science, was still covered in tattoos. Still had long hair, now graying, in a ponytail down his back. Though he had gone straight years ago, with a respectable university job, he had been very radical in his views back in grad school with Eric and Annabel. They had been in an animal rights group together. Stan had been an anarchist and knew all kinds of things. How to build a bomb. How to spot an undercover cop. How to obtain false documents. Passports. Birth certificates.

He had been glad to hear from her and had been expecting her call. ("Stan is an incredibly loyal guy," Eric had said on the phone. "He always asks about you.") He taught in the Bronx but had an apartment in Queens, to which he invited her one Saturday. Because he knew she wanted to discuss something serious.

It took her hours to get up to Queens. She had told Elizabeth she was visiting an old friend from school, and nothing more. It was not as difficult as she thought, to find the apartment, in a four-story brick building with fire escapes on the side He buzzed her in and waited at the top of the staircase, beaming at her. He was older, of course, thinning hair and fading tattoos. But with the same vitality in his smile. She grinned widely at him without even thinking about it. She missed being around people like this. People with plans. People who saw the infinite possibilities in things.

Maybe Elizabeth and I can move to the city...

He led her into the apartment, which looked like a place a very young man would live in. Futon covered in an Indian tapestry. Milk-crate furniture. She could have stepped back in time, but for the sleek laptop, its case glossy black, sitting in one corner, glowing a red beady eye.

Stan poured them some coffee, and they talked about

old times, what they had been doing, where the years had taken them both. Stan looked a little older, a little heavier, but he still had the sparkle of youth about him, still energized by new ideas and ways of doing things. He looked her straight in the eye when he smiled at her. There had always been something hungry about him. And there still was. Plenty still in him of the old anarchist.

Why don't I know people like this anymore? Annabel thought to herself, smiling, as he talked and gestured, knocking over his own coffee cup in enthusiasm. Truth was, she didn't know much of anyone anymore. She missed her old crowd from her young days.

At one point, when their conversation came to a pause, Stan clapped his hands together, and said, "Well! You want to tell me about your situation?"

Her situation. She hardly knew where to begin. She talked about the end of her marriage. About Eric. It seemed, logically, like the place to start. She talked about the business and the pressures. The pressures of success, a success that they had never anticipated when they started an environmental consulting firm.

"It was so odd," she said, looking out of the window at the fire escape, stark against the view. Brick buildings, a fleecy cloud drifting slowly through the blue sky. "He was my best friend. And somehow, he became a stranger. Overnight."

"It happens," said Stan gently. "Lifetime monogamy is one rough concept."

"I know, but I always thought we were different. And now he's reborn. Living in the desert with a girl with braids in her hair." She realized with a start that that had been years ago. She didn't know Eric's situation now, at all. "All I can say is, we got divorced. I built my house, and I lived in it alone. And it put me in a very strange state of mind."

She took a deep breath, then began the story of finding the baby girl in the woods. Slowly, haltingly, but leaving out no detail.

"Stan. I know it seems crazy, what I did. Not taking the child to the police. But … but … *keeping* her the way I did. Not telling anyone what was happening. I was afraid of losing her. She needed me! She was filthy, cold. It was a goddamn frightening thing to see. We needed each other. I thought she would be taken away from me. And … I felt so fragile, so under siege against the whole world. A little angry?" She laughed a little wildly. "Maybe it was some grand act of rebellion? I honestly now can't even tell you …"

Couldn't explain to him that it was *love* that had driven her. Love that had such an enormous, stranglehold on her. Love that had been her biggest mistake, but not her biggest regret. It had always been love that had driven her, all her life, down these unlikely avenues. Ending here, at last, at this small apartment in Queens, with a man she had not seen since she was a young girl. Practically a stranger. And she was going to ask this man to break the law for her. Get her the documents. Crazy. *Crazy.*

"Annabel. Annabel!" Stan gripped her wrists and looked into her face. "Stop, listen! You're talking so fast, you need to stop and breathe!"

She literally did this. Stopped mid-sentence and gulped down air, like a drowning woman pulled from the water.

Annabel laughed nervously and shrugged. "Stan, I can't imagine what you must think of me. Elizabeth is a young woman now who doesn't have a chance for a normal life until I rectify things. You must think I—"

He smiled warmly. "I think you are my old friend, and you did what you had to do. No judgment from me."

"But do you know exactly what it is I'm getting at?"

"Yes. And I'm going to help you. It will take a little time, but I have people who owe me favors."

"So you'll—"

"Yes. Don't worry about it, Annabel. You'll keep your girl, and give her the life you want. Your man Stan is on it."

Elizabeth stood still against the rough bark of the white oak tree, hardly daring to breathe. She watched John, waiting for her at their usual meeting spot by the edge of the creek.

She did this sometimes, just to take in the wonder of it all. Him. Their friendship. Something about it still did not feel quite real to her, even now. She longed to have someone to tell about it, to make it really *exist*. But who to tell? Her mother, of course, was out of the question. She would never understand. Her mother already seemed tense and preoccupied lately, with what, she did not know. But it was fine. Fewer questions were asked of her whereabouts. She could still say she was at the library, or on a walk.

John never looked as though he were exactly *waiting*. No glancing around for her. No impatience. In fact, he always seemed very calm, almost beatific. A man with all the time in the world. A man to whom good things always came. He was looking down into the little creek, which was running low at the moment; a dry summer. He was picking up stones and looking at them, holding them to the light, rubbing them on his pants leg. In spite of the shock of white hair, he could be a little boy, happy, humming to himself. Absorbed by nature.

In that moment it almost seemed that the thing that had gone on between them recently couldn't possibly have happened. He had always touched her quite a bit, rubbing her shoulders, gripping her hand in his sometimes as they walked to The Brambles. Touches she didn't necessarily dislike. But the last time they were alone together, in what he called the "home theatre," he had shown her a Hitchcock movie. He'd had his arm around her, casually, patting her excitedly sometimes when he knew his favorite parts were coming up.

Occasionally he would lean in to whisper in her ear. "The most compelling character in this movie is the German, don't you think? That hidden compass. His own agenda! We don't know if he's good or evil, we keep second guessing..." Suddenly, quickly, his tongue darted into Elizabeth's ear, making her jump with a gasp, the intrusive, slippery probing of it repulsed her at once. She whirled around to gape at him, wide-eyed. The look he gave her back was hurt, aggrieved, as though *she* had done something bad to *him*. He withdrew his arm from around her shoulder and sat further down the sofa, looking at her reproachfully.

She had felt confused and troubled by this ever since. Her mind went into overdrive, keeping her awake at night. In the day she couldn't concentrate. It was a relief when her mother made a day trip on her own into the city to see an old college friend. It gave Elizabeth time to breathe, to sit on the couch and process things without her mother looking at her, in that anxious, searching way she had recently that made Elizabeth put a hand to her face, her hair. Was she giving herself away?

At last, Wednesday afternoon came around. The day they had agreed to meet. (She asked for his phone number, but John said that he didn't like to use phones, which she thought odd but somehow profound, like a lot of things about her mysterious new friend.)

It wasn't until she was already on her way to the meeting spot that she knew what she intended to do. She would tell John that she did not want to go to The Brambles. The truth was, she did not like the place, at all. It was so big, it gave her the impression that just anyone could be in that house, and you wouldn't even know it. She heard odd rustles and knocks, voices. She knew other people lived there, but she had never met one. There was one that she sometimes saw from afar, watching her. The girl with the wild curly hair. The looks she gave Elizabeth were dark ones. The girl did not like her, she knew.

And most of all, she didn't want John to think he could *get anywhere* with her. She knew, surely, that John must be in love with her. She could see it in the way he looked at her, as though he could swallow her up with his eyes. The way a smile would light up his face when she said something smart or funny, and he would give her a little kiss on the forehead. The way he wanted her all to himself. That must have been the reason for his secrecy. He had told her, hadn't he, that when they were together, it felt like they were in their own world? "I just love to see things through your eyes," he'd told her once, and his love radiated off him like fever heat.

Which was why she had to do something, now. It had taken him putting his tongue into her ear to jostle her awake, into action. Although she enjoyed being with him very much, and even holding his hand, she was not going to do anything like *that* with him. That tongue, hot and furtive and slippery. Disgusting. She shuddered at the memory as she walked through the buzzing underbrush. Late summer. Autumn already creeping in. Days getting shorter. Leaves starting to fall.

And his body. It was an old man's body, though he certainly took care of himself. An old man's smell was more accurate. And the skin loose on his arms, hands knuckled and swollen with veins. It was a shock seeing her smooth, vibrant youth in her own limbs when alongside.

But I shouldn't think that way. He can't help being old. But that's just what's so wrong about it. She stepped out lightly from behind the tree. Though she made no sound, John looked up quickly and smiled at her. Had he known she was there the whole time? He made a little bow, with his hands clasped together in front of his heart. But he did not cross the creek for her. She would have to go to him.

Instead of removing her shoes as she usually did, she crossed the creek by leaping from rock to rock. John applauded her. "You're like a little mountain goat," he said. "Look at you!"

But she did not get close to him. She didn't want him to touch her.

"Shall we go then, m'lady? I thought maybe today we could watch another movie. We've done some Hitchcock. Maybe I can get you started on Kubrick? One of my favorite directors. The way he—"

"I'm not sure about that."

He looked at her, surprised. Then he moved his tongue to the corner of his mouth. Something he did when he was thinking.

"It doesn't *have* to be a Kubrick movie. Or any movie at all. We can play pool. Or I can teach you canasta."

"I'm not sure I want to go to your house. Today." She shifted on her feet, looking away from him. "I thought maybe we could just stay out. A walk or something."

"A walk? A walk wouldn't take long. I was hoping we could spend more time together than that." He smiled at her winningly.

"We could go to the library or something."

"The library?" He laughed as though she'd made a joke.

"It's where we met."

"Come on, that place is old news, honey. We can't even talk there without that nosy librarian looking over at us."

That's the idea, Elizabeth thought. She wanted other people around. Alone with John, even he wasn't touching her, there was an intensity that was beginning to feel ever more crushing. "We can sit in the little kid section," she tried to joke. "It's glassed in, so kids can make noise. And there are crayons. And puppets."

"Crayons and puppets." He nodded, looking away. Then he slid his eyes back to her, sideways. Just looking. Tongue in the corner of his mouth again. Not saying anything.

At last he sighed, and said, "Elizabeth, I sometimes worry that you don't trust me."

"It's not that! Really! I just wanted to do something different."

"Do you think I would try to hurt you or something?" He looked at her full on now, his eyebrows puckered up in distress. "Do you think I'm that kind of guy?"

"No! I didn't say that. I just—"

"But you don't want to be alone with me. Am I right?"

She didn't know what to say. So she said nothing.

John tried to catch her eye. "Elizabeth?"

She glanced up. His lip trembled. She looked away again, quickly.

"Listen. About what happened on the couch. I was just fooling around. I'm a joker. It went too far and I made you uncomfortable. Obviously."

She shrugged, embarrassed.

"Listen, Elizabeth. Maybe you're right. It's a beautiful day. Why don't you show me some nature journal stuff? I like the way you know so much about trees … and … toadstools and birds. Whaddaya call it, white oaks?" He chuckled a bit, trying to lighten the mood. He stooped down and picked something up. "What's this?"

She moved closer and looked. She laughed. "It's a crushed beer can."

He peered at it in a mystified way, until Elizabeth laughed.

He patted her on the shoulder.

"Come on, buddy. Nature walk. That's all. Scout's honor."

He winked. And she couldn't say no.

Vanessa checked the time on her phone. Ten p.m. She would wait fifteen more minutes.

She peered closely at her face in the mirror. Her red lipstick was dark and matte, garish looking and her eyes penciled in a sooty charcoal gray. Was *this* how she was supposed to look? She turned her face side to side and tried different expressions. Haughty. Amused. Surly. She couldn't tell. She merely looked like someone else. Not in a good or a bad way. She was simply a stranger.

Though she did look quite a bit *older*, she thought. And that was a plus.

She had purchased a bag of cosmetics at the drug store that day. Usually, she didn't wear them and borrowed from her mother if necessary. But her mother didn't have what she needed. She had been watching tutorials online and had practiced, drawing a face on several times. The hardest thing was keeping her hand sure and still. But she was getting better; this final face was definitely not bad.

She stood back from the mirror to look at the rest of herself. Her hair was down around her shoulders, instead of scraped back into a bun or ponytail as she usually wore it. She had even found an old curling iron under the bathroom sink and softly waved the ends.

Her clothes were unremarkable, her regular old jeans and a plaid flannel shirt over a black t-shirt. High black boots. But she didn't want to dress in a way that stood out. This was fine. This was perfect.

Because she was headed down to The Brambles, and it was Saturday night, and she'd told her parents she was going out with a friend from her college class.

She hadn't told Mack or Lil anything, either. Though they were all friends again, and very much on the same page, she told herself that she couldn't let them know what she was doing.

What she was doing was going down there to hang with her friend Bobo. She planned to become tight with The Lone Horsemen. They had *liked* her the last time. And she had loved riding, no doubt about that. It was a way she could get closer to the group.

She would seduce one of The Horsemen, she thought, sweeping a brush full of powder lightly across her cheekbones. She felt no emotion when she thought of this. No repulsion, no fear, no giddiness. Just the cool, true pleasure of *strategizing*. She loved to make a plan and put it into action.

And the plan was to spare Lil. She was just too vulnerable for this stuff. The girl *felt* too much. Vanessa used to feel irritated by Lillian's fragility. It had made Vanessa dismissive, and hard in her judgment. But somehow, in time, that had changed. Lil's softness made Vanessa want to do anything in her power to protect it.

And so it was as she took off out the door into the night, car keys rattling in her hand. She felt strong and invincible with the unaccustomed feel of her long hair flowing behind her, her face painted as though for battle. The battle was to protect Lil and avenge Elizabeth. If she had to use sex to do it, then so be it. She was ready to use whatever weapon was at hand.

People have always called me cold. It used to hurt. But my coldness can also be my strength.

She parked in front of The Brambles, where she could already hear the thumping music, and see the silhouettes of the motorcycles parked out front; she paused on the way in to admire the one owned by Flash, a midnight blue Harley, Twin Cam engine. She put her hand lightly on the throttle and imagined what it would be like to ride one, all by herself, racing down the back roads with the night wind streaming over her. At one with the bike, at one with the pavement, and thin space in between where the two touched …

I will ride by myself. One day.

She strode purposefully through the front door. This strange place was so familiar to her now, it was hard to believe she had once found these wooden double doors somewhat foreboding. They weren't even latched shut. Ever. She pushed just one open, and the beery, loud dissonance of the place washed over her, engulfing her. It was so loud, she'd need to shout to be heard. But she would not shout. She glided in, silent as an eel entering deep water. She knew who she wanted to find. And there they were, gathered on the cluster of couches pushed together in the library, the once elegant dark wood table laden with beer and whiskey bottles.

Rooster held court, telling a bawdy story about two

whores in a knife fight. "You shoulda seen the bitch shunt! Crazy ass slit from the corner of one mouth like a fuckin marionette. But she's smiling, as wide and long as Miss Universe, and says, 'look out, bitch, I'ma cut your eyeball out an' hang it from my belt loop,' and the other crazy bitch she ..."

Vanessa sidled up to Bobo, who sat at one corner of the couch, smoking a roach and laughing. There was no room for her, so she sat on the floor, draping one arm over his leg; he looked down at her, surprised for an instant.

"Hey, Bobo, your high school sweetheart is back!" It was Ghost, the one with pale blonde hair and beard, he must have been albino. His dark, dilated eyes stared crazily from the paleness of his face.

Bobo peered down at her, frowning. "You're lookin' a little different tonight."

"Yeah." She picked up one of the beer bottles and drank from it, hoping there wasn't a cigarette butt inside.

"What happened to your glasses?"

"Got contacts."

"Oh, yeah? They new?"

Vanessa shrugged.

"You turnin' a new page or something? I hardly recognized you, kid. New hair, new makeup." He leaned forward and playfully tossed the ends of her hair, then moved down so that his head was right next to hers. She smelled the beer on his breath. Also the smell of sweat and vaguely, motor oil. "What exactly are you *up* to?" he whispered into her ear.

"Who says I'm up to anything?" She would not look at him, but straight ahead, carefully making her face blank and inscrutable.

He picked up a strand of her hair and twirled it around

his finger. "Hah!" he said, leaning back into the couch, his buckled boots tinkling; the boots were old, cracked black leather with a metal cap at the end of each toe. She focused on one metal cap, intently, to distract her from the men looking at her.

"Hey, Bo, the kid wants you. Why don't you go get you some of that?"

There were yells and whoops.

Bobo shook his head. "I'm not into kids, man. I got food in my fridge older than her."

Vanessa felt less embarrassed now, and more angry; it must have been that anger that fueled her to take it a step further. She got up and sat on the arm of the couch, and draped one leg over his lap. She lifted her face up and closed her eyes as though she didn't have a care in the world. In reality, she was in a state of hyper-alertness. It was as though she could see the group of hairy faces through her closed eyelids. Somehow she knew they were grinning. Somehow she knew that Ghost was pulling straight from his whiskey bottle just as he called out, "If you don't want some, I do!"

Languidly, she took the roach from Bobo's hand and put it to her lips and lit it with his silver lighter. The skunky smoke was a welcome distraction. She held it in, then breathed out a plume and slid down further. Bobo moved over to give her more space. Then he snatched the lighter away from her, shutting it irritably with a loud snap.

"She's up for it, for real, man." This was said quietly, casually. Flash. The leader. The quietest, and most frightening, of all of them. The one who was best friends with John. Dark hair, dark handlebar mustache. Compacted. Like an explosive. "Why you givin' the poor kid the cold shoulder?" He said this in a conversational, not unpleasant tone. A quiet voice that seemed to resonate louder than anyone else's.

Bobo just rolled his eyes. "She is a *kid*."

"I'm *not* a kid," Vanessa said in a low growl, but only because her throat had tightened, making it hard to talk. She hadn't counted on attracting Flash's attention. He'd never even looked at her before. But he was now. A long, appraising stare. And she didn't know what to do. She'd planned on getting close to Bobo, whom she felt to be safe, sane and honorable. He, she could handle. Flash, on the other hand …

She tried not to let her handshake as she took another gulp of lukewarm beer. Another part of her mind clicked away rapidly – actually, Flash was just the one she should get in with. He was the one who knew everything. If she could get him to trust her, she could get all the information she needed.

"Well, then, you mind if I have a go at it?"

The word "it" snagged her thoughts immediately back into reality. Flash had called her *it?*

What have I done?

Bobo looked angry and shook his head. "Come on, that's fucked-up! You can tell this is someone's brainiac daughter. I bet she's got science awards and shit. Probably never even had a boyfriend—"

"Don't talk about me like I'm not here!" she said hotly, before she had realized what was happening, her fear making her lash out. "I'm eighteen, I'm not an idiot, and I know what I'm doing!" She would be eighteen in May. Close enough.

"The hell you know what you're doing. You're motherfucking Emily Dickinson over there. You're just play-acting that you're sophisticated." Bobo said this with a sneer, but he stole glances at her as if to say, please, don't.

She flipped her hair back and stared at Flash, head on. "I'm game for anything." She willed herself to meet his gaze. But looking into Flash's eyes was like looking down a long corridor, and she couldn't see the end of it. Anger and bravado propelled her forward while a part of her mind shrieked at her to stop *now*, that this was too dangerous.

"Let's rock," Flash said. He stood and held out a hand, chivalrously, to help her up. The hand was so tough and calloused, it felt more like taking a creature by the hoof. But she did take his hand and let him pull her to her feet.

She heard the men cheering as he led her to the hallway, and up the staircase.

He took her into one of the second-floor bedrooms and shut the door, locking it. Then he lay on the bed, a queen-sized bed with no sheets on it, just a crumpled nest of unwashed blankets.

He looked up at her expectantly. "Well?"

She didn't like the gauntness of his face beneath his dark handlebar mustache and beard. It made him seem too intense, too hotheaded. This was a man who would do anything.

At that moment, she regretted coming here. Regretted what now seemed like lame-brained teenaged schemes. She had no idea the depths she could get into. She had no idea who this man really was, or what could happen to her if he regarded her as his property.

So she stood tall, to her full height and looked at him coolly, as her mind scrambled to find a way out.

"Is this your bedroom?" she asked, summoning nonchalance.

"Not exactly. But it's always up for use. What's it to

you?"

Vanessa shrugged. She glanced around the room. Bed, armoire, mirror, nightstand table. The key. She had the key on her key ring, marked with pink duct tape.

This is why I'm here.

But there seemed to be nothing in the room that took a key. Her eyes went back to the wiry little man, who didn't mind that his dirty boots were on the bed. His arms were crossed behind his head.

She removed her shirt and tossed it to the ground. She saw herself in the mirror standing in her pink satin bra. She looked piteous, small and cold, and she hated seeing herself that way.

"Keep goin'. Don't have all night."

And so things progressed. Thankfully, Flash seemed tired, or stoned, or something. He didn't ask for much or even seem that very much into the act. She imagined that this was nothing special to him. She kept her mind shut off the whole time; she focused on the carved wood armoire, a square of filthy carpet. A water stain on the ceiling.

Just avoid the mirror.

He finished with a grunt and a sigh. Then reached over to his jeans on the floor to retrieve a pack of cigarettes.

"Not bad, girl," he said, eyeing her as he lit up. It seemed like this was the first time he really looked at her. "But you ain't no eighteen."

"I am."

"Whatever. I don't care one way or the other."

He leaned over again for something in his pocket; he brought out an amber RX bottle and shook out two small green pills, and handed her one. He swallowed his, dry.

"Take it," he said hoarsely.

"What is it?"

"Roxy. It'll make you feel incredible."

She looked at it in the palm of her hand. Small, perfectly round with a notch through the middle. There were some numbers stamped into it. It looked innocuous enough, like a baby aspirin.

Again, she froze, with no idea of how to proceed. But she had already come this far. There was no point in ruining things now. Besides, she was curious. It was as though she had written and created a character she did not know. A character she now inhabited. She was curious what this particular freewheeling girl would do.

She swallowed the pill.

Flash immediately smiled, and unexpectedly, shook her hand. "What's your name?" he asked breezily.

"Sunshine," she croaked as she felt the dry pill making its way unpleasantly down her esophagus.

This time Flash laughed, a sound more menacing than jubilant. "You're funny," he said. "You go to the town high school?"

She nodded. No need to tell him she went to private school.

"Eighteen and out soon?"

"Yeah. Can't wait."

"I know how it is. Folks at home driving you crazy, right. Why else would you be in a place like this, huh? Seems like you want more from your life." He looked at her and raised his eyebrows sagely. "Now what's your real name?"

"Jeannine." It was her middle name.

"How 'bout I call you Jennie?"

She pantomimed thinking about it for a moment, then said, "Okay," in the dullest, flattest voice possible.

"So why are you hangin' around us clowns, huh?"

She shrugged. "I like motorcycles. Bobo took me on a ride once." Wind in my hair. Velocity thrumming through my blood and bones. Just remember that feeling, hold onto it.

"Oh, yeah? So you like him, huh?"

"Sure."

"Are you a friend of John's too?"

Vanessa smiled mysteriously because she didn't know what to say.

"Well, girlie, I like you. You seem really cool to me."

"Thank you."

"And I can tell you're smart, but you don't let that hold you back any. You're the kind that likes to figure things out for herself."

She felt very perplexed now. She never remembered him speaking this much before, and it felt strange.

"Are you looking for some opportunities?"

At this point, the pill she had taken seemed to be kicking in; there was a sudden tingling coolness running through her, numbing her anxieties and misgivings. Her mind, which normally a high-powered machine that never stopped, was quiet; the feeling was not unpleasant at all.

She smiled, and a rush of pleasure went up her spinal column and suffused her whole body. She felt made of molten gold. "Always."

"You want to work with The Horsemen?"

"Doing what?"

"Baby hooker." Flash laughed at the look of surprise on her face.

"A hooker?"

"It's a clean business. Legit. You don't have to go with anyone you don't want to go with or do anything that goes outside your comfort zone. It's all part of the negotiations."

He had drawn the grimy blanket over himself but now slipped down to reveal one pointy hipbone. He looked almost biblical, with his beard and mustache and Old Testament eyes. All except the tattoo on his chest of a grinning skull in a motorcycle helmet.

"I've never even thought of doing anything like that."

"Believe me, you're fine, kid, you know enough."

"I mean, but to charge money …"

"And the scripts. "

"Scripts?" In her dazed state of bliss, she thought of actors reading for parts on a great empty stage.

"You like the roxy I gave you?"

"The what?"

"The pill. Roxy. You feelin' pretty good right now, right?"

As a matter of fact, she was. She was radiating pure love and pleasure, beams and beams straight from her breastbone. Like one of those Catholic paintings of the Sacred Heart of Mother Mary.

"You would get all the scripts you want. Roxies. Oxies. Percs."

"But how?"

"From Honeybear."

"What?" She was losing her thread of reality. As though she had gone through the looking glass, and everything was a riddle.

"You know Doctor Honeybear? He's here all the time. Sometimes he stays in one of the bedrooms, across from Mitch's."

She dimly remembered the one they referred to as "doctor," though he dressed in normal clothes. The one with a cloud of curly blonde hair, so thin and fine that you could see right through it. A head like a chrysanthemum.

"He's the one who takes care of Mitch? Puts Mitch on his IV drip and shit."

"Yeah, I think I remember him."

"Well, you should. He can always get what you need. He'll help anyone out that needs help. He doesn't make you go to an office and all that shit. He'll see you where and when you need it."

"Is he your doctor?"

"Hell, yes." Flash's eyes looked dark and dilated now, with an alarming gleam. "You can be a friend of The Horsemen, too. I can tell you're one of us."

He leaned over and opened the drawer of the lacquered nightstand. "Why looky here," he whispered.

Vanessa crawled over to his side and looked into the drawer.

It was a grenade, sitting tucked in the drawer next to a box of Sudafed and a squashed pack of cigarettes.

Her mind had trouble processing what she was seeing, and for some reason she was laughing. "Is it a toy?" One of those plastic army toys that came on a card of cardboard with a plastic dome over it. Or it could be a bank, with a slot on the side for coins …

"Hold out your hand." He picked up the grenade, and gently placed it into her open palms; the thing was heavy. Like a small iron pineapple. She was terrified to touch the lever.

"So do you think it's real now, Jennie?"

It didn't even faze her that he was calling her by a made-up name that she didn't like. She was too entranced by the grenade. The heft of it in her hand. The rampant destruction that she could hold like a heavy fruit. She remembered stealing the ammonium nitrate from the neighbor's barn when she was young, with Elizabeth –

Elizabeth! She had to keep her mind focused on her whole reason for being here. The ammonium nitrate, so cool and granular and white like snow, had given her a similar thrill.

"Whose is this?"

"It's property of The Lone Horsemen, baby."

"For what?"

"For meaning business if anyone fucks with us. We are serious. And we are for real. We're good people for a girl like you to know." He was not looking at the grenade as he spoke. He was looking right at Vanessa's face. Trying to gauge whether he had shocked her.

He's trying to impress me! She smiled. She remembered Elizabeth's look of rapt pleasure as she slid her hands into the sack of cool white granules. But she was looking into Flash's cool blue eyes as another rush of pleasure overtook her central nervous system. Seventeen years old, and she had never experienced pure ecstasy in the moment before.

"I'm lucky to get to know you, Flash. And I want to keep on knowing you. Maybe we can work something out together."

He grinned widely now. A metal tooth at the back of his mouth glinted, and he looked like a pirate from a storybook.

"Good girl, Jennie. Good girl."

Mack quietly left the bedroom and entered the second-floor hallway, key gripped in his hand.

The bedroom wasn't his. He didn't know who was using it at the moment. But since there was a party going on downstairs and the upper floors were mostly deserted, it seemed like the best time to prowl around in his socks and try to use the key.

He'd had no luck. The room had just been full of dirty

clothes and overflowing ashtrays. There was one chest of drawers that had a keyhole in the top one, but the key didn't fit. The drawer wasn't locked, anyway.

He heard footsteps coming up the landing and ducked back into the bedroom doorway. Best not to be seen. He furtively stuck his head out when the people had passed, and stiffened to see Vanessa with the scariest guy from The Lone Horsemen. The leader. The one who was friends with John.

Instinctively, Mack stopped breathing. Something in his gut made him terrified of that guy. His blazing eyes could penetrate right through the wall, into Mack, and into his head, and he would know exactly what he was up to.

Whatever scumbag evil shit John is into, that guy is, too.

He stood staring into space, straining to hear any noises from the bedroom they had just gone into. *Vanessa?* He was flummoxed. Could she really be …. well, what *was* she doing? Only one thing they could be doing.

Would he be called upon to barge in and save her, if it came down to it? There was no noise. He heard the guy say a few words, Vanessa murmuring low. She didn't seem to be in danger. Most likely she knew exactly what she was doing and would be pissed if he interfered. Vanessa was cunning. So smart it frightened him. And her mind worked in its own quiet, shrewd way that he could only guess at.

But even Vanessa could get in over her head. And since Elizabeth's death, Vanessa's whole personality seemed to have somehow morphed. She was much more daring and reckless than she used to be. But, smart or not, she had no idea what people like that were capable of. Flash wasn't some puzzle or math problem to deconstruct and pick apart, neatly, like a jeweler taking apart a watch.

He kept standing in the dark room, listening, he didn't

know how long. But there were no sounds for a long while. Then there was talking, and incredibly, laughter. What on earth would those two have to discuss, let alone laugh about?

Enough. He had plans of his own tonight. That plan was to go up to the third floor, to John and Mitch's rooms. Most people did not go up there, though, and it would be hard to explain himself if he were walked in on.

Entering the stairway, he felt the noise and chaos of the party drift up to him; he listened to try to hear who was down there. He could have sworn that somewhere in the house was John's impulsive, swooping laughter.

The third floor was strange and filled him with a sense of foreboding. It was much quieter than the rest of the house. And the doors in this hallway were all shut.

It was John's room he wanted. The most logical place to search. (But what was he looking for? And could he handle it if he found it? If he thought too much he'd become immobilized with doubt.)

Though he had never been inside, he knew it was the third door on the right. John had once chatted to a group of them, leaning in the doorway with a glass of bourbon in his hand. He had wanted to show the kids his guitar.

Mack willed himself forward again. He rapped softly on the door with one knuckle and then slowly opened the door.

Just as it had been the last time he had seen it, the room was immaculate. Bed made up tightly with a chenille bedspread and flannel sheets. No clutter on the bedside table, just a small bowl of change and a water glass.

The Stratocaster remained in its place, propped up on its stand in the corner. Mack still badly wanted to pick it up but resisted the urge.

The closet contained orderly rows of suits and shirts and pants all hung up, some still in their dry cleaning bags. John always sent his clothes to the cleaners, and they were always sharp-pressed and fresh looking. On a shoe rack at the bottom were rows of short leather boots. A particular type of English handmade boot that John spoke highly of, Mack couldn't remember the name. John had them in black, brown, and navy. Mack was hypnotized for a moment by the buttery luster of those beautiful boots.

The chest of drawers held only stacks of sweaters, all neatly folded. Funny, John was so meticulous about his clothes, but he bragged, with a sly smile on his face, that he did not wear underwear.

There was a lot about John that was odd when he thought about it. That had always been off, though Mack used to deny it, back when he was impressed by him. But even back then Mack had sensed about John a righteousness, a moral grandstanding, that somehow did not sit right; sometimes his smiles did not match his eyes.

Under the bed was the only other place he could think to look. I'll probably just find a pair of goddamn monogrammed slippers or something…

What he found there was a long, flat metal box.

His heart fluttered in excitement and occasionally lurched in fear as he pulled it out. About the size of a small suitcase. Gunmetal gray, with a lid and a handle and a *lock*.

Heart racing, he pulled the key from his pocket and attempted to insert it into the keyhole. His hand was shaking slightly. One way, then the other. But the key did not fit. Damn.

At that point, he heard the door of the adjacent bedroom creaking. Someone was coming out of Mitch's room. Mack froze in terror. He hadn't known that anyone was in there. He had not heard a sound. And this was the time that Mitch usually slept.

He was sitting right on the floor, clearly visible to anyone who walked by! He slid the metal lockbox back under the bed as the person's fast, striding footsteps came closer.

"Hey, John? Problem solved. Everything good. No more hallucinations and he should be out for a good long while—"

Doctor Honeybear. The one they brought in to hook up Mitch's drips. Large as life, with his puffy blonde curls and steel rim glasses, he peered down at Mack with frank surprise.

"Who the fuck are you?" he asked, not unpleasantly.

"I'm, uh. Just looking for some cigarettes. I'm out and can't find anyone to bum off. He told me he might have a pack in his room …" He grinned ingratiatingly, though inside he was in full panic mode. There were a lot of strange people in The Brambles, but this guy particularly creeped him out.

The doctor gave him a tight-lipped smile and shook his head. "Mmm mmm mmm. Terrible habit, my son." He reached into the pocket of his khaki pants and took out a pack of Marlboros. He shook one out, then in an unexpectedly intimate move, knelt down and put it between Mack's lips.

"Don't say I never did you a favor, kid." Then he pulled out a plastic lighter and lit him up; Mack had no choice but to inhale, his eyes watering.

Then just like that, Doctor Honeybear strode away again, actually *whistling* as he went down the stairs.

Mack exited the room with the burning cigarette in his trembling hand. He didn't smoke other than an occasional joint because he'd always played football. But that seemed like a whole different life to him, these days.

He went down a floor to the room he still shared with Sapphire, but she had been gone a lot recently. He lay in bed, looking out of the window at the moon behind the trees, listening to the low rumble of noise from the party. The red burning tip of his cigarette flashed and dimmed in his sight, like a distant airplane.

Goddamn these freaky people, he thought to himself as he dropped the cigarette into a glass of water, and after a long while drifted into uneasy sleep.

Morning came, lovely and mild, with a sunrise of pink and gold and peach. The birdsong started earlier and earlier, now that spring had arrived. But it was still raw and chilly as Lillian got out of her car in front of The Brambles.

Opening the front double doors, she was ambushed by the heavy smell of beer that still hung in the air from the night before. Along with stale cigarette smoke.

The place was strung with bottles, cans, clothes, and shoes as she made her way to the ballroom, for the morning meeting of the Ministry of Presence.

She wasn't the first in the room. People sat here and there, propped against the wall or lay prone on the floor. And John was at the front of the room, arranging candles on the makeshift altar on top of the giant mantelpiece.

Something alerted him when Lil quietly entered the room, and he turned around; his eyes lit up and he gave her a dazzling smile. He put his hands together and made a little bow.

"My dear! You don't know how happy it makes me to see you. " He strode up and kissed her benignly on the forehead.

"Well, like I said. I'm ready to expand myself. There's more to life than high school, right?" She said this brightly but was unpleasantly aware of the lingering feeling of his kiss. That little spark of puckering dampness repulsed her.

"Where are your friends?" He glanced behind her.

"I'm kind of going it alone. It's kind of a ... private decision? I keep it to myself."

He compressed his lips, then shook his head back and forth. "I get what you're saying, Lil. I do. They might not understand it, sure. But as for privacy. Privacy, like the ego, can be a prison. That sense of separateness is just an illusion. But once you've been at the Ministry a while, you may find your point of view changing. Your boundaries dissolving." He gestured with his fingers in the air, little flutters down the length of his body. "It kind of feels like dying, in a way."

Lillian involuntarily gaped at him, at the word *dying*. But she recovered herself quickly.

John hadn't even noticed her consternation. "What I mean to say is, all is one, and one is all. You will feel yourself become part of the collective. And it is *serious* bliss." He stopped and looked at her significantly.

"Do you think I'm, you know, ready? Have you ever, like, converted someone still in high school?"

"Now convert is not a word I would ever use. I don't *convert.*"

"But you're the leader," Lil said softly.

"Not a leader. I merely speak through the collective. I'm a vessel."

He smiled at her. After a pause, she smiled back. "And Mitch is a vessel, too?"

"Yes. Mitch is a vessel. He was famous, you know. Mitch was a manufactured deity in his time. His fame was enormous and *corruptive*. In a way, like the time I spent in prison, his downfall was his great awakening."

"Is Mitch, you know, *sick?*"

The smile dropped from his face, and confusion clouded it for a moment. "No. He's not sick. He's just an old man who abused his body when he was young. He's fragile. But not sick."

"I just don't see him downstairs much anymore. Isn't he usually at the Ministry meetings?"

John stroked her cheek. Lil fought the urge to slap his hand away, but she remained still and serene.

"It is so kind of you to worry about Mitch," he said softly. "But it is unnecessary. You should be concerned with yourself, and your spiritual journey you are about to undertake." He pursed his lips and nodded sagely.

"I'm excited. But I'm nervous. My parents don't even know about this."

"And nor should they. It's time to break away from old notions of who you are. They are delusions. They can trap you. Do you sometimes feel trapped by your life, Lillian?"

The question gave her pause. Actually, she *did* feel trapped by her life. Sometimes. Ladybug, the darling of the cheer squad. The one who was always there to listen and lend a hand. Working for food drives and volunteering at the nursing home. Everyone thought she was so *good*. Honestly, Mack and Vanessa didn't know her, either. Not completely.

John just smiled at her. "You don't have to say a word, Lillian. Just your presence here is enough." He put an arm around her and looked around the room. A few more people had made their way in and had been speaking quietly. But as the beacon of John's gaze swept the room, they stopped.

He cleared his throat. "Friends, I know you remember Lillian. I'm very happy that she has returned, to grow with us."

There was a murmur of assent through the group. One man said aloud, "And so it is!"

John clasped his hands at his chest. "Yes. And so it is. Lillian, since Mitch is resting this morning, will you do the honor of sitting in his place, next to me?" He pulled up the office chair that he kept covered with gold shiny fabric, and placed it where Mitch's wheelchair was usually parked, to John's left as he gave his sermon.

Lil sat in the chair and smiled modestly, looking down, with her hands in her lap.

John's voice went on and on, his voice melodious and full, sometimes swelling and filling the room like a trumpet, sometimes coming out as a quivering whisper. She watched the faces of the people watching him and saw the transference of emotion on their own faces.

What sad people, she thought, wrapped in their blankets on the floor of this ruined ballroom. Everyone here looked cold and sick. The only one full of life and vigor was John.

John's mind was not fixed on his own words, either. They flew from his mouth without him even thinking about what he was saying. In an exalted state like this, he didn't have to even think.

And exalted he was, glancing over at Lil on her golden chair. That phantom smell of church incense filled his nose again. She was a gift, a gift for *him*. And he had drawn her to him with his own holy power.

And he deserved her, too, after the unpleasantness that had happened before with Elizabeth. He thought about

Elizabeth, sometimes. It had been unfortunate what had happened. She had been, after all, his daughter. His, all his. She should have respected her father. She should have trusted him, and not doubted him. Truthfully, the way she had treated him hurt his feelings very badly. He had not only felt hurt. He had felt *annihilated* by his daughter's dismissal of him.

That feeling was intolerable. It corroded his heart, his very soul. It made his brain fill with steam, and then he went to the dark place, where he had no choice but to *act*.

And afterward, he felt nothing.

Yes, Elizabeth had hurt him. But this lovely young girl could heal him, he knew. That's why she came to him.

FOURTEEN

A Taste Of Nectar

Mack spotted Lil crossing the school parking lot. It was the first truly warm day of the season. The air was light and breezy, the trees were in bud, and students whooped and chattered as they made their way to their cars.

"Hey!" she said as he trotted up to her. She said this brightly, but her eyes looked distracted.

"I've gotta show you something," he said, reaching for his phone. He pulled something up on the screen and handed it to her.

It was a website for a doctor's office. Dr. Barclay Honeyman, MD. There was a photo of a group of doctors and nurses, smiling up at the camera.

But Lil's eyes were drawn to the one doctor in center front. "Oh, my God, it's him, isn't it…"

She scrolled down the page, and at the bottom was the site mascot. A cartoon bear, yellow, with oversized dark eyes like an anime creature. It wore a lab coat and smiled benignly. Underneath the cartoon was written, "Doctor Honeybear, the one who gives the best care!"

"Oh, my God, Mack! It's Honeybear. This guy is at The

Brambles all the *time!*"

She clicked on an info link that showed her a list of services. General family practice, physical therapy, acupuncture…

"Did you see the oxygen chamber? Guy has a fucking oxygen chamber!"

"I didn't really think he was for real! I thought he was just some skanky guy who shot Mitch full of things. He has a *family practice?*" She returned to the main page. Her eyes shot back and forth between the creepy bear cartoon, and the staff photo, where Honeybear looked so wholesome and pink-cheeked and … trustworthy.

"Who told you about this?"

"Vanessa showed me."

She looked at him, but he just smiled.

"Spill it, Mack. Why are you smiling like that?"

"Vanessa … has an appointment with Doctor Honeybear."

"Why?"

"Because *Vanessa* is getting us the inside track, why do you think?"

"Well, I hope she knows what she's doing."

"None of us know what we're doing." He put his phone back in his pocket and tipped his face to the sun. "We don't even know what we're looking for."

"But we're going to find it." She was wearing the key around her neck. She liked the feel of it against her skin. It gave her a feeling of strength. "You'd both better tell me everything. *Everything*. No secrets anymore. Remember? I'm not some little kid you have to protect."

"She's getting tight with The Lone Horsemen. Flash asked if she wanted to work for them as a hooker."

"Wha … WHAT?" She had an incredible urge to laugh,

despite her horror.

"Yeah. She slept with him. Apparently, that's the test. It makes her considered an insider now. He actually showed her a grenade—"

"A real grenade? What the—"

"These people are the real deal. Weapons. Hookers. And it seems Honeybear runs some kind of pill mill through these people. *All* The Horsemen are patients of his."

"And so now Vanessa is his patient?"

"If all goes according to plan."

She shook her head. "I can't believe she slept with him. She didn't have to go that far."

"Vanessa can handle herself."

"All *I* have been doing is joining Ministry of Presence. Playing the convert."

"And he believes you?"

"Yeah. John likes me, I guess. He touches and kisses me. It's pretty gross."

"Hey. You're doing your part. I'm just laying low. Doing my reconnaissance when I can."

"Find anything?"

"No, nothing yet. I actually made it into John's room, but I couldn't find anything the key would fit into. But check *this* out … there was a metal lock box under the bed. I need to get inside that."

Lil looked at him pensively. "If the key doesn't fit, then maybe that's not where the answer is."

"I suppose." Mack sniffed, annoyed that she didn't give him more credit for finding it in the first place.

"Hey," she said, trying to catch his eye. She hadn't meant to hurt his feelings. "We're getting there. Someday this will all be worth it."

Vanessa had not been in a bowling alley since she was a little kid. And this particular one was extremely run-down. The Bowl-a-Rama was in the seedy part of town, between the pawnshop and the all-night Laundromat.

She was overwhelmed by the loudly patterned turquoise-and-orange carpet, the neon signage, the thunderous noise of rolling balls and the clicking of falling pins.

It took her a moment to catch her bearings enough to look around the place and find the spot where she was supposed to meet Doctor Honeybear. He had said to meet him in the back corner booth in the food court.

There it was, a candy-colored neon sign that said NACHOS-HOT DOGS-COLD DRINKS. But she didn't see him. She sat down at the booth, facing the entrance door, and waited.

Why he chose a bowling alley for their "medical consultation," she had no idea. He had simply said he was meeting some other patients there later so it would be most convenient.

She checked to make sure she had the money. Two hundred dollars was the amount quoted as his "fee." She had withdrawn it from her own savings account. Money saved up from tutoring jobs. It was hers, and no one would have to know what she was doing with it. This gave her an excited feeling in the pit of her stomach. Not that she would want to explain this particular scenario to her parents, or her teachers, or anyone who thought they knew Vanessa.

I'm capable of anything, and no one knows it.

Still, a little flash of dread lit up her brain when she saw Honeybear come in; he spotted her and smiled, rushing over with an odd little skip.

The neon lights lit up his fluffy halo of hair, and reflected, blinking, off his glasses like jackpot lights; he was overwhelming to look at, like some deranged disco saint. Rather than a white jacket, as on his website, he wore a wrinkled plaid shirt with a tear in one sleeve and a pair of large, slipping down pants. A large, nylon messenger bag hung from one shoulder.

"Sorry. Sorry. Sor-*ry*," he said a bit breathlessly. "Don't like to keep a lady waiting. Especially one as lovely as you. Flash spoke very highly of you."

"He did?" She tried not to think at all of Flash; whenever she remembered having sex with him, it made her feel covered in filth. I did what I had to do, no need to dwell on things…

"Yes. And he is one whose opinion I take very seriously." His voice was loud and honking, a New York edge to it; he put the messenger bag on the table and unzipped it, taking out a notebook and pen. "So let's see here. You are … Jennie?"

"My real name is Vanessa. Vanessa Davis." This could be a misstep, she knew. Which name to go with?

"Vanessa." He had scribbled down her name. "You got a driver's license?"

She started to take it out from her wallet. She had not been expecting this. She held it in her hand and looked at him guardedly. "But why do you need to see—"

"Zoink!" In one swift motion, he snatched it from her.

She looked at him with her mouth open. "What do you think you're doing?"

"Relax, honey." He whistled through his teeth. "Seventeen years old. I tell ya. What the youth will get into …"

"Stop making fun of me. Give that back."

"I'm not making fun. Not in the least." He gave the license one more good look, then slid it back. "That's a nice part of town you live. Parents know where you're at?"

"No, they *don't*." Witticisms would not come to her. Her face flushed in anger, and she knew she had gone from sexy neophyte biker chick right back to stony-faced, pedantic Vanessa.

He looked at her askance, one eye closed, sizing her up. "Upper-middle-class. And you're smart. So what's your deal?" He asked this pleasantly, without menace.

"I like The Horsemen."

"More than boys your own age?"

"Yes."

"Hah. Sounds kinda Freudian. But anyway. Any chance you could like *me?*"

She had never really looked at his eyes before, as they swam behind thick lenses. Slightly hooded, with a reptile's indifference, they didn't match his loopy smile or the sunny dandelion fuzz of his hair.

"Okay, ignore that," he said. "But if you are my patient, then I at least have to get to know you."

She looked down and took a deep breath. She had to remember herself, and why she was here.

"So what's the deal, Jennie? Or should I say Vanessa? Which?"

"I didn't pick Jennie. Flash did."

"So he's, what, a father figure to you? Or let me guess. This is your rebellious phase. Sticking it to Mom and Dad. But in a year or two you'll be back on track, up at Princeton or what have you—"

"Fuck you. I don't need to listen to this. I only came here because Flash said you might help me."

"Okay, okay." He turned a page in his notebook. "Allergies?"

"No."

"Chronic disease in the family?"

"No."

"Ever been hospitalized?"

"Just my tonsils out when I was a kid."

He scribbled a few things down on the lined paper, as the bowling pins crashed like the surf in the background. Their booth was walled in with cheap wood paneling with one ragged, fist-sized hole punched in. Vanessa stared at the splintered particleboard and thought that this was the strangest doctor's consultation she had ever experienced. Focus, she told herself. Remember why you're here.

"I didn't mean to sound pissy or anything," she said, with a faint sneer on her lips. Remember to look tough. "I just don't like too many questions."

"Naturally." He lit a cigarette, exhaling through his nostrils. "Smoke?"

"Sure." It seemed everyone at The Brambles smoked. She would too. It was something her character would do. He gave her a cigarette and lit it.

She smiled and asked him, "So, you're one of those doctors who makes house calls? I thought they didn't exist anymore."

"I only make house calls to John's."

"Why him?"

But Honeybear didn't seem to be listening. He took a meditative puff, looking up into the smoke as though it contained an oracle. "You know this place is non-smoking? The rules, and all. But they let me. They know me here."

"But why do you come to John's house but no other patient's?"

He glanced at her, startled, as though for a moment he had forgotten she was there. His eyes, she noticed, were dilated. He reminded her of the cartoon bear on his website with the big black eyes.

He laughed. "Oh, John and I go way back. And Mitch Cooper is a special case requiring a lot of care."

"So how did you and John meet, anyway?" She had to be more careful to keep her voice flat and disinterested, as though she didn't care either way.

"That was a lifetime ago. Back when he was still a *priest.*" He gave her a salacious grin, as though this were a punch line. "Yep. Different times. He was a priest and he ran a Catholic halfway house. Through my clinic, I saw some of the tenants as my patients. Methadone patients and whatnot. John was my contact, and he and I just kind of hit it off. He's a hell of a guy. Complex, you know." He gestured vaguely around his head. "Spiritual. Great to shoot the shit with him about most anything. He sure has come a long way since then, believe me. That halfway house was a dump. Should have been condemned, honestly."

"So you're friends, then?"

"You better believe it. I visited him all the time when he had to go away."

"Go away?"

"When he was in prison." He looked at Vanessa as though she were dense. "Everybody knows about that stint, I thought. No secret."

"Yeah. It's all a big part of his sermon."

"Oh, yeah, I've heard some of those sermons. Oscar winners for sure. That John." He shook his head.

"So you don't believe in the Ministry of Presence?"

He looked at her, offended. "Of course I do. I didn't say

otherwise. It's all good stuff. Johnny Boy has done fine for himself." He dumped out the plastic box that held ketchup and mustard packets and flicked ashes into it. "He's got a handle on himself now. And that's a good thing."

"Why?" A family with three loud children was in a booth near them now. She kept her voice down in case they could guess what they were talking about.

"Oh, come on. Obviously. Why did he go to jail? For beating the living shit out of one of his tenants, that's why. Guy had some anger issues. It seemed like prison did him good." Honeybear kept talking in his loud, honking voice. He did not seem to care that two of the small children turned and looked at them curiously. He stubbed out the cigarette and shrugged.

"Did you know the guy he beat?"

"Marginally. The guy was a little piss ant. Lucky Johnny didn't kill him." He smiled to himself. "They had all used to laugh at Shorty and make fun of his south Boston accent. He was stupid to cross John over money that way. Last I heard he still has minor brain damage. Damn guy. Should have known better. John was fucking crazy back then. But you know? We all make mistakes."

"I guess."

"*Now*. The question is." Now he leaned forward and spoke in a low, confidential voice. "How can I help *you*?"

"Well, I don't know. Flash said you could write prescriptions? If I needed anything." She kept her face blank and innocuous.

"You have any menstrual pain?"

"*Huh?*"

"Don't be embarrassed. The monthly cycle can be an ordeal. Cramps. Headaches?"

"Sure. I guess."

He took from his bag a prescription pad, scribbled some things down on it, then tore it off triumphantly and handed it to her.

"This should help. Five milligrams. To be taken no more than every four to six hours. For pain."

"Okay." She could barely make out his writing. She could just make out the word *oxycodone.*

"You got any questions," he pulled a napkin from the dispenser and scribbled a number on it, "you can call me here. Or better yet, just find me at John's."

Vanessa nodded, mind spinning. He was looking at her expectantly. What more could she ask him?

"So, uh, John is a good guy, then?"

"You bet."

"I guess he does take pretty good care of Mitch. He seems really … devoted, doesn't he?"

Honeybear shook his head with a wondering smile. "Mitch! Mitch, Mitch. The guy is a legend. Do you know how lucky we are to know a living *legend?* When I was a young man, I studied him in a film class at NYU! Just an elective but man, I loved it. I wrote a paper on Mitch's characters. Something about Joseph Campbell and the hero with a thousand faces. Bullshit, maybe, but it gave me a real appreciation." His eyes shone, his hand gestures extravagant. He seemed to have forgotten about the next patient waiting in the adjoining booth. "You seen his movies, any of them?"

"I saw one about a renegade soldier in the desert. I don't know. I've mostly seen clips, I guess."

"Well, that may have been before your time. But trust me. The man was incredible. *Talented.*"

"And now you're his doctor."

"Damn straight. And what an honor it is. I could hardly

believe it when John called me out of the blue one day, when he got out of prison, and told me about Mitch, and The Brambles, and how close they had grown. John always just fell into incredible circumstances. Always has. Still does."

"Mitch is pretty sick, right?"

"He's not young. He's frail. He did a lot of hard living in his day, you gotta understand."

"I never see him anymore. He's always in his bedroom. Is he okay?"

"Like I said, babe. Man can't get around like he used to. Don't worry. Honeybear has him covered. I'm always on call for Mitch. Don't you worry." He patted her on the hand, and then a curtain dropped over his face, and he was back to sounding brisk and professional. "I'm always here if you need anything. It was a pleasure to meet you. I'll see you around."

Mitch, many times on waking up, had the sensation of falling from a great height; he would jerk, a startle reflex, and find himself in his bed. The curtains stirred in the breeze from the French doors to the balcony. His IV bag on its pole dripped its contents down the tube, into the vein in the crook of his arm.

They rarely took him out of this room anymore. These things around him were as familiar as the speckled age spots and bruises on the back of his hand, grown too tender for the stent.

He didn't mind being there, though. Because he so enjoyed the dreams of flying from which he awoke. And he could fly *anywhere*. Through the black wind of a night sky, over towns and cities and walls. Over cloverleaf superhighways, the head and taillights of the cars below like strings of bright beads. When he was a young man, he had spent a lot of time on highways like that. He had traveled constantly in cars and limos and red-eye jets. He had always been very busy, very driven. But now it all looked so very different to him from up *here*.

His favorite place to go to in the flying dreams was to his old place in Malibu. He liked to go there as the sun set and reflected on the tips of the waves that broke endlessly toward the shore. And when the sun went down he liked to smell his favorite lemon tree, and listen, alone, for the night birds to call. But his children were no longer there, waiting for him to push them in the blue wheelbarrow. The gardener was no longer there, listening to salsa music in the shed. His ex-wife was no longer there, brushing her long hair in front of her three-panel dressing mirror. All of them were gone. He, Mitch, was gone, too, even though he was brushing the glossy green leaves with the tips of his toes as he floated in the air, swaying in the ocean breeze.

Sometimes, in these dreams, he floated through the halls of The Brambles, looking for his children. Because he knew that though they were older, and though they looked a little different now, they had come to The Brambles, looking for him. His boy he searched for most of all. Because it was the boy he had let down more than any of them. He had not been home nearly enough, always on set, always away, always traveling. Never there to teach the boy to be a man. The girls, he thought, were strong. But the boy had eyes that were overly large and scared looking. And kept his head bent forward as though to duck a blow. It made Mitch sad. He had tried to say the words to make things right on that miraculous day that the boy had sat with him in the kitchen. But he did not know if he made himself understood. When he tried to talk to people, the sounds come out all wrong.

Sometimes, just when it seemed he was actually making an escape, was the moment when he woke from his dream of flying. He'd jerk back into his invalid's bed to feel Honeybear pricking him with a new needle. To find himself back there again, and no longer free, made him turn his head to the side and shut his eyes to block it all out.

Later, *later*, he would search for them again. Sometimes he could feel them in the halls of this house, trying to get to him. They were coming to free their tired father from this place where he was bound to tubes and blinking machines. They were coming to take him home.

Mack moved his hands through his bristly hair in agitation. "What exactly are you telling me?"

"I said I'm moving out. I'm getting out of here. And I have to go *now*." Sapphire moved around the room, filling a bag with clothes.

"But what about us?"

"Come on. We had our thing…"

"It's not a *thing*. Did it ever occur to you that I meant it when I said I love you?"

For a moment, it looked as though Sapphire's eyes might swell with tears. In the natural light coming in through the window, it was more apparent than ever that she was much older than him. Her eyes, though lovely, were dark shadowed and set deep into her skull. And she had a set hardness about her mouth that girls Mack's age just didn't have.

"I would have warned you. I was going to leave a note, really. This is just all really last minute, and my ride is waiting …"

"Okay, okay, but why is it all so sudden? If I hadn't walked in just now and seen you packing, you would have been, just ... gone"

"I have to make myself go now, or I'll never go. I can't tell you too much because I don't want you to know anything. My mom is living in a nice place with her new husband. In the country, right outside of town. Out by the railroad tracks. She forgives me now for running away and wants me home. She never wanted me to find John, so I get why she was mad. But we're good now, really. Now I'm going to get my life back together. Go to school or something. Clean up my act."

She walked over and put a hand on his arm, kissed him on the cheek. He saw the cigarette burn on her forearm that she would never explain to him, and it made him sick to see it. That red dot, with the welted, shiny edges where it was healing.

"I'm sorry for being a jerk," he said finally, stroking the burn lightly with his fingers, as though he could heal it. "I'm glad you're getting out of here. I'll just miss you. I just wish you'd warned me. But I just walked in here and see you with the bag and—"

She sighed and grabbed the duffel bag she had finished packing and hurried toward the door.

"Sapphire! How can I reach you?"

"You won't. It's too dangerous. I have to go, really, my ride is waiting. This place will kill me if I stay." She stopped to look at him and shrugged philosophically. "John will never love me. I'm finally accepting that. So I have to learn to love myself. You helped to show me that."

"Well," he sighed, "Can't *I* drive you? Do *something*?"

She smiled sadly and blew a kiss. "Gotta go. When they ask you where I went, you better say that you don't know.

Bye, honey. Go home. Get out of here before you get sucked in, too. Once you are *here*, it's hard to get out."

With that, she abruptly turned and rushed out the door.

Mack sat alone, head in his hands. It was *good* she was leaving. He was glad for her. But it made him sad that he couldn't be the one to rescue her. She was doing it herself. What good am I if I can't save any woman in my life?

"… and so the wife comes back to the husband's car and says 'Quick, give me a hundred dollars!'"

John and Flash looked at each other warily across the table while Honeybear laughed uproariously at the punch line to his own joke. For twenty years now they had been listening, or rather, ignoring him when he got on a roll with his jokes.

"You hear the one about the proctologist that hit the dog with his car?"

"Shut the fuck up, Honeybear," said Flash, with no glimmer of humor in his eyes. Though Flash had said very little, a heated red flush covered his face, and his eyes blazed like flames, even though they stared off into the distance at nothing anyone else could see.

"Jeez, Flash. Get a sense of humor. You've always been one morbid dude."

"I have other things on my mind."

"Yeah, speaking of …" John poured them each another round of bourbon, though it was only late afternoon. They had been lounging and drinking in the games room for the past hour and had not even gotten to business yet. "How is the situation? Any developments?"

"I have two of my guys putting their feelers out. The Vikings have it coming to them. In a big way."

"Where is it going to happen?"

"Little gathering they got planned. Steak and booze and whores. Some of our guys are going to do a drive-by. Show them a little appreciation for the shit they been doin'."

"What are you going to use?"

At first, Flash didn't answer, distracted, swatting at something above his head.

"*Flash?* What are you planning to use on them?"

He fixed John with an intense, laser-like gaze. "My boys are going to shoot those fuckers. Spray em with choppers."

"We got choppers?"

"We have two AKs. I told you I saw Jethro and got a new haul."

"What else you got?"

"We got the choppers, a Makarov, and night vision goggles."

"That Jethro is one slick dude."

"Crazy mofo. Ex-marine and shit. He made a trip down south."

"Good on him. His inventory had been shoddy for a while." John smiled lazily, relaxed as though discussing the farmer's market. "Speaking of product ..." he said, sliding his eyes to Honeybear.

"Yeah, speaking of product, I like the new girl you sent me. Where'd she come from? She's not the usual."

"Oh, you mean Lillian? Little dark-haired cutie? She's mine. So don't even think about it." John swished the bourbon around in his glass.

"No. This ain't no cutie. Tall. Dark blonde hair. Kinda … like … patrician-looking face. Cheekbones. Kinda Dutch looking. Vermeer and shit."

"Oh, you mean—"

"That's Jennie," said Flash, smiling. "I sent her your way. You take care of her?"

"Yeah, we had our appointment, and I wrote her script. But…you sure you checked her out?"

"Why?" Flash's face instantly darkened.

"Like I said. She's just not the usual. She looks like a good girl. I mean, a smart girl. She's from a good part of town. I get a doctor's daughter vibe. You better not have sent me a narc."

"Relax. I banged her. She's game."

"I trust your judgment, old friend. I just kinda got the willies from the way she *looked* at me." In the dark and neon of the bowling alley, she indeed had had that austere look of a Vermeer girl. Someone from another time and place. It was as though she'd looked into his soul.

"It's *fine*," said Flash, peering at Honeybear through angrily lowered eyebrows. "I'm not an idiot if that's what you're thinking."

"No! No. That's not what I meant—"

"Good. Then shut the fuck up, Honeybear. I do my end of the business, you do yours, and things will run just as smoothly as they ever have. Have you been disappointed with our enterprise?"

"No." Honeybear, usually inclined to ramble and clown, went quiet, averting his gaze; he'd seen Flash angry before and didn't intend to be the one responsible for setting him off. The man was insane.

"Things have been good for you, right? Booming practice? All the girls you want?"

"Yes." Beneath the sparse fluff of his curly blonde hair, which he tinted carefully with boxed color, his scalp glowed pink. As did his ears and the tip of his nose; it wasn't fair. Flash shouldn't be freaking out on him for no reason.

Flash's eyes bored into him as though to make

Honeybear's head explode. "Then kindly shut the fuck up. *Doctor.*"

"Hey, hey!" John interjected. "We are not here to fight. We are all brothers here. We are here to discuss business. Yes, indeed. Things have been flush—"

"Damn straight they have."

"—and we've been very blessed. I've got this house full right now. This house is full of love."

"This house is full of *love?*" Honeybear leered. "Blessed? My God, I keep forgetting that you were a man of God."

"And so what? I am a spiritual man. But I can love and appreciate my great bounty without being a pussy about it."

"Bounty? Like that little dark-haired girl?"

"Lillian. I am advising her. She is on a quest for truth." John blinked primly.

"Is that so?" Honeybear wagged his eyebrows; a smile played at the corners of John's mouth.

"So she's in the game? Just like Jennie?"

"No, Flash, she isn't. She might become my special apprentice, so you people keep your filthy mitts away from her. She's mine." He paused, looked up at the ceiling. "She's different, you see. Delicate sensibilities. I need to look out for her." Again, the hallucination of incense smoke that John alone could smell when he thought of Lillian's large dark eyes, and the way she looked at him – trustingly – because she did not think he was a freak or a bad person –he smelled the incense and felt the thurible swinging back and forth in his hands, the tinted light from the stained glass window warming his face. In short, he felt good.

"Bastard. Keeping all the good ones for yourself and your dirty needs—"

John, in one fluid movement, propelled himself out of his chair and grabbed Honeybear by the front of his shirt. "You dumb fuck. Don't you talk that way about me—"

"John I—" Honeybear's eyes widened in terror. He was almost more afraid of John than he was of Flash. At least Flash was somewhat predictable. John could turn on you so fast you never saw it coming.

John bared his teeth for one hissing second, his face inches away. It was a terrible thing to behold. Honeybear thought of a gargoyle he had seen once, on a cathedral in Paris when he was living abroad during his junior year; the thing's expression, twisted, rage-filled, *empty*, had scared him deeply. Probably because of all the weed he'd smoked that night. But still. He had the same sense of existential panic now as he had that dank, foggy night long ago.

"I don't have needs," John said in a terrible, quiet voice that didn't seem to come from his lips, but from some outside source, like a ventriloquist. "I have *callings*." He gave Honeybear one last shake and let him go. He sat back in his chair and calmly, even peacefully, drank the rest of his bourbon. "Needs are for dirty vermin like you, Honeybear." He pursed his lips; Honeybear could only goggle at him silently.

"I'm going to have a talk with the girl," Flash said.

"Who?" John was suddenly cheerful now, as though nothing had happened.

"Jennie. Now that she has her script, she can make a bundle selling. Rich high school kids."

"Well, I think she's just fine. Smart girl." Honeybear was careful not to set anyone else off; he *had* to get out of there, maybe swing by the office and sit in the oxygen tank for a while. Wash his mind clean by breathing that pure, silvery gas. "I gotta go, guys. It's been real. Got some appointments."

"Can you take care of Mitch first?" John asked. "He's been a little agitated recently."

"Sure, I'll look in on him, sure thing." Honeybear was glad to be put to service.

"You need me to help?" John asked pleasantly.

"No, no, you just set down there. You guys can play cards or something. I'll just hook him and get him all happy, no problem."

But the smile faded from his face as he made his way up the two flights of stairs. These people, he thought. How did I ever get so tangled up with people like this? I am so far above them, it's crazy. If it weren't for me, a trained medical professional, where would they be? Not here. Buncha skanks. Don't know how lucky they are to have me …

He was in a foul mood as he opened the door to Mitch's room, anything but thrilled to see the old guy actually standing up, leaning his weight on the top of the dresser, trying to get somewhere. His hospital pajamas hung on his bony frame. His taped and bandaged hand looked huge at the end of his bony wrist.

"Mitch? What the hell are you doing? Get back in bed before you fall."

Mitch looked at him, and Honeybear swore for a moment he saw a look of insolent hatred on the old man's face, as he tried to form words with his thin, dried out lips. "G-g-get…"

"What's that? Spit it out, old man."

"G-g-get me a c-c-car. C-c-call Alphonse to bring the c-c-car…"

"Call *Alphonse* to bring the *car?* Sure, buddy. Directly." He went over to the mini-dorm fridge in one corner of the room. He removed one of the IV bags and slammed the door shut. He knew should really let the bag warm up first. But then again, he really didn't care at that point. He slammed the bag on top of the dressing table.

He measured out the Dilaudid into the syringe, holding it up to the light. Shot it to the injection port, then shook the bag harder than he had to; those sons of bitches, humiliating him that way, like he was some worm on a hook. But what could he do? These guys were bringing him so much business. The truth was they all needed each other. And he *hated* that.

"Here we go, partner," he said, hanging the bag on the stand. "Let me stick this in your vein and get ready to blast off."

"But-but, the-the-the …. the blue wheelbarrow …"

"You are one whacked-out little tamale, aren't you?" He paused, looking to the side and smiling before he took Mitch by the bony arm, and steered him to the bed. "Hey. Is it true that you used to do blow with Roman Polanski in the south of France?"

Mitch moved his lips, but nothing came out. His eyes rolled wildly around the room, searching for something.

Honeybear affixed the tube to the catheter. "Whatever. There. You're all set. Don't say I never do nothing for you." He clapped him on the shoulder (it felt like clapping the shoulder of death itself, he thought) and whistled jauntily as he went out the door.

Lillian raised up the crinkly plastic garment bag to take another look at her new prom dress; she and her mother had picked it out the night before. It was strapless, knee length, a pale ethereal blue, with a skirt made of layers of tulle that draped and billowed into a jagged, asymmetrical hem. "It's very sophisticated," her mother had said. "Are you sure it's really you?"

But Lillian loved the dress. And the strappy, high-heeled silver sandals that went with it. She was going with Rob, the class president. Everyone thought they made a wonderful couple, and could not believe Lil's luck that he had asked her. But she felt oddly immune from everyone else's enthusiasm about prom. She was done with this life, done with high school. The old Lillian, *Ladybug*, was a personality that felt like an ill-fitting mask she had to put on every once in a while. *Ladybug* was giddy, always high-spirited, and pure as rainwater.

But Lillian wasn't. She shut the dress away in her closet and walked downstairs and out the door into the warm spring afternoon.

She thought she'd stop by Vanessa's house and see what she was up to. She heard Vanessa's little brother and a friend as they played some game, running around their house and yelling insults at each other.

And there Vanessa was, in the backyard. Swinging on the swing set. She looked so placid and peaceful as though she were under enchantment. With her dark blonde hair hanging down around her shoulders, she could be Alice in Wonderland.

Lil sat in the swing next to her. They looked at each other and didn't say anything. They just smiled.

"I can't believe you still have this thing," said Lil, pumping herself higher. "We played on this when we were little."

"Yeah. No one even uses it anymore," Vanessa said quietly. "They may as well take it down."

"Well, I still like it." Lil was swinging high. The days were getting so much longer now. It was past six and the sun was still out, though it was beginning to lower and throw shadows onto the ground, of the swing set and the two of them, strange and elongated.

Vanessa tried going higher to keep up with Lil, and then they were laughing. Laughing at nothing. Crocuses poked up from the grass, purple and yellow striped, birdsong in the air, the air that blew on their cheeks deliciously fresh and damp.

Lil tilted her head back to look at the sky. "Did Elizabeth play on this swing set with us, too?"

"No. I don't think so. Her mom always wanted us to play over there." Vanessa pictured Mrs. Gray in her mind, and the way she had begged them not to leave when they had gone over to visit; it gave her a pang of guilt to think that they had never gone back. Vanessa had tried not to think of the woman since. She had passed by her once in her car. Mrs. Gray had been out getting her mail. Vanessa had waved, but she didn't know if Mrs. Gray had recognized her. In any case, she didn't wave back. Just paused where she stood at the mailbox, gazing at her, expressionless, her eyes masked by dark sunglasses, her mane of gray curls snapping and writhing in the breeze.

"My mom sees her in the market sometimes. Elizabeth's mom," Lil allowed the swing to coast slower and slower. "She says she always seems to be in a hurry. Like she has somewhere else to be."

"Well, she always was kind of aloof out in public. I guess that's just her persona." A contrast to the pain and desperation they had seen on her face when she pointed to the ghost of the bird imprinted on her window, each feather preserved, distinct. She'd wanted to know if it had been an omen.

Maybe it was.

"Why do you look like that?" Lillian said suddenly.

"Like what?"

"Like you're about to cry."

Vanessa quickly recovered herself and made her face impassive again.

"Vanessa, I'm not saying there's anything *wrong* with it. I mean, it's kind of a good thing? I'm just used to you never showing emotion—"

"Just calm down, Lil, you read too much into things."

"Well, I …" I shouldn't have said anything. I ruined it. "I just think you've changed."

"I don't know what you mean."

Lil looked at her with a fond smile but knew to let it drop. Change the subject. To something, anything else. "Wonder where that knucklehead Max is right now?"

"Beats me," she said flatly.

"I think he'll go home soon. To his mom. I think inside, he really misses her."

"You sure seem to think you know a lot about what goes on in other people's heads, don't you?"

Lillian leaned back in the swing, lifted her feet up so that it looked as if she was standing on the pink stippled blue afternoon sky, the explosion of the sunset just inches from her toes. "Nah. I don't know so much, these days."

The next day, when Lillian arrived at the ballroom for her meeting with John, the memory of playing on the swings with Vanessa still fresh in her senses, made her feel calm and expansive. I can do this. I can handle anything.

They were planning to go for a walk in the woods. He must have been waiting for her because he opened the front double doors before she even knocked. "Hope you got your walking shoes on," he said, grinning heartily. Although he was dressed as he was every other day, black pants, ironed white shirt. Narrow-toed black boots, freshly polished.

They walked around the side of The Brambles, to the back lawn that sloped down to the woods. "Beautiful day for a walk."

"Yes, it is," Lil answered, eyeing the edge of a tattoo peeping out from under his rolled sleeve. She had never noticed it before. It looked like bird talons.

"I love to be out in nature. Frees my mind from what binds it." He took long but slow strides to allow Lil to keep up with him. "Do you feel the same way?"

"About what?"

"Nature!"

"Sure. I used to play in these woods when I was a kid."

"That's good. Wholesome."

She looked at him curiously; sometimes his choice of words was ever so slightly *odd*. Like an alien imitating a human. But he didn't notice her look. His face was tipped toward the sun, a small smile of satisfaction on his face.

As they entered the wood's edge, it was remarkable how quickly light turned to dark. It was so hushed and jungle-like with growth, even though spring had just begun.

"Trail starts down this way. Though it hasn't been cleared for a while. Should have Mitch see to that. Nothin' like a walk in the woods, no sir."

Lil was nervous now. It felt so isolated here. Did anyone know where they were? She had told no one.

The trail was indecipherable to her, but John parted the brush and held back branches as he guided her along.

"So how are things, Lillian?" His voice in the enclosure of the woods sounded flat and close, almost muffled. "School treating you well?"

"Not bad. I just had a big term paper."

"English?"

"No. History."

"I love history. Can't read enough of it. Maybe I can start tutoring you."

"Maybe."

"You going to prom?"

"Yes." Her delicate ice blue dress, hanging in the closet right now. Her closet, in her rose pink bedroom. It all seemed indescribably far away from this place, this situation, which felt more and more foolhardy and potentially dangerous. But she steeled her will. "I'm going with the class president if you can believe it."

"Lucky guy! You in love with him?" John gave her a fond, knowing smile.

"Not really. He asked, and I want to go, so …"

"I can't believe a lovely girl like you doesn't have a boyfriend."

"I did. He's in college. We broke up a while ago."

"Are you a virgin?"

Lil looked at him in shock, not knowing if she had heard right.

John put his arms up, defensively. "No need to feel embarrassed. No need to feel any shame. It's just a word. Not even a word. It is just a *construction*."

She couldn't find words to answer him. She stumbled a bit over a tree root, and he steadied her arm.

"There is no need to blush, Lil. I can see you carry shame, and that can be a heavy burden—"

"But I'm not ashamed!" And was not a virgin, either, but she did not want to tell him that.

"Well. All the same, I want you to know that I would never judge you, no matter if others have judged you before in the past. You are a pure, beautiful soul, and you should hold your head high."

They were at a wider part of the trail now, so she could walk a little further away from him.

"I hope you don't mind me talking plainly, Lil. It's just I feel so close to you that I feel I can really be myself."

"Really? I guess I'm glad you trust me." She smiled benignly, trying to hide the revulsion she felt inside. It was the first time in her life that she had experienced what it was like to truly dislike a person. The man's very aura made her feel sick and contaminated. Her head was swimming a little bit. But she reminded herself of the key around her neck. It gave her strength to remember that she was doing this for Elizabeth.

They arrived at the small creek that ran deep in the woods. It was full of clear water from the spring rains that had come through recently, but a mass of branches and brush had fallen across in one place, damming the flow; John walked down to the bank and pulled out the branches from the water, tossing them in a pile.

"Whew!" he said when he was done. "There we go. Gotta keep the creek flowin'." He crossed his arms high over his chest, watching the creek thoughtfully. Then he turned to look at Lil with an expression of great profundity. "There's a quote this puts me in mind of. 'Whatever is flexible and flowing will tend to grow. Whatever is rigid and blocked will wither and die.'"

"Who said that?"

He smiled in triumph. "It's from the Tao Te Ching. Ever read it?"

"No."

"You will, though. No doubt you will. I think that it is so, so exciting." Here he grinned widely, feverishly, as he clapped his big pink hands together, "that you have so much to learn and discover. You're just at the beginning of your journey. You know?"

She was a bit taken aback, staring at those hands of his. Muscled, squared off, so large as to be almost out of scale to the rest of his body. She had never noticed before.

He nodded, though she hadn't said anything. "Yep. I read that sacred text in prison. That's where I received my real education. Learned a lot more than I ever did in seminary. Prison's not easy, you know." He looked suddenly toward her, *fiercely*.

"I … bet it's not."

"But it made me a new man. Melted me down by fire, poured me into a new bodily mold. Yes, sir. I learned about Taoism. Tao means *the way*. The source of everything that exists …"

He talked and talked, a rapid slew of words streaming from his lips, but he also stole glances at Lil from the corner of his eye. He seemed to be *assessing*.

"Are you okay to go across the creek?"

Lil started, she had tuned out; she looked at the water now rushing along. It didn't look too deep, but appearances could be deceiving. "Hmmm, I don't know."

"I could pick you up and carry you across if you like. I bet you're no heavier than thistledown."

"Um, no, that's okay. I can just take off my shoes."

"That would work, too. I'll steady you across."

She sat down on an outcropping of rock to unlace her sneakers, and asked innocently, "What's on the other side?"

"Oh, some interesting trees and stuff. I cross over all the time."

"Are you keeping your boots on? They look expensive."

He smiled cavalierly. "No big deal to get them wet."

And so they crossed. The water's coldness shocked Lillian's feet. As did the slipperiness of the green mossy rocks when she stepped on them.

"*Whee!*" John called out merrily, gripping her arm tightly. "Don't want to lose you now!" He laughed, a bit breathlessly.

"But your boots! And your pants!"

He splashed ankle deep in the water, sodden from the knees down.

"Well, I'm the kinda guy that just doesn't give a shit, I guess. Hand-tooled, leather-soled boots, made in England." He shrugged, grinned mischievously.

On the other side, he offered his arm to steady her as she put her shoes back on, trying her best to wipe off the sand and grit from her feet. Then they walked up the bank, back into the thick of the trees.

He stopped them at one point, furrowing his brow. "I *think* it's over this way."

"Is it a surprise?" Lil asked guardedly. She knew where they were now. She imagined she could still see where all the footprints had beaten down a path in the green. Six, seven months it had been? They were approaching where the yellow crime scene tape had been wound around.

Surely this was not where he was bringing her. He wouldn't be that stupid, would he? Dread clenched in the pit of her stomach.

"Here it is!" he cried in astonished wonder. "My favorite white oak tree!"

She scarcely recognized it in its spring glory, the leaves a silvery pale pink. She had last seen it in the fall when its leaves were turning brown and dropping, its topmost branches bare as skeleton limbs. Elizabeth's tree.

She could just make out, sprouting like mushrooms in the mulchiness below, the tips of white candles, melted down to the nub. Scraps of handwritten notes. And a bit further away, a small bedraggled teddy bear.

She looked up at him in shock and surprise. He had walked closer to the tree and lifted up his hand to touch a delicate pink leaf. "It's beautiful, isn't it, Lil?"

He looked exalted as he gazed at it. But when he saw the shocked look on her face, his expression switched. He grinned in a way that was abashed. But there was something else in his eyes, too. A wing beat of fear.

Mack stood at the door of his house. Even though it had only been a matter of weeks that he had been gone, it looked very different to him now. Smaller, as though sunken in on itself in his absence; a bit shabbier. Dead growth and sticks that had lain here all winter. Maybe his mother would ask him to do some raking.

But at the moment, he didn't know how to proceed. Just walk in? But it wasn't really his house anymore, was it, since he was the one who left?

He decided to rap on the door three times, then open it, and call out, "Mom?"

She came in from the kitchen, drying her hands. The television turned to a talk show, with the volume up so she could hear it in the other room; the televised audience laughed at something and applauded as his mother came forward with a look of stunned disbelief on her face.

"Mack?" This came out as a frail bleat as she hugged him, resting her face on his shoulder, and all at once he was crushed by guilt at his own callousness. How could he have left her alone that way? Not returned her calls or her texts? His own actions seemed alien to him now. Could *he* really have done that?

"What are you doing here?" She drew back to look at him; through her gaze, he could tell how he looked. Pale and tired. Spacey from weeks of eating bad food and not sleeping.

"I just came to check up on you. You know, just see how—"

"Are you coming home?"

"I-I don't know. I mean, probably ..."

"When?"

"Soon."

Crying now, the small features of her face contorted into a grimace. "I've missed you *so* much."

"I've missed you, too. I've missed your cooking."

"Stay! I'll make you something. Anything you want. Stay and we'll talk. Oh, Mack, it's been so hard—"

"I ... don't know about tonight. But I'll stay for dinner soon." He wasn't quite ready to be drawn in completely. Even though he loved her, something in him, even as he stood there, panicked and scampered to get away before he was engulfed.

"Well." they moved over to the couch, and she grabbed the remote to turn off the talk show. The sudden quiet felt as though a roomful of people had just departed. "Where have you been, son? Have you really been living in that awful house?"

He laughed nervously. "It's not *that* bad."

"That's not what *I* heard. I hope no one is trying to coerce you there. With that, I don't know, *alternative lifestyle* stuff."

He laughed again, not knowing what she meant by "alternative lifestyle."

"Come on. You watch too many talk shows, Mom. No

one is converting me to Satanism."

"The TV keeps me company these days." She peered at his face closely now. "So what is it that's keeping you away? Is it a girl? Have you been seeing someone?"

"Kind of. But it's over now and I don't want to talk about it."

"Well, nobody's pushing you."

"*Good*." This came out testier than he had meant it to; the wounded look in her eye made him loathe himself all over again. "Sorry, Mom. Really. I'm just tired is all."

"You look it."

"So how are things?" He wanted to get the attention away from himself as quickly as possible.

"Oh. Nothing new here. But things are a little … complicated over at your dad's."

"Yeah, big surprise."

"Your brother got into a little scrape."

"What *now*?"

"Well, he had to go back to the hospital. He had a girlfriend, a young woman with a baby—"

"Oh, my God."

"Now just, shhh. It was fine, it was good for him for a while. Your father was supervising things—"

"How long can he supervise a grown man?"

"—if you would just let me *finish*, Mack! There was a breakup and Ricky had a little … breakdown. Incident. He was yelling in the street and broke a streetlight. Police came and he was put on a psychiatric hold for a while, but they released him back to your dad."

"What does Dad say about this?"

"He said it's a bonding issue. Or a trust issue? And that Ricky just needs stability and affirmation right now."

"Yeah, well, Dad is going to get burned out one of these

days. It's already killed his marriage."

"You can't pinpoint it to just one thing, son." She clutched her hands together. "Life is complicated."

"I *know* that." She thought he was still a baby. Was there nothing he could do to be seen as an adult? "I've seen some things in life, you know."

"I know you *think* you have. But you don't know what it is to have to compromise your ideals, sometimes, when you grow up. There's no way to explain—"

"Nope. I will never *compromise*." Now he was truly sorry he had come back. His sad mother, his pathetic father and brother. They were all failures, all broken, the whole lot of them.

She looked at him sorrowfully. "Well, son, I hope that things turn out the way you want."

"Yeah? Well, I don't know what I want." He sighed and turned his back to her, secretly hoping she would put her arms around him.

But she didn't. They sat in silence some moments.

"Did you see my daffodils?" she asked timidly.

"*No.*"

"I really need to prune back my forsythia."

"Is that your way of saying you want me to do some yard work?" He smiled at her. Actually, he wanted to. He wanted to be here, but not to talk. Yet.

"Not this instant, but it would be nice if you would." She went to the kitchen and started rattling around. "Do you at least want a snack?"

"Maybe."

"I made some cookies. I was going to take them to bridge club but you can have some, I'll make more."

"Thanks, Mom."

"The girls have been asking about you. Evelyn had her

grandbaby. A little girl."

"That's nice."

By the time she had brought him his plate of cookies and glass of milk, things had loosened between them in the ease of gossip and small talk.

"Have you seen the news about Elizabeth's mother?"

His eyes snapped up. "What?"

"They're bringing her back in."

"Why?"

"Word is, they think she's guilty."

"Well, that's *bullshit*."

His mother looked at him, startled. "Well, *I'm* not the one who claimed it. But it's just all looking kind of strange, isn't it? First the no birth certificate, no identification of any kind for the girl. Now they're following this trail of bizarre stuff—"

"But what *happened?*"

She stopped and looked at him, lips compressed. "If you will just give me a minute, I'll tell you. Evidently, the mother had recently gotten some false documents made through some strange man in the city with a shady past. He was some kind of fugitive, now he's a college professor. Anyway, it looks as though she was getting ready to take the child and flee."

"But maybe someone threatened them. There must have been a reason. How does this make her into the bad guy?"

"Nobody is saying that. Exactly. There just seem to be more and more threads to this story, and the woman is never straight with anyone about anything."

"So?"

"*So.* She's under a lot of scrutiny right now. Let's just say I don't think she'll be leaving town anytime soon."

"Well, I think it's ridiculous." He looked out the

window to a clear blue sky. Telephone wires with birds on them. He felt righteous anger imagining their harassment of Mrs. Gray.

"Oh, Mack. I keep forgetting you knew her when you were a little boy. Of course you think well of your friend's mother. Honestly, I think you're still shaken up by Elizabeth's death. You just haven't been the same since."

"It's not just me being sentimental. Her mom didn't do it, period. Let's drop the whole thing, please."

They sat in tense silence for a few moments. The unfinished cookies sat on their plate; the milk growing warm and leaving a ring on the table. His mother put a coaster under it in one swift, silent motion. Mack had lost his appetite.

"Some things came in the mail for you," his mother said, adding with a glimmer, "one thing in particular I think you'll be glad to see."

"What?" he asked absently. Money from his grandparents? His birthday wasn't until next month.

But his mother brought him a large, fat envelope. In its corner was the insignia of Cleaver College.

"When did this come?"

"On Friday, I think."

It had been the one place he had applied to after the other had rejected him. The one school with no admission deadline. He tore the envelope open.

"They accepted me," he said, a slow smile spreading across his face.

"That's great, hon! I knew you could do it! You'll be a college boy before you know it!"

His smile faded a bit. "I still don't know if I'm going to say yes, though."

"Why ever *not*? It's a fine school."

"I didn't apply in time for financial aid."

"Work that out with your father. You know he owes you."

"For what?"

She shrugged. "Not being there for you. Ricky takes up all his time. I know he feels guilty about that. I think he would give you whatever help you needed."

"I don't want his help. I can't stand to even be around him!"

"Mack! He's your father!"

"Just— Mom, I haven't made a decision yet."

"But what else will you *do*?"

Mack didn't answer. He tried to imagine the next autumn and couldn't picture anything at all. He had the feeling he would just fall over a cliff into oblivion.

"I don't know. I was thinking about going back to the road crew."

"*Mack!* For a living?"

"Never mind. I can see how this conversation is going." He shoved a cookie into his mouth, swallowed so fast he almost choked. "But, hey, why didn't you tell me when the envelope came?"

She gave him a hurt look. "Well, I didn't think you wanted to hear from me."

"I would want to know something if it's this important, Mom!"

"I ..." Now she ducked her head and looked up at him through lowered eyelids, almost flirtatiously. "I was just waiting for you to come back, so I could surprise you. And I *knew* you were coming back."

"Oh yeah? How?" He became a bit nervous. He couldn't always shake his childhood belief that his mother could read his mind. "You can't fool me, I know exactly what you're thinking," she would often say to him, triumphantly, when he was a little boy and had tried to pull something over on her and got caught.

She smiled at him. "Oh, you know. Just a mother's ways. But then you've always been like that. You were never the type of boy to walk away from something without seeing it through to the end."

WHERE ARE YOU NOW

Vanessa paused in the hallway at school to read the text on her phone. She had given Flash her number, true, but she was still surprised to see that he had contacted her.

At school. Where r u?

A long pause, and then, JUST WOKE UP. U COMIN 2 THE PARTY SATURDAY?

She waved her friends along, and they headed to lunch without her.

I might be.

MIGHT?!

Yeah I'll be there

She had just seen them all the other night. Not at The Brambles, but at the little ramshackle house on the edge of town that they used as their clubhouse. She had taken a pill before she went riding with them, riding on the back of Flash's bike. The two things together, the drug and the motorcycle ride, had been a transcendent experience. The sense-memories of it made her feel blissful even now, in this crowded hallway of private school kids who were talking about trips abroad and lacrosse teams and kegger parties; they could never know what true joy really was. But *she* knew.

She remembered what it was like to feel that speed and velocity mixed with the luminous melting feeling in her nerve endings that the drug had given her. It had made her feel one with the road, the fleecy sky, and her own surging youth and aliveness. All was one. Everything.

On that bike, she felt multidimensional, connected to other times and places. For periods of their ride into the countryside she felt like a Viking goddess, on the prow of a great ship sailing into the ocean wind, the gruff hairy men around her worshipful warriors. They were sailing in a flotilla into strange new lands that they would conquer, and it was all balanced upon her grace and will and strength. She'd held her head regally as her long blonde hair had blown in the wind …

BETTER BE THERE!! C U BABY GIRL

She smiled and slid her phone back into the pocket of her khaki uniform skirt. What am I doing, she thought to herself for what felt like a thousandth time. If anyone here even knew, what would they think of me?

What do *I* think of me anymore?

She wasn't sure. She knew the things she had done. And she knew that she enjoyed them. Well, *some* of them. In the beginning, she had been playing a role. Projecting a false image, to get these men to trust her. But now it seemed she had played the role so well that she was *becoming* it.

She had taken drugs. Serious drugs. And wasn't ashamed, and she looked forward to doing it again. But she had made a promise to herself that she would not fill her prescription. She would not do it when she was not *on the job*.

Oh, but then, at times like this, going about her normal everyday life, she felt so dull and drained of color. She felt a bedraggled thing, washed up on a rocky shore. She longed to fly and be free again.

In the outside pocket of her backpack, was a neatly folded white cotton handkerchief. Embroidered lightly on the sides in an almost Greco Roman design, that reminded her of the moldings on the walls at The Brambles. And there were initials stitched in one corner. *JD.*

It had been Bobo who had given her the handkerchief, after their ride. Her hair had been wild, her face stung red from the whipping wind. Her mascara in rivulets down her face, but it wasn't from the wind. She had been so moved by the beauty and wildness of the day, their Viking voyage on endless phantom seas, that she felt overwhelmed and could only quietly cry in a corner while the guys sat around the scarred old kitchen table talking business. To her, they looked like ruffian warriors of old, not drinking beer and playing poker but gulping mead from carved horns, counting their pillage …

"Hey," Bobo had said, quietly on his way back from the fridge. "I see you crying. Why don't you take this?"

When he handed her the neatly folded handkerchief, she was so confused that all she could do was laugh.

"Hey, it's no joke. I got a bunch of these when I was young. From my godmother. I carry one everywhere. They're sharp as shit."

"For … real?"

Bobo looked at her, unsmiling, but with amusement twinkling in his eyes. His reddish beard was slightly patchy high on his cheeks. She wondered what his real name was.

"For real. You take that, now. You look like a girl who could use a handkerchief."

"Why?"

"Because you're the kind of person who feels a lot."

She touched the delicate edge of the handkerchief now;

so odd, so unexpected that this was kept in the snap pocket of Bobo's oil stained, patch-covered denim vest. It went to show, she thought, that you never knew when you would discover the unexpected in people.

Vanessa took out her phone and texted Mack.

R U still living there?

He didn't answer at first. She thought maybe he was in class, but then:

Yea

Will you be at the party?

Yea

Me 2.

The hall was empty now, all the students in the cafeteria or sprawled outside on the stone steps. Next, she texted Lillian.

U going 2 the party 2morrow?

This one came instantaneously, as though she had been watching and waiting:

YES

Lil looked across the lunch table at Mack. She put her phone back into her pocket and smiled.

"Speak of the devil. That was Vanessa. Looks like we're all on for tomorrow night."

Mack looked up from his Styrofoam plate of spaghetti and meatballs, which he had been shoveling quickly into his mouth. "Why are you looking at me like that?"

"Because I want to get this motherfucker once and for all."

"Don't curse."

She laughed at him, then saw he was in earnest.

"Why not?"

"Because it's not you, Lil. Come on."

"Well, there's a lot you don't know about me, Mack Mackenzie."

John opened the French doors and stepped onto the balcony, enjoying the feel of the cool air on this fresh spring morning; he was always the first in the house to awake, six a.m. sharp, and it was his favorite time of day.

The sloping back lawn was already shaggy. The ornamental trees along its borders used to make the area look park-like, but now they were overgrown. The boughs of the trees needed trimming, many of them heavy and dragging down to the ground. Oh well. From where he was standing he could enjoy his view of the Japanese cherry blossom, and the way its petals blew in the breeze like confetti or rice at a wedding. The sight always made him feel celebratory.

And he *should* feel celebratory, he thought. There was a lot to feel glad about, these days. Things were finally going just the way he wanted them to, instead of the way someone *else* wanted them to be, which was the way it had been all his life. Until now.

It was mornings like this that he could truly appreciate the beauty around him. The majesty of The Brambles. And it made it all the better to realize, truly and deeply, that he was the one who had willed this, willed it all.

He hated to even think anymore about some of the places he had lived before. The old rackety wood-framed house with the dirt yard of his boyhood, mangy dog tied to a tree running in circles. His dad had been a salesman, always on the road, until the day he stopped coming home. His mother was a damn whore, truth be told, taking strange men into the back room. John always knew, even back then, that he was destined for greater things once he left that place.

It depressed him to think about the seminary, and the

cramped and threadbare quarters he'd lived in when he was a priest. Or the halfway house with those filthy squalid men. He didn't mind prison, compared to these places. At least in prison, he had a following of people who felt real to him, for once. The prisoners respected him more than the people in his clergy. He knew his power there. He knew who to be friends with, and how to get favors. He almost hated to leave and go back to "real life." (How he hated that term. Life was never real, not to him.)

But then, by fate, he had found The Brambles. That piece of trash loser guy had led him there. Martin. John had just been released with only his wallet and the clothes on his back. He'd followed Martin, another released prisoner. Martin, a loser and a weakling, a non-entity in the prison; John at first thought he'd mug and rob him, just because he could. But he thought better of it. He followed his intuition, which told him, watch. *Wait.*

His intuition had been correct. It led him to Mitch, and The Brambles, and the richest life he had ever lived. Of course John knew his good fortune. Of course!

The only thing was, he wished he did not need Flash and Honeybear like he did. He knew he was better than them. Smarter. More evolved. *Special.* He had needed those two in the beginning. He had called them as soon as he was settled in with Mitch. They had done well together over the years. Done lots of favors for each other. But now he wished they were gone.

He drank deeply from his mug of coffee. *Damn,* there were grounds at the bottom! He spat them out with an angry hawking noise, tossed the rest of the coffee off the balcony, then threw the mug after it. It made a tinkly *crash* as it landed on the back patio, and the sound made him feel a little better. Then he promptly forgot about it and went back to his reverie.

Yes, it would be so ideal if it were only him running the show. He was sick of the other two. He would especially like to murder that annoying Honeybear. He hated his levity and his unfunny jokes. Honeybear's glibness made him feel disrespected in some deep way he couldn't name. It was as though he didn't take John or The Brambles or the genius of the whole operation seriously. And he knew Honeybear made fun of his sermons. As though the Ministry of Presence was the biggest joke of all. Well, the joke would be on that motherfucker if one day John took it into his mind to cut his throat with a piano wire. Because the Ministry was *no joke*. John never felt more alive, more holy, than when he communed with and saved those poor bedraggled souls who sat in the ballroom to watch his sermons.

And as for Flash, the guy was a dirtbag who had far too much power allotted to him. John was afraid of him, he had to admit deep in his gut. Because Flash, in all of his pill-popping, bug-eyed craziness, was capable of anything. With that droopy mustache and burning, mirthless eyes, he reminded John of a painting he had seen of Vlad the Impaler. John wouldn't cross him because he *couldn't* cross him. The unfairness of it all made him sick.

Oh, well. To be honest, the person he most liked being around was Mitch. Mitch was special in the same way that *he* was, or else he wouldn't have been so famous back in the day, and gotten so rich. Mitch was on his level. But Mitch didn't question him or talk back. And for that, especially, he actually loved the man.

In fact, he knew it would cheer him right now to go look in on Mitch. So he went back inside and into the bedroom next door, where Mitch lay asleep in bed, one arm strapped to the headboard. Honeybear had had to restrain him because lately Mitch had been wandering, trying to get out the door and to the stairwell without his wheelchair.

He had even pulled the IV out, and had ended up tearing the tender skin by ripping off the tape; he'd left smears of blood on the wall where he'd tried to steady himself, and John had scrubbed them away with a sponge all by himself.

Now Mitch was asleep, his face turned to the side so you could see how handsome his profile really *was*. He looked like a different person when asleep. Like this, he still resembled a matinee idol, and it made John feel proud. It even made him feel a little sorry for him; the way his hand was secured by the restraint couldn't be comfortable.

But he loved Mitch, and it was for the best. He would do *anything* to keep him safe, and he had everything he needed, so why would he want to leave, anyway? He remembered that time one of Mitch's no-good kids came to the door looking for him. "Patrick." John sized him up right away. West Coast, tan skinned, white teeth. Not terribly tall, but obvious that he worked out. Just in his early thirties, and obviously he was the type who had it all in life. Camelhair overcoat. He spoke with a kind of ease and largesse that seriously rankled John for some reason.

"How do I know you're really Mitch's son?" he had asked, remaining two steps up on the stairwell so he could look down at him; the kid didn't even look like Mitch. Weak chin, slightly jowly already.

The kid held up his driver's license, asked to be allowed in, sounded oh-so-reasonable and well-spoken and *patient*. So John had to get two of The Horsemen to escort him right back out the door and back into his car, a rental Audi. "And you stay the fuck away, your father doesn't want to see you, now or ever!"

Well, why should he? Where had his kids been all these years? Probably just wanted something out of Mitch. At least, that's how John *explained* it to Mitch. And John wanted to protect him (Mitch got too emotional sometimes for his own good), so he never told him about his son's visit or the letters that came in the mail. There was no need for him to know.

John gave Mitch a kiss on the temple, so light as to not wake him. "I love you, brother," he whispered, then quietly exited the room and went back into his own.

Need to shave, he said to himself, looking into the mirror in his small private bathroom. But other than that, he didn't look too bad. His mother had always told him that his blue eyes were his best feature. "You have the eyes of a movie star," she had said. Even though she was a whore, she did love him best of all of the brothers. She told him so. She was dead now. He occasionally thought about her. But not so that it troubled him.

He drew himself up, held back his bathrobe and looked at his body, standing to this side and that; not bad. Underneath he wore what he slept in, sweatpants and his favorite Che Guevara t-shirt. But even so, he looked good. His stomach was larger than it had once been, but his chest and arms were still massive. He visited the basement gym and lifted every day and it paid off. Here he was pushing seventy and he could still kick Mitch's son's pansy ass if he wanted to.

He finished shaving and changed his clothes, choosing an Arrow shirt that had just come back from the dry cleaners, a pressed pair of black jeans and his pointy-toed, hand-tooled English leather boots. It had been Mitch who turned him onto these shoes, and he couldn't go back to anything different. They made him feel like a king.

He went back onto the balcony where he sat on a raffia chair and had his first cigarette of the day. In his mind, he went over his day's agenda. He would go into town, stop by the bank to cash a check Mitch had written, then the market and the liquor store. Everyone was coming over again tonight. Which was just as well. He could use a little fun. It had upset him to learn that Sapphire had left, back to her mother's place, he knew. She hadn't even warned him after he had let her live there, her own bedroom and everything, all those years. Ungrateful. His own daughter! Oh well. She'd never truly felt like his daughter, anyway. She wasn't bright enough. She wasn't a *thinker* like he was. And she was a junkie to boot. He hated junkies.

It made him feel better to know that Lillian would be at the party that night. She had told him so, and he believed her, though she looked a little quiet and strained by the end of their nature walk the other day. She had said she felt a migraine starting. He told her he could give her a pill for that, but the girl had declined, so he merely kissed her on the forehead in a fatherly way and told her to go home and sleep it off.

Oh, Lillian. Now there was a good, proper girl. A real girl. Pleasant, respectful, eager to learn and be taught. But that wasn't all. There was a real depth to her, too. A real intellectual curiosity. They felt so natural together. If Flash or Honeybear even tried to lay a finger on what was *HIS* …

He smoked a filterless, French tobacco, Gauloises. Richer and darker than American cigarettes. These he kept to himself and did not share. He liked the way they scorched his lungs and made him feel slightly giddy on the exhale.

He wondered if it had been foolhardy to take Lillian to

the tree. He didn't know why he'd been compelled to do it. It was as though he couldn't help himself. The memory of Elizabeth comingled with the anticipation of what was to come with Lil was just too delicious to him. And truth be told, it made him a little afraid, to take her there. The daring of it, though, was like jumping off a ledge that he knew was too high up, but instead of breaking his bones, he landed on his feet, breathless and exhilarated, looking up at the great height in wonder.

But didn't that describe his whole life?

Elizabeth. The whole thing was unfortunate, in a way. But it depended on how you looked at it. She was his daughter, in a much more *real* way than Sapphire ever was. He *deserved* to possess her completely. She just didn't realize that this was a good thing. He was nothing but a benefit to that poor girl! And things went very well, for a while. They had had some really good and gentle times together.

The problem was that there came a day when Elizabeth lost her faith in him. Lost her *trust.* She began looking at him differently, almost slantwise, as if she observed something about him only she could see. A couple of times he even saw a flash of repugnance on his daughter's perfect young face, while looking at him! Her *father!*

And that time he tried to kiss and caress her, and she misunderstood. She didn't understand that his intentions were pure. She thought that he was a *repugnant,* dirty old man, and then she started to avoid him. And then she had the gall to try to break it off entirely with him. And that's when things went very wrong and came to the unfortunate conclusion that they had.

It wasn't his fault that things had to be that way.

But the funny thing was, killing Elizabeth had been an

almost holy rite for him. Like giving communion, or conferring a blessing. And it had changed his life. She lost *her* life, which wasn't worth much anyway, and in doing so, made him *more* alive than he had ever been. And he loved her for that.

Oh, that last day when he and Elizabeth arranged to meet down at the creek. A warm sunny day in autumn that still felt like summer. The leaves in the woods just beginning to change. He knew something was different by the way she stood on her side of the bank, just *looking* at him. She stood tall and straight and looked at him steadily, with no shine or glimmer in her eye at all. With her dark hair and dark eyebrows, she resembled an Indian maiden who was considering whether to take out her bow and shoot.

"Ahoy, Pocahontas," he had called jokingly, holding one palm up and making a droll face. But she did not even smile. And she kept her shoes on; usually it was she who removed her shoes and crossed the water to him. Damned if he was going to be the one to do it.

"Are you coming over or not?" he asked, lightly, with a friendly tilt of the head.

"I don't think so," Elizabeth said.

"And why not?"

Another of those long, level stares. "You know why."

John felt stung, as though she had indeed taken an arrow from her quiver and shot him straight through the chest! He felt hurt. And then he felt mad. But it was a slow building anger, like putting his foot on the gas pedal, and depressing it, little by little. The burn and throttle of it thrilled him just a little bit.

"I don't know what it is you think happened," he said, in a kind, sympathetic voice. "But it didn't."

For some time they remained on opposite banks, talking back and forth. John explained that he loved her, as a father would. That he missed his own children and that his relationship with Elizabeth was very dear to him. But she remained unmoved. She said that while she had enjoyed their time together, something about it made her uncomfortable, and she didn't know why.

"Maybe what's making you uncomfortable is something inside *yourself*," he said solemnly. "You think that the problem is me, but it's not. You're projecting something that's not real."

"I don't think so," she said and had the gall to play around, to gather up stones and practice skipping them across the deep part of the creek. The insolence! He felt his foot press the pedal another millimeter…

He put his head down and sighed. "Maybe you're right," he said. "Maybe I am a bad person. I've just been tricking myself."

She said nothing, but her movements slowed, became more absentminded. As though she were actually listening.

"People always told me when I was growing up that I was a bad person. I wanted to prove them wrong. But maybe I was fooling myself all along. I used to … do drugs. Drink a lot. I did some things I'm not proud of. But I tried really hard to …"

He shrugged, and looked up at the branches, swaying in a breeze so faint that the movement was all that gave it away.

"… to turn myself around. I grew up. I found religion. I tried my best to help other people, as much as I could. But I guess deep down it's all a sham."

The girl was still now, though she didn't look at him.

"I think it all comes from the fact that I didn't have a

mother. Never knew her. She died in childbirth. I guess it just made me damaged." He walked to the very edge of the creek, just barely getting his toes wet.

Elizabeth had looked up at him when he said the word *mother*, and now she watched him, her lips slightly parted in thought.

"So I want to apologize to you, Elizabeth, if I did anything to make you uncomfortable. I guess you can say I'm a needy person. And I should never have tried to put such weight on the shoulders of a mere child—"

"But I'm not a child."

He smiled fondly, regretfully. Raised his hand as though to say goodbye.

"I'll leave you now before I cause any more harm I think it is time for some self-reflecting. Alone. So I guess this will be the last we see of each other."

There was a slightly wounded look in the girl's dark eyes. Precisely what he'd been going for.

"You aren't *that* bad," she murmured.

He laughed sadly. "You don't know the half of it, child."

"You were just trying to find a friend, John, that's all."

"I should find more appropriate ones." His bottom lip trembled a bit. "I should have known better, considering your youth and everything … but it's just that you are so different from *other people your age.*"

The girl looked down and smiled shyly. He thought he saw a bit of a flush in her cheeks.

He paced back and forth a bit, as though thinking. Then wheeled toward her. "I'll tell you what."

She looked back up at him, still half-smiling.

"Why don't you come up to my place one last time?"

She stopped smiling.

"Just to say goodbye? I just want it to be special. Because you have been a good friend to me and have shown me so much, Elizabeth."

She didn't answer. But her hesitance showed in the softening of her expression and drove him to press on.

"Just come to the back patio with me. We don't even have to go inside. I want to drink a toast to us. I have a really good bottle of Chenin Blanc. *French*?"

She looked up at him and smiled at his earnestness.

"Okay, I know you're under twenty-one, but one glass won't hurt you. I want to teach you about wine. Because I know that you are smart and sophisticated, and when you grow up you should know how to order."

"I don't know if I'll like it."

"Sure you will. It's very light. It's like apple juice. I was saving it for you."

She sighed. "I guess so. My mom won't even have to know because she's out."

"Out?" He tilted his head to the side, like a bird that had spotted a shiny object.

Elizabeth's face went back to looking guarded. "I mean, she'll be back really soon."

"Right. We won't be long, anyway. She can just call you, right?"

"Yeah, I have my phone."

"Well then." He held an arm out to her, though he didn't move any closer; Elizabeth was wearing a long, crushed velvet skirt in a green so dark that it looked almost black. The green flashed in the patches of sun, like the shell of a beetle. She lifted it up so the hem wouldn't get into the water.

"Don't you want to take those shoes off?"

"No, I can do it," She carefully balanced, going from

rock to rock, in her black ballet flats. At last, when she got close enough, John reached over and took her by the hand.

"There, there you go ... Oops! There goes your hem!"

"It's okay, I'll wring it out."

"Why do you wear such long skirts, anyway?"

"Makes it easier to bicycle."

He laughed at this fondly and gave her a little kiss on the forehead.

Elizabeth pulled back at him and shot him a look. "Don't kiss me."

John blinked at her, stunned by her abruptness. "I wasn't—"

"You know I don't like that."

"I was merely showing you how fond I am ..."

She gazed at him, her brow lowered, her face dark and heavy with anger like a storm cloud. John saw something in her face he hadn't seen before. He saw *himself*. This young girl could be just as formidable as he could! Her look, the way she had her arms crossed high on her chest. The silent beat before the predator struck out. She reminded him of himself the moment before he tore someone apart.

Words faltered on his tongue, he shifted on his feet. How dare she make him feel not only ashamed but also afraid? He cleared his throat. "I'm sorry, Elizabeth."

"I've heard that before. Now I'm leaving. 'Bye."

"But you're already across the creek. You've already gotten wet. At least let me pour you that glass of white. We'll sit on the patio and maybe we'll see the sun start to set."

She sighed. He didn't think she would budge. He'd ruined it.

"*OK*, John."

"You'll come?"

"Yes. But honestly, if you touch me again, I'll leave."

He nodded in a courtly way and motioned for her to follow him. Jesus Christ. What had *happened* to the girl? Turning on a dime like that! She had been so sweet and obliging before. She used to trust him. Had someone else influenced her? Had she been watching some goddamn feminist talk show or something?

He kept his head raised high in a dignified manner and did not move near her. "You can keep all the books I gave you."

She looked at him, confused.

"You know. The Burroughs. The Ferlinghetti poems. Those meant a lot to me. But I would love it if you kept them to remember me by."

Elizabeth nodded at him. But she did not even say thank you. Anger flared again in him silently, the pedal edging down just a little more.

He walked a bit faster now, sweating in the heat of the afternoon, the leaves at the very tops of the trees turning autumnal red and yellow and orange, blazing against the perfect blue sky.

"It's beautiful, isn't it?" He said, gesturing up.

"What is?"

"Fall. Early fall. My favorite times of year are the in-between times."

This did draw her interest. "Me too. Like, I love it when it's spring but not quite. I love seeing snow on the daffodils."

"Aw, you're painting a picture for me in my mind," he said, dreamily. "Very evocative. I know *exactly* what you mean. Times between seasons! Like years between decades. Though you might be too young to have experienced that."

"I can imagine it, though," she said quickly.

"We're more alike than you think," he said with a smile.

Nearer to The Brambles, the path became narrow and choked, as it always did. John held aside branches for her and helped her get her green velvet skirt unstuck from the pricklers.

"I'm afraid you'll get a little tear," he said. "That would be a shame. Your long skirts make you look like a queen."

"I get them at the art festival when it comes to town. It's handmade."

"Then your clothes are as unique as you are!"

But she had stopped remarking, or blushing, or showing pleasure. She was acting like a stony-faced *bitch* again, John thought, clenching his teeth though he was still smiling.

At last they broke through to the edge of The Brambles' long, sloping back lawn, still impressive even though crabgrass and dandelion had invaded long ago. And the grass now ankle high and tickled when they walked.

John was a bit out of breath now. With a stab, it hit him that he wasn't getting any younger.

"I don't even know who's up at the house. We were all up pretty late last night, so they might even be just waking up. No one will bother us, though. No one will even know we're there."

"I don't care if they do."

He didn't know what to say to this; they continued walking, and the back of The Brambles loomed closer and closer. From far away, it was still impressive. John almost felt tears as he tried to imagine the greatness of the place through this poor, silly girl's eyes.

"It is incredible, isn't it?"

She didn't answer, as he gestured grandly with his

hands. "Sometimes I can't believe my own good luck in living here. It was built, I thought, in the 1890s? By some kind of mail-order magnate? Imagine it back then with a full house staff, carriages rolling up to the front door … pretty wild stuff."

Elizabeth nodded. "Wild."

"And I can just imagine you, Elizabeth, as a guest back then. The way you wear your hair pulled up in a bun with the curly tendrils, and your long skirts, you would fit right in at the grand lawn party of 1896!" They reached the flagstone patio, and he pulled out one of the heavy iron chairs so that she could sit at the heavy glass table. "You have that look about you, you know. You could be a Gibson girl."

"I saw pictures of Gibson girls in my history book."

"You resemble one. Except for the corset."

She glanced up at him, a flash of embarrassment in her eyes.

He motioned about his own waist and protruding stomach. "Corsets were so tight back then, they'd crush a lady's internal organs. Make you faint dead away in the name of beauty. Aren't you lucky you never had to endure that?"

"Yeah. I guess."

"But ladies rode bicycles back then. At least there's that."

John found that he was chattering longwindedly. And saying nothing, really. At least the girl was seated at the table. The heavy iron chairs and table. If she were already sitting down, she surely would stay, wouldn't she?

"You sit here, I'll go in and get the drinks."

He went in through one of the French doors, crossed the games room through to the enormous kitchen. Gorgeous copper pans and pots hung from racks, but they looked so dusty because no one here ever cooked. They always ordered take-out. He would polish them later.

He opened the refrigerator, empty except for some old looking milk, leftover Chinese food, and the bottle of Chenin Blanc. Simonsig. The bottle was a pale, luminous green, like the grapes it came from. He enjoyed the cool heavy weight of it in his hand.

Next, he rummaged through the cabinet for two of the heavy red glass goblets he liked to use. They had a raised pattern of stud-like designs on the outside, and intricate, floral-and-vine stems.

Corkscrew. He could never find the goddamn thing when he needed it, and he needed it fast, he was so afraid that the girl was going to change her mind and leave if he took too long. So many junk-filled drawers in this filthy place. Bunch of animals live here who don't put things back where they belonged.

He noticed, with distaste, that his hands trembled as they scurried about. Large, muscular hands, sure. But riddled with veins, covered in speckles of liver spots. He was aging well, he thought, except for the hands. They looked like his grandfather's. And sometimes they did feel stiff from arthritis.

Damn it to hell! he thought. He wouldn't look like a fool who couldn't open his own fancy wine bottle. Was it someplace he was overlooking? Had he by any chance gone senile and not noticed? He forgot things more and more. Maybe others here had noticed but were not telling him. Maybe they even laughed at him behind his back. He slammed the drawer shut with a curse.

But then, he saw it. On the counter next to the wine rack, a rack that was always empty because all the pigs here drank so greedily. It was a wonder no one had touched the Chenin Blanc. He would have killed someone if they had.

Easy. *Easy.* He tried to keep his hands still as he turned the screw and pulled out the cork with a *pop.* Didn't know why he was shaking so goddamn bad. He filled the two glasses and put the wine back.

After considering what he was doing for only a moment, he reached up to one of the high shelves where there was a cookie jar shaped like a baby elephant holding a red-and-white striped ball. Goddamn ridiculous thing belonged to Mitch. But this was where John kept a few roofies in case he ever needed one. He didn't think anything, really, as he shook out one small white pill from the bottle and dropped it into one of the drinks. His nervous system automatically felt calmer as he watched the pill sink down into the wine, tinged red now by the glass.

If he tilted his head right, looking through the kitchen window, he could just see the girl, sitting on the patio, looking dreamily out toward the woods at the end of the lawn, from which they had just come.

Almost languidly, he came out again, holding the glasses.

"Here, you are, young lady. I hope I didn't keep you waiting too long." He rolled his eyes. "Couldn't find the bottle opener. 'Til I saw it right where I left it before! That's aging, I guess."

He set the glass before her, then sat down.

"Cheers, then? To us?"

Elizabeth was looking down at the screen of her phone; she typed something in, then when finished, nodded, and held up her glass, clinking it against his. John watched carefully as she took her first sip.

"Ha ha! Nice face. You think it's bad?"

"I don't know what I think of it."

"Oh, that's just because it's your first sip of wine. Believe me, you'll get used to it. And even acquire a taste for it. I think you will have a taste for *all* the good things in life. I mean, I didn't always. I had nothing when I was a boy. Now I have everything I could possibly need or imagine. And you know what?" He leaned forward conspiratorially. "It's *great*."

This inspired Elizabeth to smile, the tiniest bit.

"This bottle of wine cost me seventy dollars, but it's nothing to me. Because I wanted you to taste the good stuff."

She dutifully took another long sip.

"So, what are your plans in life, Elizabeth? You never mentioned college."

"I will go to college. Just not now."

He looked at her keenly. "You know what I think? You don't need it either way. You'll find your path no matter what. Because you're special."

"My mother wants me to go, though."

"Was that her you were texting just then?"

"Yes."

"So how does that work, being homeschooled?" The wine was already relaxing him. It was delicious and tart. It tasted of peaches on his tongue.

"I'm not sure, exactly. But she says she'll work it out. She went to college, and grad school and everything."

"Sounds like a smart woman, your mother."

"Yeah. She was an environmental scientist. Still is. She sold her business, though. To pursue her own stuff." She was smiling a bit proudly, John noticed, annoyed.

"So what will you do in the time being?"

"My mother is talking about traveling."

"Oh. Gap year, huh? Trip to Europe?"

"I don't know. She's talking about living somewhere else for a while."

"Moving *away?*" His eyes fixed on her, slightly widened.

"Yep."

"Permanently?"

"I think so, yeah. If we decide to." She took another sip, and this time did not make a face.

"And how do you feel about this?"

She thought for a moment, then said, "Happy."

"Why?"

"Why not? I keep telling her I want to move to New York. That's the place I love best. We make trips into the city for museums and plays and stuff and it's my favorite thing *ever*—"

The girl's eyes lit up, and she looked alive in a way John was not accustomed to seeing her. As she prattled on about Soho and her favorite Cuban restaurant, he fumed inwardly. The woman who had stolen her, this woman who wasn't even Elizabeth's parent, had made the decision to take her away? Impudent little bitch. He had seen her from afar, with her haughty hatchet face and long gray hair like a witch. With her Ph.D. and environmental business or whatever. Probably sanctimonious as hell.

"But Elizabeth, are you sure this is best? This is your home."

"Well, you keep telling me to expand my horizons, right?"

He said nothing. She wasn't drinking fast enough. Too much talking.

"Well. Anyway. I was going to teach you about wine,

wasn't I? Now, I want you to take a big gulp and swish it around in your mouth like this …"

The nerve of that bitch, taking his daughter away.

"Now, after you swallow, think about the flavors you were able to taste."

She swallowed, then paused. "It tasted like fruit."

"Yes. You could taste apple. And orange …"

"And peach."

"Very good. But could you taste the flavors underneath? The oak flavors, from aging?"

"You mean like the *wood?*

"Yes. Something like that. Flavors that give it complexity. Almost like popcorn."

"What?"

"Take another mouthful and see what emerges. There's more than you realize."

She took a sip, holding it in her mouth thoughtfully before swallowing. "I can taste nectar."

"Nectar?"

"Like eating honeysuckle."

"Well, that's a different take!"

"I'm a hummingbird!" She said this loudly, suddenly, with a goofy grin on her face.

John smiled, looking at her closely. "You don't say!"

"Look at my wings going so fast they're invisible!"

"I always knew you were more bird than girl!" Wow, it was hitting her so suddenly.

"I feel like I'm vibrating."

"Did you taste anything else?"

"I don't know. Something strange. Slightly bitter."

"Did it remind you of anything?"

"Nothing. Just aspirin or something, I don't know …" her words were slightly slurred.

He took a sip of his own drink. Crisp and delicious. "So tell me, Elizabeth—"

"I *said* I'm a hummingbird."

"So tell me, hummingbird, what does your *father* think of your plans to move away?"

She rolled her head around and around, languidly, looking up at the sky. Then finally, "I don't see him."

"Isn't that kind of strange?"

"No. My parents are divorced. What's so strange about that?" She listed a bit to the side, arms outstretched.

"It's just odd never to see him at all. Doesn't he care about you?"

"I don't know …"

"Well, he sounds like a real asshole."

She made a humming, burring sound with her lips.

"Are you listening to me, Elizabeth? I think it's a goddamn shame if a father does not have the decency to care about his child."

She looked at him; though her eyes had glazed over in a drugged torpor, a spark of anger showed through; it was Elizabeth's clear daytime self, still emerging as though looking at him up through murky water. "It is not a shame if I never knew my father. I told you, we don't need him! DON'T NEED HIM!"

Her impertinence was truly pissing him off, but he intentionally softened his face and voice. "I'm sorry. I just care about you, that's all."

"Well, I don't need you or your caring, either." But her attention was caught by something up in the air. "Look," she said softly, "at those chemtrails in the sky. It almost looks like a design."

John glanced up. "Just looks like random streaks to me."

"What do you think they break up into? What do they become when they dissolve, I wonder…" her voice trailed off.

"Never mind all that! Let's finish our glasses! One-two-three GO!"

She swallowed the last of the wine, eyes on the sky the whole time. John just pretended to drink, his was already gone.

"Motion, in the sky, caught like a *brush mark*…" She slumped down in her chair as she said this, head lolling a bit more.

"You're a very pretty girl, you know that?"

"Yes."

He had expected her to feel flattered. Why did she not? "And you have a great mind for such a young girl."

"Yes, I do."

"Promise me one thing. Promise you'll never let others corrupt you."

She didn't answer.

"Did you hear me, Elizabeth? Keep the world *out*, and keep your integrity *in*."

"But I love the world."

"Well, that's just naïve. Be more vigilant. It's a corrupt place with small, bad people in it."

"Small and bad like *you*?"

This time he nearly stood up in rage. His hands had the urge to smash something. So he took his glass and smashed it on the flagstones.

"Ha ha!" he said after, "It's kind of a tradition to, uh, smash your glass after a good glass of wine."

"Huh?"

"Never mind. You're next. You finished? *Break the glass!*"

Bleary-eyed, she let the glass roll out of her fingers and onto the ground. It did not break.

"So, are you telling me, my dear, you are happy to leave this town?"

"I didn't ... I ..."

"You must hate it here."

"No. I love it."

"But you don't have anyone here. But me, right?"

"I have everyone. I know this town. I've watched it all my life. I watch the people here go about their lives every day. I know them all. I love them all. Just from afar ..."

"You feel okay, hon? You look a little peaked."

"The town doesn't know I watch them all. I keep them all in my head like a snow globe. Sometimes I think I am their secret guardian angel. Because I keep them all safe in my dreams at night. Sometimes I think I dreamed all of this. That I dreamed up *you*. That I'm dreaming right now ..."

"Would you like to lie down?"

"I feel light as oxygen. I'm here, but I'm other places, too."

John sat up tall and crossed his arms over his chest as he watched the girl's head slumping like a rag doll's.

"The things you are saying make no sense to me, Elizabeth. You kind of remind me of your mother."

"But you don't know my mother."

"Oh, but I do. Your real mother. Little meth head from the Ukraine? Pretty enough, but half her teeth rotting. She used to have all these odd sayings. Like 'a crow will never be a falcon.'"

"Huh? Wuh ..."

"A *crow* will never be a *falcon!*" He hawked this out in a high-pitched, Slavic accent. Elizabeth looked at him, stunned.

"I always wondered what the hell she meant by that, your mother. What do *you* think it means?"

She said nothing, leaning her arms heavily on the table, as though to press it down, to stop the world from reeling.

"I'm talking to you, girl!"

Fear in her eyes, just a glimmer. She was like a girl stuck in quicksand.

"Yeah, that's right. Your mother is not some stuck-up Ph.D. Your mother is a toothless whore. Mail-order slut! Not a brain in her head. Still listened to eighties hair metal because that was all she was exposed to. Black market cassette tapes. Bon Jovi. Can you imagine the ignorance?"

"I-I don't know...." Her voice sounded like a cassette tape itself, one that had been left in the sun and warped so that the sound was distorted.

"You're just as trashy as me, Elizabeth, if it's any consolation to you. So don't you dare look down on me!"

"I-I ..."

"What did you call me a minute ago? Small? And *bad?*"

"I don't ... feel right ..."

"Damn straight you don't feel right. You just let a small, bad man give you a drink of alcohol. Don't you know you shouldn't let strangers ply you with booze? What if there were something in it? Huh? See, you're not so smart."

"Take me home ..."

"You are home. Stop whining and face the music. This is all your fault."

Her face twisted in anguish. "I ... *hate you.*"

John smiled, baring his teeth, panting, and dog-like. If he had dog ears, they'd be flat against his head. "It really hurt my feelings, the way you treated me."

"What?"

"I tried to love you. And you just blew me off."

Her head was all the way down on the table now, her back hunched in a defenseless way. He almost pitied her.

"I tried to love you, and you wouldn't accept it. You made me feel like a dirty pervert, you know?"

She was motionless and silent.

"It's not right, you know? And this is all *your fault*. You did this to yourself."

He sighed, just watching her for some moments. Head down. She was *breathing*, her back rising and falling with long, ragged breaths. But she was *out*, for sure.

Time to act. He didn't want to bring her into the house. People were usually up by now, people might bother him.

He would take her to the woods, he thought. No one would see them there. And he could just leave her if he wanted. He didn't need her passed out in his room. Too much of a hassle.

He lifted her up from under her armpits and dragged her back, chair scraping. She made a couple of indistinct, muffled sounds as though murmuring in her sleep. Then he easily slipped one arm under her knees, one behind her back, and lifted her up. She was not heavy at all. Bird bones, just like her mother. Didn't come from him, that was for sure. John was built as solid as a black bear.

One of her ballet flats fell off her foot as he headed toward the woods. He jostled her until he was able to knock off the other one. He'd deal with them later.

It was still afternoon, but the sun had sunk a bit lower in the sky. Cicadas hummed, a strange, almost digital hum, like a machine whirring. No one at all was there, but John was tense, his mouth drawn in a straight, tight line as he made his way through the narrow, choked path.

A doe crashed through the brush in front of him, almost

mowing him down; John let out a little cry of surprise. *"Motherfucker!"* Scared the hell out of him. The thing had moved so fast, it had practically been a blur. There was an afterimage, though, burned on his retinas. The faint dusting of spots on its side. The black eye on the side of its head, that looked at him in oblique animal terror. "Jesus Christ," he muttered to himself, feeling foolish now to have been so startled by a dumb animal.

A little deeper, and then the creek. He couldn't balance with the girl's weight, so he went straight through the water. *Plunk, plunk, plunk.* There was a little turtle on the other side of the bank, and he came close to stepping on it in his haste. It seemed to John that his vision had changed. He could see everything around him in astonishing detail. Just as it was said of birds of prey. He saw the little wrinkled head of the turtle thrusting forward, its withered little legs scrambling to move his bulk forward. He saw the dash and whirl of tadpoles in a sunbeam down into the water. It was as if he was flying overhead from a great height, but could zoom in on anything he chose. Maybe Natasha was wrong. Maybe he *was* a falcon after all.

Just a little bit further, and he stopped. Listened. Looked all around him, and then he lay the girl down on the soft pine needles on the ground.

Her eyes slightly open, he could see the smallest sliver of the whites and the edge of the irises; they seemed to be scanning back and forth, though what could she possibly be seeing?

Her hair had come undone and was spread out around her head, like a mermaid under water. He kissed her on the forehead. He could kiss her as much as he wanted now. But her skin felt clammy and cool under his lips, and it was off-putting. None of it seemed to count for anything if she wasn't awake.

So he drew back to just look at her, instead. Her lips parted, and the smallest bit of drool glistened at the corner of her mouth. It seemed he could see the slight pulse in her neck, and at her temple. One eyelid twitched sporadically. Was this what she looked like when she slept every night? As she had for seventeen years, not knowing who her father was?

He laid his head on her chest, listening to her young heart beating. That was a good sound. A steady sound. He stayed like that for some moments, trying to feel close to her. Like she was actually *his* now.

But it was as though her body in its dormant state was shutting him out. The girl herself was in some dim corridor of consciousness that he couldn't find, couldn't get to.

"Elizabeth," he said at last, rising up on one elbow. "Wake up."

He shook her a bit, gently. And though she made a small murmuring sound, she would not open her eyes to see him.

"Girl, it's your father speaking to you. Open your eyes and look at me. Now!"

He began to feel foolish. He had drugged the girl and brought her out here. For what? He didn't even have a plan! He'd brought her here so he could love her, at last. But he couldn't. Looking into her pure and ethereal face, he knew he was not worthy of her. Of course she would not have him. Of course she turned him away. Because she was his *real* daughter, she was the only person on this earth who could see right through him. That he was a small, sad man. That he was nothing.

"How dare you make me feel like nothing," he hissed into her face. "*Girl.*"

Anger flooded his brain again, and he became like a ticking furnace about to blow. He couldn't hear anymore, only the sound of steam whistling in his ears. His vision, no longer falcon-like, shrank to a tight tunnel. It was like looking through binoculars the wrong way. Everything looked small, drained of color, and insignificant. Including the fish-pale girl lying on the ground in the middle of the woods.

The blackness spread quickly through his brain and nerves, interspersed with a strobing, incandescent red. All rational thought obscured as he hurried to the place his throbbing instinct was sending him; there was one word that flashed in his thoughts again and again. Shed.

SHED SHED SHED SHED SHED

It was as though his synapses had synchronized into a tribal drumbeat, louder and louder, propelling him forward. Urging him to act. Compelling him to annihilate.

He didn't even notice the cold water of the creek. He didn't notice the pricklers snagging at his clothes. He tore through the brush, unseeing and unfeeling, like a machine.

It seemed he had teleported himself in an instant back to the edge of The Brambles' property. The gardener's shed was at the very edge, a small white clapboard building that needed paint and a new roof. It had been a long time since John had been in there.

The door creaked open with a groan, and it took a moment for his eyes to adjust to the dim. There was a riding lawnmower. A wheelbarrow. Various scythes and clippers on a wooden rack. An electric chainsaw.

But none of those things was what he was looking for.

There were still signs of the gardener who had once worked here, must have been decades ago, because he hadn't been here since John arrived. There was still a hotplate and a can of coffee. A small radio and an ashtray full of cigarette butts. Some tacky paperback horror novels from the supermarket, one featuring a leering skeleton with blonde hair and wearing a prom dress. Through his blind rage, John felt some small contempt for this man who was surely a lout.

At last, one by one, the correct items emerged. Canvas garden gloves. A large, curled length of rope.

And, his attention snagged on a pair of rubber boots lying in a corner. He held them up to his own feet. Bigger. The lout must have been a big one, because these boots looked like size twelve. John removed his elegant, English leather shoes and stepped his feet into the monstrous boots. They felt, cool, and stiff. They flapped and shifted around as he walked; they would have to do for his purpose.

He put on the garden gloves, then took down the rope hung neatly on a peg. Must hurry, before she comes out of it.

The little bitch. Stupid little bitch. Letting this happen to herself. What a waste.

Flap, flap, flap. It was just like walking to school in the snow as a kid, wearing his older brother's boots that didn't fit him. Wearing a cheap nylon parka patched up with electrical tape. How he hated those days. Stepfather always knocking the shit out of him. His mother told him he would grow up to be wealthy and important because he was smarter than other people. And she had been right.

Hadn't she?

These woods were really *his* in a way, weren't they?

The branches at the top of the trees swayed and rocked. Breeze coming in. There would be rain, the forecast said.

He plowed on ahead, rope slung over his shoulder. Must hurry, no turning back. Elizabeth wasn't worthy to be his daughter. (At least Sapphire would do anything for him, even if her desperation made him dislike her all the more.) He'd had such high hopes as he'd watched Elizabeth from a distance. That had been when he'd felt closest to her, really, when she was an image that lingered in his mind as he fell asleep at night. Quiet, studious, old-fashioned-looking girl, riding her bicycle by the side of the road.

He had known who she was for longer than that. But he hadn't cared. Back when he was using. He'd been out of his mind all those years. Drugs, women, partying. He didn't recognize himself, in those years. Being in prison had filled him with a yawning appetite for freedom. He was only human. Being human, he had succumbed.

But he had sobered up, mostly. Things were no longer out of hand. He knew there had to be more to his life than wasting away in The Brambles with a bunch of pathetic freaks like Flash and Honeybear. He wanted meaning. Longevity. He wanted to claim his daughter so there would be more to live for. Because, honestly, was there anyone else who truly loved him? Since his mother wasted away in the cancer ward?

But his daughter rejected him. He had made her, and now he must unmake her. It was the only thing to do.

She still lay there, in the hushed, dark woods like a fairy tale princess under a sleeping spell.

He walked past her though, because he wanted to find the right tree. The most beautiful one. And he saw the one Elizabeth had pointed out to him, the white oak. The limbs were sturdy, and he picked the one that seemed the best height, and he tossed the end of the rope over it.

Not right. Higher, it would have to be. He pulled it down, then shimmied up the trunk a bit, up to the branch he wanted. He looped the rope around, pulled it through, then tried to remember exactly how to make a hangman's knoose.

Muscle memory in his fingers made it all come back to him (He'd made them when he was a young man, to terrify his younger brother.) The canvas gloves made it a bit tricky, but before long he had it. A noose big enough to fit over his own head. He first made six loops, then seven, because that was a sacred number.

He stood back and looked; the empty noose swayed gently back and forth in the breeze that was picking up more as the clouds rolled in. It was, he decided, the right height for his purpose.

John picked up the girl in his arms. Her eyelids fluttered, and she said something quietly that sounded like 'wormhole.' He ignored her, shifting her body so that her head rested on his shoulder.

It was a bit of a struggle, leaning back to accommodate her weight while fitting the noose with his left hand. And then he stood holding her, rocking her back and forth slightly, thinking to himself, this is the last time I'll hold my daughter.

He tried hard to remember the first time or any of the time he might have held her when she was a baby. But he couldn't. Those years only brought back the memories of music so loud his heart vibrated, screaming out to tell people a story, heart always pounding, and the acrid drip of meth at the back of his throat. An infant howled back there, somewhere, but her cries were mixed in with all the other noise; he couldn't see her face at all.

"Sorry about all this," he said rather hollowly, like a man uttering his line on a stage.

Then, with a grunt, he tossed the girl into the air. And

free, he strode away.

But now, smoking on his balcony and remembering that day, it felt so long ago. John took it as a sign and blessing that he was never caught. *Of course*, the police asked him questions, but they'd asked everyone in town questions. The truth was, he had gotten away with it, which said to John that it was meant to be. He was every bit the special man his mother always said he was. Destiny was his friend and ally.

He pulled his robe tighter around himself, spit once off the balcony, and went inside.

FIFTEEN

THE VIRGIN OF THE GATEWAY

Mitch woke with a start at the sound of a yelled curse, then what sounded like glass breaking. John. He was awake, and apparently, just thrown something off his bedroom balcony. The windows of Mitch's own next door room were cracked open, so the noise carried in easily.

He drifted a bit back into sleep, but knew John was still out there because he could smell his cigarette and hear him muttering to himself as he sometimes did when he was alone "having a think." Nothing unusual. But Mitch still didn't like it when John was in one of his mercurial moods.

Plus, Mitch was tired. Though his body had been lying supine in bed, his spirit had been elsewhere during the night. These kinds of splits between body and mind had been happening more and more easily since they had put the restraint on his arm. Either that or it was caused by the new medication Honeybear was pumping through his veins.

It didn't matter to him *why* he could do it, just that he *could* do it. He could go anywhere. He could fly, he could move through walls as though they were mist. Some of the places he visited, he recognized easily like his garden back at the house in Malibu. Certain back alleyways in Brooklyn where he played among the ash cans as a boy. He even sometimes liked to wander the rooms of this very house, to see what he could see.

But the night before he had been in a place he hadn't traveled to before. It was a clearing in the woods. Possibly his very own woods at the back of his property, not that he ever bothered going there much over the years. But it was a field, bright with blazing wildflowers, flame-colored, yellow and orange and occasional bits of violet.

And he wasn't alone there. There was a girl, a teenaged girl, dark-haired like his daughter. Except she wasn't his daughter, she was a stranger.

Because he was dream-traveling, he didn't know if he could talk to her. So he simply looked at her. She was across the field from him, but she was walking his way. Black t-shirt, a long skirt made of crushed green velvet, like something his first wife would have worn back in '72. Was this girl from his Laurel Canyon days? Mitch became a bit nervous.

So many things he had done wrong in his life at that time. Such hedonism that came with fame! So many people he had hurt. People he probably didn't even remember now. He didn't know if this place was the past, present or future. Or what this approaching figure had to say to him.

The girl was close now. He heard the brush of the tall grass on her skirt. He lowered his eyes to the ground, resigning himself to this reckoning because surely that was what this was.

He could only bring himself to look at her feet. Which were bare. Also, they didn't quite touching the ground but hovered a few inches above.

"I'm sorry. Please have mercy on me," he said, head bowed.

"For what?" her voice was low and gravelly for such a young girl.

"For whatever harm I've done. I repent, I repent it all, even if it's too late."

"I'm not here to judge you."

She said this with what sounded like humor in her voice; he looked up at her and she was smiling. This girl did not look wounded. She looked radiant and full of life. The color in her cheeks was high, her dark eyes sparkled with a quiet benevolence.

Mitch wrung his hands together and looked down again. Such loveliness. He didn't deserve it.

"I abandoned my own children," he muttered out of nowhere. "And I killed my first wife."

"It wasn't your fault."

"I got her on dope, so yes, it was my fault."

"She forgives you."

"Well, she shouldn't." His voice was choked with anguish.

"And your children forgive you."

"I don't even know where they are."

"They are looking for you. That's what I'm here about." A small purse of colorful woven yarn hung across her chest. She took something out of it. "They want to find you. But you will need this."

She moved forward and held something out to him. A small, sheath-shaped silver key, just like the one he used on his roller skates when he was a kid. He took it in his hand and stared at it.

"What's this?"

"This is to open the lock on your wrist restraint."

"I'm not supposed to have a key."

"I don't care."

"It will make them angry. John and Honeybear."

"Soon, that won't matter anymore."

"They said I could have just the one wrist restraint if I stopped pulling out the IV. They trusted me …" his voice died away.

"Mitch, it's time for you to take your life back. You don't have to apologize, and you don't have to feel afraid. You don't deserve this, even though you think you do."

But still, Mitch shrugged forlornly. Even though he was free in these dreamscapes, he knew for a fact that earthbound Mitch was too weak and beaten down to ever escape.

This lovely girl sought out his gaze. "Mitch? It's true. I'm here to help you. And in return, you'll be helping me. You want to do that, don't you?"

At some point, she had drifted closer still. She smelled like dewy grass and nectar, with a damp undertone of dirt. Wild and fresh smells that made him close his eyes and breathe in.

She was right there when he opened them again, her eyes on his, pleading and earnest.

"What can I do to help you?" he asked at last.

"The three young people need your guidance."

Instinctively, he knew who she meant. He remembered the first time he had seen them through the window, crossing the back lawn. The boy and two girls. His children? He wasn't sure anymore. Time and space were intersected, all mixed up. Too many reference points.

"They will be at The Brambles tonight, and you need to speak to them."

"And say what?"

"You need to show them to the doorway behind the mirror."

He knew what she meant. The floor length mirror in his room, the one he hated to look at because of the image of a wasted, pathetic old man in it. He liked to pretend it wasn't there.

But if the mirror were lifted up on the right side, it swung out on hinges, and there was a small utility door hidden behind it.

"Why do they need to know about that?"

"They need to know what's behind the door."

"But there's nothing. It's just a storage room full of junk."

For some reason, this made the girl smile and it was as if she glowed brightly, all the colors of her flaring.

"Mitch, there's more in there than you know."

"I doubt it." It was a smallish room, he knew. Lined with built-in shelves. The man who had lived here long ago had intended it as a safe room where the family could hide when under threat; he had had the room put in about the time of the kidnapping of the Lindbergh baby.

"Have you been in there yourself?" She tilted her head to the side, mischievously.

"Can't say I have." Even when he had lived there alone, there were many areas of the house he didn't go into. He had mostly camped out in the games room.

The girl's face now serious, she stared at him for a beat. Then said, "All you need to do is guide the three of them to that room."

"It's locked."

"They have keys."

"What do I tell them?"

"Tell them what they are looking for is in that room."

"And they will know?"

"They will know."

"And then what?"

The girl was becoming smaller again, moving away from him. "And then you will see your children again. And good things will happen."

"What kind of good things?"

But she receded further, and faster. It reminded him of when he was young, the old black-and-white televisions, where when you turned them off, the screen shrank away into a small bright blip.

Who are you? he thought he yelled, then realized he was only yelling in his head.

It was about that time that he was awoken by John yelling and throwing something off the balcony.

Now as the memory of the dream gathered around him, he felt a deep, abiding peace; a feeling of purity as though he had been baptized, falling back trustingly into strong arms, head down into fresh river water, and out again, dripping, cleansed, and amazed by the new world he saw around him.

And in his closed hand, nestled snugly, was the key.

Flash realized, with a start, that he had been standing, staring into the bathroom mirror for a very, very long time.

Toothbrush in one hand, toothpaste tube in the other. Something had arrested his thought at some point and made him freeze, looking into his own eyes.

He was not a good-looking man, he knew. Not that that had ever mattered. It had always been raw power and force of will that drew the things he wanted to him. People were afraid of him. Something about his eyes, those eyes looking straight back at himself from under the unflattering light from the fixture above his head, bowl-shaped, with a shadowy heap of dead flies at the bottom.

"Shark eyes," one of his old girlfriends had told him once. "You see me, but you don't see me."

Truth was, he didn't feel much for most people. Even himself.

He lifted up one of his eyelids to look at the rolling, yellowish eyeball underneath with its threaded red veins. He had deep bags under his eyes, from years of being too wired to sleep. Mostly he felt nothing, and more often than not, thought nothing. Nothing of any consequence, anyway. Not only did people find him frightening, but they found him mysterious. Simply because he did not talk very much.

What was his life all about, then, anyway? He thought this, lifting his lips into a sneer, the better to see his pale and recessed gums. Pleasure, and the pursuit of it. He liked good food. He liked women, though not to talk to. He liked riding his bike at the head of the pack, deafening roar in his ears.

Most of all, he loved the look of fear on another man's face when Flash was about to hurt him. It made him feel most alive. Though he was mostly the one who strategized The Horsemen's strikes, he liked the feel of a cold metal weapon in his hands. He'd shot a man before, right in the gut. He'd never forgotten seeing his rival sink to his knees in disbelief before he had even known what hit him.

He had never killed a man, though. Of that he was sure. But he liked to think of himself that he could if he needed to.

He splashed water on his face and watched the rivulets roll down his face, from the tips of his handlebar mustache, becoming more gray than black. He thought about the party that night and tried to get himself stoked about it. But then again, what was the point? Another night of getting shitfaced with the same people he was so sick of seeing. What was the end of it? Another snort, another girl, and then what? His life had grown predictable. And to him, that was worse than death.

Something new, he said to himself in his mind. What he was feeling was both dullness and immense pressure. Not a pleasant feeling. There was an overriding tension that he wanted, *needed* to break. He wanted to hurt someone, but he didn't know who. Not the new girl, Jennie, though he still didn't quite trust her. Sometimes she looked just as inscrutable as he did, and he knew she was hiding things. But he at least respected her for that. At least she was someone new in his tired, sorry life. Her eyes were pale gray like a husky dog's. Even banging her had made him somewhat nervous, but in a good way.

And that's what he wanted. Nothing made him feel new things so much as that girl had. He would be glad to see her that night.

He walked out, still bare-chested, and looked out of the window. A clear bright day out there. He could do anything he wanted. Hell, he wasn't yet sixty. There was a lot left for him.

One person he was for sure sick of, was John. Arrogant son-of-a-bitch. Thought too much of himself. Thought he was clever. Sometimes he thought John and Honeybear looked down on him and talked about him behind his back. He could slit either of their throats and not think twice about it. It was like being married to two skanks he didn't even like anymore. Both clever, smug bastards.

If they ever double-crossed him …

Flash had had only a tenth-grade education, but he

wasn't stupid.

Maybe I just need to get out, he thought. Maybe it was being chained to these guys that was making him bummed. If he had half a brain, he would break out on his own. He knew about the cash box under John's bed. He could grab that, move out all the stuff before anyone knew what was happening.

And then what? Who knew. He could go down south, change his name. Go into business on his own. He had connections. He could trade and sell the weapons himself. That was the part that interested him anyway. Not dealing in whores and pills with that freak Honeybear. The way things were going, it was Honeybear who would go too far and call attention to himself and get them all arrested. Flash always had a sort of sixth sense about things. And what this sense was telling him was that the time had come to get out, and think of himself.

Flash had the key to the secret room. It was on a large key ring with a bunch of other keys. But he took that one off and stuck it in his wallet, so it would always be on hand in case he needed to think on his feet. Or when an opportunity would unexpectedly present itself.

He returned to the bathroom to take one more look at himself. This time, he liked what he saw a little better.

"Let's do this, motherfucker!"

Mack, Lil, and Vanessa had been group chatting each other all morning, in a lazy kind of way as each lounged in their respective bedrooms on a beautiful, warm morning in May.

Lil: What r u all going to wear?

Vanessa: Dunno. I'm going for biker bitch.

Mack: U R a bitch. Just different kind.

Vanessa: ?

Mack: Ivy League, debate team bitch. U ain't no biker.

Vanessa: Shut up Max, you little boy.

Mack: Just cause my mom is making me pancakes don't mean I'm a boy.

Lil: GAWD STOP FIGHTING!

But things were free and easy between the three of them. Lots of laughing, jokes, and rides out to the country in Mack's truck. Rides in which they looked out at the scenery of rolling hills and farmhouses and horses as they discussed their plans for bringing down John.

"It just feels weird to be talking about stuff like this, on a nice day like this when we're looking at a *cow*," Lil said this with a smile on her face, though. A lightness had come over her the past month. A tightness in her chest had been relieved; she had never known it was there until it was gone.

"Yeah, well, if you take it too seriously you go mad. You do what you have to do. And then you keep moving." As Vanessa said this, she glanced over at Lil uneasily. Lil was the one who was going to distract John that night, and Vanessa was afraid for her. No one knew what could happen, what could go wrong.

"We're all together on this," Mack said, firmly. "If anyone is in trouble … well. Nobody *will* be in trouble." There was the merest hint of wavering in his voice. He was the one who would be in the most dangerous position. He would be on the third floor, where this time he would find what needed to be found. He *had* to. Graduation was next weekend. No matter what they said, they would all be going their separate ways after that. Vanessa would be gone next month.

"I'm going to miss you guys," he said, bashfully.

"You won't get rid of us that easily." Vanessa yawned.

"You can come into the city and see me."

"Yeah. No matter what, after this, we're linked for good." Lillian said this casually, but there was a steeliness in her eyes and a determined look about her mouth that was new and unfamiliar. Because she was thinking of the white oak tree, with its tender leaves blazing pink. The beauty and terror of it.

She was going to make John pay, and the sweetness of this thought rose through her veins like spring sap. She was an arrow, flying toward the heart of its target.

Spring had started to shade into the verdant greenness of summer. The tall irises bloomed in their containers in front of the Town Hall. The people of Wellesley mowed their lawns for the first time, and the smell of sweet cut grass filled the air. People sat on their front porches, played Frisbee in the backyard, and shopped for garden mulch, much as they did every year at this time on a lovely Saturday afternoon.

But even as summer songs already played from cars' open windows into the sunny day, there were a few people in the town distracted by something they saw, a vision of the dead girl. These people were among the very elderly and the very young. One little boy named Cody, four, was sitting in his booster chair in the backseat of his parents' car, idly watching the blur of trees and houses go by when he saw a shimmering vision of the girl in the long green skirt, walking by the side of the road.

She looked, to Cody's eyes, like a princess from a Disney movie, or a lady who would dress as a character and read books aloud to the children at the library. Was she a character? Or was she a real girl, like his babysitter? He couldn't tell if she was real or not. He looked at her, wide-eyed, as the car got closer; she turned and looked directly into his eyes and smiled a dazzling smile.

This made Cody feel confused, and look away quickly.

"Did you see that princess fairy girl?" he asked his parents, arguing over where the best place to go for wallpaper paste was.

"What do you mean, Cody?"

"Walking, right there, right there …"

His mother frowned into the rearview mirror. "Don't see her, sweetie."

"She's right back there, she waved at me."

"Well, that's nice, Cody."

The very young didn't know who Elizabeth was. But the elderly did. Ruth Brown saw her when she filled her birdfeeder; the apparition was very sudden. Elizabeth swooped by on a bicycle, hair caught up in a messy bun, cheeks pink, eyes wide and looking into the distance.

Ruth felt the cool breeze of the girl pass through her very body, right through her eighty-five-year-old bones, an electric feeling, like a rush of adrenalin that was sorely missing from Ruth's life these days. Not an unpleasant feeling, but a shock nonetheless.

Ruth took a long look at the girl's retreating back until the girl vanished, as though swallowed by an invisible mist. Birds flew up and flocked around the feeder, but she hardly noticed them.

It was not fear Ruth felt; it was just the unspoken thought that the dead girl is back. In superstition or faith, she couldn't say, but she crossed herself. Lord have mercy on our souls for not seeing her when she was alive.

Honeybear pushed open the door of The Brambles, and it gave a loud creak as he stuck his head in and called,

"Hellooo?"

There was no answer, so he proceeded in. "Jesus! Someone needs to oil those hinges. It sounds like I'm opening a fucking crypt!"

It was five o'clock, the sun just beginning to lower in the sky. A time when he knew there would be very little activity at The Brambles. Which was just what he wanted.

"Hello?"

The usual losers and burnouts, he saw, were slumped here and there on couches in the various rooms. In the library, he saw the older guy who was always there, pudgy and balding and middle-aged but in a child's clothes. Camouflage cut-off shorts and a Burning Man t-shirt.

"Hey, Junior," Honeybear said, with a leering smile. "What's shaking? Is John here or what?"

The guy at first didn't look up, but then sighed heavily and rolled his eyes up like a martyr. In a put-upon voice he said, "Yeah, he's *around*. I think he's in the back, working on his puzzle."

Honeybear stood there for a moment, nodding. "Yep. John and his fucking puzzles. What an old maid kind of thing for him to take up. Right? You know. Queer."

The guy ignored him. Honeybear's smile amped up wider, as he tried to get the guy to look at him.

"May as well take up knitting sweaters, or bingo, eh? Canasta?"

"Hmmm."

"You ever heard the joke about the guy dressed up as his own mother, to play canasta and pick up babes?"

The guy didn't even answer this time; all Honeybear wanted to do was make him laugh, for Chrissakes.

"Well, fuck you, Charlie," he said, as he walked back to the games room, his steps echoing on the marble floor.

Sure enough, there John was, with a chair pulled up to the ping-pong table. The net was down and spread out before him was a large jigsaw puzzle, all done around the edges, but a large, jagged hole in the center.

"Degas," Honeybear remarked, looking over his shoulder.

"Huh?"

"*Degas*. The puzzle! It's one of those paintings of the ballerinas."

John seemed to snap out of a trance he had been in, gazing down at the table. "Huh? Oh, yeah. I like that shit. Those dancers knock me out."

"I know, man. *Impressionism*. I saw some of these, at the museum when I was living in Paris. *Very* lovely. The light in those paintings, you can't imagine. I love the impressionists. Because they captured not just the object itself, but the *life* of the object. Like, how it inhabits space. Glow of the protons. A fleeting impression of life force, you know? Those fuckers were for real. They could paint the way *air tasted* if you catch my drift …"

"Are you high?"

Honeybear barked a laugh. "Why would you ask me that?"

"Because of the way bullshit is spewing out of your mouth."

"I get passionate about things that turn me on, man."

"And I can feel you flailing your arms around, even though I can't see you."

"Guilty as charged."

"You know the party isn't till nightfall, right?"

"I know."

"Then what do you *want*, Honeybear?" John turned around now, to look him straight in the face.

"Just wanted to talk."

"You can go bother plenty of people with your rambling tonight. I am personally not in the mood right now. I come here to do my puzzle so I can relax."

"Well, I'm sorry to bother your mood, John, but I wanted to discuss something serious, and I didn't want Flash around."

"Why?"

Honeybear sighed and pulled up a chair. "Because it's him I want to talk about."

"Well, spill it."

"I think he's holding out on us."

"Why?"

"Things just look fishy, is all, when you look at our numbers. I think he and his guys are snorting all of our product up their noses and not selling it retail."

"I don't know what you're talking about."

"That's because you don't involve yourself too much with the business side of things."

John was turning over a puzzle piece in his fingers. "It's their business."

"Yeah, but I'm a big part of it. And you know, I get tired of feeling disrespected. And so should you."

John put the piece down and closed his eyes. "You are a smart man, Honeybear. You graduated from medical school. You are also a moron."

Honeybear's scalp flushed red through his candy-floss hair. "Sometimes I think you're just as bad as they are."

"Keep things gentlemanly, is my advice. We do each other favors. And they *do* respect us. But The Lone Horsemen bite the heads off chickens. They'll shoot a man in a kiddy arcade. They're good guys, except when they're not."

"If we just stood together, you and I, I think they—"

"Just shut the fuck up, Honeybear. You always get your fair cut. They get you patients, *and* you get the girls. I don't know what you're bitching about. But I was in a pretty good mood until you came in here."

"Oh yeah? What's to feel good about?"

John suddenly slammed his fists on the ping-pong table, making the puzzle pieces jump in the air. "What's to feel good about? I feel good that I'm not a whiny little bitch like you. When I have good fortune, I appreciate it. As far as I'm concerned, I'm the luckiest man alive."

"Because you live in a dump like this? You have only Mitch to thank for that. And honestly, he's not in such great shape. If I were you, I'd be packing my bags now because—"

"Don't give me that shit. You're the one supposed to be keeping him healthy. Or at least, alive."

"—because his blood vessels are going to dissolve like tissue in water. He's a fucking ephemeral being at this point—"

"Well, he's not my savior. The universe shines kindly on me. Good fortune will find me wherever I go. And you wanna know *why*, numbnuts?"

"No, why?"

He smiled engagingly. "Because I'm *special*."

"Oh, will you give me a fucking break ..." Honeybear got up, knocking over the chair, and walked out of the room. He kept going, across the alcove and out the front door and into his black Mercedes, and then he was roaring down the carriage path and down the long, winding driveway.

Jesus Christ, he thought. Imbeciles.

He had been feeling okay when he had driven up, but

now his mood had taken a turn for the worse. John had been right, in a sense. He didn't appreciate what he had. His big, beautiful Tudor house with a lake view. Thriving business. More patients than he could hope for. Then why in God's name am I wasting my time here?

Just the other day he had screamed at one of his nurse practitioners over a small mix-up. Wrong of him, he knew, but at least it had made him feel so good to catch her crying the in the break room, her narrow back heaving.

He was a success. He was a rich doctor. He was cultivated and had traveled the world. Slept with a different girl every week, each younger and fresher than the last.

So why did he feel so damned empty all the time? Why was a low-life redneck like *John* having a richer, more satisfying life than him?

Delusion. Arrogance, that's why. Honeybear was just too smart for his own good.

I won't come back here again, he vowed to himself.

Knowing, of course, he *would* be back, to seek out those elusive *good times*, again and again and again.

Annabel Gray lay on her couch, wine glass in hand, and gazed in an unfocused way out of the floor-to-ceiling window, out to the dark woods that lay beyond. The sun was starting to set and for her, this was always the worst part of the day. In the morning and afternoon, she was able to uphold her willpower to hold herself together. She kept herself busy and distracted with errands, going around town in her dark sunglasses, not speaking to anyone but content in her stream of forward momentum.

Pay a parking ticket. Go to the store for groceries. Visit the dentist.

She did the things she had to do, but no more. She knew people were talking about her. She knew she was in the papers. She felt the cloud of suspicion follow her everywhere she went.

That's the mom of the dead girl.

That's the freaky homeschool mom who kept the girl in a closet.

That's the mom who tried to fake the birth certificate.

That's the woman who might have killed her own daughter.

When Annabel saw them staring, she imagined a bright golden shield of imperviousness around her, protecting her. Then, it was like the town around her did not exist.

Sometimes things did break through her shield, though.

"Witch" she once heard someone whisper in the humid, dripping garden section of the hardware store. Over stacked trays of petunias, she looked ahead at the person who said it. Elise Tilbury, the minister's wife. The two women gazed into each other's eyes for a long, still moment. And then, Annabel fled.

Can't believe I'm so weak. But I can't stay strong forever. And for all I know, they will come to arrest me any day.

Her ruminations began when the sun began to set. What if I hadn't gone to New York? Why didn't I look into her bedroom, just to peek and make sure she was sleeping? Should never have left her alone. I'm paying the price, for stealing what wasn't mine. For disturbing the natural order of things.

She remembered the first time she'd heard Elizabeth cry, the thin and dirty toddler in a diaper. Should have called the police. Probably even would have been better for everyone if she had just turned away and gone home.

But she hadn't. She had gathered up the girl child in her arms and never wanted to let her go.

Selfish love. Greedy, selfish, mother love.

Annabel's mind slammed away in her head, spun in circles like a trapped animal, until, aching and bruise-tender, it exhausted itself and she lay in a stupor, the wine bottle near empty on the floor.

The tops of the trees thrashed back and forth. A storm blowing in? She rarely checked the weather anymore. Because what did it matter?

The swaying movement was soothing to watch, though. In spite of the fact that her daughter had gone into those woods and never came out, those trees were still beautiful to Annabel.

Dusk, that hour of beauty and sorrow; she lay back and surrendered to it.

As she did, her brain registered that she had just *seen something*, movement in the woods. Nothing she could detect with her naked eye, just a sense. And, a gradual illumination. A glowing from between the trunks of the trees, maybe some strange reversal of nature, the sun setting from inside the woods. A softly glowing pale green, as though the woods were full of fairies with glowing lanterns.

She rubbed her eyes. Had it finally happened? Had her drinking led to hallucination, psychosis?

For a flash, she was terrified, because light reminded her of those crowds coming to build a shrine to Elizabeth. The woods had been all lit up then, too.

But this was different. A gentle glow at first, that grew stronger and stronger. A luminous celadon color. Silent and soft and beautiful. The glow intensified to a cool green blaze, spreading out over the treetops until it receded again. It gave Annabel the same rapturous feeling as when she spied a shooting star. Something fleeting and precious, and gone before her mind could process what she had just seen.

And then Elizabeth's voice spoke in her ear. "You don't have to worry anymore. Everything is fine now. Don't worry."

Mack, Lil, and Vanessa walked through the woods, cutting through the back way to The Brambles.

"You sure we shouldn't just drive?" asked Mack. "We could get out of there quicker if we needed to."

"No, it's better this way," said Vanessa. "We don't know what will happen. It could be a liability to have a car there. Make things worse. This is simpler. If we're in any trouble, it's easier to just disappear this way. Anyway, it's just like the first time, isn't it?"

The light of dusk was enough to see by, but it made everything look so different. The leaves on the trees looked eerie and blue-tinged, as though they were at the bottom of an ocean.

After walking in silence for some moments, Lil sighed. "Does anyone else feel … heavy?"

The others looked at her quizzically.

"I mean, like in your chest."

"Are you okay, Lil? You look a little sick." Vanessa peered into her face anxiously.

"I'm alright. I just hate The Brambles. I hate the way I feel there. It just makes me feel so dirty, you know? The closer I get, the heavier I feel."

"Just shut down your feelings. Go numb. Pretend you're a robot."

"Vanessa, not *everyone* can do that. When I'm there, I

just feel … contaminated."

"Well, it *is* a depressing place, but we're almost done," Mack tried to smile hopefully, but felt conspicuous and fake.

"It's not depressing. It's evil." Lil looked straight back into his eyes. "Don't call it anything less than what it is."

"Lil, are you up for this?" Vanessa had stopped and put her hands on the smaller girl's shoulders.

"Absolutely." But though her jaw was set stiffly, her eyes looked full of pain. "I know what we're here for, and I—"

"Hey! Did you see that?"

Mack had stopped, and stared into the path in front of them and pointing.

"I don't see anything," said Vanessa after a moment's pause.

"But I did. It was a flash."

"Huh?"

"I don't know. Like a spark from a campfire? Kind of floating by?"

"I don't smell any smoke, though." Lil's voice was small and shrunken.

"Look!"

Now Vanessa had her finger trained on it. At first, it looked like a small piece of paper, sizzling with greenish fire at the edges. It drifted in the darkening air, floating up and forward; the three followed.

"Look, there's two of them now!"

It was larger than they had thought, about five inches across its wingspan …

"Luna moth," Vanessa whispered, and as though in response to its name, it flew close and settled on her finger.

Glowing, pistachio green and tufted. Its eyespots

seemed to look back at her. Its delicate feet tickled as it fluttered its wings.

"How do you know?" asked Mack, coming close to look.

"I've seen one before, camping in the Catskills."

"Do they always glow?"

An emittance of light came from up ahead, so they followed to see where it was coming from.

It was Elizabeth's tree. Hundreds of glowing luna moths perched on its branches, blazing.

"My God, it looks like a Christmas tree," said Lil, the light reflected on her face making her look otherworldly and fairy-like. As she stood looking, a small moth flew to her and landed on her temple.

"What is it doing?" She felt it moving around, the wings brushing against her cheekbone.

"It's drinking your tears," Vanessa said quietly.

"But I didn't even realize I was crying."

The tracks down her cheeks glowed with reflected green light.

"I'm serious. Some moths and butterflies drink tears. For the sodium. They pass it on to their offspring."

Mack looked at her dubiously but didn't argue. Vanessa had always been queen of arcane facts. He felt a moth scrambling in his hair. It made his scalp tingle, but he did not raise a hand to touch it.

"It feels like a blessing," Lil said.

"More like Moses and the burning bush," Vanessa murmured.

"Don't go all Bible school," Mack said, with a smile in his voice.

"Well, it's a sign. That we're on the right track." Lil looked at the others "We're doing the right thing, aren't we?"

The others didn't answer. They didn't know what to say.

The three of them lingered some moments more, before following the trail again. They got to the creek, which was running low and dry from lack of rain, so it was at least easy to walk across. No one said a word at all, the rest of the way, as each mused over what they had just seen.

It seemed almost too soon when they broke out of the brush, and there was the wide lawn of The Brambles before them. It was even darker now than it had been when they left. The house stretched before them in the distance, like an ocean liner on a calm sea. The windows blazed golden, and they heard the music, amplified in an echoey, tinny way; it made it all seem as if the scene was already a hazy memory at some point in their future.

"Why hello!" John came forward to greet them in the front foyer. He had been in a knot of conversing people, but his ice blue eyes had trained on them immediately when they entered.

He kissed each girl on the cheek, and extended his hand for Mack to shake, but then grabbed him in a bear hug.

"My favorite high school gang! My three peas in a pod. How ya doin'? I'm always so happy to see you. You bring so much fresh energy to this place. And my *life*." He turned to look each one in the eye, individually. "You know that, right?"

Mack shrugged and looked sheepish, not knowing what to answer.

"Because you do. I think we came into each other's lives for a reason. And I hope I bring as much to you as you do to me. Ya know?"

Vanessa nodded.

"Ya know, earlier today I was telling …" John motioned vaguely behind him, "I was telling Asshole over there, I told him, 'I'm the luckiest man alive.'" He raised his eyebrows. "And it's true. And you are the luckiest kids. And this is the luckiest place. Because this house," he stamped his foot, a sudden and startling sound, "is full of love."

The three of them smiled. They were all nodding now, in a synchronized, automatic way.

"I love you," John held a red glass goblet in his hand, and raised it toward each one of them, in turn. "And don't you forget it."

Abruptly he turned away from them and shouted to someone else. "Hey, Marty, where's the guys with the keg?"

"Whew," said Mack under his breath. "He's drunk off his ass. It'll be easy to keep tabs on him."

"He's not drunk," whispered Lillian. "He's always like that."

"Well, I think *I'm* going to get drunk just so I can stand it," said Vanessa with a sigh.

"Don't you dare!"

"Kidding, Lil. Jeez."

"Well, I just want us all to stay sharp."

They made their way to the kitchen, where Lil poured from a bottle of pinot noir into three plastic cups.

"Not for me," said Mack. He went to the refrigerator and got himself a bottle of Corona. "I'm good. Gonna go chill for now. I'll be checking in later."

He peeled off the cap, took a long guzzle, and headed to the front of the house.

A group of guys sat on the staircase. John's hippie underlings.

"Hey, Mack, where ya been?"

Andy was the one who spoke. He had a patchy blond beard and wore some kind of voluminous striped pants, almost like pajama bottoms. He was not much older than Mack, but had dark pouched eyes and smelled like a homeless person; Mack sat on the step above him, but not too close. They fist bumped in greeting.

"Uh, yeah, I've just been livin' back at home for a while."

"You getting along with your parents now?"

"Well. My mom. I've been helping her around the house and shit. I don't see my dad."

"Yeah, well, we miss you, dude. But mom, right? She needs you and all …"

"It's cool. I don't mind her." There actually was a new tranquility since he'd moved back. Things were easier. Quieter. The air less fraught. "Probably did us good for me to get away for a while, you know?"

"You heard from Sapphire?"

Mack's face darkened into a blush. He swung up the bottle and closed his eyes.

"No."

"Ha! Sounds as though you don't want to, either."

He shrugged. It still caused him a hollow feeling in the pit of his stomach just remembering her long, tangled hair, and how he'd liked to hide his face in it. To think, he had felt *safe* with her. And she vanished, anyway. The things these people did to her. In spite of his sadness at losing her, he hoped she was safe and happy.

"Closed chapter," Mack croaked into the bottle at his lips.

With that, there was a momentary lull. Mack reminded himself why he was here. He trained his eyes on the front door. He would need to remember each person who walked in, and where they were.

Smoke, a bluish haze, had wafted through the evening up at the high ceiling. The repeat medallion plaster moldings on the ceiling were crumbling away; the crystal chandelier had dropped by a foot, exposed wires dangling.

How many decades of parties has this room seen, wondered Vanessa as she looked around in her Vicodin blur. Surely the walls and ceiling and floorboards were soaked with trace evidence and echoes of human folly for generations.

"Toot?" asked the Horseman sitting next to her, a large man with what looked like a chemical burn over half his broad face. He held up a vial.

"Naw, I'm good," she said and focused on the conversation on her other side. The one that they called Ghost was speaking.

"Yeah, you shoulda been there that day. This was, what now, twenty some years ago? I saw this fuckin Hell's Angel comin' outta the auto parts store. Saw 'im in the parking lot, I knew who he was. I'd been keeping track. And I was still green, I was still young, you know, so my mind was kinda running crazy, it was my chance, you know. But I had the grenade in my saddlebag, and you know what I did? I threw it at the motherfucker! No one else around us. I swear to God he turned and made eye contact with me right when it landed. Not *on* him but close enough. I was the last thing he ever saw, ha! Motherfucker is blind and half deaf now, still got the puncture wounds all over his body. Lucky to live, they say. And even though he knows it was me, fucker never squealed ..."

The drug in her system made her feel very calm and

centered. She listened to Ghost's story without the usual horror, but with a sort of benign detachment. These were the people they were. Could it ever be any different for them? Was it really in her to judge them? She felt like an anthropologist studying a foreign society and taking notes.

Every once in a while, her eyes darted to Flash's face; in profile, he looked as though he was deep in his own thoughts. His eyes, usually alert and darting in their sockets, missing nothing, trained on some inward vision. He didn't laugh at any of the stories the guys were telling. Didn't tell any yarns of his own. He just *sat* there, and it made Vanessa nervous, despite her mellow high.

"What's up?" she asked him quietly at one point, perching on the arm of his chair.

He glared at her and said, "Who wants to know?" His eyes had snapped back to life and bored into her with a paranoid fury. She shrugged and looked away nonchalantly, though her pulse had jumped.

In turning her head, she noticed that Honeybear had just entered the front foyer. Damnnit, she thought to herself. She had to keep an eye on him, too. He was the only other one who ever went to the third-floor bedrooms. As far as she knew, Mack might be up there, now.

She got up to get another drink. Then she went back to find him in the doorway of the library, where he talked loudly to a girl with long blonde dreadlocks.

"… and then I said, what do you think the stirrups are for? Ha ha ha ha!"

Honeybear stood too close to the girl, who had a vacant smile on her face, turned away from him. She flashed a look of gratitude when Vanessa approached and slipped away.

"Hi," Vanessa said, tilting her head flirtatiously. "I got

you a drink if you want it."

"No thanks, sweetie. Red wine makes me flush all over and get the sweats."

"Oh."

"Well, thanks, though." He fixed her with his gaze, which was queer looking from the way his metal-framed glasses distorted his eyes. He smiled at her, but the smile wasn't pleasant. "So what's going on these days?"

"Nothing much."

"Graduation coming soon, right?"

"Uh huh." This was the conversation she'd had too many times with all her older relatives.

"And what did you say you were doing next?"

She had inferred to him, last time, that she was planning nothing. But something compelled her this time to tell him the truth. "I'm starting college soon."

He raised his eyebrows. "Oh, really? That's different from the usual girl around this place. Where at? The community college?"

"No. I'm going to Columbia."

He looked at her keenly. "No way?"

"Yes. I'm starting this summer."

He looked at her for a long moment, nodding. "I went to NYU myself for undergrad."

"Oh, yeah?"

He took her by the elbow and led her over to a settee in an empty corner.

"So you're a smart girl."

"I suppose."

"And yet you're at this place, slumming it with those wheelie boys."

She looked back at him, unblinking.

"Can I ask why someone like you is getting involved

with a hellhole like this?"

"Reasons."

He raised his eyebrows, then leaned in close, and said quietly, "Expanding your horizons. Seeing who and *what* is out there. Just because you're smart, doesn't mean you're dead inside. Am I right?"

She mimicked his expression, raising her eyebrows ironically.

He nodded. "I know how you think. Because I am exactly the same way. There's more to life than going to school and educating yourself and taking your assigned place in society. I mean, I've always had a nice house. Nice cars. Member of the golf club and all that shit. But you know what that stuff does not make me feel?"

"What?"

"ALIVE." His eyes rounded, his grin bordered on maniacal. "There's always more to life. Mostly in the dark back alleys. But then, you seem to know that."

"I like these people."

He drew back, looked at her askance.

"It's true."

"Well, what a good intentioned little girl. Because I will tell you, in spite of your optimistic nature," he leaned in and whispered, "these people are *scum*."

"Are you scum too, then?" She smiled gamely. But her mind was on other things. She kept glancing over his shoulder at the staircase. Mack had been sitting there a few moments earlier. But now he was gone.

Honeybear looked at her mock-sternly, waved his finger. "I don't like your insolent tone, young lady."

"You what?"

"Listen. I'm talking to you seriously because I can tell you're a serious person. It gets to be sometimes, believe it or not, that I desire serious conversation."

"Well, fine. I'm serious, then."

"Good." He came closer to her until his face was inches from hers. "I can tell that we are two of a kind. I understand you."

Vanessa said nothing. The conversation was taking a strange turn that she had not anticipated.

"We're smarter than the others. And that's a burden, it *is*. You know why?"

"Why?"

"Because we *see more*. And the reason we are driven to chase down more of everything is because we know, deep down, that nothing really means anything."

His eyes met hers, swimming behind the thick lens of his glasses like paramecium under a microscope.

"We know that deep down, underneath, there is no meaning. Nothing really means anything."

Now she gaped at him, stunned. He studied her with intimidating intensity. And she had the terrible feeling that maybe he *did* see her in a way that others couldn't and had seen her for the empty person she had always feared herself to be.

"It's not true," she whispered.

But then suddenly, his demeanor snapped back again. He smiled and shrugged.

"Sorry, young lass," he said brightly. "Didn't mean to take a philosophical turn on you. Not the time or place, is it?"

"It's okay, whatever."

"Columbia, huh. Terrific. I used to date a girl who went there. But her roommates hated me. Called me The Stalker. Don't ask. I preferred Sarah Lawrence girls. Columbia tended to be snobs. Not that you are. You're different. Just sayin'."

"I, uh—" She saw, over his shoulder, Flash walking around by himself, scanning the room restlessly. His eyes met hers for a flicker, then he looked away.

"You think you wanna do a little business up there?"

"What do you mean?"

"You know, at school. I'll keep giving you scripts. Because I'm your doctor."

"You aren't really my doctor, though."

"Oh, but I am. It's all up and up. You know how much you can sell even one of those pills for? And there are some rich kids up there. They have the money, believe me." He drew closer. "This can just be between the two of us. We don't have to involve ..." he jerked his head in the direction of Flash, who had strolled to one of the front windows, peering out. "Or any of those clowns."

Vanessa forced her eyes back on Honeybear. "Just us?"

"You need some extra money, don't you?"

"I have a scholarship."

"Full?"

"No." How could she get away from him?

"I was National Merit myself. But that was a million years ago. Watcha gonna study? Pharmacology? Hah ha ha ha!"

"Linguistics."

"Ah! Semantics. Syntax ..."

"You got it."

"'Language is a virus from outer space.' Ya know who said that?"

She didn't answer because Flash went up the stairs.

Mack! She had to warn him.

"I'm going to go sit down for a minute," she said. She would text him. They had already agreed that the warning would simply be the letter X.

"You okay? You look a little pale."

"I'm fine, I just want to be alone," she said more curtly than she meant to.

"Alright. Get back to me before you leave if you want to talk about things."

She walked around the corner and sat on a spindly decorative chair. She texted the letter, but didn't know what else to do; her mind raced but she felt helpless.

Mack felt his phone vibrate and took it from his pocket. X.

His heart pounded. It could not be a worse time. He was in John's room. Moments later, he heard footsteps coming up the stairs. Try to slip out? No time.

He slid into the closet and eased the door closed, hoping it wouldn't creak. He was afraid to make a noise by clicking the latch, so he left it ajar.

I'm a dead man, he thought, head bent low, arms wrapped around himself, pressed in among the suit jackets. What can I say if John opens the door?

I'll pretend to be high. I'll pretend that I'm freaking out on mescaline …

A presence entered the room. Somehow, it didn't sound like John. John moved swiftly and decisively. This person was slow-moving, with a heavy tread and the sound of a rattling chain.

Hardly daring to breathe, Mack twisted himself to get a view through the cracked door. Flash. And he was sneaking around himself, from the way he paused inside the doorway and listened. He wanted to make sure no one was there.

Mack felt his stomach reel with panic. What if his phone buzzed again? What if he sneezed? He had no idea what

Flash was really capable of.

He was moving forward again, into the room. Now his movements were quicker. He squatted beside the bed and pulled out the metal box that Mack had found earlier.

Flash pulled out a key. The box rested on top of the tightly made bed, open, and full of cash. He took out stacks of hundred dollar bills, laying them in rows, counting them up. Thousands of dollars. Transfixed, Mack's, heart leaped into his throat. Was he here to steal it?

Flash counted, his lips moving silently. And when he was done, he just looked at it, his brow furrowed darkly. Then he whispered, "Motherfucker."

Swiftly, he put it all back into the box, locked it again, slid the box under the bed, and left. Again the sound of footsteps, this time going down the staircase.

In the silence afterward, Mack remained still, too afraid to move. He buried his face in the soft weave of a camelhair coat, taking deep breaths, in and out.

"What do you mean, dear?"

Lil bit her lip and looked down. It was noisy where they were, beside a group of guys shouting across the foosball table. John's gaze was soft with concern.

"I mean, I'm just feeling a little sad right now."

"Why is that? How can I help?" Now he crouched on one knee, in front of where she was sitting on the sectional sofa.

"Well, I—"

"Can you speak a little louder?"

"Well, it's just so noisy in here …"

"Yeah, the games room is always a hub of activity, isn't it?" He smiled, as one would smile when trying to cheer a petulant child.

"I. Well. I'm wondering whether to get back together with my boyfriend and I just feel really confused."

"Oh. I didn't know you had had one." His eyes turned steely, though his lips smiled encouragingly.

"Yeah. We broke up in the fall, but he just called me and we were talking." A lie. She had not spoken to Jack since the breakup. But looking up through her lowered lashes, she saw that she had provoked the effect she wanted. His entire focus was on her.

"Do you love him?"

"I don't know. I used to. I still might."

"This must be very confusing for you," he said soothingly, taking her hand in his. His hand was freakishly oversized, dwarfing her own.

"Yes."

"I mean, you are a different person now. You've come a long way since you I've met you."

"Do you think so?"

"Why, of course! Since you became a full-fledged member, or rather ... since you joined the *family* of Ministry of Presence, I've seen a huge change in you. Why, you were like a little *girl* when I first met you."

"I was?" She smiled in a way that she hoped seemed shy.

"Yes. But not anymore. You've opened yourself up to all the knowledge of the universe."

She only just contained a snort of laughter.

"You put your trust in me, for which I am immensely honored and grateful."

"I do. Trust you. You've been like a father to me, you know."

At this, his expression changed subtly; he didn't speak, but regarded her closely. Solemnly. "Do you want to go somewhere else quieter?"

"Okay."

"Shall we go up to my room? Quietest part of the house!"

"No! Um, I mean …" She thought frantically.

"I don't mean anything by it. I'm not going to try anything. It's just that no one will bother us up there. These rug rats aren't allowed on the third floor."

"Well I, um … is there anyone in the ballroom? I kind of want to be by the altar. I want to mediate with you, if that would be okay?"

John seemed pleased by this. "Oh, I think that would be wonderful. I'm so happy that you would share that intimacy with me." He stood up, held out a hand to help her from the couch.

As they walked from the room, John wheeled around. "HEY!" His shout was loud, piercing. The noise in the room dropped. "Get away from that!"

He shouted at a couple of hippies leaning on the ping-pong table, where a large jigsaw puzzle was laid out.

"Get the fuck away from my project! Do you know how many hours I spent on that?"

Lillian glanced at the nearly completed puzzle, ballerinas with young spindly limbs in rose-tinted tutus.

The two hippies took their drinks and backed away, eyes large in fear.

"Fucking assholes," he muttered, linking his arm through hers. "Sometimes I feel they don't respect me. Like they don't respect anything at all."

Vanessa stood in a corner, watching the staircase, until she saw Flash come back down the stairs again and head to the kitchen. She followed him.

He rummaged through the fridge for a Budweiser. She stood behind him, and said, softly, "Hey."

He did not answer. He shut the fridge door and removed the bottle cap, flipping it onto the floor. He took a long draw, glaring at her.

She felt herself contract in fear. She couldn't read his face. Had he found Mack? She made her voice flat and bored. "So what's up?"

"Nothin', why do you keep askin'?" he growled and softly belched.

"Is … anything wrong?" Her nerves were aflame, though she kept her face still.

"Why the fuck do you wanna know?"

Vanessa shrugged. "I guess when you came downstairs you looked pissed off or something."

He looked at her closely now, not saying anything. Then, "I saw you schmoozing around with Honeybear earlier."

Was that the problem? "Yeah. We were just talking."

"You aren't fucking him, are you?"

"No!" The very thought made her queasy with revulsion.

"You better not be."

"Are you mad at him or something?"

"Hmm." He turned to walk away.

"Flash?"

He turned back, an exasperated look on his face.

"Can I go ride with you?"

"Why?"

"I don't know." Her mouth had been moving faster than her mind could keep up. "I just like to ride." This was true. And she wanted to, terribly, right now. Honeybear's words had made her feel sick and hollow.

There is no meaning.

Nothing really means anything.

"Please?" And then surprising even herself, she started to cry, pressing the heels of both hands against her eyes, to try to stop the tears.

"Fine. Come on, a short one," Flash said, leading her out the door, and then soon they were on his bike, flying into the night, the engine's roar drowning out all thought, the night wind drying her tears so that it was as though they never existed.

Mack quietly stole from room to room, moving as quickly as he could, trying to inspect every bedroom, every closet. He kept the lights off and shone the flashlight from his phone, the blue-tinged light making the view feel claustrophobic, like tunnel vision.

So far, he had found nothing. Nothing unusual looking, nothing he could open with the silver key in his front pocket.

The memory of Flash with the box of money felt dreamlike and hallucinatory and left his frazzled nerves humming. He wanted to work as quickly as possible and get *off* the third floor. If he found nothing, he would at least know that he'd done everything he could.

At one point, he leaned against the wall in the hallway, needing to clear his head. Without realizing it, he had been taking deep, ragged breaths. He felt as though he had run a marathon. His mouth was dry and his muscles tense and sore.

A thump, a knock, like furniture being moved, sounded in Mitch's room; the door was closed, but light escaped from under the edge.

Mitch's room. He had been leaving it for last. Thinking

of it filled him with dread. The medical equipment, the mini fridge full of IV bags. He had caught glimpses of the room before, a sickroom. A room to die in.

Thump, thump, drag. Wasn't Mitch asleep now? He hadn't heard a sound the whole time he'd been up there.

Then, he all but leaped from his skin when the door creaked open, spilling light into the hallway. Mitch, barely upright, steadied himself by the door jamb.

Mack'd never seen anyone as frail actually standing vertically. Mitch's skin was so pale, it looked transparent, stretched over the shadowy skull sockets in his face and delicate bones stood out in each hand; the shock was almost enough to make Mack cry out.

He looked into the old man's eyes. The moment seemed to stretch on and on, as though they were the only two people in the whole world.

The moment held a sense of unreality. Mack wondered if he were really there and if it were really happening. Mitch's eyes didn't have their usual glazed, unfocused appearance. He saw Mack and gazed straight at him. The shrunkenness of the old man's face, his very lack of physical substance, transformed him into an elemental being, filled with light.

At last, Mitch spoke. He said, "Son."

Light radiated from him and haloed him in the doorway. It poured into the hallway, onto Mack.

"My ... my son."

Mack felt his heart lift in his chest. It had been such a long time since a man had called him *son*, and looked at him in an all-encompassing way that made him feel that he was truly being seen, for himself. The intensity frightened him but made him feel whole and alive.

He cleared his throat, and said, "Yes."

Mitch's face relaxed into a smile of relief and gratitude. He nodded, reached out his thin fingers toward Mack, but drew short, as though afraid Mack was a mirage that might be shattered by his touch.

Then he motioned for Mack to come forward. "C-c-come. Come."

With difficulty, he turned his body around. His back was so frail, exposed by the hospital gown he wore; his ribs, the jutting shoulder blades, the slack skin with dark moles.

But he was moving, and Mack slipped into the room. It had a close, sickroom smell. Though large, it felt crowded, with the wheelchair and IV poles taking up so much space.

Mack stood gingerly as Mitch tottered over to the foot of the bed; a leather arm restraint attached to the headboard hung open and empty.

But Mitch called his attention away from the bed, slurring his words, "Here. Through here."

He gestured at a mirror that reflected a young man and an old man, surrounded by medical detritus.

"It's … just a mirror."

Mitch walked closer to the mirror, and with shaking fingers, he worked the tips under the edge of the frame.

The mirror swung forward, on hinges. The reflection, the boy, the old man, and the entire ruined room and its sickbed, slid smoothly to the side. And Mack was looking at a hidden door.

Mitch pointed and said, "You … have the key."

Dumbfounded, it took Mack a moment before he said, "Yes. I do."

Lil and John sat cross-legged on the floor, looking up at the altar and the usual collection of objects, the brass Ganesh, the candles and the geodes. But there was something different.

"The painting. Is that new?"

It had no frame, it was painted on a piece of canvas and propped up in the center of the altar. It was a painting of a girl meditating or praying, her eyes downcast, her hair a mast of stylized waves which also contained many small objects. Tiny stars, tiny books. Cups and daggers, little yin/yangs …

"Do you like it?" John eyed her sidewise, a small smile on his face.

"Yeah … well, it's very colorful. It's like those psychedelic posters from the sixties …"

"Do you want to know what it's called?"

"What?"

"*The Virgin of the Gateway*."

"Huh."

"Notice the keyhole?"

"No." She leaned closer.

In an intimate voice, low into her ear, he said, "It's in her solar plexus. It's the entrance to her being."

"Cool." It was certainly a *busy* piece. It made her eyes hurt to look at it.

"Would you like to meet the artist?"

"Sure."

With a manic smile, John turned and offered his hand. "Pleased to meet you!"

Lil looked at him in confusion and he laughed. "It's *me*! I'm the artist!" He stood up and helped her to her feet. "Here. Come get a closer look."

"I-I didn't know you painted."

"Oh, I play around with it, now and then. Just a little hobby. I work in oils. I keep a little easel upstairs and take it out onto the balcony. I like to paint outside. There's something about it I find centering." He looked at Lil significantly. She blushed in confusion.

"Who, umm, is the girl in the painting?"

He sighed, wistfully. "It's my daughter."

"I never knew you had one ..." her voice trailed off hoarsely, but he was already speaking over her.

"I've had more than one. Daughter. Both on the physical and spiritual plane."

A creeping sense of panic washed over her when he turned to give her a soulful look.

"The one in the painting is my oldest daughter. But I had to paint it from memory. Because she is dead."

"Oh ... I'm sorry to hear—"

"Suicide. She was a very confused girl. Woman. She was twenty-two. Had gotten into drugs. She was a drug addict with about five different low-life boyfriends at any given time. In the end, she was about a hundred pounds soaking wet and out of her mind with hallucinations. Those are what you see in her flowing hair," he gestured at the painting. "I guess I'm trying to capture what a mystery she was. To me and to others."

"You must be—"

"I was told she killed herself on a railroad track after one of the lowlifes ran out on her. Lay down on the tracks and let the train run her over. Can you imagine?"

He gazed at her, and she realized he was waiting for an answer.

"Yes, I mean no, I can't imagine ..."

She felt him gauging her reaction, looking from one eye to the other. He's trying to see if I believe him.

"So, there are ... other daughters?"

"Yes. Luck of the draw, I guess. I make girls. And that's

fine by me. I don't want any lousy boy. There's nothing I love more than little girl babies. I love their soft skin. I love the way they smell. I love the way a girl is always loyal to her daddy."

Lil didn't like the way he leered. She despised *him*, certainly. But she knew she had to remain steady, and not show her fear.

But he was so *close*. She could smell his scent, a mix of cigarettes and an odd, an ozone-type smell, like rain on hot pavement.

"I love talking to you, Lillian. What is your middle name?"

She paused, then told him, "Grace."

He put a hand to his heart, as though he had just been stabbed. "You don't say," he whispered. "Of *course* it is Grace." He took her by the hand, and looked at her, urgently. "I always suspected you were special. Now I know it."

She smiled, uncertain of where this was leading.

"'For by grace you have been saved through faith. And this is not your own doing; it is the gift of God.'" He kissed her hand with a smack. "Ephesians, 2:8."

"Wow."

"Yes. I read the Bible, front to back, back to front. Prison was my great teacher. A curse that became a blessing. I can appreciate the wonderful things in life now." He said it in a rush, as though by rote.

"That's good …"

His eyes were strangely alight. His expression rhapsodic. "I'm going to ask you something."

Her heart lurched in dread. "What is it?"

"Would you like to be with me?"

"In what way?" Her throat had gone dry.

"Would you allow me the honor of entering your body?"

"I—"

"You are a virgin, yes?"

"I, um, well—" Fast-rising panic. Her vision became patchy...

"I know about your boyfriend. But I can forgive you that. I *will* forgive you that."

He put a finger to her lips when she tried to speak.

"Shhh. It's okay. You are Lillian Grace, child of God. You don't even have to ask to be forgiven. Because you already are."

Now he had both her hands in his, and he looked like a man hot and rambling with fever. "If I could be with you, it would be in honor and tenderness. He didn't love you. *I do*."

She drew back, trying to slip her hands from his. "This is very confusing for me ..."

"Nothing to be confused about, if you follow your instincts." He lowered his voice, into a tender croon. "I can see myself giving a baby to you."

Her eyes wide with alarm, she stopped breathing.

"Picture it, Lillian Grace. Not now, but someday in the future. A child of your own. A little living being, folded up inside you, nurtured by your own blood."

"But I—"

"It's an amazing thing, that women can give the gift of life. You are such a sweet and beautiful person. It only seems fitting that you would one day have a beautiful little daughter of your own—"

"I CAN'T—"

"There is nothing like a daughter. One day, you will see ..."

"You're hurting me. Let me GO!"

"Shhh. You're not listening to me!"

"Because you're CRAZY!"

His face reddened with anger, but his voice was controlled, though trembling. "I can see that you are a bit overwhelmed, but you need not be. Shh, calm down. You are beautiful, and I would like for you to be mother to my next daughter."

He held her fast, hard enough to bruise; she wondered if she had to bite him to get free, but just at that moment he let go and took her face gently between his palms.

"Don't be afraid, Lillian. I love you."

"You don't know me."

"But I *do*. And I'm a lonely, lonely man." His mouth drew into a grimace. "I have lost both my daughters. Have some compassion, can't you? I'm a human being, you know."

Lil felt deep revulsion in her gut, like scalding bile. "You don't *deserve* compassion," she whispered.

"Excuse me?"

"You're *sick*." Her voice came out still and flat. "You're a predator. And I would never give a daughter to you. I wouldn't even let you *touch* me."

He looked into her eyes, his face stony and blank. Before she knew what was happening, he drew back and slapped her across the face.

"Little slut!" he cried, in an oddly high voice, not the deep, modulated voice she was used to hearing; this sounded as though he had breathed in helium.

Lillian clutched at her face in shock. No one had ever done that to her before.

"How *dare* you!" John moved closer and grabbed a handful of her shirt, and shook her. "I showed you my heart and this is how you speak to me?"

Her teeth rattled in her head and she saw sparkles of light flicker around the room.

"You were an honored guest. In my house."

"It's not your house," she whispered, her throat too constricted to speak louder.

"I ministered to you. I educated you. And this is the thanks I get?"

Lillian's mind was a blur, blinded by terror. "Dirty killer," she said, "Dirty murderer ..." An incantation of protection ...

He reared up, pulling her with him, propelled by fury. A force of nature, a tsunami, he hurled her across the room like a rag doll.

She thudded hard against the altar and tumbled onto the floor, knocking over the brass Ganesh statue with a bang. Winded, she couldn't even make it onto her feet before he loomed over her again.

"I don't have to take this from trash like you. That's what you are. Trash." He swung a leg bag to kick her, then stopped short. He laughed at the way she flinched.

"Damn right you should be scared of me. I could snap your neck like a twig."

"If you hurt me ..." She didn't know what to threaten. She could not think at all. Limbs all tingling and weak. She fumbled for her phone in her pocket with shaking fingers. John slapped it out of her hand. It flew across the room and hit the wall before falling to the floor with a crack.

She made it to her feet and ran toward the door, but he overtook her. She felt his hand on her shoulder, and a scream escaped, a long wailing scream like a cornered animal. She who had never screamed in her life. Now it was coming out of her, and she could not stop.

But it did not stop *him*. He grabbed her by her upper arm and yanked her to her feet, a demonic fury contorting his face. He shook her by the throat.

"Little bitch, little bitch. I'll teach you what's what!"

Nothing, she had nothing to protect herself with, and his face was so near, she could see the cracked irises of his silvery blue eyes, threaded with red veins. His teeth bared at her, she saw one crooked eyetooth, as pointed as a dagger. Breath that smelled of raw meat. This terrible face was all she saw. There was nothing else. *No escape.*

From the library, Vanessa heard the scream. Faint, but definite. She looked at Flash, his hair still wild from their bike ride. He had just entered with a bong in his hand.

"Did you hear that?"

Flash shrugged. The other men in the room did not respond, either, as if a woman's screams were commonplace at The Brambles.

It came from the ballroom. She ran as fast as she could and pushed open the double doors to see John manhandling Lil, shaking her small body, his face consumed with rage.

"Let her go!"

Quickly Vanessa crossed the room and grabbed a silver candleholder from the altar, and hit John with it. She landed some blows, but he was so tall, and his wide back was so wide and thick with muscle, that it was like hitting a water buffalo.

John laughed in little huffs. "I'll kill both you little bitches." He held fast to Lil and kicked at Vanessa, but she jumped away. She grabbed the brass Ganesh from the floor and threw it at him, and overshot. He cackled, a high, weird laugh as it landed behind him with a *clang*.

What else could she use? In the center of the altar was a hideous painting, amateurishly done psychedelia in lurid colors, painted on a piece of canvas board. She grabbed it and hit him on the head with it.

"Hey!" he barked savagely. "What the fuck do you think you're doing? Put that down!"

She hit him again, hard, and she had his full attention. He tried to grab Vanessa while he gripped the struggling Lil with one hand.

"Don't you *touch* that you impudent little bitch! That's mine! That's real art in case you didn't know. It took me—"

Vanessa drew back from his hands. She beat the painting on the side of the mantelpiece. Then she held it up and licked it, in one long swipe down the center, and grimaced at the faint bitter taste of linseed oil.

"Goddamn you, *defile* my work, oh, you little cunt! I'll *end* you for that!"

His grip loosened more on Lil. He only had her by the forearm. Thinking quickly, she remembered the silver key that she wore around her neck. She yanked the key hard, breaking the chain. Holding it firmly between her knuckles, she made a stab at the face.

The terrible silvery eye, the eye of a predator, felt jelly-like and yielding as she drove the key in, and pushed in with all her might, and *twisted*.

The howling he let forth was blood-red and anguished – a demon resisting release from his body; he let go, drew back swearing, and clasped his face.

"Oh my God, Lil, are you—"

Vanessa stopped short when Lil turned to look at her, her lips parted in shock, her eyes bright and alert, blood on her hand.

John yelled and wailed, his hands covering his face.

This time, people *did* come running at the sound of a scream. Two horsemen and a trio of hippies burst into the room and gathered around John.

Vanessa grabbed Lillian by the arm and said, "Let's go!"

She had to yank Lil away; transfixed, she watched John in wonder. She tugged again and the girls ran out, down the hall, through the kitchen and out through the back door.

"But-but Mack—" Lil panted.

"I'll text him when we're safe."

They raced, gasping for breath, lungs burning, across the wide, sloping lawn, shaggy and verdantly green in the daytime, a washed-out lunar blue in the moonlight. Desperation drove their legs to longer and faster strides, fear gave them wind as they sought the shelter and safety of the woods.

Crashing through branches, dodging tree roots and fallen logs, almost at the creek, Vanessa's phone vibrated in her pocket. Without slowing down, she took it out, and read the words.

I FOUND IT

The two girls collapsed in the basement rec room at Lillian's house. Catching their breath, willing their yammering hearts to slow down.

Each felt their stomachs lurch when Mack knocked on the sliding glass door. They expected him but adrenalin still surged through their veins.

"You guys okay?" he whispered.

"Yeah," Vanessa said. "Just kinda rattled. Although," she took hold of Lillian's chin and lifted it up to the light.

"Jesus," said Mack, coming closer. "What the hell

happened?"

Lil shrugged. "That's what you get for crossing John."

An angry red mark on her cheekbone stood out starkly against her pale skin. She smiled ghoulishly at Mack's consternation and laughed. "You think anyone at school would believe me if I told them how I got this?"

Mack didn't smile as he traced the mark with his finger. "Bastard," he said.

"Never mind that," said Vanessa. "Back to business at hand. Show us what you got."

Mack appeared to be stuck in a ruminating trance for a bit before he took his phone from his pocket and opened the lock screen.

"I haven't looked at these yet," he said, punching around, brow furrowed. Then scrolling; his face lit up.

"Bring it here," Lil said, motioning him to sit between them on the couch.

They brought their heads close together and looked at the photos, slowly, one after another.

Images of a room the size of an extra-large walk-in closet, one where most people would keep out-of-season clothes or stacks of linens.

But this room was full of deep shelves stacked with guns. Assault rifles, haphazardly piled and hung from pegs on the wall.

"My God," said Vanessa. "Are those things *real?*"

"Looked real to me," said Mack, scrolling to the next, and the next. "I tried to get some close-ups, but I was working fast, flailing around ..."

There looked to be dozens of them. They gasped when he zoomed in on a photo of a plastic binful of grenades, Mack's hand and knee visible at the edges of the shot.

"Where was this?" Lil asked, dumbfounded.

"Mitch's room."

For some reason, this made the girls laugh.

"Serious. Hidden room."

"How'd you find it?"

"The man himself."

The next photo was a picture of Mitch, gaunt and frail but standing tall in his hospital pajamas, looking right into the camera. A ghost of the cinema idol he was once showing through.

And the last was a picture of his rumpled hospital bed, with its leather wrist restraint clearly visible, empty, its lock sprung open.

LOCAL AND FEDERAL AGENTS RAID
HOME OF ACTOR MITCH COOPER

Ten people were arrested in connection with a raid that took place at 1315 Bellehook Lane, the home of celebrated local resident Mitch Cooper, movie actor and director who starred in such acclaimed films as *Midnight Outlaw* and *The Man and the Serpent*.

In response to a report of elder abuse, police visited the home. The officers had been tipped off to the location of a cache of weapons. In a hidden room they found multiple automatic machine guns, knives, and grenades. Elsewhere in the house, they found a box containing $50,000 in cash.

Implicated in the raid were members of The Lone Horsemen motorcycle gang, an organization described by local police as a "highly structured criminal enterprise." The gang had been subject to memos exchanged between various local law agencies. "We had already been keeping a close eye on them," said police chief Robert Coor. "But because of an insider tip, we were able to move forward and make arrests."

One person arrested, John Leary, 71, had been residing in Mr. Cooper's home and was described as his "caregiver." In addition to aiding and abetting in weapons trafficking and prostitution, Leary is now being questioned in the death of local teenager Elizabeth Gray, as personal effects of the girl, plus a birth certificate, were found in the hidden room.

Also arrested was Dr. Barclay Honeyman, 55, who owns a medical practice in Wellesley and has been charged with illegal prescriptions and sales of opioids, including oxycodone and methadone. Honeyman has been charged with running a "pill mill" in coordination with The Lone Horsemen.

The investigation is in cooperation between local officials and agents of the Bureau of Alcohol, Tobacco, Firearms, and Explosives. The investigation is ongoing. Police believe there will be more arrests to follow. STORY CONTINUED 3A

Most of the front page of that day's newspaper was taken up by a composite of mug shots, most of them bearded and straggly haired members of The Horsemen. One solemn photo of Dr. Honeybear holding up his number, glowering at the camera. And one at the top of John, head at an arrogant slant, one eye hidden behind an eye patch.

The paper sold out in supermarkets and kiosks. No one could believe that it had been happening in their town, all along, and no one had guessed.

Strangest of all was the birth certificate for a baby girl born seventeen years ago, to a Natasha Andrushko and a father unnamed. The baby was named Darja. The certificate was found in a box along with Elizabeth's ballet shoes, a woven yarn Guatemalan purse, and an elastic hair band that still had strands of Elizabeth's hair stuck to it.

The facts came fast and furious, new data flowed in every day. Cars full of curiosity seekers drove up to The Brambles regularly now, up the carriage path, slowly, people taking pictures with their phones. The story was national news.

It was People Magazine that ran the big feature on the rescue of Mitch Cooper. How poor his health had been, the drugs he had been given, the infections, the bedsores. The abuse. They ran the photos that Mack had taken, of frail Mitch and his shackled bed, alongside a much larger, newer photo of Mitch reunited with his children. He was in a wheelchair, smiling and bright-eyed, surrounded by his three adult children and seven grandchildren, a sweeping view of the California coast behind them.

Mack and Lil sat separately in a crowd of 120 graduates in royal blue caps and gowns, as they listened to the valedictorian giving his speech.

"We stand, here, at the open doorway of the future. We entered high school as children, and have become grown adults. Though all of us will go our separate paths, we will always remember to …"

The valedictorian was a tall, gangly boy, mocha skinned with a soft afro standing out like an areole above his head. Though delicate in frame, his eyes scanned out boldly over the crowd, his voice rich, full and steady.

When at last all speeches were finished and each student had received their diploma, there was whooping and hollering as the hats were thrown up to the ceiling of the gymnasium. The air was warm and stifling, and the large industrial fans around the room did very little to move it. The graduates were very happy when it was time to line up and march back into fresh daylight again.

Students drifted out to the athletic field in back of the school, where friends and family converged on them; in the confusion and press of the crowd, Mack and Lil still found each other. He drew her up into a big hug, lifting her in the air.

Mack's mother and father had arrived separately, each hugging him and snapping photos.

"Your brother would have loved to have been here," his

father said, wiping at his eyes.

"It's okay, Dad. I'll see him again when his thirty days are up."

"Well, I think the judge could have given him a more lenient sentence, with his little brother graduating high school and all. But instead the lousy bastard—"

"Tom. Please. None of that now." His mother smiled tenderly at Mack, and he smiled back.

Then someone put her hands over his eyes from behind and said, "Boo."

"Vanessa!"

"Congrats!" She kissed him on the cheek, reaching up on her tiptoes.

"Congrats to you, too. Wish I coulda come to yours!"

"Yeah, well. Smaller school, smaller guest list. Way it goes." Her graduation had been the week before, in the chapel on her school grounds. Instead of caps and gowns, Vanessa and the other girls had each worn white dresses and drifted down the aisle holding single red roses, like eerie teenage brides. "It was really cool of your parents to invite me along."

"How could we not?" asked Mrs. Mackenzie, putting an arm around her waist. "You've always been like a sister to Mack, you and Lillian both."

"Speaking of …" Mack walked a few paces over to where she was hugging her sister and grandmother. "Lil," he said, "Look who's here to see us."

Vanessa threw her arms around her and said, "Congratulations!"

"Oh, thank you! I'm so stoked you were able to make it. When are you going off to school?"

"I move in in ten days."

"I can't believe it!"

Mack's mother came over. "Hey, you three! Why don't I get a picture while I have you in one place?"

The three posed, grinning, arms around each other. The red mark still stood out on Lillian's eye. She had told everyone that she had walked into a cabinet door. The cheerleading squad had laughed and said, "That's our Ladybug!" Lillian had just smiled, a serene and secretive smile.

After they had walked around, greeting and hugging and chatting and posing for more photos, the three drifted together again and walked a little way off from the crowd where they could talk without being overheard.

"Wow," said Vanessa. "Can you believe this is the first time we've been together since …"

"*That night.*" Lil shook her head. "Crazy. There was just so much to process. I just kind of wanted to check out for a while."

Vanessa punched Mack in the arm. "And hey, congratulations on the *other* thing."

"You mean the money?" He winked. "Hey, I *told* you we could split it three ways."

"You split five thousand dollars three ways and it's not much." Lil smiled, head tilted thoughtfully. "Anyway, it was you who took the biggest risk. It was you hiding in John's closet. If Flash had caught you …"

"Hey. I did what I had to do. Either of you would have done the same. I still can't even believe it, though. Who knew there was any reward for *tip-offs*? Easy money!"

Vanessa laughed. "Well, my *God*, I guess they had wiretaps on these guys for *months*. They just didn't know where they were hiding the stuff. I think they should have given you more than that, actually …"

Mack shrugged. "Well, hell. I wasn't expecting anything

at all. But I can sure use it."

Lil sat down on the grass and motioned for the others. "What are you going to spend it on?"

"Haven't decided yet."

Vanessa looked at him sidewise. "Tuition, maybe? Huh?" She elbowed him in the ribs.

Mack shrugged. "Don't know. Not in the near future, anyway."

"So what *is* the plan?"

"Haven't decided yet." At that, he set his mouth in a straight line and looked away.

Vanessa looked at him for a long moment, lips parted as though she were about to speak. But then, she saw something that made her decide a change of subject would be a better tack. "Look who else was here to watch us," she said, waving at someone emerging from the crowd.

It was Mrs. Gray, walking toward them wearing a dress of bright, grass green silk. Her hair was sprung around her head in her usual wild style, silvery white curls bobbing in the breeze. But she wasn't wearing sunglasses as she usually did. Her eyes sparkled like flecks of mica.

"I'm sorry I was hanging back," she said, "I ... didn't even know whether to come or not ..."

"Oh, Mrs. Gray," said Lillian, getting up and walking to her, "I'm so glad you decided to come, after all! We so wanted you to be here."

"Yes, well," The exuberance made Annabel shrink back just a bit. But then her happiness showed through again. "I wanted to be here more than I wanted to hide! I'm so happy to ..." Her voice became faint, a little distant, for a second. "I'm so happy to see my daughter's first friends starting their new lives together. And I wanted to say congratulations, and ... thank you."

She approached each of them individually, gave them a long hug, and kissed them on the cheek. When she came to Lillian, she paused a moment longer, staring, and gently stroked the red mark on her face. "Thank you, for everything," she said, quietly.

Then she walked away again, her vibrant green making her stand out even as she disappeared into the engulfing crowd.

"She looks … *better*," said Mack, shrugging.

"Did you—" asked Vanessa.

"My family invited her. I thought no way she'd come." Lil had a smile on her face that looked happy and sad at the same time. "I want to visit her one more time before we all go." She sighed. "I can't believe we're finally leaving this town."

"Yeah," said Vanessa in a mild, dreamy voice. "I kind of like this town more than I used to. I miss it already."

"Said the girl getting ready to move to New York City," said Mack with a smile.

"Well, you know what I mean, right?"

Mack had been picking dandelions and weaving them into a crown. He put the finished product on Lillian's head.

"Queen of suburban green lawns," he said.

Lil smiled obligingly. But there was pain in her eyes.

"What is it?" asked Vanessa, putting a hand on her narrow shoulder.

She looked away, then back again. "I don't know how to explain it."

"What?"

She touched the flower crown on her head, lightly, with her fingers. "I don't *feel* her anymore."

"Elizabeth?"

Mack ambled off to the side, kicking at the dirt.

Lil aimed her eyes upward, so tears wouldn't spill out. "I used to feel her all the time. At school. In my bedroom. At The Brambles. And now that she's not here, I feel kind of ... *lonely?*"

"But you always have us," Vanessa said, putting an arm around her.

"Yes. We'll always have each other."

But each knew, inside, that this might not always be the case. Already, since the last night in The Brambles, they felt themselves drifting away from each other, in small ways, bit by bit. They didn't phone or text each other every day the way they used to, when the murder drew them all together.

As they walked together, arm in arm, back toward the colorful group of graduates and families, each kept their own secret thoughts to themselves.

Mack knew he wasn't going to school, that he was going to take a year and travel. He had money now, and he'd never seen the West Coast. It was time for him to escape the crabbed greenness of New England and see new landscapes. His dad was going to take his truck in for a tune-up, and then he would leave. He couldn't wait. His eyes thirsted to see something foreign and new.

Lillian had never told her friends about the dark times she had had, the desperate racing thoughts, cutting lines into her own skin on her rose-covered comforter just to feel the relief and release. Though the wounds were now healing, there was no need for them to know now. And though she would miss them, the two people who knew her best, better than her own family, she was relieved to be leaving. She needed time to focus on herself. She had applied for a private dorm room at her new school, where she planned to study psychology. And no one there would know that she was once a cheerleader named Ladybug. She could be anyone she wanted.

Vanessa smiled to herself, and touched the lucky silver key in her pocket; it had been the key that turned in her heart, springing its lock open. She would always keep it.

Watching the ocean of young people in their fluttering blue robes made Vanessa think of one of her favorite words. *Offing*. An old nautical term. The most distant part of the sea that could be viewed from the shore. A place you could not anchor. The near future.

She had not told the other two that she was applying for a motorcycle permit. She had the manuals, and she had enrolled in a driving course. Because, for her graduation present, she had picked out a used red Honda Shadow. Black rims with silver highlights. A V-twin engine with a deep, sonorous sound that sounded like a life force itself. Already, she imagined herself, riding low, hand on the throttle, going, gone.

Acknowledgements

I would like to express my great appreciation to Rebel ePublishers and my lovely editor, Jayne Southern, for her hard work and discerning eye. I would also like to acknowledge RMD, whose valuable guidance and insight made this work possible.

About the Author

Leah Erickson has been published in many journals and magazines, in print and online, including *The Saint Ann's Review*, *The Fabulist*, *Eclectica*, *Pantheon*, and *The Coachella Review*. Her debut novel, *The Gilded Lynx*, was published in 2016 by Kraken Press. She lives in Newport, Rhode Island with her husband and daughter.

Also by this author …

The Gilded Lynx

And for more from this author …

Please turn the page for a preview of *Blythe of the Gates*

Blythe of the Gates

ONE

"Luna. Open your eyes and look at it!"

Very old, covered in cracked brown leather, with rows of hammered brass tacks along its edges, a heavy latch of blackened metal held the box shut. Only the Magician was allowed to use the key, and he kept it in his breast pocket at all times.

Luna knew the box was lined in faded red velvet. And she knew how the antique metal hinges would creak when he opened it up. There would be an ancient smell of mildewed newspaper, the smell of trapped life, the smell of time passed by …

"Luna. Open your eyes and look at it!"

Why the Magician did this to her, she did not know. But some nights when he was in a particularly wicked mood, he would take the box down from where he kept it at the top of his closet, and make Luna look at what was inside.

She tried to turn away, and shut her eyes to it.

This made him laugh. "Luna, I am your husband. Listen to me! Look at it."

But it was unbearable, to look straight into it, because it hurt. Looking straight into the thing was like looking straight into the sun; when she shut her eyes, she saw pulsing blood-red, and floating orbs…

"Look …"

To look inside the box was to feel her own dissolution, deep down in her very center, spreading out and out until she had no more edges to her.

But once she did look, it was so hard to look away again.

The stage. The hot, bright light of the stage, from which she could not escape. For all around her was the audience, in velvet seats, on balconies and in private boxes. Like the theatre of a surgeon about to perform a procedure on a patient. And she was, in a way, anaesthetized.

At her cue she joined the Incomparable Cosmos onstage, where she walked from one end to another in her beautiful white dress of which she had been so proud. But now she felt like a girl in a nightgown, living some kind of dream or nightmare, but unable to wake up. Unable to run from the stage and down the short flight of steps, down the halls lined in red brocade silk, through the marble and brass lobby, until she was free.

She could not do that. She moved from one end of the stage to another, turning, spinning, waving with one flat palm as though she were royalty, in just the way that the Magician had shown her.

And then, when the audience applause died down, she stood in the bright beam of spotlight. With grand and imperious gestures the Magician beckoned her to come forward upstage and stand before him. One by one, he pulled long stemmed roses from his sleeves, red ones, which he gave to her one by one, until she held a dozen. But as she held them, smiling, he made a swift movement with his hand, and the petals all loosened and swept, alive, through the audience like a swarm of bees: gasps and incredulous laughter, then enormous applause.

Next, he approached her for a tender kiss on the lips. He stepped back, and she opened her mouth, and a tiny blackbird emerged from her lips. Its small dry feathers and the skittering of its feet nearly made her gag, she had to control the impulse, but the little fellow stirred and took flight, somewhere toward the high molded ceilings of the theatre, and she looked after it with a blank expression as it flew away. And now the applause showered down over them like a hailstorm.

Again she bowed and curtsied, trying to keep her face smiling, still and serene. But when he led her to the table, something in her always changed. Her inner vision choked and narrowed as though she saw and thought only through a dark tunnel.

Because the table was where her soul wanted to leave her body, and follow that little bird. She forced herself to lie supine and inert as a sarcophagus as the Magician opened a case of silver knives and held it forth, striding the stage for the audience to inspect.

He set the case on a small table, and selected the longest of the knives and held it up so the stage lights glistened down its length.

"Be still, my darling," he said in an overly loud, yet tender tone. "This will not hurt you."

He drove the knife into the center of her chest. The audience not only gasped, but some cried out in terror.

Though it was true that she felt no pain, Luna was aware of the coldness of the blade, invading her insides. Her eyes, huge and trembling, stared straight up ahead, seeing nothing. Her body shuddered at the invasion. *Saint Michael the Archangel, defend us in battle, be our protection against the wickedness and snares of the devil ...*

Shuddering and silently reciting the prayers of her

girlhood, she endured as he drove five blades into her torso, the handles protruding like arrows in the hide of a fallen gazelle.

Silence enveloped the great hall when the Magician held up a hand, sweeping the audience with a grave, thundering look. "Behold!"

He pulled each of the knives, with a brandish, out of Luna and then held out a hand to help her up. She stood to show them that her dress was still white, she had no wounds, no blood to mar the snowiness. The applause was overwhelming, louder than ever, but she was beyond hearing it.

The Magician led her back to the table and helped her lie down. He stood behind her, facing the audience. For some long, dramatic moments he paused, gazing at them with an indefinable intensity.

Until he pronounced, "My darling wife, you will ARISE!"

Her eyes closed, and she heard the hush, the sound of hundreds of people in a room together being still and silent. A white roar, like the sound inside a seashell.

And she felt the energy of their focused attention on her, and she clung to it, because it made her feel safe. She was only dimly aware that her lover was out there, somewhere, and watching as well. He, his love, the memory of their shared afternoon in bed, now seemed as far away as the moon.

Overriding this all was the terrible force of will of the Magician: he was inside her now, deep at her very core. Suffusing what was once her, Luna. It was as though someone had gently but firmly clasped a hand over her mouth, and she couldn't breathe.

She heard the murmurs as her body, little by little, rose

off the table, her long gossamer skirts grazing softly against its edges as her body lifted up. And up.

It was such an indescribable feeling, being weightless. There was nothing to do but give in to it. The terror and blankness of it.

She remained horizontal for most of her ascent. Halfway, she dared to open her eyes, just a little, and looked around her. Hanging above the stage from hidden beams were large, glittering cutouts of a half-moon and stars. She idly noted the way they swung back and forth, stirred by the air coming through vents placed high on the wall.

She tried to imagine that the force holding her up was like the sea, the green Irish Sea she remembered from her youth. That pebbly beach where she liked to collect driftwood. There were so many secret places that she liked to go to as a girl, and she tried to go there now. The grassy moors. The old village graveyard with her favorite headstones she visited, those for children with angels and little lambs that were friendly to sit by. She was more afraid, and ashamed to be afraid, of her mother's headstone, too new and immaculate, the earth still fresh and dark where it had been dug.

Did those places still exist? Sometimes it seemed as though they vanished when she crossed the ocean to this new country. Was she still Luna Mulkerrins of County Clare? Was that still her family, father and sisters and cousins, who were somewhere in the faceless and unknown crowd below? Would they judge her if they knew her true thoughts and deeds?

At the highest place, she gently rotated so that she was upright, high up like a Christmas angel, and she held her arms straight out as he'd told her to do. She hovered there, and the audience not only applauded, but cried out and whistled; it was the grand finale of the show. An ocean of upturned faces, aimed up at her. And all she could do was concentrate fixedly on a crack in the plaster ceiling, and a small drift of spider web. She was so alone, so high up.

Slowly, slowly she descended, weak and lightheaded as though deprived of oxygen. She trembled, had been trembling the whole time, her muscles shuddering in a quick automatic fashion that she would feel later as a general soreness. The lower she got, the more she was embraced by the warmth and effusion of the crowd, the unseen thunderous audience, because all she could see now was red, her vision flooded with blood-red like the velvet that lined the Magician's box.

Her feet in the ivory satin slippers touched the hardwood of the stage: gravity, her friend! The pull of it felt a shock, it was nothing she ever noticed or appreciated until it was gone. The strong invisible pull each body feels to the planet. She whispered a silent prayer of thanks, to be held fast again.

Her legs wobbly, she feared they might buckle and fall. She walked gracefully to the front of the stage with the Magician beside her, who held her hand up in the air in triumph. They made a bow together.

Now able to focus, Luna stole a glance at the Magician, surprised by what she saw: a look of rapturous wonder was on his face as he looked forward, letting the applause wash over him in great waves. Covered in a light veil of sweat, looking a little pale, he trembled a bit himself. It was an exertion for him, too, to keep Luna aloft so high and for so long with his willpower. The magic didn't always come easily. But in spite of his fatigue, he looked exuberant, like a man who had just burst through the surface of a body of water, diamonds of droplets sparkling in the edges of his hair, his eyelashes, which were long as a woman's.

She had never seen him this way before. In awe. Electrified. Reborn. He did not turn to look at her, though. He looked around, and up, into the balcony seats; the audience giving a standing ovation.

At last they walked offstage, she feared the noise had been enough to deafen her, because even as the staff working backstage smiled and held arms out to her, she could not hear them as they mouthed … something … to her. She could not hear their words, only the rush of blood in her ears. And she saw the expression in their eyes shift from jubilance to confusion to fearful concern as, finally, her legs did go out from under her, and she surrendered to sweet gravity once and for all as the floor came up to meet her.

www.ingramcontent.com/pod-product-compliance
Lightning Source LLC
Chambersburg PA
CBHW020910110726
47900CB00001B/98